I0564904

Founders' Effect

War of the Second Iteration

Book Two

Thomas Watson

Cover Artwork by Fiona Jayde Media
Copyright © 2018, All Rights Reserved

DESERT STARS PUBLISHING

ISBN: 0615773745
ISBN-13: 978-0615773742

For my parents.

Thomas T. Watson Jr.
Doris E. Watson

CONTENTS

Other books by this author:

The Gryphon Stone

The War of the Second Iteration
Book One, The Luck of Han'anga
Book Two, Founders' Effect
Book Three, The Plight of the Eli'ahtna
Book Four, The Courage to Accept
Book Five, Setha'im Prosh

Short Fiction:
Chance Encounters
179 Degrees from Now

Nonfiction:
Mr. Olcott's Skies
Tales of a Three-legged Newt

ACKNOWLEDGMENTS

With thanks to Brian Gross, Frances Gross, Molly Black, and Stephanie Hansen for their assistance as beta readers, and to my wife Linda for assistance with combined beta reading and proofreading.

Cover art by the author. Cover font created by Neale Davidson/Pixel Saga's Freeware Fonts

CHAPTER ONE

Endmost System
Uncharted Space
Two Months After Contact...

Alarms rang and warning lights flashed as the ship suddenly appeared in the node. The gray-clad crew on duty all flinched, and any who were away from their duty stations rushed to take their places. On the tactical display that floated near the wall opposite those stations, blue and red icons showed the system's defense force scrambling as ships pulsed their engines, moving in on the intruder. Weapons platforms signaled target locks.

James Calavone glared at the main display as the large ship barged in and passed uncomfortably close to a smaller outbound vessel just then approaching the node. No one entered Endmost system unannounced without challenge. The new arrival would have only moments to establish an acceptable identity, and failing to do so, all aboard would die. In the meantime, the outbound ship announced an emergency shutdown of its matrix drive field, a frantic attempt to prevent a cross-amplification that came a heartbeat from failure.

"Warship! A heavy cruiser," Pete, the officer of the watch and nearest Calavone, announced. "They're sending a signal. It's... " He turned and stared at Calavone. "Sir, that's the *Vengeance!*"

"I'll be damned," Calavone said quietly to himself. Out loud he said, "Answer them and determine their status. Maintain red alert."

Pete nodded and said, "RDF *Vengeance* from station traffic control, stand down immediately or you will be fired upon. Advise of your status. Do you require assistance?" There was a pause, then he turned toward Calavone and said, "Sir, the commander of *Vengeance* wishes to speak to you directly."

"Go ahead." Light swam and then coalesced in front of Calavone's station, forming the image of a pale, familiar face, square-jawed but a step back from handsome, clean-shaven from crown to chin. He wore the dark blue uniform of the Republic Defense Force, but with no sign of rank or decoration.

"James? Good, you're still doing the first watch thing. I wanted to come through when you were on duty. We're nominal. No immediate emergency to report."

"You almost created one, Andrew!" James Calavone replied. "What the hell did you think you were doing coming across without warning?"

"It's been almost seven years since I last had direct contact with you. We have the entire Republic Defense Force out to get us. I couldn't simply take the chance that Endmost was still a free outpost." Kester shrugged, but somehow did not seem the slightest bit apologetic. "If we were flying into a trap, I wanted the element of surprise."

Calavone shook his head, unable to believe what he had heard. "We almost launched, you damned fool!"

"Good thing for us you're so old school," Commodore Andrew Kester said with a smirk. "And it's nice to see you, too."

"What the hell *are* you doing here?" Calavone asked with all the patience he could muster. "Wait, you said the RDF is after you? What the hell is going on?"

"Big trouble, but it's nothing I'm going to talk about over an open com. We need to speak face to face, as soon as possible."

"Trouble? You? That's *two* surprises in one day! I'll order the main dock clear and *Vengeance* can..."

"Don't bother," Kester interrupted, shaking his head. "I'm already in a shuttle and about to head over. I'll be alone. Meet me in the dockyard." The projection shimmered away.

"Right. See you soon," Calavone said with a trace of sarcasm to the now empty air before him. "Some people never change," he added under his breath. Then he glanced around and nodded to the first watch officer who occupied the com station. "Pete, you're in the hot seat. I'll let you know what's going on as soon as I can."

"I'm on it," was the man's calm response, and Pete stepped onto the central platform that held the Station Master post slightly above all the others.

Calavone left the post and crossed to the narrow end of the instrument-packed, brightly lit room. The door in the plain bulkhead opened to a small, gray-walled passage illuminated by a light strip that ran all the way to the lift terminus. There was a capsule waiting — standard operating procedure — and he stepped inside. As soon as the door closed, the capsule moved him swiftly from the operation center's offices in the administrative ring straight to the core, then with a soft bump switched rails and rushed up the main axis to the docks. By the time he found himself free-floating in the bright, cool vault of the station's docking facility, white-clad workers were already escorting Andrew Kester away from the port through which his shuttle had entered.

"Thank you, gentlemen," Kester said politely to the station hands as he approached. "I know my way from here." He grasped a slider on the nearest come-along pole and pushed away from the port.

Calavone watched as the workers saluted the departing Fleet Commodore, and when Calavone gave them a nod, turned their attention to other tasks. "Andy," Calavone said as Kester slid within range of easy conversation.

"Jimmy!" Kester clasped Calavone's hand firmly and gave him a broad, square-toothed grin. "Good to see you again."

"Likewise. It's been far too many years."

"That it has! Much too long, which of course can't be helped. Endmost is not a place for casual visits. How's Carla?"

"Doing fine. She'll be delighted to know you're here." Calavone released Kester's hand and worked to remain composed. His annoyance with Kester's careless arrival was difficult to suppress with pleasantries. Each man held himself in place with an easy touch of the pole, veterans with no need to clutch and hold. "You can't be in it *too* deep. You're in a good mood."

"Being careful." Kester glanced around, as if admiring the facility, and kept an easy smile on his face. "You have a secure office here on the station, I assume?"

"Yes." His friend's smiling face did not jibe with the change in the tone of his voice, the hardness of his eyes. Calavone knew Kester well, and saw the signs of real fear in the man. Annoyance was replaced by a mix of curiosity and concern. "We can be there in just a few minutes." He gave a practiced flick of the wrist and began to float backwards, the way he had just come. "Does *Vengeance* need attention?" he said a little louder, to be heard by the crew over the noise of the docking facility.

"As a matter of fact, life support needs a thorough overhaul, but it's not an emergency. When it can reasonably be scheduled."

"Consider it done," Calavone replied.

"Good enough."

They were at, and then in the lift, the noise of the busy place closed off when the capsule shut the hatch at Calavone's command. As the trip back to the full-g torus began, Calavone said, "You've got all my feelers twitching."

And then Kester dropped the act, looking grave and tired, and older than his sixty-seven standard years. "You know me well enough to pick it up, I suppose. Things aren't going well, out there," and he made a vague gesture outward with his left hand. "But we really need to be buttoned up before I can give you the complete story."

"Bad enough to risk coming back here? The authorities have always suspected a connection, you know." When Kester did not reply immediately, Calavone said, slightly exasperated, "Artie, is this capsule secure?"

"It is secure," a quietly neutral voice said from the com speaker.

"It's bad enough that we had no other choice," Kester replied. "There are no ports in the Republic we can use that won't result in my arrest, and the loss of my ship."

"Good God, Andy, what have you — No, okay, we'll hold off until we're at my office," Calavone said, holding a hand up to forestall the objection he saw coming.

"Yes."

They finished the tube ride in something less than a companionable silence, and then walked briskly down the forever sloping, up-curved main corridor of the green and white administrative ring. It was not a long walk to the office complex that served as Calavone's home away from home. They passed through the quiet outer offices, occupied by workers seated at terminals surrounded by pale green walls, monitoring progress elsewhere in the stellar system for which Endmost Station served as capital and nerve center. Everyone wore gray uniforms with only a name over the pocket to distinguish them. Off to one side was a projection containing a large system schematic showing worlds, stations, habitats, and ship traffic. Endmost was a busy place, with a respectable-sized population.

The inner offices were pale blue, with the same gray carpet underfoot, and there they found Calavone's secretary, an attractive young brunette, waiting. She left quickly after a polite acknowledgment of the order to do so; Kester's eyes lingered on her until the door closed between them. Calavone tapped a key code into the terminal on his desk. "There. Only way we could be more secure would be a life pod out in the cometary halo. I do hope we won't need to go *that* far?"

"Ah, no," Kester said with a quick grin and an equally quick look around. "Got anything to drink?"

"Whiskey." Calavone shrugged and added apologetically, "It's synth."

Kester shrugged off the clarification and said, "I'll take it. Neat."

Calavone poured amber liquid into a pair of squat, heavy glasses. The smell of the whiskey was assertive and obvious.

"To the ones who died with honor, for freedom's sake. And to those who will." Kester held his glass up as he spoke.

The words were all too familiar, and hit so close to home. Calavone's father had said exactly that, years ago when he and Kester had been young boys, as he led the forces covering his followers' retreat from the Republic. That was the last Calavone had heard of his father, who he now knew to be long dead. The words had been remembered, and were now the standard, one might say traditional, toast for those who called Endmost their home. "Amen," Calavone said softly in reply. They tossed back the first helping, then Calavone refilled their glasses. They looked at each other across a long, black desk, made of iron and stone, polished like a dark mirror. After each of them had taken another sip, Calavone said, "Out with it."

"The Leyra'an have made contact with the Human civilization centered on old Earth."

"God save us!" Calavone whispered, and set the glass down with a thump. His stomach seemed to clench around the whiskey. "Are you sure?"

"Yes. I led an invasion into Pr'pri system, hoping to anchor our flank for an intended sweep of the Leyra'an systems in the Disputed Zone. One last shot at securing the border before politics at home renders it all but impossible. We found a ship there from what's called the Commonwealth. They helped the Leyra'an halt the invasion, after the scalies sprang a trap. Our intel missed a large fleet of warships, disguised as civilian freighters. All we could do was hold the node and wait for back-up. These folk from the Commonwealth *claim* neutrality, but

I'm not buying it. They were letting scalies crawl all over this probeship, as they called it. A little too cozy, if you ask me."

"People from the home world... " Calavone shook his head, having paid little attention to the rest of what Kester said. He took a solid drink of whiskey. "My God. Andy, if anyone else came to me with that story as an excuse for violating security protocols the way you just did, he'd be out the airlock right now."

"You really didn't know already?" Kester frowned and said, "So much for your network!"

"It's a secure network, Andy. Unfortunately, that means news sometimes comes in slowly."

"We knew they were out there," Kester went on, and then to Calavone's apparent surprise added, "Never mind how for the moment. And we had a pretty good idea where to go and look. Suffice to say that was part of the reason for trying to button up the DZ now. Protecting our flank was a convenient cover story that had some virtue in being more than half true. We tried to move on a broader front to hide this, but the scalies put up a hell of a fight along the inner corridor."

"They knew," Calavone said suddenly. "They were herding you."

"Pretty sure now that's the case," Kester admitted. He sipped whiskey and shook his head, a rueful half-smile on his face. "And we fell for it. Came in with guns blazing and shot up a bunch of transports full of civs that were right in our path." He grimaced. "A year ago that would have been overlooked. But these Commonwealth people, they saw it and were appalled. In response the Admiralty made a big show of calling my tactics excessive and dismissed me from the scene when the political types came through to handle matters to do with contact."

"Stinks, being set up like that," said Calavone.

"As you know all too well." Kester took another sip.

Calavone grunted and tossed back the contents of the glass. "More?" he asked, and Kester extended his glass after first draining it. "Don't get me started on ancient history. So this all happened — when?"

"Two months ago. Don't know where things stand at the moment. We've been a bit out of touch since then." Kester finished speaking with his eyes on the whiskey.

Calavone's eyes narrowed in suspicion. "Out of touch, huh? Andrew, what the hell *else* is going on?"

Kester sighed and sipped the whiskey, grimacing slightly, as if either the taste no longer pleased him, or what he remembered was a bitter pill. "My crew and I set a trap for Kr'nai Ersha and his ship the *Han'anga*. We knew the *Han'anga* would be escorting the Commonwealth's embassy into Leyra'an space. When they came through, we hit them. There were unforeseen consequences." He hesitated and his hard gray eyes looked up at Calavone for a moment, then shifted back down to the glass he held before him.

"Go on." He didn't bother to question Kester's decision to go after their old acquaintance. He understood the power of old grudges.

"The Commonwealth ship came through the node before we expected them, and we fired a warning shot to back them off. Turned out to be a really bad idea. These ships are *huge,* bigger than anything in the Fleet! Hell, it was bigger than Endmost station! They create a lot of residual stress in transit. That must cause their matrix field to extend further and to take longer than I expected to dissipate. Our shot intersected their field while it was still hot. The field snapped. The next thing we knew, the forward sections had sheared off and the bulk of the vessel just disappeared. The flux from the field when it collapsed caught us and did more damage than *Han'anga,* when she returned fire. We let the *Han'anga* run for it and went to the debris field looking for survivors, but we were too late. There weren't any."

"Somehow I doubt you came away empty handed, though."

Kester shook his head, then finished his whiskey and set aside the empty glass, apparently done for the moment. "No, indeed. The nose of that ship contained their docking facility. We salvaged several smaller ships and managed to remove and shut down their onboard memory cores before some sort of self-destruct completely erased their databases. We're hoping it contains a record of the stealth technology they displayed during the battle of Pr'pri... "

"Stealth? You left that part out," Calavone said.

Kester leaned forward and stared at him. "This so-called probeship was a traveling space habitat, Jimmy. This station would fit *inside* of it! But when we emerged into Pr'pri system there wasn't a *trace* of it on our scans, not so much as a ghost of an echo! I thought I was speaking to a Human aboard the *Han'anga* when suddenly — *wham!*" He reached out and slammed his hand down hard on the desktop. "There it was, like a space station from the core systems materializing out of *nothing!*"

"This is beginning to sound like something out of a drama vid," Calavone said mildly.

"Look for yourself, if my word isn't sufficient." Kester nodded toward the terminal, clearly annoyed. "I've set things so you can access our records."

"Wasn't calling you a liar, Andy," Calavone said, raising his right hand in a defensive gesture.

"I wouldn't blame you if you did," Kester replied. He subsided and shook his head. "I wouldn't believe a word of it without proof, if I hadn't been there and *seen* it all." He pointed to the terminal and said, "You should review the record anyway. You need to *see* this for yourself."

"I'll surely do so." Calavone looked thoughtful, then said, "So now you're in the deep dark with the Admiralty?"

"The Admiralty, the government, and more than likely the Commonwealth," Kester replied with a frown. "Instead of following orders and falling back, we went after *Han'anga*. By itself, that act might have been overlooked. Then we messed up with that Commonwealth ship. We really *didn't* mean to do them any harm. Next stop we made we found that they'd suffered enormous casualties. We've been declared a rogue ship."

"You ran for it when you found out."

Kester nodded and said, "With such crew as remained willing. Turned the rest out. They don't see it, Jimmy, meaning the government and the Admiralty. They don't see where the danger lies, with the Leyra'an having already won over the Commonwealth. I screwed up, trying to take out Ersha, but I'm right about what's going on, and Fleet just isn't listening."

"Andy, you're one of a handful trusted with the coordinates to this system. What were you thinking, bringing all this to our doorstep?" Calavone made no attempt to conceal his annoyance. "You can't hide here forever!"

"We're not here to hide!" Kester snapped. He closed his eyes and shook his head. "Jim, we need to understand and make use of Commonwealth tech. We've got an enormous amount of data from that wreckage. We have small craft built with Commonwealth tech. My people, the ones who stayed with me, are good enough to get a sense for how important that data is, but a heavy cruiser doesn't have the facilities to exploit this stuff. Endmost does. That is, if you can make sense of it."

Calavone stared at his friend in silence for a moment, then said, "The download code?" he said.

Kester looked up, visibly relieved, and said, "Kester-flagcom-alpha-zero-zero-one."

"Artie," Calavone said, "download the data. Secure and review."

"Right away, Jim," said that same neutral voice as heard in the lift capsule.

Kester was visibly startled, and his pale features took on a pinkish tint. "You said this office was... "

"Relax, Andy, that was a computer talking. One that responds *only* to my voice print unless instructed to do otherwise." He laughed as he waved off Kester's attempt to protest further and added, "Hell, it won't even talk to my *wife!*"

"That didn't *sound* like a computer," Kester said.

"Well, it isn't exactly standard issue," Calavone replied. "I'll explain later. Now, tell me what it is you hope we can do with this treasure trove you've brought me?"

"We need to find ways of adapting it and using it to neutralize the advantages it gives the Commonwealth over us, or might give the Leyra'an if my worst fears are realized," Kester replied. "I don't necessarily see the Commonwealth as the enemy. Not yet anyway. But we'll be better able to deal with them if we have at least some understanding of their technology. I can't go to the powers-that-be with this. Oh, they'd use the information, but they'll also take me out of the game. I've become too much of a liability."

"What makes you think I'd be interested in rushing to the aid of the Republic?" Calavone demanded. "I'm surely no more popular there than you, even if they *do* think we're all dead!"

"Ah, but if you suddenly came to the rescue, wouldn't that change how things are? And just possibly give you the chance to achieve the goal your father was denied."

"We might also ruin what's left of his legacy out here," Calavone replied.

Kester looked grave and shook his head. "No. What little I saw of the Commonwealth quite frankly scares the hell out of me. Their tech is that far ahead of us. You master that tech, even a small part of it, and the Republic is *yours*. And then we can turn about and make the whole thing safe from the Leyra'an *and* the Commonwealth."

"My, aren't you ambitious these days," Calavone said, raising one dark eyebrow. When Kester opened his mouth to object, he held his hands up in a placating gesture and said, "Calm down, Andy. Give me some time to look this stuff over. Let me get up to speed. Then we'll see what we can, or should, do."

"All I ask, Jimmy. That's all I can ask."

CHAPTER TWO

It never really surprised Robert MacGregor that so many survivors from the *William Bartram's* crew remained in Pr'pri system. Serch'nach station was a beautiful place, full of life and light and good people. There was something about the unwavering and unquestioning support of their Leyra'an neighbors that made it difficult to say goodbye. Very few did so, and the Leyra'an made it plain they were welcome for as long as they desired to stay. Nor was he surprised that the survivors in due time organized themselves, pulling together the fragments of their former space-faring community, and asked permission to build a habitat to house them and such of the Leyra'an as wished to join it. He saw this as a sign of healing, this desire to rebuild.

He was, however, deeply surprised by the course the planned habitat followed.

"They want to do what?" he asked his wife Alicia, the evening she brought the news.

"The new habitat will incorporate the remains of the *William Bartram*," she repeated. "I do wish you'd attended the meetings."

"Couldn't be in two places at once," he replied. "And when a harvest is ready... " He ended with a shrug.

"Well, there's a recording, so you can do the next best thing," Alicia replied. She relaxed in the shallow bowl of a disk chair built from plaited *mi'pat* branches, head back, her red hair bright against the black cushions. "We're going to salvage the probeship. Everything is to be recycled as building material in some fashion. The habitat will be stripped first of useful artifacts and... " She hesitated for a moment, then finally said, "and of organic debris that will be processed and used to build the ecosystem of the new habitat."

Organic debris. Robert knew that their dead shipmates had already been removed and their remains added to the cycle of life of Serch'nach station. Livestock and plants remained, however, locked in the frozen, airless stasis of the Void.

"It makes perfect sense," said Rost'aht Holm from where he reclined in another disk chair nearby, Kr'nai Melep close beside him, her head on his shoulder. "Take what remains of your past as a foundation for the future." He slid his arm around Melep and hugged his wife to him briefly. "It will, of course, be home for Rost'aht, when it is done."

Alicia bowed to him, her only reply and all that was really needed.

"It does," Robert conceded. "But it's also, well, unsettling. The idea of disturbing the wreck, I mean."

"It will be recycled, one way or another," Melep pointed out. "What more fitting use, than a living, breathing monument to those we lost?"

"In this case, that's literally what it will be," Alicia said. "I'm leading a team that will do a genetic salvage. Before anything is removed, we'll take and inventory samples for the purpose of cloning the plants and animals that shared the probeship's habitat with us. In a way, we'll be bringing them, as many as we can, back to life."

"Can you do that for the people you lost?" Holm asked.

"The option exists," Alicia said quietly, not quite looking at the Leyra'an half of her family as she spoke. "DNA was collected, to make certain of identification. The sequences are stored and can be used to make clones. I imagine some of the children that grow up in the new habitat will be clones of those we lost."

"The new habitat will be a living memorial, indeed," said Holm. "Life will be created from what was lost, and mingled with the life that you have found here in Pr'pri system."

"May others take it as a hopeful sign, this resurrection and mingling," said Melep softly, her amber eyes bright with emotion.

There was a quiet moment, then, and Robert looked from one to the other, his still new family, and the three of all living beings he most loved. Whatever his surprise or initial misgivings, he knew exactly what he should say in that moment.

"I don't suppose you could use a pilot?"

And so Robert joined the grand effort of creating a new spark of life in the Void, a habitat for Humans and Leyra'an to set an example in plain view of those who must negotiate a permanent peace between the two species. Such lofty goals, all around. When the time came, he flew Alicia's team to the probeship.

Nothing could prepare him for the sight of the *William Bartram* looming before him, dark and dead, the abandoned hulk of what once had been his home. It literally hurt to see it, a dull ache in his chest. Pale, almost ghostly in the glare of Pr'pri system's blue-white star, the dead probeship bore little resemblance to the ship he remembered. The prow was missing, almost a quarter of the ship's length, and jagged, broken bulkheads and twisted metal framework marked the end from which it was torn. There was no way to connect this mournful wreck with the giant ship of exploration, once home to three thousand people. Now it was a ghost ship, a ship of memories, haunted by the deaths of those killed during an unprovoked attack by a rogue warship from the Republic.

Alicia had been aboard the *William Bartram*, had faced the terror of the great ship's violent death while Robert was elsewhere, caught up in his own desperate adventure. He looked to his right, where she sat beside him in the shuttle's forward compartment. He could see the tears welling up in her eyes, glittering as they reflected the instrument lights.

He reached over and took her pale hand in his. "You sure about this?" he asked.

She nodded, never looking away from the image displayed before them. "I've *got* to do it, Rob." A simple statement, without explanation or rationalization. It was enough. Robert gave her hand a gentle squeeze and then released it.

"We will be with you, sister," Melep said from behind.

"Indeed," Holm said in his deep voice, seated directly behind Robert. "You will not face this alone. Neither of you."

"Makes all the difference," Robert assured them, with a catch in his voice.

He glanced aside at Alicia and saw her eyes staring forward, her jaw clenched. Robert gave his wife's cold hand a gentle squeeze, but there was no response.

He flew their ship around the bulk of the wreck, until they found the temporary docks rigged to a section of undamaged outer hull. The docking area was bright white with green and blue lights further setting it off from the shadowy hull of the dead probeship. Robert guided them through the traffic already on station, and gently brought them into dock. Other ships were attached around them, and crews were already inside the vast, dark chamber of the old habitat, gleaning the samples and bringing out salvage that would bring another place to life.

They joined the crew in the aft passenger compartment and led their team of twenty volunteers into the docking facility, where they donned equipment-laden EVA suits. Alicia fumbled with one of the samplegrabbers on her suit and lost it for a moment, then snatched it and slammed it back into place.

"Need a hand?" Robert asked. She seemed pale to his eyes, and her hands were shaking.

"No!" she snapped. Alicia closed her eyes for a moment, then drew a deep breath as if to calm herself. "No, Rob. Sorry. Didn't mean to be short, it's just... "

Robert nodded and patted her suited shoulder. "Come on, let's get it done!"

"Right," she said, and sealed herself into the suit and gave him a thumbs up. Her eyes stared back at him though the visor, white around the edges.

He told himself her anxiety was only to be expected. Alicia had told him the tale of her narrow escape from the crippled probeship, of seeing those only a step or two behind her being lost to the Void. Being here was surely a hard thing. He suppressed his misgivings, and trusted her strength.

The salvage crew entered an airlock large enough to hold them all. Robert felt his suit stiffen and heard the tiny ticking sounds that said the joint servos were active. He flexed his fingers, and his hand moved freely and naturally. The opposite hatch of the lock opened and they floated down a long, bright tube that passed through the thick hull of the wreck. Alicia and Robert, flying slowly side by side, led the way.

When the tunnel ended it turned them loose into an immense darkness, sprinkled with clusters of lights that slowly moved around. Some represented teams doing the same sort of work as Alicia and her group. Others worked to salvage bulkier things deemed too fragile to be taken by the bulk handler robots, items not meant for simple recycling. Structures were being dismantled and their components cataloged for reassembly. Personal effects, left by the survivors as they fled in desperate haste to air-tight refuges and escape pods, were being secured. Artifacts the survivors wanted in the new habitat, to decorate the interior with landmarks representing the look and feel of their former home, were being removed. Only when such items were safe would the robots be turned loose to deconstruct the ship, salvaging and rendering what remained into resources to be reshaped as needed.

"Mother of us all," Robert whispered as he looked out into the vast darkness that once had been their home. Thirty years of his life had been spent here and he thought he knew the place well. This place of patchwork light and darkness was unrecognizable. Flood lights cast stark shadows around them. A grove of shadowy trees, dead, frozen leaves black in the glaring light, seemed to huddle below them. His heart rate went up, and he had the feeling of one lost in a nightmare.

"Every time I think I've faced the hardest thing life can hand me," he whispered, "I discover that I'm wrong."

Alicia continued to drift forward as he paused to try and take in the silent, frozen horror before them. She seemed to be headed for the dead trees beneath their feet, and it seemed as good a place to start as any. He nudged his jets to fully face the grove.

A shriek cut through his head; someone had screamed into the comlink. Too startled to think at first, Robert hit his jets to turn and see who was in distress. Too late he saw that Alicia's arms were waving wildly, fingers clutching as if to claw at the darkness. She screamed again and then started to babble, her voice panic-stricken, but forming fragments of words and sentences that made no sense. Robert shouted her name and pivoted toward her, but her suit's jets came on full power and she sailed with rapidly increasing speed back the way they'd come.

Chaos reigned in the comlink as normal radio discipline was briefly supplanted by shock and surprise as Alicia plunged into the group and through it, sending several spinning out of control into the dark. Melep cursed in Leyra'an and told them all to shut it down. Three suited figures launched after her, Holm being one, identifiable by his size.

Robert knew they wouldn't catch her in time. Instead of racing after them he used his suit's emergency systems to call up Alicia's controls. In fractions of seconds that seemed agonizingly slow, he overrode her flight capability, turning her and increasing thrust in a bid to limit her impact with the hull. She was not aimed squarely at the exit, and would hit the ring of bare bulkhead that had been cleared around it. With relief he saw that Alicia's own systems sensed the impending impact and braced for it. Her velocity would not be reduced in time to prevent a heavy blow.

All the while Alicia wept and babbled, clearly terrified. Robert brought up her vital signs and was appalled by her heart and respiration rates. The nanomed in her body was fighting even then to restore normal balances, but the effect would not be instantaneous. Robert aimed and fired his own jets and moved as quickly as possible to where she would slam into the inner hull; by then all the group who remained in control of their own motions were either on their way to the hull, or launching into the dark to assist those with whom Alicia had collided.

She hit hard and rebounded, suddenly silent and limp. Robert felt his heart lurch and glanced at the readout from her suit. Alicia was alive, but unconscious, and mercifully the stats gave no indication of serious injury.

Holm glided into her path and caught her gently in his arms, putting them both into a quick spin. Jets flared as he slowed the rotation, then the two crewmembers with him were able to grab hold. In moments the small cluster of suited figures was stable. Robert sailed in to join them, Melep less than a heartbeat behind.

"Oh, gods of all... " Melep said, sounding out of breath and near tears.

"She's okay," Robert said, with one more look at the readout to be sure. "There'll be bruises. But — she's okay."

"Physically," someone said.

"Indeed," said Holm. "Come, let us take her from this place *before* she wakes up."

"Agreed," Robert said. "Where's Hilde?" he asked, naming Alicia's usual lab assistant.

"Here, Rob." A hand gripped his shoulder; she'd been right beside him.

"Take care of the others, make sure everyone else is okay," he said. "Carry on if that seems right to do. We'll take her out of here." And he pointed to Melep and Holm.

"Got it. Keep us in the loop, will you?" Hilde asked.

"Promise."

As they flew slowly to the airlock it opened and an emergency response crew in orange suits appeared. They met them halfway and let the medtech take charge, the three family members clinging to each other as they trailed along.

In the hours that followed Alicia was checked out and found to be free of serious injuries. From the damage done to her suit, this was little less than a miracle. When she woke up she could only cling to them each in turn, weeping uncontrollably, and at last was given a sedative. Sound asleep and strapped securely into a med pod, she traveled with Robert, Holm, and Melep back to Serch'nach station. The medic who met them there checked her again, revived her, and they finished the journey home in a lift capsule. Alicia clung to Robert the entire time, saying not a word, and walked to their apartments as if in a daze, with Holm on one side and Robert on the other, and Melep going ahead to see to doors.

The small family of Rost'aht was home and safe, but in a somber mood, a thing no Leyra'an could tolerate for very long. They steered Alicia to a wide and well-cushioned disk chair, mindful of her bruises, and settled her in. She refused being put to bed, reluctant to be alone. Robert crawled in beside her and curled around her, feeling altogether wretched and helpless as he saw the vacant stare in her eyes and the bruises showing on arms and face. No worse than bruises, trivial work for the nanomed, and they were damned lucky it wasn't much worse, he knew. But her mind... there the molecular sized 'bots could not go. They addressed the physical, responded to the hormonal and neurochemical swings her fears induced, to keep them from doing harm. They restored balance, sustained homeostasis. The dread of the blackness that filled the *William Bartram*, the fear of falling into that darkness — these were the province of Human intervention, and all Robert could do in that regard was hold her close while Holm and Melep went about household business.

He was not at all surprised to see Melep and Holm turn on the red and blue and silver lamps they had strung around the perimeter of the open-air dining area. Elf lights, Alicia had taken to calling them, and they knew how the lights pleased her. Gentle Leyra'an evensong drifted from the sound system, and soon the smells of dinner being prepared drifted through the apartment. Robert *was* surprised by this, thinking food would be the furthest thing from Alicia's mind.

He was wrong about that. "I'm hungry," she said softly. "Are you hungry?"

"Yes," he replied. "As a matter of fact, I am."

Alicia sat up and scrubbed at her eyes, rubbed her nose. "I feel like a fekkin idiot," she said.

Robert didn't argue, and merely breathed a sigh of relief. "We all have our limits," he said. "You crossed one of yours, today. You don't always see that coming."

"I should have," she said, still clearly angry with herself. "You know about the nightmares, about how I still can't sleep in the dark. I should have known this was a bad idea. What the *hell* was I thinking?"

"You were *thinking* you had it under control," Robert said. He sat up beside her and took one of her hands. She squeezed his hand hard. "You were wrong, but I doubt there was any way you could've known that without going in."

They sat in silence for a few minutes, then Alicia said in a small voice, "I'm not going to try again. I can't go back. Not into that... darkness." She shuddered and her eyes grew wide as she said the word, then she turned to hide her face against his shoulder.

"Then join us under bright and colorful lights," Holm said. He had approached unnoticed, and stood there holding a broad, scale-backed hand out to her. "There is food and drink and light, and we lack only the other half of our family to make it all worthwhile."

Robert got out of the chair and Alicia took the offered hand and let Holm draw her out. He led the two of them out onto the patio, where the evening meal awaited them on the round black table made of polished *ma'lotma* fungus wood, the white dishes and steel utensils laid out in strong contrast to its glossy black surface. Colorful highlights from the lamps glowed from the black table edges. The dining area of the suite was on the uppermost floor, so they could look out over feathery treetops, and beyond to the gentle upward sweep of their inverted world. The sounds of the busy space station murmured all around them.

They sat and passed a long-necked bottle of *bosh'sh* around. When all their cups were full they raised them, but no one spoke at first. Then Alicia said, in a rough voice, "Gaia, how I love you all!" And drank a healthy dose of the potent liquor.

Robert and the others saluted her and drank, then plates were passed as they turned themselves to normal things, determined in that way to fend off the darkness that seemed lurking all too near. Just as he wondered what they should talk about, what would be safe, Alicia looked at her cup and said, "This new habitat will have *boshna'ti* vines in it."

"I would hope so," Holm replied. "If only in our family allotment. Rost'aht could hardly be called restored if we do not grow *boshna'ti!*"

Robert smiled at his friend and nodded, knowing Holm would understand the Human gesture as assent. Rost'aht, in its previous incarnation, had been *boshna'ti* growers and brewers of *bosh'sh*, before all but Holm were lost to war. "I'm hoping for an entire vineyard, not just a part of our private garden," he said.

"You aren't alone. It's been discussed as part of the overall plan," Alicia said. "And not just *boshna'ti*, but hops as well."

"Ezra's idea," Melep said. "He's anxious to drink beer that hasn't been hauled all the way from Eriola."

Alicia did not respond, and as quickly as she introduced the topic, she dropped out of it. They ate in silence for a time, an awkward pause that Robert finally needed to break. The way Alicia's gaze kept drifting off into the distance was worrisome. "Ezra and his folk made good beer," he said.

"The best beer and ale," said Melep.

"He will again, soon," Alicia said firmly, her gaze back in the here-and-now, eyes glittering. "He *will*!"

Robert nodded and then said, "We should grow wine grapes, too. I know wine doesn't appeal to the Leyra'an as strongly as beer, but... "

"I like wine," Melep said. "Especially the pales."

"Whites," Robert corrected.

"Yes, those."

"That, too, is already part of the plan," Alicia said. "After all, there were wine grapes on the *Bartram*, and we'll soon have their clones... " She stopped suddenly, and took a deep breath before continuing. "*I* will have their clones in my lab. I can surely do that much. And you," she looked at Robert, "will grow them out for us."

"Count on me to be *part* of that effort," Robert replied. "I'm in no way qualified to take charge of it!"

"You will be," Holm said. "Of that I have no doubt. That memory thing in your head probably has all you need to know by now."

"It probably does," Robert replied. "But until I've applied enough of it directly, gotten hands-on with it, the information alone doesn't count for much. I'm knowledgeable, but I lack the true expertise that comes from experience."

"Such a strange concept," said Holm, the dark scales of his forehead puckering together on a frown.

"But one I would be willing to endure," Melep said. "That must be an amazing thing, to have a database in your head."

"Must seem that way, from your perspective," Robert replied. "I wouldn't know. I've always had a memory hoard, so it doesn't seem in the slightest bit out of the ordinary."

"We're making some progress on that," Alicia said. "Someday we'll be able to make memory hoards for the Leyra'an. It's actually a more complicated process than adapting nanomed, learning to grow an extra organ in a living brain."

"Does the nanomed have a higher priority?" Holm asked.

"No." Alicia replied. "We have separate but equal efforts underway. But even with comparable resources, the one will just take longer. The nanomed will be easier to accomplish."

"If you had to choose," said Melep, "I know which one I would vote for."

Alicia frowned and sipped *bosh'sh*. "The Republic *still* hasn't taken us up on our offer to share med tech, have they?"

"I would know, if their position changed," said Holm, who was assistant to Melep's uncle, Kr'nai Ersha, the chief Leyra'an diplomat in Pr'pri system. "The offer went to the central government by way of a regional governor, but there has been no response except to say the offer will be studied. They respond to messages and inquiries from the Commonwealth, but initiate no contact on their own behalf. And there is still no sign of the requested representatives for the Trilateral Commission. That does rather slow the process of negotiation."

"What are they waiting for?" Alicia muttered.

Robert saw his wife frown in anger. She looked tired and distracted, and even with rapid healing, the bruises were prominent on her cheek and forehead. She sipped her drink with her eyes closed. All that had taken place that day was, after all, a direct result of conflict with the Republic.

"They are afraid," Holm replied. "It has literally been an article of faith for the people of the Republic to believe that Humans can only live one way. The existence of my people shook that belief deeply, but we are not Human, so there was a way out for them. Now they have found the Commonwealth, filled with Humans living much as we do. How can they respond? The truth would be too costly to embrace, so I believe they hesitate and delay, and no doubt work to keep their population from knowing contact has taken place at all. If your most basic beliefs were suddenly not merely challenged, but proven flat out wrong, how might *you* react?"

"With fear," Alicia replied, with a sigh. "And perhaps anger. And stupid decisions."

Holm gave her the slow, deep nod of the head — almost a bow — that among his people meant complete agreement.

"Still," Alicia persisted, "to deny their people perfect health and near immortality? That just isn't *right!*"

"I agree," Holm said. "I fear the consequences of this denial will be a greater upheaval than they might endure if they simply said yes."

"It would help if they'd send those representatives. Get someone here to see what they are dealing with, and see that we mean no harm," Robert said. Unspoken came the thought, *So no one else will ever endure what happened to her.*

"But you will harm them," Melep said sadly. "Just as we did before you. You will not mean to do so, but seeing what you are will upset their way of life, perhaps beyond hope of repair."

"As for sending negotiators, where would they be sent?" Holm asked. "They have refused the offer of facilities on Serch'nach, even though this is now neutral territory. They cite 'security concerns.' The Confederation, I regret to say, has declined to send its people into the Republic. This leaves the Commonwealth, which presents a unique problem of its own."

"What have we done *now?*" Alicia demanded.

"They won't hold negotiations on or in anything of the Commonwealth where an Artificial resides," Robert reminded her. "Artificial Intelligence is anathema in the Republic. We still don't know why. And we don't build anything meant for permanent habitation without an Artificial as part of the basic design."

"Well, it needs to happen *somewhere!*" Alicia said. She looked and sounded increasingly angry. "We need to make sure what happened to the *Bartram...*" She stopped abruptly and her lips became a thin, tense line.

Her eyes filled with tears and she looked away from them, struggling for control.

The awkward silence returned to the dinner table. They all picked at their food for a time, or sipped *bosh'sh*.

"We have no artificial intelligences in the Confederation!" Melep said suddenly, as if it were a great revelation.

"This is known," Holm said mildly.

"Hear me, husband!" But she looked around at all three of them. "They will not use Sersh'nach because there is no way they can be sure they have blocked all our attempts to spy on them. But what if we invite the Republic to settle their diplomatic mission in the new habitat? Set up the Trilateral Commission there? They could have their people on site from the very beginning to oversee construction, make sure it suits them. We would use Confederation and Republic computer tech, and leave out the Artificial Intelligence. Perhaps *that* would be neutral enough for them." She looked around at them and blinked. "Why not?"

"Would they even consider it?" Robert asked.

"I do not know," Holm said slowly, looking up at them with large, amber-gold eyes shining in his dark face. "But it is an idea worth considering. Yes, it should be discussed at the next meeting of your survivors' committee. They would need to agree to such a plan before it could be suggested to the Republic. And the suggestion should come from the *Bartram* survivors, to make it more difficult for the Republic to gracefully refuse."

"It'll be a rough orbit to fall into," Robert added. "With all that's happened to us — I don't know about this. Lots of people have hard feelings toward the Republic. I expect this could be a *very* divisive issue."

"Yes, it *will* be," Alicia said. "Maybe it'll be too much." And for a moment Robert thought she was about to tell them all why it couldn't work. But instead, she went on with, "It's still a good idea. We need to give it a chance. Something *must* be done, and I haven't heard a better idea!" She reached out to Melep and took her hand, with a fond smile for the Leyra'an woman. "I will present the idea at the next meeting." Alicia's voice changed, lost the weariness and gained a sort of grim determination. "Holm, you should come with me to the next meeting and lend your support."

"I am willing," Holm said. "But I am puzzled. How might I help?"

"No one I know among the Leyra'an understands what my shipmates suffered better than you," she said gently, looking the man in the eye. "Essentially the same thing happened to you, and if you of all people can embrace this idea... "

"She's right," Robert said.

"Then I will come," Holm replied.

CHAPTER THREE

Eb'ara Kai Station; Pa'haronsa System
Leyra'an Confederation of Clans
Two Years After Contact

The now familiar warmth against his back shifted slightly as John Knowles drifted up into the fuzzy consciousness of early morning, and gave a brief prayer of thanks. It still seemed both strange and wonderful that she should be there, and just plain strange that any of what was happening to him could possibly be real. A year ago Wirolen's people, her *species*, had been his enemies. Now one of the Leyra'an was the love of his life, a strange concept all by itself for one who saw himself as a perennial bachelor. Looming over all of *those* adjustments, he would this very day request asylum within her clan and family. How had he gone from a loyal officer of the Republic Defense Force to a refugee in the alien realm of the Leyra'an? *How did I come to this?*

Through death and doubt. The death of a man he would never truly know, who died in a selfless act of courage that saved John's life, and abruptly crystallized long-suppressed doubts regarding the life he lived and the duties he embraced.

I wish I could have known you, Eb'shra Mosin. I hope I can make my life worth the terrible price you paid. I intend to do so.

He caught himself as the words half-formed a prayer. How could he ever have known Eb'shra Mosin? Not that long ago he would have shot the man on sight. He might not even have acknowledged him as a man! Yet now he acknowledged the greatest of all debts to this man of the Leyra'an, who had died in his place without the two of them ever exchanging a single word.

The doubts had been there all the while. As an officer of the RDF Intelligence Service, John knew all too well how often the government he served lied to its people. Necessary lies, he had believed in those days. Humans were so easily drawn to the way the Leyra'an lived. Casting that way of life in a bad light was seen as essential to the defense of the Republic.

But how can it be, he wondered as light levels in the room slowly and automatically rose to full daylight, *that a corrupting influence might change a man for the better?*

He had been well-rewarded for his loyalty and entrusted with a delicate mission, to serve with and spy upon one of the Republic's most decorated heroes. A man also considered a possible link to the most notorious criminal in all of the Republic's history. The mission changed John's life, though not in any way he could have expected. Between then and now he'd been an unwitting participant in a massacre, had witnessed contact with the long-lost people of Earth, had been sent to a prison station to set a trap for his commanding officer's greatest foe, and then led a revolt by the prisoners he found being abused there. He'd fallen in with enemies of the state, formed a common cause with the Leyra'an, and turned his back on his oath of loyalty to become a traitor, a refugee.

In a desperate fight at the end, John was wounded and rendered helpless. A young Leyra'an named Eb'shra Mosin came to his aid, saved his life, but died in the doing. John could not forget the look in the eyes of

Eb'shra Mosin, the look of naked terror and pain as life left him.

How could a race of beings capable of such a thing be evil?

The area of warmth at his back pressed in closer. They often slept back-to-back, so when John rolled over toward her, he was able to curl around her slim form and draw her in close. Eb'shra Wirolen grasped the arm he slipped around her and pulled it snug against her breasts. He knew from recent experience that she was not really awake when she did this. It was a reflex, like pulling the blanket up to your shoulders without being truly awake, but aware of the chill. John for not the first time marvelled that the texture of her skin, covered as it was with smooth, tiny scales, no longer felt strange against his. It was simply how she felt. He marvelled all the more that she had chosen to be with him. Her cousin had died saving his life, and when she saw how deeply this troubled him, Eb'shra Wirolen sought to comfort him, reaching out to him in that way her people had. That's all it had been, at first.

Did the Leyra'an know love as Humans experienced it? It was hard to say for certain. They seemed a more openly passionate people than Humans, given to loud and heart-felt declarations and celebrations to match. They were also capable of grief so deep that John had been afraid for her, when the ceremony to release Eb'shra Mosin's soul was held. Offering comfort in return, he sparked a relationship that showed no sign of cooling off. Whatever the answer to the question of how the Leyra'an felt love, John Knowles found himself deeply and passionately in love with this woman of another species who was, all the same, so very Human in the ways that mattered. John held Eb'shra Wirolen close, and yet again gave thanks.

This was the day he would either become an honorary member of her family, or seek refuge elsewhere. They were aware that the clan as a whole was divided on the matter, but her immediate family, and that of Eb'shra Mosin, were determined to petition the Matriarch for acceptance on his behalf. A Human brought into a

Leyra'an family was hardly without precedent, with a substantial population of Human refugees from the Republic living within the Confederation. In fact, his friend Robert MacGregor and Robert's wife were now joined to a Leyra'an family, Rost'aht, as part of that family's restoration.

Robert MacGregor was a piper. Bagpipes. John shuddered at the thought that his friend might offer to perform for them in celebration, and for a moment almost blessed the light years between them. But he would gladly have endured the bagpipes for the chance to see his friend again, and to meet Alicia MacGregor. He wouldn't even mind seeing Rost'aht Holm again.

Wirolen rolled over within the curve of his arm and faced him, deep amber eyes open and completely awake. Her people were like that, a legacy of their predatory past, sound asleep one moment and wide awake the next, with none of the morning fuzziness normal for Humans. "By the way of Human, I would be your wife?" She spoke Leyra'an until the last word.

"Not by the way of Human," he replied. He spoke only Leyra'an to her, having decided early on to immerse himself in their culture and language to better understand her people. "By the way of Leyra'an."

"It would be for the best if both ways were satisfied."

John thought for a moment, then said, "You are right, of course. For now, though, the way of your people must suffice. I will abide by the Way of Leyra'an, for it will bind me to you and to your people, if the Matriarch approves. Nothing would please me more."

She gave him a Mona Lisa smile. Her people generally considered a smile that showed teeth a sign of aggression, a challenge. It showed poor taste, and poorer upbringing. "Even though you have been warned that I cling like a smothering vine?" she asked with a narrowing of the eyes that meant mirth.

"Feel free to cling and smother," he replied.

Wirolen rolled over on top of him and did her best to comply.

They dozed off again afterward, and when they woke again there was just time enough to prepare for the meeting with the Matriarch and the Elders, to see if his petition was to be accepted. John ran through what he had been taught regarding the customs involved, feeling suddenly like a schoolboy studying at the last moment for an exam. *Speak only in Leyra'an... bow slightly each time you respond to her... do not allow her to rise without offering your hand... address her as Matriarch...* It was about as formal as the brash Leyra'an ever got, and was more than formal enough to set John's nerves on edge.

"Be easy, *sip'ya'a*," Wirolen said in the Human tongue, but using the Leyra'an phrase by which a woman addressed her lover. "You will do fine."

"You know, I doubt I have ever done anything more important, much less been more worried," he said, staying true to his decision to use only her language.

"I understand," she replied, in kind. "And you must expect that the Matriarch surely knows this, and will make certain allowances for your lack of experience. Be honest with her, and show no fear. She respects honesty and courage." She took his hand between hers and gazed into his eyes. "This is very important, what you do, for both our peoples. She will understand this, as well."

"Well, yes, all of that," he replied. "Mostly, I fear embarrassing you."

She smiled, almost looking shy to Human eyes not entirely accustomed to reading Leyra'an expressions. "You will do no such thing, ever. For I know you will do your best."

He held her for a moment, briefly touching his forehead to hers in the Leyra'an equivalent of a kiss, and then returned to dressing himself in styles suited to a Leyra'an gathering. For a moment he had wondered if his RDF dress uniform might be suitable; Wirolen asked him if he had gone mad, and that was the end of that. So he found himself dressed in a fine suit of Leyra'an clothes, with a tunic-style shirt of cinnamon brown, trousers of a darker shade, and black belt and boots that seemed made of some sort of leather, though Wirolen assured him it was a synthetic organic material, grown for the purpose. Over it all was a loose, long-sleeved robe of dark gray cloth, worn by ancient tradition to represent his nature as a supplicant. Lacking was an *es'ava*, the colorful braided sash that would announce his clan and family affiliation; for the moment, at least, he had none. Wirolen wore similar colors, with a long-waisted blouse, a long, loose, swirling skirt, and dark brown slippers on her feet. Across her chest, cutting a line from shoulder to hip, was her colorful *es'ava*. Bands of coarse cloth, crimson and aqua and lavender, were wound loosely together. He told her she was beautiful, and she said the same of him, and they stepped out of their sleeping quarters to wait in the garden.

Their escort soon arrived, two sturdy young men with the brown scale coloring typical of Eb'shra, with stripes of darker brown around their arms and on their cheeks, wearing shirts and trousers very much like John's, but of looser, more casual fit and in warmer browns and deeper greens. The colorful braided *es'avas* crossed their broad chests from shoulder to hip. At first glance John wondered at such informal dress, then realized that it allowed these muscular gentlemen more freedom of movement. They were surely bodyguards, likely present as much to protect the Matriarch from him as they were to lead him to her presence.

"The Matriarch is ready," said one, after both had shown proper respect to a guest by bowing.

"As are we," Wirolen replied.

John held out his arm and with Wirolen attached to it, nodded to their escort. "Please, lead on."

They walked out into the concourse of the enormous main ring of Eb'ara Kai station. John wondered if he would ever make sense of the apparent chaos he saw around him. Tall trees, with leaves of silver-green or feathered bronze, grew around and loomed over multilevel structures that seemed a jumble of open frameworks and panels that served as movable walls. The buildings often sat in pairs, with a single-floor domed structure between them. There seemed no plan to where buildings were located, and the only straight lines of travel were the main walkway and the tram line that paralleled it. The station was well lit in the day cycle; the

Leyra'an came from a brighter star than the Human species. The place was lush, flowers and shrubs growing from any spot in which a container could be accommodated. To John's eyes it was extravagance compounded upon luxury, a station lifestyle only great wealth could sustain.

But the Leyra'an knew nothing of costs and accounts. Unrestrained by such concerns, the places in which they lived were unrestrained as well. For John, it was nearly overwhelming, and seductive.

They drew stares as they marched along, for although it was common knowledge that a Human had come to the station, this was not a part of the Confederation in which Humans were often seen. For all that he was properly dressed for his location, John knew he was exotic, and felt terribly conspicuous.

It was not a long walk, as it turned out, to the council chambers of Eb'shra, Clan Pa'haronsa, yet another pair of open-air structures flanking a dome. Only in scale were they different, being much larger. There were also more of the movable, lightweight wall panels in place than usual. Brown vines with pale gray-green leaves climbed the posts and struts of these buildings, dangling over the curve of the dome.

The escort did not slow down as they came to the council building, entering and striding confidently forward. The interior of the dome was broad and open, divided only by low walls that doubled as planters, from which spilled bright green, feathery-leaved vegetation, nurtured by bright and ornate lamps suspended by chains over their heads. These subdivisions of the dome were occupied by Leyra'an men and women, some sharing desks and others moving about on errands of various sorts, the scribes and clerks who saw to the management of clan affairs. On either hand he could see other entrances such as the one through which they had just passed, leading into the structures flanking the dome. And in the center of the dome stood a large gathering of Leyra'an, looking their way, waiting.

In the midst of that gathering, facing them, was a low couch, on which was seated the first truly elderly

Leyra'an he had ever seen in the flesh. She looked like a well-dressed collection of sticks and taut, scaly skin, and her cheekbones stood out prominently. White hair, which he had not seen before on a Leyra'an, was cut short, stiffened, and curved around her head like a helmet. She held a cane with an ornate silver head, fashioned in the likeness of a sharp-snouted beast he did not recognize. The Matriarch held the cane upright with one hand on the head, and the beast head seemed to peer out at him from between long, almost fleshless fingers. Golden eyes, sunk into her dusky-scaled face under sharp brows, seemed to glare out at him as they approached. The escort stopped John and Wirolen a few paces away from the couch, then moved to stand on either side of the Matriarch. She briefly flashed her teeth at him, and there was nothing aged about that challenging smile. John restrained himself, met those eyes and ignored the pointed teeth, and when they were motioned forward, they approached and bowed. "I hope the morning finds you well, Matriarch," he said in Leyra'an.

"Well enough," she replied. If his presence offended or angered her, nothing of that showed or came across in her words. "You speak our language well, and with sufficient courtesy."

"Thank you, Matriarch. I have had good teachers." He bowed again.

She looked him up and down, slowly turning the cane around with her fingers as she did. Her assessment completed, she looked at Wirolen and said, "Granddaughter, for a Human he is not at all unattractive."

"No, Matriarch, he is not." There was nothing deferential in Wirolen's tone.

"That would be reason enough for me," the old woman said with a sharp laugh, "but others would be offended. Tell me, can anyone other than grandchild Wirolen with her odd taste in men give reason why he should be welcomed among us?"

A woman stepped out from the crowd around them and approached. When she stood beside John, she bowed. "Eb'shra Vil," the Matriarch said. "You are the mother of Eb'shra Mosin. *You* will speak?" She looked and sounded genuinely surprised.

John certainly was.

"I would, Matriarch," Eb'shra Vil replied softly.

"Well?"

"To honor the memory of my son," Vil said quietly. "To honor his sacrifice, we would have this man among us. *My* house will take him in."

John restrained the urge to reach over and place a comforting hand on the woman's shoulder. They had spoken at length the night before, and much to his surprise, there was neither animosity nor blame in her. She saw it as a choice her son had made in a split second, and was proud of Mosin, even as she grieved. When she explained that to John she wept, and it broke his heart. But nothing in that awkward and painful meeting gave him any reason to expect to hear her speak on his behalf. Her grief was still there, for all to see, and more than anything at that moment, he wanted to see this woman comforted. But it was not his place to speak, and he could only stand there and feel an echo of her pain.

"You are pained by his death?" the Matriarch asked John quietly.

"Very much, Matriarch. Her son put himself in harm's way for my sake, and died."

"You would not have done the same?" the Matriarch demanded. "Were your roles reversed?"

John did not answer at once, then sighed and said quietly, "I do not know, Matriarch. Perhaps not. I am not the man I was the moment before Eb'shra Mosin made his choice. The man I was — likely not. And knowing this shames me." He looked up and met her gaze. Wirolen and various members of her immediate family had urged that he answer honestly, and he had done so. And now, for the consequences.

"And well it should," the Matriarch replied quietly. "Mosin was a good lad. Intelligent. Strong. And he had a good heart. What he was as a man is now lost to Eb'shra. Do you think you can fill that void?"

John considered his answer carefully, then said, "No, Matriarch, I cannot. Nor will I try. I do not believe it would be appropriate. It is not why I have come."

"No? Then tell us all why you have come. Not, surely, for the desire of this lady, alone? Or are you that shallow?" She glared at him, and her teeth flicked in and out of sight for a split second.

Knowing he was being baited, John nevertheless kept his tone even and locked his eyes on hers. "Matriarch, there is nothing shallow or convenient about my love for your granddaughter. For her sake alone I would *indeed* have come." Wirolen's grip on his arm tightened. "But I found her *after* I started down this path." He looked at Eb'shra Vil pointedly, then back to the old woman. "I follow this path, set before me by the God I worship, in the hope that what I learn might somehow prevent any other parent from knowing her pain."

Some of those gathered, the current elders of the clan and family, scowled, but they had done so all along. But others were nodding, now, clearly impressed by the Human in their midst. The Matriarch glared at Vil. "And you believe in him? You trust his motives?"

"I do, Matriarch," Vil replied, without so much as a moment's pause. "I do not know this man well, and I have only met two Humans before now. But I have seen his pain. I *believe* his pain. It is a mirror of my own. He does not say so, but my heart tells me he has come to seek healing, as well. It is my wish that he find it." She looked at him with tear-filled eyes and repeated, "It is my wish that he find it."

John closed his eyes for a moment, and prayed that the Matriarch would not address him immediately after hearing what Vil said. He did not think he could speak, just then. His hands were shaking; he felt Wirolen tighten her grip on his arm. He was thinking of that first meeting with Eb'shra Mosin's family again, of telling them how their son had died, and how he tried to express something of the burden, the debt, now on his soul. Of how he had lost control in the end, and wept in his own confused grief, suddenly desperate to understand it all. And here was that man's *mother*, trying to help him find a way to be absolved of guilt. He wondered if such a thing would ever be possible.

"I would know your minds in this matter," he heard the Matriarch say in a hard, raised voice, a voice accustomed to command. "Let the Elders here assembled add their judgment to mine."

"We would know *your* judgment," said a man with streaks of gray through his hair and thin, rust-colored markings on his face. He and six other white-robed men and women drifted into the open and stood behind the couch.

"My judgment?" the Matriarch replied. "Well then! Here is my judgment. This man before us, this Human, is a good man. He comes to us bearing a terrible burden. He comes to us seeking help and healing. He seeks peace. He seeks acceptance. And I say we will give these to him! Who opposes?" Two closed their hands into fists and brought them to their chests with a thump. "Who supports?" And five held up one hand apiece, fingers spread and palms outward. "My judgment is supported." She gazed up at John and said, "Be welcome among us."

"Our house will take him," said Vil again.

"That is well done, daughter. Be honored for that." The Matriarch looked around and tapped her cane on the floor, and John responded to the tug on his arm from Wirolen, which told him it was time to leave. As instructed he said no words of thanks, and merely bowed to the Matriarch in visible acceptance of her judgment, then turned and followed Wirolen and Eb'shra Vil away.

CHAPTER FOUR

Pr'pri System
Neutral Space

On the day of the *Bartram* survivor meeting, family Rost'aht gathered for their midday meal in the establishment of one Rir'lek Traloph. The short, spritely proprietor greeted them with his usual enthusiasm, silver and copper arm bands clattering together as he rushed to greet them when they arrived. Robert, Alicia, and Melep were shown to a table on the very top of the structure, which gave a grand view of treetops and the upward sweep of the torus on either hand. Holm arrived shortly after they were settled, with important news as an excuse for his tardiness.

"We have a protocol in place for managing the Trilateral Commission," he declared as he dropped into the chair between Melep and Alicia. The metal chair creaked when he landed.

"That would imply representation from the Republic in the near future," Robert said.

"I would like to think so," Holm replied. One of the Rir'lek household helpers came by with glasses and a tall pitcher of pinkish *a'boshna*. "In essence, the protocol requires two representatives from each domain, and chairmanship of sessions, which will be public, will rotate between them. There is much more to it than that, of course, with staffs of varying size supporting the work, among other things."

"The overall structure is in place, though," Robert said. "That's progress."

"To progress," Melep said, and they all drank to it.

"Does the protocol set out the meeting place?" Melep asked.

"No," Holm replied.

"In that case, here's to the success of *your* endeavor." And Robert raised his glass yet again, saluting first Alicia, then Holm.

"This will be an interesting meeting," Alicia said after they drank.

Holm regarded her for a long moment, then asked, "Is there really any chance that they will go along with this idea?"

"It won't be all that well received, by some," she replied. "Under the circumstances, that's only to be expected. But," she paused and took a drink, "I think I know how we should present it in order to improve our chances."

They spent lunch working over Alicia's idea, an act that ran counter to the usual Leyra'an habit of discussing lighter matters over a meal, especially in public. They were still trying to finesse it when the time came to head to the meeting site used by the survivors. It was a bit of a journey, by tram and lift capsule and then tram again, to another ring of the station altogether. The site, when they arrived, was a shallow amphitheatre built into a turf-covered artificial hill. Dozens of tiers of seats stepped up and away from the stage at the bottom of the bowl, behind which was a wall of tall, slim trees with disc-shaped, pale green leaves. A crowd had already gathered inside when the four of them arrived, and many more were following them. Most were Human, the probeship's surviving crew, but it seemed to Robert that nearly a full quarter of those gathered were Leyra'an. The Leyra'an contingent grew with each meeting.

Alicia paused, looked around, and said, "He's over there." She led them on to where Ezra stood in discussion with a small group of Humans. They were all dressed in a mix of Human and Leyra'an styles, all of it in the browns, reds, greens and dark blues favored by the Leyra'an. All of the Humans wore a gray arm band with a blue stripe around the middle. These were the colors of the Commonwealth Survey, to which they had all once belonged. It was a mark of remembrance and solidarity; Robert and Alicia had slipped theirs on before entering the amphitheatre.

The chairman was Ezra Ashe, once the proprietor of the Willow Lake Inn, the most popular food and music venue aboard the lost probeship, a gathering site so crowded and noisy at times that in hindsight it had seemed almost Leyra'an-ish. His wife and all their children save one, his eldest boy, had perished in the disaster following the attack.

"Good day, my dear friends," Ezra said. His voice had little of the cheerful energy it once contained, and his smile wasn't quite as broad and easy as in better days. No one was surprised when it was suggested that stout, black-haired Ezra be named to the chairmanship. Robert hadn't expected him to accept the position, but Ezra surprised him by seizing the opportunity as a way to deal with his own grief by providing support for others. "What's on your minds today?" Ezra asked.

"Are we that obvious?" Alicia asked with a brief laugh.

"Have you heard of a game called poker, my dear?" Ezra laughed when she shook her head and then said, "I would not recommend it to you."

Alicia laughed again and shook her head, then explained to the man what she and Holm wanted to do. Ezra did not react visibly to Alicia's words. "Yours will be the only bit of new business, then. And I wish you luck with it." He gestured to the lowest rows of seats, where other speakers waited for a chance to address their fellow survivors.

"Thanks," said Alicia in reply, and the four of them found seats in the waiting area.

"Just a gut feeling," Robert said into Alicia's ear. "But I don't think he likes this idea."

"It just took him by surprise," she replied.

There followed a long series of reports by various committees charged with designing the many aspects of the habitat. These were summaries of smaller meetings and conferences over the station network, given in this form to provide an excuse for gathering together. All of it mattered, though some of it was of more interest to Robert than others. It turned out that Robert's idea for vineyards had indeed occurred to a number of people, and the idea was enthusiastically approved by those assembled. He put his name forward to be part of the team that would see it done.

The result of the comprehensive poll regarding the name of the new habitat was formally announced, and Robert nodded in approval when he learned that their new home would be named Bartram. At that point, Ezra came back to the stage, a giant holographic image of him floating in the background display, through which the trees were dimly seen.

"My friends," he said. "We have one item left, our sole bit of new business for the day. It will be presented by Rost'aht Holm and Alicia MacGregor." He looked into the front row and gave them a nod.

Alicia and Holm climbed the steps to the stage, dressed alike in dark green tunics and brown pants and boots. Each also wore the braided, colored sash, the *es'ava* of gold, green, and electric blue that marked them as members of family Rost'aht. Alicia's red hair stood out brightly in the plain surroundings; Holm seemed to loom over her. They stood side by side and then bowed to the audience.

"I have no doubt that you are all aware of the slow progress in establishing diplomatic relations between the Republic and the Commonwealth," Alicia said to her fellow survivors. "The building of a peaceful and constructive relationship with our lost brethren has faced numerous obstacles, as have negotiations aimed at a permanent peace between the Republic and the Confederation." There was a quiet but definite stirring of those assembled. There was no small amount of animosity held by the survivors of the *William Bartram* for the Humans of the Republic. "One such stumbling block, we have been given to believe, has to do with the selection of a venue for long-term negotiations."

Holm then took his turn. "The Republic," he said, "has among its many objections a grave reservation regarding the beings you call Artificials. The development of such artificial life forms is forbidden in their domain. This has created a quandary for those trying to start the Commission of which we have all heard, for the Republic will not meet with us in any facility containing such an entity. Nor will they agree to a site within this station. To provide an alternative, we of Rost'aht propose this: that the Bartram habitat be built using non-sentient computer technology designed for habitat management by the Leyra'an and the Republic." A grumble of objection rose from those seated behind and above Robert. He resisted the urge to turn and look back. "By foregoing the use of artificial intelligence... " The objections rose in number and volume. "... we could invite the Commissioners and their respective staff members and support crews to live with *us*. Let *our* community be a truly *neutral* community, where folk of all three domains may be welcome to mingle in safety and comfort."

"Welcome!" someone shouted. "You can't be serious! This so-called Republic murdered more than half our crew!"

"No!" Alicia shouted back. "They did no such thing! One man... " The crowd noise rose and she pitched her voice to rise above it. "*One man did that!* One man alone, in defiance of his government's instructions... "

"If they weren't at war with the Leyra'an," another voice shouted, "none of it would have happened!"

"They *are* responsible!" a new voice insisted.

"Not all of them!" a different voice shouted.

Divisive, Robert thought. An understatement. The audience suddenly dissolved into a myriad of heated arguments. Robert did turn and look, then, appalled by what was happening. In all the years he'd served with these people aboard the *William Bartram*, nothing approaching such a thing had ever happened! Faces were red, profanity was shouted, hands were waving around.

"Madness!" said a man in the next row behind him.

Robert wasn't sure he was being addressed, but he responded all the same. "Not madness," he shouted over the uproar. "Sense. Negotiations are necessary, and they aren't going to happen if a site can't be chosen!"

"Perfect sense!" a woman in that same row shouted. "Listen to them! Do you want anyone else to go through what happened to us?"

"'Course not!" was the shouted reply. "But why do we have to cater to these bastards and their backwards idea to get it done?"

"One problem at a time," Robert suggested loudly. "Their superstitions are a minor matter."

But the two were no longer paying attention to his input. Disgusted, Robert turned to face the stage again, where he saw Holm standing a step in front of Alicia, arms folded across his broad chest. Alicia looked past him with a pale face and frightened eyes, with the sort of expression she wore when she woke bolt upright from one of her nightmares. Holm shouted something at the crowd, but the only evidence of it was the baring of his teeth when it did no good. He looked to one side and waved at Ezra, made an upward gesture with one hand. Robert saw Ezra nod, then pull a small device from his jacket pocket and touch it. He looked to Holm and nodded again.

Holm addressed the crowd again, but this time his words were amplified to an almost painful volume. "Hear me!" he shouted, and the words rolled over the crowd, many of whom turned, startled, to face the stage. Once was not enough. "*Hear me!*" thundered over them, as Ezra tweaked the volume yet again. And this time the noise dropped down to a few muttered conversations, last words being given, as they all turned to listen to Rost'aht Holm.

"Believe me when I say I understand your pain," he began.

"How can you possibly understand *our* pain?" a shrill voice demanded, and Robert looked over his shoulder toward the speaker, aghast. How could anyone in the *Bartram's* crew not know?

"Because I have felt it!" Holm shouted. "I feel it even now! I watched while everyone I ever knew or loved died in an instant. My parents, my brother and my sister, the grandparents on both sides, cousins, uncles and aunts. All of them gone, lost forever. One nuclear detonation, and everyone who truly mattered to me was *dead!"*

Robert stared at his friend, a man who was now so much more than that, and a lump formed in his throat. You could hear the pain and grief in Holm's voice. All of them could, and the survivors of the *William Bartram* were shamed into silence. Robert suddenly wanted to be down there with his Leyra'an brother. Alicia *was* there; she stepped forward to stand beside Holm and take his hand between hers.

Into the silence of embarrassment, Holm went on, casting aside their carefully considered presentation and lashing out at them with his voice. "You should know this tale by now! I let that horrible instant light the fire of hatred in my heart, and hatred *consumed* me. I swore to kill every Human I could reach. For hate's sake I walked to the edge of oblivion. But a man stood in the path of my hatred and did not flinch. A Human, and one you all know very well! And now," and Holm looked down at Alicia for a moment, then looked up and raised their clasped hands into view, "Now, two of those I love most in all the universe are *Humans!"* He swept his gaze across those assembled. "I let grief rule me, and blamed those who were blameless. Now *your* grief threatens to lead you down that same path. *Yes*, you should feel grief. It is only right that you do so. This is part of how we honor those who are lost to us. But will you, in your grief, give in to hatred and risk losing a chance to end this war forever? To free those who come after us from the same sad fate we have known? This is the question you must discuss, not whether or not all the folk of the Republic are deserving of your hatred. Will you step over the edge into the abyss that nearly took me? Or will you turn from it, and honor your dead by finding the peace that will save so many others?"

Alicia suddenly raised her free hand and rubbed tears from her face. Holm did not move his gaze from those assembled before him.

Ezra Ashe walked slowly across the stage to stand beside Holm. His face was pale, his expression one of a man deeply unhappy. A muttering of voices rose up as he took his place before them. Ezra held up a hand and waited, but said nothing. Such was the respect the others held for this man that the noise of debate fell away quickly. Ezra waited a moment more after the noise subsided, then lowered his hand and began to speak. He was not a tall man, equal in height to Alicia, but broad-shouldered and muscular, with a broad, pale face under black, curly hair.

"This is a proposal worthy of serious consideration," he said, his deep voice booming out and needing little amplification. "And one that cannot avoid arousing powerful feelings one way or the other. So we will not decide now, what to do. We will wait until this time tomorrow, at which time I will put a poll up on the net. We will each of us record our decisions privately, after due consideration. Do not decide in haste. Do not decide right now. Discuss this with one another. Think about it carefully. Vote tomorrow."

That ended the meeting. Robert and Melep hurried over to Alicia and Holm, embracing them one after the other. "Well done," Robert said when he could find his voice.

"I take it this was a Rost'aht idea?" Ezra asked as he stepped down from the speaker's platform to join them.

"Yes," Robert replied.

"You upset and then embarrassed a lot of people," Ezra told Holm.

"It could not be helped," the tall Leyra'an said gently. "The idea has merit, but they will not consider fairly unless they look beyond their anger. And I understand their anger."

"Yes," said Ezra. "Yes, you do." He looked down at his feet.

"Ezra?" said Melep gently, reaching out to touch his arm. "Ezra, what is wrong?"

"I heard what he said," Ezra replied. "And I'm still angry. I can't help it." He looked up and around at them, then fixed his gaze on Holm. "And now I need to find out if I'm half the man you are."

CHAPTER FIVE

Pr'pri System
Serch'nach Station

The vote, when it was taken, was close, with fifty-seven percent in favor of the proposal, and forty-three percent against. The decision was made: the Bartram habitat would be built with the sensibilities of the Republic in mind, and the offer to host the Trilateral Commission would be made. The vote decided the matter, but it cost them. It split the survivors of the *William Bartram,* and roughly a third of their number simply could not accept the decision. They formed themselves into a separate group, and announced that when the first of the grand liners visited from the Commonwealth, they would depart.

Robert and his immediate family were stunned by the news of this unintended consequence of their idea. They made various appeals to the dissenting faction, but won very few converts. In the end, all anyone could do was simply say goodbye, as those who could not forgive the Republic for what had happened removed themselves to places where the Republic could never directly touch their lives.

Among those who chose to depart was Ezra Ashe. It was a somber night in the apartments shared by Rost'aht when Robert brought the news home.

"They mean to rebuild the Willow Lake Inn," Alicia said, that evening. They sat in chairs on the patio and looked out into the inverted world of Serch'nach Station, in quiet twilight mode at the end of the day. The elf lights gleamed around them. "How will that work without Ezra?"

"His son isn't leaving," Robert said quietly.

"Ira isn't going with his father?" Alicia asked, clearly appalled. "Mother of Life!"

Robert rose from his chair and went to the table behind them for the wine they'd left there. He went to each and poured the clear liquid into their glasses; no one refused. "Ezra gave me the news himself. They both voted against the proposal, but Ira had a change of heart when talk of leaving began."

"I feel very bad about all this,"Melep said softly and sadly as Robert filled her glass.

Robert reached down and stroked her thick mane of black hair. "Hush, Melep," he said gently. "You are in no way responsible. The idea was a good one. If it hadn't come from us, it would have been suggested by others, eventually." He returned to his seat between Alicia and Holm. "I've spoken to several who admit to thinking of it before we made the proposal. We merely got there first."

"But... *families* are being broken up by this," Melep said. "Oh, this is *not* what we intended!"

"No," said Alicia. "It wasn't. And we should have foreseen such consequences." For a moment Robert saw that distant look in her eyes, one he knew meant she was seeing the darkness within the *William Bartram* again. Her eyes focused on the glass of wine in her hand and she took a sip. "But I'd have gone on that stage and made the suggestion all the same! It's hard, but the consequences of *not* doing this will be harder. Things must change, and if we don't make it happen, who will?"

"Indeed," said Holm. "It must begin, and where better than here?" He sipped the wine he held and wore a thoughtful frown. To Melep he said, "You are quite right, my love. It is an easily acquired taste."

"Word went out to the Republic today, didn't it?" Robert asked.

"Yes," Holm replied. "The *Cygnet* took its stacks of printouts and flew home this morning. The Bartram Proposal was sent with the highest possible priority."

"Printouts," Alicia scoffed. "Gaia, what nonsense!"

"For it to be so deeply rooted and unquestioned," said Robert, "I'm guessing something really bad happened to these people, long time ago. Why else go to such trouble to make sure nothing of a digital nature can pass from the Commonwealth into the Republic?"

"Someday we must learn the reason for their animosity toward Artificials," Holm said. "So far, they have said nothing of their reasons."

"How soon do you think we'll hear back?" Alicia replied.

"If recent events are any guide," said Holm, "it will be weeks, at least."

And so it proved, but though the delay was considerable, the reply was a surprise. It consisted of a team of engineers and other observers from the Republic, sent to supervise the construction of Bartram. They were blunt about their motives, their primary mission being to make sure no computer technology they did not understand was installed. They were soon an integral part of the design and construction of the habitat, recording and questioning everything.

A matter of days after the return of the *Cygnet* with the agreement to go along with the Bartram Proposal, the grand liner *Thomas Say* arrived from the far side of Pr'pri system, after a month-long transit. For most of the residents of Pr'pri system, the passage of the *Thomas Say* was cause for celebration. As routes into the Confederation from the Commonwealth were discovered, grand liners were adding Leyra'an systems to their routes in an effort to facilitate cultural exchange. Robert wondered, when he heard of this, how long it would be before the Republic permitted such exchanges; so far there had been no word. But while the rest of the system celebrated, there were those on Serch'nach who did otherwise, as they watched friends and family board the liner and leave Pr'pri system behind.

There was no send-off. The partings were private matters, and painful. In the case of Ezra Ashe, his final message to Rost'aht was a polite request to *not* come see him off.

"We will honor this request," Holm said. "And we will keep the door open, should he return."

Pr'pri was the turn-around point for the *Thomas Say*. When its visit ended, it fired its massive engines and left Serch'nach and the remaining crew of the *William Bartram* behind.

It seemed to Robert the community of survivors who remained behind drew together and became more tightly knit. Meetings were held more frequently to plan the interior of Bartram, and gatherings for the sake of gathering became more common as well. They had endured yet another adversity, and as before, responded by holding more tightly to what was left to them.

In the months that followed, they watched the habitat's infrastructure take shape in space, less than an hour away from Serch'nach. Exhaustive safety tests followed, and then were repeated when the habitat was pressurized and put into spin. When it was proven the habitat was stable in all mechanical aspects, Humans and Leyra'an began the task of bringing the mesocosm to life. The monitors from the Republic wandered the interior of the habitat, watching and recording.

Where the lifeless hulk of the *William Bartram* had drifted, cold and silent, there was now only empty space. All that remained of it was, one way or another, incorporated within the inverted world named Bartram. Robert stood one day on a concrete foam feature, a bare rise that would soon be covered in manufactured soil and planted in turf. There were already patches of green to be seen as he looked up and around. The vineyard he intended to build would sweep away in both directions from where he stood. Robert grinned as he thought of being part of the crew bringing life into this place.

When the date was set for permanent inhabitants to move in, most of the Republic's crew of monitors returned home to report on all they'd seen and measured. They left behind a trio of watchers, to make sure nothing was changed while they were away. Another month passed, then the *Cygnet* returned, bearing with it the Republic's Commissioners and support crew.

"Ha! It is a *major* achievement!" Holm sounded both pleased and amazed by the event. "There will be a Trilateral Commission after all!"

"They timed their arrival well," said Alicia. "Tomorrow is Moving Day. Are they aware of the event?"

"Yes," said Holm. "And according to the leader of the Republic's Commission, they will participate."

"From that I assume they've picked a spot to live," Alicia said. "I wonder which one?"

"Give me a moment," said Melep, and a display drifted up from where she sat and filled the center of their living room. "It should be a matter of public record. And here it is!" A bracket formed and flashed around a modest complex of buildings on a bluff overlooking one of the larger bodies of salt water, one that would be stocked with marine creatures from Old Earth. The image for that part of the map was recent; it included palm trees over the white sand around the deep blue lake, still propped up by poles.

"They have good taste," said Robert.

"I am surprised anything there was yet untaken," Holm said.

Robert made a gesture and the area under the bracket scrolled data. "All the residents are Human," he observed.

"Ah," said Holm. "They wanted to make sure they had acceptable neighbors. I suppose we should not be surprised."

"We're over here," Alicia said, and a new bracket flashed less than a quarter of the way around the interior from the salt lake. "And here are the residences for the Leyra'an and Commonwealth Commissioners, minus brother Holm, of course." All of the highlighted residences were within walking distance of the restored

Willow Lake Inn, in the middle third of the central park in which most of the inhabitants chose to live. "The Trilateral offices are near alpha hub, so everyone has a bit of a commute."

"I'm glad they're joining us," Robert said. "Moving Day is a good time to meet people."

"And they *will* meet *my* people, whether they live next door or not!" Melep said. "All the pubs, inns, and restaurants will host celebrations at the end of the day. They will hardly be able to avoid mixed crowds!"

"It has been suggested that the Commissioners join the big party at the Willow Lake," Holm said. "Both the Commonwealth and the Confederation contingents will be there. Those from the Republic were politely noncommittal."

Much of that day had been devoted to packing, and the rest of the evening went into similar preparations. The following morning the transport crew arrived, stripped their Serch'nach apartments and hauled everything away.

"So strange to leave the place where we became a family," Melep said wistfully. She stood just within the doorway and looked around at the bare, empty space.

Holm stood behind her and wrapped her in his arms. "When you leave a place with regret, it means it was worth being there," he said. "Change has come. It is a needful thing and we will accept it."

"We'll be there together," Alicia said.

They all nodded and said yes, and turning around walked away from the empty suite of rooms. It was a quiet trip through the tube system to reach the docks, where they boarded a shuttle full of survivors of the *William Bartram*. Holm and Melep ended up the only Leyra'an aboard, aside from the flight crew. The new habitat looked fresh and new where it slowly turned in space. Soon enough they were inside, riding a tram to the cluster of residences that included their home. They passed several such neighborhoods, each a blend of open-air Leyra'an and blocky Commonwealth architecture. Some structures incorporated elements of both at once.

Everywhere he looked Robert saw the rawness of gray foamcrete, and the bare lines and angles of the basins and pipes, fittings and planters that would, through time and intensive cultivation, eventually be lost to sight, even as they went on performing their functions. The light of the core lamp over their heads seemed a bit too bright, as if even the light itself had a raw newness, the result of having no mature trees to cast pools of shade and soak up the glare. The living mosaic he recalled from the probeship was visible only in outline. It would take years for that to change and fill in completely, and many willing hands to work the change.

Robert looked around and smelled the still too-pure air, recycled for the time being entirely by machinery and algae vats. That sharp eagerness to get into the work struck through him again as he looked around and contemplated the changes ahead. Something of his feelings must have been visible in his face, for he saw Alicia looking at him with a fond and knowing smile. "We're going to be just fine, here," he said to her.

"Yes," she replied, giving one of his hands a squeeze. "We will."

The tram slid silently, carrying passengers who were anything but. There was sadness noticeable, as people saw restored structures and landscapes that brought back memories of what once had been their home. But the words he overheard spoken by those around him expressed an eagerness to move on, and to bring this new place fully to life. Robert's feelings reflected the words spoken around him. "This was the right thing to do," he said quietly.

When Alicia did not respond he looked at her, and saw the round-eyed stare, eyes peering into darkness remembered. "Hey," he said, with a gentle nudge. She blinked and focused on him. "Here and now's the best place to be."

"Yes," she replied, standing a little closer.

The complex in which they'd chosen to live overlooked a long, winding stream, one that eventually flowed into Willow Lake a moderately long walk away. It was one of those with a blended architecture: ground-level, pueblo-inspired private spaces with split-level, open-air Leyra'an structures that rose beside and extended over the house proper. They stepped lightly off the tram as it slowed, but never quite stopped, outside their complex, waving at the people who went on from there.

They walked around to the entry for their residence, and then passed through a still empty courtyard garden space. Robert immediately began to amend the mental list of ideas for what to plant, a task his family left entirely to him. The entry led to the wide family room, which opened to bedrooms, guest rooms, office space, and a dining room. Outside and above were spaces that could be configured into new rooms as needed and on top an outdoor patio dining area reached by a spiral stair made of black iron.

There was a bare quality to the place that was much like that of Bartram itself, but this quality, too, would change in time. Robert was absolutely sure of it.

Room by room they worked as a team to unpack. When the kitchen was done they moved on to the bedroom chosen by Holm and Melep, then to that selected by Robert and Alicia. They paused for a midday meal brought along for the purpose and eaten out on the still bare upper-level patio, and then worked on into the evening. Most of the time they were playful, in high spirits. There came the moment, though, when Robert found the box containing his bagpipes in their stasis shell. He stood there with the dull-surfaced, black rectangle in his hands, then noticed Alicia watching him, with that frightened look back in her eyes. Melep and Holm continued to open boxes and remove contents. They both looked up at their Human companions for a moment, then politely turned their attention to other things.

Robert went to the wall farthest from their bed and opened one of the cabinets built into it. He slid the case inside and closed it, then turned to see that Alicia had drifted along behind him. She was staring blankly at the cabinet.

He put his arms around her and whispered, "Hey, love. Here and now. Stay with me, okay?"

Alicia clung to him for a moment, then stepped away and nodded. "Here and now," she replied. "No better place or time. Come on, let's get back to work."

As the light began to dim for the night cycle, they had the place arranged well enough to start living there, and tired as they were, it was time to step out and celebrate the grand event. Already they heard strains of music drifting through the twilight, heard people laugh and sing. It was Moving Day, and for the members of Rost'aht it was time to visit the Willow Lake Inn.

They decided to walk, and they weren't alone. Familiar voices called them, and their quartet soon became a crowd that strolled between the silver lamps set along the pathway. The stream flowed on the right, sometimes rushing over stones and sparkling in the lamplight, but usually flowing smoothly and quietly along in the gathering dusk. The path curved around the lake, into which the stream fell two meters over a noisy spillway. Small paddle boats dotted the surface, decorated with multicolored lights, and a few people swam nearer the shore. Willows dotted the shoreline, not more than shoulder high, but engineered to reach mature size in a matter of months. Robert ran his fingers through the thin leaves of one as he walked by it, and was not the only one to do so. Cloned trees, essentially the same trees they had known before, resurrected. Over a broad, low arch of a bridge, they crossed the narrow end of the lake. Water tumbled and splashed down another spillway and the stream resumed its course off into the habitat. The loose crowd walked out onto the wide, stone-flagged patio of the Willow Lake Inn. On the far side was a stage.

For a moment, they all paused and looked around. No few of them wept. The reconstruction was perfect. It was almost possible to pretend nothing had ever gone wrong. Then Ira, not his father, appeared from within to welcome them, and the illusion faded away.

"Will you be playing tonight?" a man asked Robert.

"No, not tonight," Robert replied with a forced smile. And beside him Alicia took his hand and held it tight.

Holm led them through the growing crowd to a large table near the shore of the lake. A Leyra'an and two Humans were already seated there, and the Leyra'an was waving them over. It was Melep's uncle, Kr'nai Ersha. With him were the Commissioners from the Commonwealth, a man and a woman, Yu Sei Ho and Sarah Badesha. Robert knew who they were from the common newsfeed, though he had not seen them before in person. Introductions were made all around, with appropriate courtesies in the form of handshakes and bows. Ersha concluded all of that by waving them toward empty seats.

"Having a good Moving Day?" Ho asked. He was a small, slim man with long black hair tied back and braided, and more than enough Asian characteristics in his face to suit his name, a rather rare combination in the Commonwealth. Beside him sat Badesha, a dark-skinned woman with black eyes and black hair so shiny it had bluish highlights in it from the lamp on the pole behind her. Both wore the sort of loose, colorful, but casual clothing to be expected of Commonwealth Humans on such an occasion. Ho wore a jacket that seemed more gray than green in the lamplight. Badesha wore a short-skirted yellow dress that left her shoulders bare; color and style both suited her perfectly.

"A new experience for some of us," Melep replied with a glance at Holm. "Waiting to occupy a new habitat or station until it could be done by way of a group migration, and then treating that day as a sort of holiday, that is something of the Commonwealth that could become popular among *my* folk. It has been a most enjoyable experience for Rost'aht."

"A Moving Day is always at its best when you participate as a family," Sarah said.

"I have to admit this is new to me, as well," Robert said. "I went walkabout from the station where I grew up, then joined the Survey. This is the first brand-new place I've ever lived in, and it's the first time I haven't relocated as a singleton." Not strictly true, but he didn't count losing the *William Bartram* as a relocation.

"Is there word on how the folk of the Republic are settling in?" Holm asked.

"We know they're here," Ho replied. "They were told of this gathering. The reply was a polite acknowledgment, but nothing more." He shrugged slim shoulders and added, "We shall see."

Someone brought pitchers of beer and mugs to the table; it was impossible to tell whether Ira had taken on an apprentice or someone was just pitching in to help. The mugs were raised in a succession of toasts, and the celebration at their table began in earnest. The party grew around their table, as well, and across the way to where the refurbished stage, salvaged from the probeship, sat in its usual relationship to the stone building. Several Human musicians had gathered, the remnants of the old pub band, and music rolled over the crowd. Soon several couples were dancing, more joining them as time passed and beer was consumed.

At the tables around the wide patio people laughed, talked, raised glasses and cups, and sometimes wept for times gone by even as they celebrated a new beginning. Robert felt a lump in his throat when he heard the music. He had been a part of that band, had played the jigs and reels that were moving men and women of two species around and around on the flat, fitted stones. He almost stood up, could feel the urge to join them, but the same block of hard emotion that left the pipes sitting at home kept him in his seat.

One thing Robert knew only too well about himself was his inability to keep his feelings from showing. And the moment of distress surely showed. A large, warm hand closed over his wrist. Robert turned his head and met the amber-eyed gaze of Rost'aht Holm. He raised his mug and Holm followed suit; they tapped the mugs lightly together and drank, then Holm patted his arm and leaned back in his seat to watch the people dancing. If the others noticed the exchange between the husbands of Rost'aht, no comment was made or sign shown.

"I believe we have found them," said an unfamiliar voice, one clearly projected in their direction.

Kr'nai Ersha looked up, as did Yu Sei Ho and Sarah Badesha. "Ah, so you have come after all!" said Ersha. "Very good! Please, join us."

"Don't mind if we do."

Robert turned in time to see two men come around the table and pause as space was made available for them. Ho rose to his feet and introduced them. "This is Emerson Worth, chief Commissioner from the Republic, and his associate Drake Bristol."

The first named was a clean-shaven, rather stout man with close-cropped, light brown hair gone gray at the temples. He wore an open black jacket over a pale blue shirt that was buttoned snugly around the neck, and pants that matched the jacket. The effect would have been severe, and this did indeed seem the fashion of the Republic, except for the broad, bright smile on the man's face. By that smile and his overall body language, he was clearly quite pleased to be there. His eyes went from face to face as the introductions went around the table, with a nod of acknowledgment to each one. His assistant, on the other hand, seemed otherwise. Leaner and dressed in dark brown with a white shirt, he *did* make the style seem severe, and looked anything but at ease. He was fair-haired and like Emerson Worth he was clean-shaven. Unlike Worth's brown eyes, alive with emotion, Drake's were as cold as they were blue. Those eyes flicked hither and yon, drawn by every flash of distraction.

Everyone else rose and hands were shaken, bows exchanged, and Robert said, "Mr. Worth, Mr. Bristol, you are both most welcome!"

"Call me Emerson, please." And Emerson flicked a quick glance at his younger associate.

"I'm Drake." It was said quickly, as if recovering from a missed cue.

Emerson and Drake took the offered seats just as a new round of pitchers was brought, along with a multi-course evening meal of Human and Leyra'an cuisines. The aroma of food seemed to loosen Bristol up a bit; his expression lightened further when Alicia filled a mug of beer and passed it to him.

"We weren't sure whether or not you would brave the evening madness," Ho said as dishes were passed around and plates began to fill.

"Well, it was by no means certain we could get away," Emerson replied with a sidelong glance at Drake. "But in the end the lure of the Commonwealth's legendary beer was overwhelming."

"Legendary?" Robert asked with a short laugh.

"Among those who were here during Bartram's construction," Emerson replied. He took a long drink from his heavy glass mug, raised his eyebrows and said, "I would find it very difficult to argue with them!"

Drake lowered his mug with a nod and said, "This is very good, as a matter of fact."

"Glad now that we succumbed to temptation?" Emerson asked.

"Oh, I suppose so," Drake replied with a reluctant smile. The Leyra'an politely ignored the brief display of teeth. "All work and no play, after all."

Something in the way he said the words made it seem to Robert that Drake was being somewhat less than sincere. Even smiling, the man looked like he would prefer to be light years away.

Sarah appeared to take him at face value. She laughed and said, "Perhaps that could be the basis for the first round of negotiations. We will exchange brewers!"

Emerson saluted her with his mug. "Dear lady, I can think of few more promising avenues for discussion!"

They ate and talked and learned of one another, as strangers met in the midst of celebration so often do. Robert learned surprisingly little from Drake, who answered questions with as few words as possible, while clearly taking in every scrap of information he could. Emerson, on the other hand, seemed as eager to talk as he was to listen, which he did in equal measure — when not eating. They learned that he was a career politician and a professor of 'societal sciences,' as he called it. He had been married for more than thirty years, with both children and grandchildren, all of whom he claimed vexed him terribly, even though his love for them was abundantly obvious in his tone of voice and choice of words.

He also made it plain he had high hopes for the Trilateral Commission, even while acknowledging that progress — while inevitable — was likely to be very slow and require patience. Drake gave him a strange look, as if surprised by these words in some way. But he said nothing, and Robert was left puzzled by what that glare might mean.

"So, together you form a single family unit," Emerson said at one point.

"Two marriages joined," Holm replied with a slow nod. "*Es'avami g'ru,* as it is rendered in my language. We seek to restore my own family, Rost'aht. At one time I alone remained. Then Melep consented to join with me. You would say, 'marry.' A single couple would be a slow start, and the Way of Leyra'an permits an offer of joining to otherwise unrelated close friends. Something more than aunt and uncle to the children who will come. Our love for these two," and he pointed to where Robert and Alicia sat together, "was such that we chose them, for all that they are Human."

"And other Leyra'an *approve* of such a thing?" Drake asked.

"Most do," Ersha said. "A few do not. Such arrangements, including mixed marriages between individuals, have taken place many times in the Confederation. We have learned to accept these as good things."

"You *feel* like a family," Emerson said, leaning back as if to take in the four of them at once. "The way you look at each other, speak to each other. You make it obvious, without being, well, obvious about it." And he raised his mug to them. As they drank, it seemed to Robert that Drake did so reluctantly, frowning a little as he looked at Emerson over the rim of his mug. If Emerson noted the faint scowl, he did not react to it. "I can't help being curious how such a relationship came into being. Perhaps one day, if it does not seem too much like prying... "

"It is a matter of pride for us, and nothing we are ashamed to tell." Holm's eyes flicked toward Drake and away, and Robert realized he was not alone in the feeling that Drake was not perhaps as easy with all of this as he might seem. "It is not a short tale, and if I were to tell it I would want to tell it in full."

Emerson glanced at Drake, who shrugged a little. "As we are not scheduled to begin official proceedings for a few days yet, I have no incentive to turn in early. Tell it as it should be told, by the way of your people."

And Robert saw a certain hardening of the look in Drake's eyes, as Emerson made his request.

Rost'aht Holm assumed the mantle of first husband and lore master of his small family, and told of how his original family had been killed during the last major operation launched by the Republic, a beginning that brought a sad frown to Emerson's face and something like a scowl to Drake's. Holm wisely did not dwell on it, and spoke gravely of the black oath of *setha'im prosh* he had so rashly taken. He told of his first encounter with Robert and Alicia, and from there the tale unfolded to the ill-fated flight of the *William Bartram*, the attack by Kester's warship, and the sequence of adventures that followed aboard the warship *Han'anga*. He spoke of the ultimate consequences of his oath, the forfiture of his own life, and of how Robert had intervened and saved him. He told of how they saved each other's lives more than once in the adventures that followed, and how, by the time their journey took them back to Pr'pri system, they were more brothers than friends. The tale went on, with pitchers of beer brought around to them over the time it took, but all eyes were on Holm, who with his deep voice told a compelling tale. Robert relived the story, and it was both fascinating and a little disturbing to hear it from another point of view.

It ended with a homecoming, the discovery that Alicia yet lived, though so many others dear to Robert had died, and ended with the joining of the MacGregors to Rost'aht.

Emerson seemed honestly moved by it all; his eyes were bright with emotion. "Well told, Rost'aht Holm,"

Emerson said. "An inspiring tale of redemption. You have done me a great honor in sharing it."

It was very much the sort of thing one Leyra'an would have said to another.

Holm put one hand to his chest and bowed slightly toward Emerson. Drake sat there looking into his mug, a scowl on his face.

"The Republic comes across as the villain," Drake said, an edge of complaint in his voice.

"I see *Andrew Kester* as the villain," Holm said mildly. "He is responsible for the deaths of those I lost, and for those who died with the *William Bartram*. I do *not* hold the folk of the Republic accountable. I *cannot*. Learning to see things that way was a hard lesson," and he flicked a glance at Robert, "but I have learned it."

Emerson, after a stern look in his colleague's direction, said, "I am especially intrigued that you went from trying to kill Robert to being, for all practical purposes, married to him."

"Ours is a universe of ironies, is it not?" Holm asked.

"It is indeed, sir," Emerson agreed with a gentle smile. He drained his mug one last time and rose somewhat unsteadily to his feet. "Good people, it is an honor to be among you. I look forward to working with you all in ways that benefit all our peoples."

"As do we," said Ersha, who rose and bowed deeply, if unsteadily.

The men of the Republic made their way through the thinning crowd, and were gone. It seemed to Robert that as they departed Emerson looked around in wonder, while Drake stared resolutely straight ahead.

CHAPTER SIX

Pr'pri System
Bartram Habitat

In the months that followed, meeting protocols were debated and adopted, issues brought up and tabled, arguments patiently heard, and — to hear Holm describe it — the work of the Trilateral Commission became yet another set of discussions that resolved next to nothing at a very slow pace. In Bartram, crops were planted, supports for Robert's vines erected, and the residence of Rost'aht came to look more and more like home. Holm was busy with the ever more complicated negotiations, and chaired numerous committees, duties he shared with Ersha and Melep, who had remained her uncle's apprentice through it all. Alicia focused her attention on the research to adapt Commonwealth nanomed to the Leyra'an, an effort she was able to relocate to Bartram. And Robert was adopted by a han'anga.

The heraldic animal of Clan Pa'haronsa, the han'anga was one of the most popular pets kept by the Leyra'an, assuming the role long held jointly by cats and dogs in Human society. Rir'lek Ninit, one of the Leyra'an with whom Robert worked, brought her obviously pregnant han'anga to the vineyard with her, reluctant to leave the animal alone with her time near at hand, and no doubt hoping the precocial offspring would bond with her coworkers and relieve her of the burden of placing pups in good homes.

"As long as she doesn't get in the way," Robert said, "I have no objection." He patted the beast's head as he said that, and was rewarded by a low crooning, a han'anga's way of saying you were acceptable. She was a large, handsome creature, powerfully built and yet graceful in her motions, dark gray with dark brown eyes and bands of cinnamon coloring on her flanks. Robert guessed the beast was half a meter tall at her broad shoulders and around 40 kilograms in weight. Add size and weight to the teeth in her broad, scaly muzzle, and this was not an animal to be trifled with if angered. By reputation they were both amazingly gentle and affectionate creatures, and fiercely loyal. A crest of boney spines bristled from the back of her head, covering the neck, and each spine was a kaleidoscope of alternating blue, green, and reddish-purple bands. When she nuzzled his hand, Robert assured her that she was the most beautiful han'anga in the Universe, and the creature's owner beamed at him.

And of course, halfway through that very day, she gave birth down inside one of the long troughs that would soon hold soil and the roots of hop vines. Stacks of brown poles, made of cultured wood composites, were piled in a pyramid nearby. The crew, Human and Leyra'an alike, sat on the poles or at the edge of the trough, legs a-dangle. Drawn by their shouts and laughter Robert made his way over to the group to see what had come of it all. They were at the end of the long trench, where rolls of turf awaited planting, along with large pots of lilac clones clustered nearby. The han'anga was on her side below him, looking absolutely exhausted, as Ninit worked to clean up the messy consequences of birth. A small herd of miniature han'angas, recently cleaned by several volunteers, wandered around, squalling. Now and then one would investigate a Human or Leyra'an in the crowd. Soon several people were holding babies and being nuzzled by them, with looks of delight on their faces.

"Well, congrat... " he started to say, when an especially large example of baby han'anga leaped from the trough and scrambled up the front of his trouser leg, then hitched itself up on his chest, small but pointy claws prickling as it climbed. Almost in self-defense he caught it up in the crook of his arm. "What have we here?" he said with a startled laugh. Perched on his arm, forepaws braced against his chest, Robert looked into the warm brown eyes of the grayish-blue scaled pup. Its flanks marked with pale rust-colored stripes, the pup was the size of a half-grown cat.

"A very happy little boy," Ninit replied. "He has found his fosterer."

"His what?" Robert asked warily. The han'anga pup warbled at him as if asking a question.

"Han'angas are born able to fend for themselves," Ninit said. "But they need guidance. In a pack, in the wild, they attach themselves to other adults, who watch over them until they have grown. Of course, with domestic han'angas, they never quite outgrow that bond."

"Oh, no," said Robert. "This is not a good idea. Really bad timing!"

"If you set him down firmly, right now," she said, "he will bond with another."

But it was much too late for that, for Robert had made eye contact even as he demurred, and the delighted han'anga pup was nuzzling his neck and warbling like the happiest, luckiest han'anga ever born. Robert looked at Ninit, then sighed and said, "You can tell me how to take care of him, right?" And found himself surrounded by laughter.

Back home, Alicia looked at him and said, "You're joking."

Melep took one look and said, "Oh, he's *beautiful!*"

The han'anga hopped from Robert's shoulder into Alicia's arms, who gave a little shout of surprise, then laughed, and in a moment the pup had the undivided attention of both women. After they fussed the little fellow for a while, he made his way back to Robert by leaping from Melep's arms into his. "Oh, he knows who daddy is!" said Alicia, and she laughed aloud as the pup pulled himself up onto Robert's shoulder, balancing by clutching his hair with one forepaw.

Holm walked in through the entry and cocked his head to one side as he assessed the situation. "Now, here is a pleasant surprise! Welcome, little one!" He reached over and scratched the pup under his chin. The han'anga quivered where he sat on Robert's shoulder. "He will not be riding your shoulder for long," Holm said. "He will be a big one."

"How can you tell?" Robert asked.

And Holm replied, "Look at the size of his feet."

Robert looked around and said, "So we all agree he can stay?" When all nodded and voiced agreement he said, "Great! Now, what do we call him?"

It became a debate to rival any discussion between Trilateral Commission members, except for the laughter. In the end, they gave him a Leyra'an name, and called him Gava'mi. In a remarkably short time Gava'mi learned to respond to his name. A more pampered han'anga could scarcely be found within Bartram, and yet they never quite seemed to spoil him, for he proved both mild-mannered and undemanding. Holm and Melep considered Gava'mi an unusually intelligent example of his species. In fact, one scolding for a misdeed was usually all he required, and a potential problem behavior never developed into a bad habit. Very soon it was hard to imagine their residence without the Beast, as he was often called. It seemed he had always lived there.

For all that he showed affection to the entire household, and was very attentive to guests, his fosterer was indeed Robert. The others could come and go as needed, but Robert's departure put Gava'mi in a state of great anxiety.

"So, where I go, he goes?" Robert asked Melep one morning, early on.

"While he is young," she said. "A mature han'anga develops the habit of guarding what he or she thinks of as the nest. This will be true especially when we have children in the house. But for the first few months of his life, he will find it difficult to be apart from you."

"That could be inconvenient," Robert said, frowning. The Beast was in the crook of his arm and poked his broad muzzle into his ear. "You will grow accustomed to it," Melep said. "Many of your vineyard crew is Leyra'an, and they will understand having a young han'anga around. In fact, he will no doubt spend much of your working day playing with his siblings, since all were adopted by members of your group."

"Stop that," Robert said mildly, and shifted Gava'mi so he could not reach Robert's ear. The han'anga's own short, pointed ears came erect and cocked toward him, a sign of concern. Robert puffed air into Gava'mi's face, imitating something han'angas did to calm the young of their species.

And so Gava'mi became Robert's shadow. Concerns over inconvenience never materialized, and the han'anga's constant companionship was soon just a fact of life. As Gava'mi grew, something he did rather quickly, Robert found he was not looking forward to the mature phase of which Melep spoke. He would miss having Gava'mi always around, when the time came.

In the meantime, Robert went about the work of establishing a mixed vineyard of grapes and hops and *boshna'ti*. It was set on the beta docks side of the central green zone, and was large enough that the rows of young vines on their wires and poles, when examined down their length, seemed to be grown in a shallow bowl or valley that curved gently up in front and behind, to vanish in a pseudo-horizon of misty distance. There were three sets of support structures, one for each species and containing one hundred rows, set end to end in a band that ran almost all the way around the inner surface of Bartram. Between each segment of the curved plantation a knoll had been built, covered with artificial soil and planted to thick, flower-sprinkled turf that also covered the paths between rows.

On the top of each knoll, pairs of tall, wide, dark gray stone seats were set back to back, carved from asteroidal rock. The stone chairs were an ancient Leyra'an tradition, the posts occupied by the guardians of the vines. There were no pests aboard the habitat, of course, but the Leyra'an seemed quite convinced that it would not be a proper vineyard without the chairs, and no matter that two of the three plant species didn't originate on the Leyra'an home world. Robert liked the idea of these guardian posts and the old tradition they maintained, and so supported the installation of the seats.

Robert spent the days working the vines and checking the drip system that delivered water and nutrients to roots, then resting at the end of each day, before going home, by perching on one of the guardian seats and contemplating the day's progress. He was never alone. Other workers would sit beside him, or in the turf around the seat, chatting while han'anga pups played in the grass and around the nearest vines. On rare occasions he would stay after the others left, with only Gava'mi to keep him company.

The day cycle would end with dinner and long conversations, sometimes at home, sometimes at the Willow Lake, where the willow trees grew swiftly and young ivy was soon to be seen over most of the walls of the pub. And more often than not they took the same table by the lake, a willow on one side and a silver lamp on the other. They were such regulars there that young Ira began to reserve the spot for their use.

Emerson Worth, Yu Sei Ho, and Sarah Badesha often accompanied Kr'nai Ersha to the Willow Lake after a session's end. Drake would make an occasional appearance, but it only became more obvious, not less, that he found being out and around the Leyra'an uncomfortable. They made him welcome when he showed up, but put no pressure on the man to join in.

"Well, no, not tonight," Emerson said one evening, when Sarah inquired after Drake's absence. "He seems to have some special business of his own. And to be honest, he has become no more at ease in my company than in yours." This was said with a nod toward the Leyra'an. "We've been on the outs, you see. He feels I spend too much time fraternizing with the other elements of the Commission. He has complained more than once that we should keep our distance and remain 'objective.' I suppose he bows out to set a good example."

"You see it otherwise," Alicia said.

"Oh, very much so," Emerson replied. "I believe that those of us involved in these discussions must know each other very well indeed, and through each other at least glimpse the constituencies represented. There will, in the end, be compromises necessary, however much my government prefers to believe otherwise. We *must* find a way to achieve peace with the Leyra'an. We need to find ways to allow the marvels offered by the Commonwealth to make their way into the Republic without bringing everything we've built crashing down around our heads. How can we manage any of that if we don't know who we're talking to?" He sighed and drank deeply, then sighed again in satisfaction. "Drake is young, and full of belief in the rightness of his cause. He is not always wrong, but he hasn't yet learned that the art of compromise is the key to success in politics."

"That sums up nicely why we're here," said Yu Sei Ho. "We relax, we talk off the record, eat good food and drink fine beer and ale and wine. At times, I find it difficult to believe we have any chance to succeed. Then we're here, among friends, and certain things make a little more sense."

"Exactly!" Emerson said, raising his heavy glass mug in salute. He took a drink, then paused and looked distracted. When he set the mug down he looked a little pale, and there was sweat upon his brow.

"Emerson?" Melep asked. "What is wrong?"

"What?" He seemed to shake himself and gave them a polite half-smile. "Oh, nothing, dear lady. I think I ate those sausages a bit too quickly."

"No, you've done this before, though not so obviously," Alicia said quietly. "Please, what is wrong? Whatever it is, quite likely we can fix it."

Emerson rolled the mug around between his hands to the degree possible with the handle in the way. "I rather doubt it, my dear. You see, I have developed a condition known as Founders' disease. It's, ah, very unpleasant. The shared library contains entries on the matter, if you really must know about it. Not exactly pleasant dinner time conversation."

"Actually, I *have* heard of it," Alicia replied, grave and concerned. "It's a catch-all phrase for a variety of problems caused by genetic instabilities. Which form do you have?"

"Stage three Alpha," he replied. "Very slow, and found usually in those of advanced age. And I *am* well along, as my people measure such things, well past my century mark. Our medicine may not be up to the fantastic levels of the Commonwealth, but we do live long and healthy lives, all other things being equal. It's considered a birthright, in the Republic. When you need medical care, it's provided, a tradition that developed during the Foundation, a time when keeping as many alive and well as possible was our highest priority."

"But it can't handle this disease?" Robert asked.

"No. Founders' is rooted in our limited genetic diversity, and since we don't practice what you call genetic engineering... " He shrugged and gave them a wry smile.

"Emerson, it's possible that our nanomed tech *can* handle it," Alicia insisted. "Adjustments would be necessary, to compensate for the genetic bottleneck through which the Republic passed long ago. But I'm *sure* we could help."

"Perhaps," he said, and he looked tired and sad. "But we are not permitted to partake of your medicine, Alicia. My government is trying very hard to conceal the tremendous longevity of the Commonwealth, for my people would surely demand access to its source, and it would be profoundly disruptive of my culture to allow that without first planning for mitigation."

"Emerson... " then Alicia paused, and Robert stared at her. It was most unlikely his wife not to voice her thoughts. "Gaia," she whispered instead. "Will you at least ask your superiors if we can provide palliative and support care? To help you bear up under the pressure of the negotiations."

"Another ale is all I really need," he replied. And then to the look she gave him, added, "Yes, sweet lady, I will ask."

"As will I," said Ho. Ersha and Holm voiced support of the idea. "We need you hale and hearty, my friend, if you're to carry your weight. I'll send a message to your government requesting permission to give you limited treatment, enough to stave off your illness while we work."

"All right," Emerson replied after a moment. He looked up from the interior of his mug. "I will agree to that." Then he laughed, for Gava'mi was beside him, sitting up with his forepaws on Emerson's leg, begging for a handout. Robert opened his mouth to scold the Beast, but a bit of sausage had already been obtained, and Gava'mi had rambled off under the willow tree to consume the treat.

CHAPTER SEVEN

Pr'pri System
Bartram Habitat

The matter of children was quickly taken as a given, for how else could the family regrow? Robert assumed parenthood was in his near future as soon as the joining of his and Alicia's marriage to that of Holm and Melep was formalized. Just before Contact, he and Alicia had set their plans for starting a family, eager to do so. The tragedies that followed First Contact derailed those plans, and then the building of a new home for the *Bartram* survivors diverted them. The desire for parenthood revived after moving into the Bartram habitat, and yet for all of that, when their wives felt the time had come, Robert and Holm were somewhat taken by surprise. The most recent discussions had seemed to lack immediacy.

"Just like that?" Robert asked. "The time is *now?*"

"You are very sure of this?" Holm asked. "Much as we all desire it, there is no need for haste."

"Very sure," Melep said. They happened to be on the path home from the Willow Lake that particular evening, and she walked hand in hand with Alicia, as they did so often.

"We must be," said Alicia, and at that moment Melep giggled. "We're both of us pregnant."

There was a long pause in the conversation as they strolled slowly on and the husbands of Rost'aht assimilated the news. Of a sudden, Robert realized it was one thing to consider parenthood, and quite another to be confronted by it as inevitable. A moment of eye contact with Holm convinced him immediately that his brother-in-law felt the same. At length, as both women began to laugh at their looks of befuddlement, Holm said to Robert, "I wonder which one will be the Matriarch of Rost'aht?"

"They'll take turns," Robert said. Then to Holm's scandalized expression he laughed and said, "What? You think we'll have a choice in that matter either?"

And so in the fullness of time a Leyra'an family that was now Robert's own was reborn in a most literal sense. Rost'aht was increased by two births, one Human and one Leyra'an. With the birth of those children, Rost'aht became a family refounded as such things were seen by Leyra'an law. The children of Rost'aht Holm and Rost'aht Melep, and of Robert and Alicia MacGregor, were born within hours of each other. They gave birth in the same room, with a group of friends and a midwife crew made up of both species in attendance. Two boys, both as perfect as could be, making noise to do a Leyra'an celebration proud, although the outrage in those cries was hardly a sound of celebration.

"To be expected," said Melep after she'd caught her breath. "Who would willingly leave such comfort and security?"

"We'll make it worth their while," Robert said, and he stared in wonder at his son and his exhausted wife. He reached down to gently brush a lock of her hair, limp and sweat-soaked, off of her forehead. "Whatever it takes. We will."

Holm came to him when he said those words and embraced him, holding him tightly for a long moment, unable to speak. Robert returned the embrace with a will.

Recovery from the trial of birth, as the Leyra'an called labor, was a matter of a few hours, thanks to Commonwealth medicine, though somewhat quicker for Alicia than Melep. A few days later, family Rost'aht took their new children, an assortment of Human friends, and members of Melep's original family Kr'nai to a quiet observation bubble near the beta pole, where they turned out the lights and stood looking out at the stars. There would be Leyra'an customs to observe and celebrate, but by prior agreement they would honor first the quieter way of Humans in the Commonwealth. It would all be recorded and sent into the Commonwealth, to Alicia's and Robert's distant families.

It did not take long. First Melep, then Alicia, raised their newborn sons up to the stars, and as each infant was held aloft, Robert said their names and spoke the words taught him long ago by his Gaian parents.

"Rost'aht Vurn, behold the stars. Rost'aht Pali Paul MacGregor, behold the stars. From the stars of old, all from which we are made was born. Of stardust are we made. And as those stars shine, so shall your lives be points of light and life in the lifeless Void. That Void is vast, but in light and life there is hope, and in hope we find the strength to face that emptiness. May your lives shine brightly and long, and know that you are not, and never will be, alone."

"Mother of Life," said those Humans present who shared such beliefs. With a hand over each heart, all assembled bowed toward the new mothers.

And with that, they went out into the happy madness that rang through the confines of Bartram. But it wasn't the rebirth of Rost'aht the folk of Bartram celebrated. It was the news that the Leyra'an were no longer subject to aging and death that sent the *bosh'sh* and beer flowing. The medical technology used by the Commonwealth to heal injuries and eliminate old age had finally been adapted to Leyra'an physiology. The distribution of what quickly came to be known simply as "The Cure" was well underway, with Holm and Melep being among the first to receive it; little Vurn, like his brother Paul, was literally born to it. The by-then well-planted, if not fully grown interior of Bartram was aswarm with happily inebriated Humans and Leyra'an. Bands of musicians, some of them strolling along as they played, sent music into the air from parks and gardens; pubs and restaurants of both Human and Leyra'an style overflowed with food and music and drink; people danced wherever music could be heard. Leyra'an passed them wearing brilliant sapphire blue bands on their wrists, a symbol that marked those who had already received the new medical treatment. The bands flashed and glittered in the white light of the great fusion lamp that ran high over head.

"How's all this looking to the representatives of the Republic?" Robert asked Holm, raising his voice to be heard. Several well-wishers had surrounded Melep and Alicia and were singing, some literally, praises of the newborns. Gava'mi pressed close to Robert's leg, and he finally gave in to the frightened animal and lifted him, a substantial weight by then, and puffed air into his face. The crest of spines flattened as the Beast calmed down.

"They are, as usual, both confused by and confusing on the issue," Holm replied. "Your people made them the same offer, of course, out of simple fairness. But where my people are eager to accept this gift, *they* remain cautious, concerned with how it will disrupt their society."

"Emerson said as much. And it would certainly *change* the way people live in the Republic," Robert said. "How could it not? But — disrupt? That almost makes it sound like we are trying to harm them in some way!"

Holm raised his hands, palms outward, approximately chest high, the Leyra'an equivalent of a shrug. "So little of their ways make sense to me that I sometimes wonder if they really are Human. Or if *you* are." There was a brief flash of teeth as he smiled, an indication he was being playfully rude. "Let us leave our friends of the Republic be, this day," he added, looping his arm around Robert's shoulders. "In the end, though we must offer to help, they must find their own paths through these changes."

"You're right," Robert replied, and let his brother-by-marriage steer him into the thick of things. He felt a little chagrined bringing it up. Holm no doubt had little desire to bring his work into the celebration, frustrating as that work was proving to be for many of those involved.

And not the sort of thing to be thinking about at a time like this. The crowd surged around them, a nearly equal mix of Humans and Leyra'an, all laughing, shouting and singing, badly, in two different languages at the same time. Robert stopped and shook his head, confused, then realized it was the translation system making a mess of things. There was too much input. Robert disabled his implant.

The family Rost'aht strolled along the path to the familiar lake with its young weeping willows planted around the shore. The willow tree that would one day overgrow the pub seemed larger than it had just a few nights before. Robert was pleased by how well the cloned trees had grown in such a short time. In a very real sense they *were* the trees that had grown aboard the probeship. Robert had nurtured and then transplanted the saplings himself.

The patio between the pub and the lake was in a state of happy bedlam, and blue wrist bands flashed everywhere he looked. A number were wrapped around Human wrists as well, apparently for no other reason than to fit in, the Human population having been born to the treatment. Every now and then a sparkling blue band sailed up into the air, and those that landed in the water were retrieved by swimmers who raced each other to the glittering prizes.

Ira Ashe waved and shouted a greeting that could not be heard from where they stood; Robert just grinned and waved back. Ira looked much like his father, with the same black, curly hair and stocky build. Robert stood for a moment, scanning the crowd and seeing so many familiar faces. In a reflection of his own depression, there was a time when he would have scoffed at the idea that these people would ever smile again, much less laugh and sing and dance. And yet here they were, and by all accounts the scene before him was replicated throughout the habitat. There were small children in the arms of parents, some of them only weeks older than the babies in slings worn by Melep and Alicia. Robert was pleased and deeply touched by what he saw.

"Holm!" Someone shouted. "Rost'aht Holm!" It was a Human voice, and male.

Off on the edge of the madness, very near the shore and seated at the usual table, they saw Emerson Worth with Kr'nai Ersha. Both had tall tankards of heavy dark green glass which they waved in the air to make themselves more visible to the young family. In the space between, the delirious crowd ebbed and flowed. Heedless of Leyra'an custom, Emerson was grinning hugely, eyes on the young mothers. Rost'aht Holm nodded toward the table and Robert began to make his way in that direction as his friend gathered up their wives and children.

"Well, hello, Emerson! Hello, Ersha. We wondered where you'd gotten to," Alicia said warmly, bending down to kiss Emerson's cheek and then touch her forehead to Ersha's. They each greeted the two men at the table after their fashion, handshakes, forearms clasp, or a brief touch of foreheads, then they joined them at the table.

"I went on ahead to make sure you would have a safe haven in this madness," Ersha said. "Along the way, I came upon Emerson, who was being swept up and carried off with the crowd. He seemed in need of rescuing."

Emerson still grinned and then laughed at Ersha's words, looking a bit foolish. "I expected there would be a party to mark the release of the Leyra'an treatments, but I really had no idea! It's a bit overwhelming if you aren't accustomed to such things." He looked from Alicia to Melep. "The new ones have come out to play, I see. I do apologize for not attending the service. A messenger arrived in system from the Republic and I found myself trapped by yet another briefing."

"It is understood," Holm said.

"Indeed," said Melep. "And here at last is Rost'aht Vurn. And my sister holds Paul MacGregor, who among my people will be known as Rost'aht Pali."

"Oh, they are beautiful!" said Emerson. "I'm so glad you brought them with you. Amazing that they can sleep through this!"

"They won't," said Alicia. "At least, not indefinitely." She gave him a close look. "How are you feeling?"

"I'm better, sweet lady. The medical staff aboard the *Perseverance* has used the advice of your physicians to good effect. I may yet be granted time enough to see these negotiations through."

Holm uttered a short bark of laughter, which Robert knew by the sound to be derisive. "I fear you will need the Commonwealth's full treatments to have hope of *that*," Holm said.

"There are days I would agree with you," said Emerson with a tired sigh. "It's hard, you know. So much of what our fellow Commissioners suggest makes perfect sense. We could improve life so much, back home, and quite likely without upsetting the proverbial wagon. But... " He was clearly about to launch into the topic, then looked from Melep to Alicia and said, "No, not now. Let's let it be for the moment."

"Forgive me," said Holm, left hand over his heart. "And here I so recently admonished my brother," and he nodded toward Robert, "to leave these matters aside."

"Hard to do, when it occupies your every waking moment," Emerson replied. "No harm done. Now, give me a better look at these sweet ones of yours."

Robert sat back, accepted the mug of beer that made its way to his hands, and watched as Vurn and Paul each had their turn in the crook of Emerson's arm. He handled the newborns as one well accustomed to such things, which was to be expected of a grandfather. That one child was not Human seemed to matter not at all. Emerson assured each one that he was the handsomest newborn boy he had ever seen, and sounded perfectly sincere each time.

Time and priorities were different in the Republic, in ways Robert still only half understood. In the

Commonwealth Robert and Alicia were of an age, their early ninth decade, at which most couples began to have children. The ability to bear children was no longer limited by time. The folk of the Republic routinely lived a century or more, but according to Emerson generally had their children before half that time had passed. For Emerson, the time for raising children was a matter for memory.

"I take it Drake will not be joining us this time?" Robert asked.

Emerson replied without looking up from the baby he held. "He is away bearing messages and updates to our superiors regarding recent events." He still did not look up, much less look pointedly at the celebration surging around them, yet his meaning was obvious enough.

Robert looked away from their friend and into the crowd, afraid his expression would give him away. It was galling to know of the illness Emerson endured, while living among people who could cure it completely. There was no reason for it. There was no excuse. And there was nothing he could do about it. Emerson was a law-abiding citizen of the Republic, a man who led by example. There was no way he would allow them to cure him of a disease from which so many suffered, when the many were denied. His endurance was bolstered by the powerful religious faith that was part and parcel of so many citizens of the Republic; he trusted in that higher power to see him through. What was meant to be, would be, he kept telling them. If there was fear beneath the faith, it was very well hidden. Robert knew the man well enough by then that he did not believe there was much fear at all. It was admirable, and yet it made Robert both angry and sad.

"We are in danger of running dry!" Ersha declared suddenly. He stood up and studied the loud, dancing crowd. The sound of the pub band nearly drowned him out. "We will need to launch an expedition, I fear. Friend Ira's people are overwhelmed!"

"Follow me!" Holm shouted. He dropped the bag of child care necessities he carried into a chair and lunged into the crowd. Rost'aht Holm was tall and powerfully built, and people just naturally got out of the way when he moved with purpose. Kr'nai Ersha walked briskly forward to stay in the bigger man's wake. The Beast darted after Holm, then looked wildly around at the crowd, and just as abruptly scampered back to Robert. The two Leyra'an gentlemen were quickly lost to sight, with Gava'mi peering after them while warbling concern over their apparent lack of judgment.

"Easy does it," Robert said, hugging the young han'anga to his chest. "He'll find his way back." Gava'mi tucked his head under Robert's chin and warbled softly.

Robert caught a quick glance between Melep and Alicia just as Ersha and Holm disappeared; Melep with a faint nod of her head directed Alicia's attention toward Emerson, who sat with little Paul in the crook of his arm, beaming with pleasure. Robert knew something was bothering her from the look in her eyes, and examined Emerson as closely as he could, without seeming rude. Whatever caught Melep's attention was not obvious to Robert, but that she was worried left him uneasy, and he paid close attention to their friend from that moment on.

"Ah, my dear ladies," Emerson said. "Very well done, indeed. They are both so very beautiful. May all the blessings of Divine Providence be upon them, always."

"Thank you, Emerson," Melep said gravely, placing her hand over her heart and bowing her head. Robert and Alicia bowed as well. And then Holm and Ersha returned with trays of clean mugs and two very large green glass pitchers, held high enough to pass safely over the heads of the crowd, Holm balancing his easily on his right hand.

"Ira sends his regards, his congratulations, and his apologies," said Holm. "I doubt we will see much of him this evening, though somehow he seems certain food will make its way to us before evening is well along."

And evening it was, as the great axis lamp array began to fade to the programmed twilight. Where before there had been a brilliant bar of white light, rendered hazy but still dazzlingly bright by the ambient humidity of the habitat atmosphere, there was now a zone of soft blue-white light, darker blue at each end. The bar would never darken fully, and glittering points of light would hang above them in the haze all night long; the minimum setting of the great lamp always looked to Robert like a band of stars.

The night cycle settled in. The blue arm bands worn by recipients of the Cure turned out to be self-illuminating. Some had a steady sapphire glow, while others flickered and flashed. The crowd of people dancing nearby was liberally sprinkled with these blue lights. The dancers were as visually distracting as they were noisy.

The beer was distributed by Alicia, who poured for all. Her red hair fell forward as she bent over the table. Emerson handed Paul over to Robert, and took Vurn from Melep. He cradled Vurn in the crook of one arm, and raised his mug with his free hand. The noise, incredibly, seemed to increase as night descended, and Robert was just about to suggest that the infants had probably been out enough for this occasion, when a stricken look came to Emerson's face.

"Emerson?" Robert half shouted over the crowd noise.

"Take him!" Emerson said suddenly, his voice tight and strained. He was clearly, and suddenly, in great pain. He thrust little Vurn out to Melep. "Quickly!" And Melep did so, lifting the child from her friend's trembling hands. The baby began to cry, but his infant expression of fear was for the moment overshadowed by Emerson's obvious distress. He was panting for breath and deathly pale. "Something... wrong... " He glanced around at them with wide, frightened eyes.

"*Emerson!*" Melep cried, leaping to her feet as the man toppled backward toward the lake.

Holm made it just in time to keep Emerson from rolling into the water. Swimmers just offshore turned to stare. The people nearest their table became suddenly quiet as Melep's cry of alarm cut through all other noise, and people crowded around with looks of puzzlement and concern, their voices murmuring inquiries regarding what had just happened. Some distance away, other celebrants, unaware of any trouble, carried on in time to the lively Celtic music, blue arm bands flashing and twinkling, creating a surreal background to their situation. Emerson appeared unconscious, breathing in short gasps, and Alicia was summoning aid over the open com, uttering a terse description of the situation into the open air. Holm carried the man lightly to a chair capable of reclining, and with a kick pushed it open and nearly flat. Very gently he placed Emerson on it and said, "He is still breathing, at least."

"What is it?" Robert demanded. "What happened to him?"

"I don't know!" Alicia snapped, almost in tears. Her face was almost as pale as that of Emerson. "I'm an emergency medic, not a doctor!" She touched his wrist with the fingers of one hand, laid her other hand on his pallid forehead. "His pulse is erratic, and he's feverish. We have to get him to a shelter before the air... I mean... No, no, to the... to the...to the... " Her hands were shaking.

"Alicia!" Robert took one her shoulders and gave it a shake. "Here and now! We need you!"

Alicia shrugged him off. "Infirmary! He needs to go there *now!*"

Gava'mi whimpered and retreated under the table.

Emerson was trembling, twitching, his face contorted and yet seemingly unconscious. Robert watched in horror. He had seen men wounded, even killed, in battle. Had killed one of them himself. But the sudden onset of illness was unheard of in the Commonwealth. There was no frame of reference and there was absolutely nothing he could do. He held the now fretful child in one arm. Paul joined his brother in crying for comfort.

The emergency response vehicle soared over their heads, emitting a buzzing pulse of noise designed to get people to pay attention and move out of the way. It settled swiftly down on the patio, vacated just a moment before by the revelers, all of whom now realized something was wrong. The music was stilled and anxious murmuring was all that could be heard from the crowd. A Human med tech jumped out of the sleek teardrop-shaped pod and rushed forward with a float board to where Alicia remained bent over Emerson. With a soft word of instruction he moved her out of the way and guided the board to the side of the recliner. Holm did not need to be told; he lifted Emerson lightly and deposited him on the board with great care. The board lit up as diagnostic instruments began to scan him, surrounding him with a pale yellow glow. Straps looped out automatically to secure him to the board, and the tech steered his patient with quick, measured steps back through the hatch in the rear of the ERV.

Melep, with her still squalling child clutched to her heart, stood with her face pressed into Holm's broad chest. Ersha was speaking aloud to himself, clearly using the open com, though Robert could not hear who he addressed. Paul still cried a little, but seemed to be settling down. Gava'mi crept out from under the table, shivering and with his spines bristling. He stood with his shoulder pressed to Robert's leg.

Another moment, and the ERV rose into the night above the pub's silver lamps and, with a soft whine and a rush of air, was gone. As the red lights dwindled, Alicia said, "Come on. I know where they'll take him." She reached out and took Paul from Robert, secured him in the sling, and led the way through the crowd to the tram depot.

CHAPTER EIGHT

Pr'pri System
Bartram Medical Facility

Emerson was moved swiftly to the habitat's infirmary. Limited to the tram system, Robert and his family arrived significantly after the fact, with Robert last of all, having made a brief side trip to return Gava'mi to their home — to the Beast's evident displeasure. He offered such reassurances as he could to the frightened animal, but Gava'mi wailed piteously all the same as he left. Alicia sent him a brief report that Emerson was at the hospital and had been stabilized, but that the medical staff did not believe he would remain so for long.

When Robert caught up with them at the hospital, Alicia was in deep conversation with a tall, slim Human male in the pale blue coverall of a Commonwealth doctor. She held Paul in his sling and nodded gravely to whatever the doctor was telling her. Robert stepped up beside Melep, who stood close to Holm and had one arm wrapped protectively around the sling holding little Vurn as he nursed, oblivious to events around him. "How is he?" Robert asked in a low voice.

"It has not been good," Melep replied. She took a deep breath to steady herself. "His heart stopped... " Her voice choked up.

Robert slipped his left arm around her waist, and Holm put his right arm around her shoulders, and the three stood in silence, waiting for Alicia to bring them the latest update. The conversation between the other wife of Rost'aht and the surgeon seemed to go on for hours. At last, she laid a hand on the doctor's arm and nodded, though whether in agreement or reassurance, Robert was not sure. The doctor seemed ill at ease, and this did not in any way reassure Robert.

"He's alive," Alicia said.

She did not look at them directly when she spoke."Alicia, what is it? What's wrong?" Robert asked.

"He was in something called critical organ cascade failure," she replied, speaking with some difficulty. She couldn't seem to find her breath. "It has to do with the blood cancer his form of Founders' causes. Organ system degradation. They stabilized him, but it's temporary. The required time to grow compatible organs for transplant, well, he won't last long enough."

"But then, what can they do?" Melep asked.

"The Cure," Holm said.

Alicia nodded at Holm and said, "It's the only thing we have that could work quickly enough, and even that was only possible with a bunch of artificial supports in place. Rather than struggle to keep him breathing while replacement organs could be produced, nanomed is even now being applied to repair and restore his existing organ systems."

"The Republic *allowed* that?" Robert asked.

Alicia shook her head. "The medical staff here contacted the Republic's Commission office for permission, but no one would take responsibility for a firm answer. The doctor on call found himself faced with the risk of a diplomatic problem on one hand, and the certainty of Emerson's death on the other. Rather than wait, Dr. Grosslin made the decision to apply nanomed in conjunction with mechanical aid. The combined effects of the two seem to be moving Emerson in the right direction. Too soon to say for certain that he'll be okay, but there's reason to hope."

"This will not be a popular decision with the Republic," Holm said.

Robert saw Alicia drawing a deep breath, which she always did before issuing an angry retort, but before he could intervene Melep said, "That may be, but at least he will be alive to deal with the consequences."

"Yes," Holm replied. "Emerson is a man of great influence in the Republic. He sees the possibilities in peaceful relations between all three realms. And for many years he has been a calming influence on his own government when dealing with the Republic's internal dissent. We need him, and so do his people."

"How will he feel about it?" Robert asked. "Consider his beliefs, his faith. Did we really have the right to make this decision?"

Alicia met his gaze without flinching, clearly irked that he would even voice such a question. "No, we probably didn't. But we were out of options. *Emerson* was out of options, and had lost the capacity to decide for himself. A person with Founders' who goes into what they call 'steep decline' has only days to live, at most. If nanomed was going to save him, it absolutely had to be applied *immediately*. The physician on call made the decision and, frankly, I'll back him up without reservation. Call it selfishness on my part, if you want, but I can live with that."

"As can Emerson, now," Melep added quietly.

Robert looked at Holm and asked, "But won't this compromise his position in the negotiations?"

"Only if others know," Melep replied.

"*Emerson* will know," Robert pointed out with a glance her way.

"Then whether or not his credibility suffers in the eyes of the Republic is up to Emerson," Holm replied. "It will be for him to decide if this treatment should be revealed."

"The medics here aren't going to volunteer treatment details," said Alicia, "unless pressed. But even if no one asks, he will recover and then remain in remission. His illness will not return."

"He'll cease to age. Won't be able to hide that forever." Robert shrugged when Alicia gave him a look that said he was belaboring the obvious.

Then she looked chagrined and said, "Worse than that. Someone who has grown up without nanomed, exposed to it now, responds in other and more visible ways." She looked around at them and said, "The nanomed will treat his *age* as a disease and cure him of that, as well. Within a few weeks he'll actually begin to look *younger*."

"*That* will be a problem," Holm conceded with a brief flash of teeth, an indication to those who knew him of just how serious the situation seemed to him. Then he sighed and said, "But it is a problem for tomorrow. First we must find a way to make him understand what was done, and why we could do no less." He turned his amber eyes on Alicia's colleague, who had drifted up to them as they spoke, and asked, "When will he awaken?"

"Any minute now," the doctor replied. "He should be able to understand what you tell him. There's been no detectable brain damage." He did not look to Robert like a man comfortable with his situation and added, "He'll be physically exhausted, but most likely, mentally alert."

"We should be there," said Holm. "And we need to explain things to him as soon as he seems capable of handling the news. He must know, if he is to manage his situation without revealing himself accidentally."

The doctor paused as if listening to something else entirely, then said, "I've just been informed that Mr. Worth is coming out of the anesthetic, already. He's a tough one! You should go to him now. This way," and the doctor led them to a quiet room with pale green walls; the lighting was reduced to a soft glow that lacked any glare at all. The members of Rost'aht, infants sleeping soundly in their slings, gathered around the bed in the room, Holm and Robert on one side, Melep and Alicia on the other; the doctor hovered just inside the doorway. Emerson was covered to mid-chest by a light blanket, and what they could see of him above it was covered by a lightweight white linen shirt. His hair was a dark, tangled halo around his head on the pillow. He seemed to be completely awake and aware. "What happened?" he asked in obvious bewilderment. "All I can remember was being suddenly dizzy and sick... and *terribly* confused. Somehow, I don't think it was the ale!"

"It wasn't," Alicia said, resting a hand on his shoulder. "Emerson, you went into cascade failure, steep decline as your doctors call it."

Emerson looked tired, sad, and old. He sighed deeply, then said softly, "I had hoped to be spared longer. There is so *much* yet to do!"

"You will have that time, and more," Alicia said. "The decline has been arrested, and the damage it caused is being reversed. In a few weeks... " she paused and looked at Robert as if seeking support. "In a few weeks you will be completely cured of Founders'."

"What are you talking about?" Emerson's face was pale and puzzled, his eyes opened wide.

Dr. Grosslin moved to the other side of the bed from Alicia and looked gravely down at his patient. "Your condition was deteriorating with frightening speed. The only effective treatment we could provide was nanomed. We had no choice."

"It wasn't *your* decision to make." The strength of his voice surprised Robert, as did the anger it contained.

"A decision was necessary," Grosslin replied. He seemed unfazed by Emerson's tone. "Your own people refused to respond to the situation expeditiously, and you were incapacitated. Under the circumstances, my oath as a physician left me no other course of action."

Emerson closed his eyes and was silent for a long, awkward moment, then nodded. "I can't fault you for doing what you believed was right. You couldn't have known that I'd placed myself in the hands of God, and accepted my fate, some time ago."

"Well, we couldn't accept it!" Alicia said suddenly, angry and unapologetic. Her eyes glittered with tears and she struggled to control her voice. "It was too late to do anything less. We *need* you, Emerson. And you deserved better than to die of a *curable* illness." Once started, the angry words seemed to come without any real control; her voice shook as she continued and she clutched the rail along the side of the bed as if to anchor herself. Seeing her white-knuckle grip, Robert suddenly saw her spinning off again into the darkness of the *William Bartram*. He moved around the bed to be closer to her. "Everyone in the Republic deserves better! All of your people. I won't pretend to understand why the Republic is so reluctant to allow us to share this gift with you. I don't *need* to understand. It's wrong, just flat out wrong! People will die for no reason!"

Before Robert could intervene, Emerson reached out a shaky hand and laid it on one of hers. "Gently, my dear. You are upsetting the little one." And Paul was indeed fussing a little. Alicia looked abashed and cupped the child's head with her other hand. "You are right, sweet lady. *Know* that I believe so. But as things now stand, there's no other way to handle this thing. It hurts my soul, knowing what could be, but is not. It hurts more than you can imagine! But you must trust that I know what I'm doing, that the path I am on *will* bring about what we both desire."

Alicia straightened, and Robert put an arm around her shoulders to steady her. He felt her weight shift toward him.

Emerson looked around at them all, then up to the doctor and said, "Just so I am completely sure about what's happened, you've treated me as you've done the Leyra'an?"

"Yes," Grosslin replied. "I supplied you with a generalized version of nanomed. When treating someone who has not already received such, it's referred to as a 'flush.' A lot of it, all at once. The nanos read the DNA of cells in damaged organs and begin immediately to correct, generating a stable sequence. The cells in those organs first return to normal function, then with the assistance of the nanos begin tissue restoration, while eliminating cells too badly damaged to contribute. You'll feel very tired for a few days, and there may be episodes of mild fever. And you will experience a sharp increase in appetite. Eventually you will establish a new level of homeostasis, which when stabilized will last indefinitely."

"I will never grow old," Emerson said. "That's what you mean by that."

"Yes," Dr. Grosslin replied.

Emerson said nothing to them for a moment, eyes closed as he considered what he had just been told. Robert found the man's expression blankly unreadable. Then, at last, Emerson asked, "Can this be undone?"

Alicia almost gaped at him, and looked up at her other family members, then to the doctor. When she met Robert's eyes all he could offer was a small shrug. He did not know the answer, though he was sure Alicia did. In any case, there was no answer he *should* give. It was Alicia's turn to be silent for a long awkward moment, though in her case the distress she felt was easy to see.

"Yes," said Grosslin. Alicia flinched, but did not quite look toward him. "At least, I can shut down the nanos when you're out of danger. I *won't* do it before then. The repairs they make between now and then will be permanent, but the Founders' disease would likely return if they aren't allowed a few days at least, to restructure your DNA. Is that what you want me to do?"

"I truly don't know what I want." Emerson looked grave and sad. "To be sure, I don't want to be sick again! Who in his right mind would willingly embrace such an unpleasant fate? And I certainly was not anxious to die, though if that is what God has indeed decided for me, then so be it. But there is so much yet to do, and I don't feel that my time has come!" He sighed and seemed to sink into himself. "To take the decision from me was wrong. But under the circumstances your options were truly limited. How can I be angry with you for that? But — this is all so confusing, and I'm very tired, just now, too tired to think straight. I need time, good people. Time by myself. I need to think about this, and to pray for guidance." He glanced around at them, plainly looking to see that they took the hint.

Robert did. He took Alicia by the arm, then said, "Of course, Emerson. You know how to contact us if you need us." As he steered Alicia around and toward the door to the room, he saw Melep and Holm bow to Emerson. When he reached the corridor outside, preceded by the doctor, they were behind and then beside him. Seeing that their newborns were once again growing restless and knowing that by now the Beast was a nervous wreck, he said, "We should go home, now. We all have some thinking of our own to do."

CHAPTER NINE

Pr'pri System
Bartram Habitat

A month after Emerson's crisis, Drake Bristol
returned from the Republic bearing a formal protest
from his leaders. The exact nature of the protest was not
immediately known, though the rumormongers pointcd
immediately to the Commonwealth's distribution of the
Cure to the Leyra'an. Shortly after Drake's return,
Emerson stopped showing up at the Willow Lake, and
according to Holm was not much in evidence in the
Commission compound. When he was seen, he seemed
ill at ease.

The time for a special session to hear the protest was
soon announced. This one, like the regular meetings, was
declared open to the public. Robert decided on impulse
to attend in person with Holm and Melep, while Alicia
and the boys remained at home to comfort Gava'mi in
his absence. They traveled with Holm to the complex set
aside for the Commission, a set of strictly
Commonwealth-design buildings. Everything to do with
the Trilateral Commission was held inside. The people
from the Republic found working out in the open too

distracting. When they arrived Robert and Melep parted company with Holm, who served as co-Commissioner for the Confederation of Clans. The two made their way down a short hallway to the auditorium and gallery for those who came to witness the meetings in person. Usually their numbers were few, and most of the five hundred available seats remained empty. This time Robert and Melep made it to seats just in time to miss a general rush of arrivals that literally filled the place to capacity. Early arrival also gave them seats just behind the reserved VIP front row.

The crowd settled and the Commissioners filed in and sat around a shallowly curved gray table that opened toward the audience. Emerson glanced just once at Drake, with obvious anger in his expression, then appeared to ignore him. Drake avoided the older man's gaze. From where Robert sat, Emerson and Drake were on the left wing of the table, Kr'nai Ersha and Rost'aht Holm on the right, with Yu Sei Ho and Sarah Badesha side by side in the middle.

Emerson rose slowly to his feet, the very picture of a man reluctant to proceed. The gallery was silent. Emerson carefully avoided so much as a glance at Drake, who sat stone-faced as he waited, dressing in a stark black suit and white shirt. "Colleagues," Emerson began, as usual, and as usual he looked around at all assembled as he spoke, Human and Leyra'an alike. "I will yield my time to my associate, Mr. Bristol, who has recently returned with new instructions for our mission and a message for the Commonwealth from the duly elected government of the Republic." He bowed and sat down, still refusing to look at Drake.

"New *instructions*?" Robert whispered into Melep's ear. "What the hell does *that* mean?"

"I have no idea," Melep replied. "Somehow it does not sound good." She moved her hand off the armrest of her seat and took Robert's hand in hers, holding tight. "Emerson looks *most* displeased."

Robert watched Emerson sit down and wondered if anyone else in the room understood that the senior Commissioner from the Republic was now a man in perfect health, and likely to remain so for centuries to come. Assuming he didn't have Dr. Grosslin deactivate the nanomed. So far, there was no sign Emerson had made such a decision. Robert wondered how long the illusion that nothing had changed for the man could be maintained. And then he wondered, with a sudden sinking feeling, just what Drake Bristol knew of the matter.

"Thank you, Mr. Worth," Kr'nai Ersha said. The Confederation of Clans held the chair that day, and he was the senior member. "Mr. Bristol, you have our undivided attention."

Drake rose to his feet and addressed the Commission with cold formality. "I have been instructed to protest the current and planned exchanges of information, technology, and genetic resources between the Commonwealth and the Confederation of Clans. The people of the Republic respectfully demand that these exchanges be ended immediately and remain suspended until the Republic has made a decision on its response to the similar offers made by the Commonwealth to the Republic. We believe it is necessary that all three parties move forward in the same direction and at the same rate. We also respectfully demand that further travel between the Commonwealth and Confederation be restricted to official business approved by this Commission. The loose intercourse between our neighbors is simply not acceptable while these negotiations, which are aimed at finding agreeable ways to expedite such exchanges, are ongoing. Last, the Republic is aware that a Leyra'an-specific variant of the Commonwealth nanotech-based medical technology now exists, and that the Commonwealth plans to make it immediately available to the Confederation. This, also, is unacceptable. The Commonwealth must desist until such time as appropriate agreements on the exchange between all three entities involved have been reached."

No one responded for a long moment, long enough that Bristol began to look distinctly uncomfortable, standing there before them. He was slow to take his seat and his look became a glare as the silence persisted, and his eyes shifted from his colleagues to the gallery and back repeatedly.

Yu Sei Ho glanced at his associate; her only response was a slight upward twitch of one dark eyebrow, to which Ho nodded. "Since an objection of this sort was anticipated, I am prepared to respond on behalf of the Commonwealth," he said to Ersha.

"Please do so," Ersha said.

Ho looked at Drake for a moment before speaking. "Mr. Bristol, were your superiors able to provide any indication that, in the near future, citizens of the Commonwealth and the Republic will be free to travel between their respective civilizations?"

"No, sir. I was not given a specific time for that."

"Did they provide an indication that they will be ready to accept direct representation from the Commonwealth to the Republic?"

"No, sir, not at this time." Drake's answer was quiet, and guarded in tone and expression.

"Did they send, with their requests, *any* indication at all of when exchanges may begin of information and *medical technology?*" Ho clearly emphasized the last phrase.

"No sir, they did not." A light flush of color appeared in Drake's face.

"Does the Republic honestly believe the Commonwealth should hold off developing relations with the Leyra'an indefinitely?"

"Your choice of words overstates the case, somewhat," Emerson said mildly.

"With all due respect, Mr. Worth, I don't believe that's the case," Ho replied. "The Commonwealth understands the need for careful consideration by the Republic. The differences between our life ways are considerable, far greater than those that exist between Commonwealth and Confederation. We are willing to respect a need for caution, but have come to the reluctant conclusion that what we are dealing with here would more honestly be described as obstructionism. From what you have told us, the Republic has not moved forward on a single suggestion or proposal offered by this Commission."

"This has been explained before, more than once," Drake replied, with first a hard look at Emerson. "Until we've had a chance to thoroughly study the effects of such things on the Republic and its people, and have a plan in place to mitigate possible social and economic disruptions, we *cannot* simply open our borders to Commonwealth ideas and technology."

"Can you provide us with *any idea* of just how long such studies are expected to take?" Yu Sei Ho asked.

"My government does not believe it is wise to place an arbitrary time limit on such a complicated process." Drake's reply was as stiff as the collar of the white shirt under his black suit.

"No such concern exists within the Confederation," Yu Sei Ho said. "That is due, of course, to the similarities in our life ways, and cannot be helped. And, of course, it is not for the Commonwealth to dictate how and when the Republic should respond to what we offer. But as a representative of the Commonwealth, I find it difficult to justify leaving our relations with the Leyra'an suspended indefinitely while the Republic drags its collective feet. My instructions from the Councils are currently to pursue the development of relations with the Confederation and Republic at whatever rates each is willing to manage. Your people wish to follow a more cautious approach than the Leyra'an. That is your right, and your choice. But how can the Republic justify a demand that we must match that pace with the Leyra'an? Can you tell me why the Leyra'an should suffer unnecessary illness and death because the Republic cannot examine this matter expeditiously?" The expression on his face changed, but it was only a narrowing of almond-shaped eyes that were locked on Drake, where he sat very much on the spot. "Your policies do not dictate the policies of the Commonwealth, and should not. We are, after all, prepared, and in fact quite eager, to provide the Republic with *exactly* what we intend to give the Leyra'an. We are not offering them any advantage that is unavailable to you."

Drake looked ready to explode, and his face had taken on an unhealthy shade of red, but Emerson spoke before Drake could react. Drake visibly clenched his jaw and stared at the table. "Our way of life is very different from the ways pursued by the Leyra'an and the Commonwealth, as Commissioner Ho has himself pointed out," he said. "That this is the source of the problem has also been placed on the record, more than once." He looked down for a moment, as if considering his words. "What you are offering, though it is of course a most generous gift, would alter the acquisition and distribution of wealth in our society in ways not easy to predict. The effect it would have on the building of family fortunes alone is nearly incalculable. We need to consider carefully the management of these effects."

"I don't believe you can fully manage such effects in advance," Ho replied. "There are too many variables, many of which will surely become known only after the fact. But in any case, the Republic is surely free to take as long as it deems necessary. While I find it disturbing to think of the many lives we could save while these studies are made, it truly isn't for us to decide what is right for the Republic. I am frankly baffled, however, that the Republic presumes to restrict access to these techniques to the Leyra'an while they slowly examine issues of their own making."

"My people share the concern over unnecessary suffering within the Republic," Ersha said. "Surely the folk of the Republic, given lives of indefinite length, will find ways to sort things out as they develop? After all, they will have plenty of time."

Robert knew Ersha very well, and so could easily see the enormous restraint required to keep his outrage from showing. The Leyra'an had less understanding of the Republic's archaic system of exchange than the folk of the Commonwealth, for whom it was at least a part of their history. The Way of Leyra'an had always followed a different path.

"I truly wish it were so simple," Emerson said. And he sat there looking old and tired.

Robert was shocked. He knew Emerson's gift for speaking extemporaneously, and expected the usual eloquent evasion from the man. Instead, Emerson yielded his position and sat there with all the signs of a man defeated.

Yu Sei Ho wore a puzzled frown as he looked from Emerson to Kr'nai Ersha. "As I said before, this situation was anticipated. If the chair permits, I am prepared to *formally* and for the record answer the Commissioners from the Republic."

"Please proceed," said Kr'nai Ersha.

Drake stiffened and opened his mouth to speak, but a curt gesture and a sharp, definitely angry look from Emerson stifled the intended response. Instead, Drake sat glaring blankly at the section of desk before him.

"The Commonwealth has no desire to aid either side in the conflict between the Confederation and the Republic," said Ho. "Our official stance, as it already exists, is to mediate negotiations at such time as both parties indicate a desire to carry such negotiations forward. Until that time, the Commonwealth as a matter of policy will continue to explore and develop its relationship with each party to the extent allowed by that party. We will do so with the ultimate intent of improving the lives of the citizens of all three civilizations in whatever ways we find possible. We have not, and will never, offer the Confederation of Clans anything that we do not also make freely available to the Republic. It is up to the Confederation and the Republic respectively to decide how to respond to the Commonwealth and its offers of technology and information. We will not deviate from our current policies because the parties in conflict choose different ways to respond to our overtures.

"And so, the Commonwealth *respectfully* refuses the *request* of the Republic to suspend trade with and travel between the Confederation of Clans and the Commonwealth. I will take this moment to reiterate that the people of the Republic are free to join in these exchanges, and are indeed encouraged to do so. We would welcome you among us, and are eager to learn how our long sundered peoples can enrich one another."

"We do not resist your generosity without good reason," Emerson replied. "The differences between the Commonwealth and the Republic are no small matter. The differences between the Republic and the Confederation are even greater. Our initial experiences with such shocks to our culture ultimately led to open warfare between our people and the Leyra'an. We have no desire to risk a repetition of that experience, hence our caution."

"We can assure you that risk of such conflict simply does not exist," Sarah said. "By itself, such a fear isn't a valid reason to bar meaningful communication. Quite the contrary, I would think. That we offer, first and foremost, a way to free your people from the dread of illness and death should make that abundantly clear."

Emerson seemed frozen for a moment. "I am inclined to agree with you on that matter," he said softly. The words brought Drake's eyes up from the desk. Robert could not see, from where he sat, the other man's expression, but doubted from the way Drake quivered that it was a friendly regard.

"May I make a suggestion?" said Holm.

"We are open to your input, of course, Rost'aht Holm," said Ho.

With a nod from Kr'nai Ersha, Holm said, "Of all the things that might flow from the Commonwealth to the Republic, this gift of life they offer carries with it the greatest potential for immediate change. So, rather than release this technology to your people all at once, perhaps you could bring it to them a little at a time."

"How do you mean?" Emerson asked, frowning slightly, but clearly interested.

"Take it to those in the greatest need," Holm replied. "Those with grave illnesses such as Founders' disease, or the consequences of extreme old age. Let it seem a treatment for dire circumstances at first, and then, when you have had a chance to gauge the reactions of your people and your economic system, perhaps then carefully release it to the general populace."

Emerson slowly shook his head, as his colleague frowned and glowered. "But word will surely filter through the Disputed Zone of the more general nature of the Cure and of its use by the Leyra'an. In fact, rumors of its existence are already being passed around. How do we account for such a disparity?"

"Point to limited supplies," Sarah said. "The need to bring production up would make it seem quite plausible that setting certain priorities might be necessary, at first."

Robert stared at Emerson, anxious to see how the man might respond. Pointedly ignoring Drake, the senior Commissioner from the Republic nodded thoughtfully and said, "Something of the sort has in fact been suggested, back home, by the opposition party. The idea was not taken seriously. But if the Commonwealth is determined to move forward as planned, it might provide a way out of our quandary." He gave Drake a quick look, then said to the Commission, "I will see to it that our government is reacquainted with this suggestion, in the context of these new developments."

"And although I have answered by proxy," said Ho, "I will see that the message from the Republic is received by the Councils of the Commonwealth, for their consideration."

"Fair enough," said Emerson. Addressing Ersha he said, "As far as I know, sir, there is no other business pending. Unless Mr. Bristol has something else... ?"

Drake Bristol sat as still as stone and did not speak. Robert could just see the tiny head-shake the man made in response.

"We are adjourned," said Ersha after a brief silence.

"That might be a first," Robert said to Melep as people rose to their feet and sought the exits. They stood together, but held back to let the crowd thin. "They actually resolved something."

"What was resolved?" she asked, puzzled.

"How to juggle relations," he replied. "The Commonwealth just made it as plain as starlight that we're going to work separately with the Confederation and Republic, if the Republic won't end the foot-dragging." They worked their way down the row of seats toward the aisle leading to the door. "The Republic doesn't get to dictate the policies of the Commonwealth."

"Which is as it should be," Melep replied. "A line had to be drawn, I suppose. But will the Republic respect it?"

Robert glanced back to the meeting table and saw Drake and Emerson still there, apparently arguing about something. Emerson made a dismissive gesture and turned abruptly, heading for the door at that end of the room. Robert caught sight of the look on the face of Drake as he followed Emerson toward the door, the rage that seemed about to burst forth in Emerson's direction. Then the two were through the door and gone. Worry formed a knot in his gut.

"I wouldn't count on it," he replied. Hooking his arm through Melep's, Robert led her out, and they headed for home.

CHAPTER TEN

Endmost Station
Disputed Zone
Two Years After Contact

"Interesting algorithms," James Calavone said quietly, and half to himself. He took another sip of coffee and let the movements of his eyes determine the rate of flow of information down the screen hanging in the air before him. "I'm surprised the Commonwealth isn't infested with self-replicating machines, by now." He smiled to himself as he said this, thinking of how vid-dramatists in the Republic depicted the Human civilization the Founders left behind. It was assumed that one day the two branches of the Human race would meet again, and in fictional renderings it was always a brave band of folk from the Republic saving Humans from cybernetic fates worse than death.

As it turned out, the dramatists had missed just how dangerous, in a rather subtle way, the other Human civilization would turn out to be. Rather than a race of half-living, half-machine hybrids, they were perfectly normal people who lived lives that were the seductive antithesis of everything normal Humans should embrace. Lives supported by a technological base so sophisticated it had taken many long months to put together the analysis before him.

"Depends on how you look at things," Kester said. "Sounds to me as if they *are* infested with machines. From what I've heard, and you've found in those files, these Commonwealth folk haven't done a real day's work in a couple hundred years."

"Longer than that," Calavone said over the top of his mug. "Though I suppose it depends on how you define 'work.' " He thought for a moment, then said, "I have to admit I can see some immediate uses for this, given our current predicament. For instance, we could build a fair-sized fleet in a hurry, if we adopt this technology. Of course, we'd need to make use of self-aware computer technology ourselves."

"Become a monster so the monster won't break us?" Kester said, quoting an old proverb.

Calavone grinned at his friend and said, "I'd rather be that monster than stand by while everything I believe in is swept away. Besides, this wouldn't be the first time I've bowed to expedience."

"I don't see how you can accept such a thing so easily, when there are other possibilities we might explore," Kester said.

"To control *this* tech? No," and he shook his head. "We need computer tech of a comparable nature to run this stuff."

"It's a moot point," Kester said with a shrug. "The self-destruct protocol we aborted had already wiped the high-level functions from the computer cores on those smaller ships."

"The point is hardly moot, Andy," Calavone said. He raised his mug and grinned at Kester across the rim. "I don't need the Commonwealth's tech for *this* part."

He could see from the change in Kester's expression exactly when things finally fell into place, the look of someone who suddenly saw something that should have been obvious long before. "You already have a machine mind here!"

"Of course I do!" Calavone replied with a short, hard laugh. "And yes, as you've no doubt guessed, it's the one I address as Artie."

"'Artie'," Kester said again, shaking his head.

"Oh, come on. It's a suitable nickname." Calavone took another sip of his coffee.

"How the hell did you manage this?" Kester demanded. "The old records were purged when the machines the Founders built ran amok."

"The purge was not entirely effective, as a matter of fact. And we had very useful information my network *gleaned* from those who managed the, ah, *initial* Commonwealth contact." He shook his head and set down the mug. "Pray that these people of the Commonwealth never learn the truth about what the Republic did with that crew they found marooned out here. I believe it would be the end of us!"

"I doubt they're *that* much of a military threat," Kester replied. "They're more numerous than we are, but... "

"After all the months we've spent reviewing... " Calavone was openly aghast. "Wake up, you damned fool! If they were to turn this production technology to the manufacture of military hardware, the Republic would cease to exist! I'm looking at a single application, here and now, to produce a small fleet in a matter of months. They have tens of *thousands* of such facilities that could do the same in a few *weeks*. We wouldn't stand a chance against them!"

"I don't think their *culture* is capable of warfare," Kester said defensively.

"How much are you willing to bet on that?" Calavone shot back. "If they *ever* see us as a threat, they'll remember war, sure enough. That's simple Human nature. Even the most conservative estimates put the Commonwealth at several orders of magnitude of our size. We goad them into it, and they'll take us apart in no time!"

"You're underestimating the strength of the Republic," Kester replied shortly.

"Oh, not at all! I'm being realistic, here. Because of what's going on in the Disputed Zone and out beyond the Rift, the Republic is one crisis away from disintegration. The Commonwealth would have little trouble exploiting our internal divisions. They'd crack us wide open! Unless I can find something here," and he waved his free hand at the display gleaming in the air before him, "that can be used to provide some sort of leverage."

"These data stores might *eventually* give us parity, facing the Commonwealth," said Kester. "Short of using their tech to suppress our own people militarily, I can't see how it'll help with internal problems. You'd never win the general populace over using such tactics."

"You're too short-focused, Andy. We might not need strong-arm tactics. There's med tech in here, too. We're in the process of extracting and analyzing their cure for old age. If we can replicate that and make it available to the general populace, a big attraction for the Commonwealth will be gone, and being the source, I'll have what I need to rekindle the revolution my father began." He bit his lip as his eyes strayed back to the display. "That will be tricky. We'll need a way to convince the general population that long life is desirable, but that the ways of the Commonwealth are not. I'm not entirely sure how to approach that one!"

"I'll leave that stuff to you," Kester said with a shrug. "Just tell me where you need *Vengeance* to enforce the decision. We've been idle for much too long! Do we have any sort of time frame here? When can we expect usable results?"

"Well, we've adapted some of our own automated mining and construction facilities, but between glitches and a shortage of personnel, tangible results have been slow in coming." Calavone finished his coffee and set the mug aside. "Ironic, really. Once we get even a single set of these things fully operational, we'll be independent of manpower in the usual sense. Which is handy, Endmost not being a major destination for emigration. We'll need the personnel freed up from construction to help crew the ships we build."

"We do this right, finish what your father started, Endmost won't *need* an immigration policy." Kester frowned and said, "Of course, if this works out, we'll have to deal with what to do with all of this. The rest of the Republic gets hold of this production technology, and whatever we accomplish becomes a moot point, in a hurry!"

"That won't be allowed," Calavone said calmly. "It will be restricted to Endmost. Artie is more than capable of making sure no files are copied or transported out of here. But we're getting ahead of ourselves. My father grew impatient, and look where that got him!"

And what it got me, Calavone thought, but did not say. *Stuck out here off the far end of the DZ, hoping no one accidentally stumbles over what we've built. Especially now that it looks like we can develop the means to protect our independence and maybe save the Republic from itself.*

"To be sure," Kester said. "We've waited this long." He sighed and added, "God, that's so easy to say."

"I know what you mean," Calavone replied. He held the coffee decanter out when he saw Kester drain his mug. Kester held the mug out without hesitation. "Careful with this stuff. Get used to it and synth or *mi'pat* will never go down right, again."

"It's been such a long time since I tasted the real thing," Kester said, as he inhaled the steam with obvious pleasure. "Never touched the scaly brew, and the synth crap we make on the ship... How the devil did you get access to real coffee, anyway?"

"Same network that keeps me up to date on affairs of the Republic," Calavone replied. "Now we grow our own, down close to the star. Natural light apparently works better."

"I hope you gave the fellow who absconded with the seeds, or whatever, a medal. Being caught with the stuff without a license gets you ten years hard labor."

Calavone laughed and said, "He's a legitimate grower with connections that have no idea where his true loyalties lie." He sobered and added, "We have a lot of good people in our network. There's no way we would have survived without them. I doubt we could attempt what we're contemplating without those people, no matter how much Commonwealth technology we managed to choke down. Keep *that* in mind when the machines worry you. We're using this stuff to help people who have everything to lose, should we fail."

"So, we're really going to build our own fleet of ships, presumably to take on the RDF?" Kester asked.

"Not the entire RDF, immediately," Calavone replied. "I intend to secure the DZ for them, first, a *most* patriotic gesture. That will relieve the Republic of the need to take on the Secessionist movement growing out there. If that all works out, we shouldn't have much trouble building support with the purists of the trans-Rift settlements."

"How do you plan to handle the Secessionists?" Kester asked.

"We'll let the Secessionists think we're secretly with them on eventually breaking away from the Republic, and use the population to provide crews for the ships we continue to build here. By the time it becomes clear we're playing one side against the other, we should be in a strong enough position that the RDF won't be able to dislodge us, and the Secessionists will have been neutered."

"You're assuming the RDF will sit still for this," said Kester.

"That's going to be tricky," Calavone admitted. "We can't have any conflict with the RDF in the beginning. We'd lose. But if we can get the upper hand in the DZ fast enough, then wave the olive branch, there's a good chance they'll talk first. Now, what exactly we'll say to cover ourselves remains to be developed. I'll think of something. In the meantime, the Secessionists will sit tight if we convince them it's a ruse. Which it will be, of course, in more ways than one. In time, we will be a power capable of holding the unwholesome influences of both the Commonwealth and Leyra'an at bay. A power capable of guiding the citizens of the Republic back to the path chosen for them by the Founders."

"You seem pretty sure of all this," Kester said.

"Oh, it won't be so easy as all that," Calavone laughed. "I have no illusions about it! But it's a good outline on which to build our plans. And it's always easier to amend a plan, than to create one from scratch!"

"You know, that long life business might come in handy," Kester said. "I think you may be right. If you can nail that down it would give you a very powerful sort of leverage. Imagine how cooperative the right sort of people might be, if you could promise them they'd live forever?"

"Good idea!" Calavone didn't have the heart to tell his friend that it had already occurred to him. "Leverage indeed! I like it! Now we just need to be able to build stuff fast enough."

"A fleet first, I trust?" Kester asked.

Calavone nodded. "Last intel on preparedness isn't up to date, but word is the contractors for the fleet rebuild are over budget and crowding deadlines."

"Business as usual," Kester replied with a smirk. "The Republic won't maintain control of the border if that goes on. And that sets our priorities, then. We get the cure for old age available to use as leverage *after* we build our fleet and *before* they restore theirs."

"And then we appear in the nick of time to save the Republic from another civil war," Calavone agreed. "Which would be ironic, since it was *losing* a civil war that landed us way the hell out here in the first place!"

CHAPTER ELEVEN

Eb'ara Kai Station
Pa'haronsa System

It took a long time for John to feel anything less than conspicuous, a lone Human on a station otherwise populated by Leyra'an. The feeling ranged from peculiar to alarming, depending on the situation. He was treated cordially enough by those with whom he interacted, since his acceptance by the Matriarch gave them little choice, but it was easy enough to tell when a Leyra'an was being polite because he or she felt giving the Human half a chance was the right thing to do, or because the word of the Matriarch gave them no alternative. Misunderstandings were fewer now that he had a facility with their language, but he still acted like a Human when trying to handle unfamiliar customs and situations. He stood out like the proverbial sore thumb. The looks that followed him everywhere he went were reminder enough, and months passed before the station folk were simply so accustomed to him that he no longer drew prolonged stares.

And so it was, the morning he and Wirolen joined the station's populace to receive what was being called the

Commonwealth Cure. He walked through the main torus of Eb'ara Kai station with Wirolen clinging to his arm and pretended not to see how many still did double-takes at the sight of a *Human* among them. He was dressed in the casual tunic and trousers style of Leyra'an males, in dark red and darker green, colors Wirolen assured him looked very good with his fair skin and black hair. He wore the braided *es'ava* of her clan and family, crossing his chest from right to left instead of left to right, to indicate his adopted status. Some of those passing by offered the couple polite nods of greeting that he acknowledged in kind. A few greeted them aloud with friendly words.

They walked together along a broad footpath inside the main ring, a route paved with closely fitted, dark gray tiles. Beds of bright blue, yellow, and pink flowers lined the path, over which arched willow-like trees with feathery, pale gray-green leaves. The foot traffic was heavy, and increased as they walked. They found themselves part of a large and noisy crowd moving along toward the same destination, the nearest of the three distribution centers set up in the main torus for the dispensation of the Commonwealth's great gift to the Leyra'an. The gift of centuries — at least — of life lived in perfect health. People spoke of it around them in excited voices, though many were openly skeptical that such a thing could be true.

A ship had come with the means for producing this medical miracle, a ship crewed by men and women of the Commonwealth, and they were now ready to dispense the Cure. John wondered if the same gift was being given to those he had left behind in the Republic. The Commonwealth would surely have made the offer, if Robert MacGregor was at all representative of that society. And it would surely be an easy thing to do, there being no special adaptations necessary.

The crowd stopped and people sorted themselves out into an ever-lengthening line. As they waited, a trio of very official-looking members of Clan Pa'haronsa's station management crew came toward them. Badges clipped to their clan sashes identified them as such. It was obvious from the way they peered into the crowd that they were looking for someone, and when they spotted him it was just as obvious *who* they sought in the crowd. For a moment John felt a pang of anxiety.

"John Knowles," said the eldest of the three, the one with streaks of gray in his mane of dark brown hair and prominent black stripes curving from his cheekbones into his hairline. They all three bowed, with a rattle of golden arm bands and badges of office.

John bowed in response and said, "I am John Knowles." It was always best to respond to formal courtesy with the same, even when it was ridiculously redundant. Who else could he be?

The eldest of the station officials said, "You must come with us, please. The folk of the Commonwealth wish to speak with you." He then bowed to Wirolen and said, "Eb'shra Wirolen, you may come as well, if it pleases you."

"It does," she said with a bow in her turn. And they followed their escort away from the growing noise of the crowded queue.

As they followed the officials, they encountered people with bright, excited eyes walking briskly across their path, all of them with fluorescent blue bands around their wrists. John sensed a large and very public, possibly station-wide, celebration in the near future. He and Wirolen were led into a lift cluster that shuttled people from the gathering place up to one of the station's infirmary units. A group of Leyra'an, wearing blue arm bands, filed out of a capsule, which was then appropriated by the officials. It was a short trip to the middle deck, where he found himself somewhat taken aback to see Human faces for the first time after so long. He caught himself, forcing himself not to gape at them, or babble greetings as if finally seeing his own kind was a relief; he doubted such would sit well with Wirolen. There were five of them, three women and two men, all wearing pale blue uniform coveralls, and all with that same strange combination of youthful appearance and mature bearing he remembered from Robert MacGregor.

It was a busy place. Leyra'an shuttled up through the same lifts, then were led by station crew to padded benches that lined the hall. People who had received treatment were being led back to the lifts, clutching the blue bands being handed out by various station crew members along the way. Each Human doctor had a small crew of observant Leyra'an med techs in attendance. Everyone was talking in quiet tones, and from time to time laughter was heard. One of the Humans glanced up, then strode over to meet them. Without thinking John stopped short and bowed, as the Leyra'an would have done.

"Hello, John," said the woman who first bowed in response and then stepped forward to greet him, right hand extended in the ancient Human custom. Her voice was deeper than he was accustomed to, for a woman, but was quite beautiful, as was the speaker. "I'm Ursula Ashrama, from the Commonwealth. I bring greetings from Rob MacGregor and his family. My ship has a message from him, by the way. It's been downloaded to the station database for your convenience." She spoke the Human language.

For a heartbeat John just stared, then rather self-consciously took her hand in a grip firm enough to match hers. She was as tall as John, though slimmer, long-legged and graceful in her movements. He had never seen a Human with skin so dark, and her wide, black eyes were unlike anything he had ever seen. Her hair was black as well, straight and cut short. John knew all too well that the original population of the Republic included a rather small and not entirely representative sample of Human genetic diversity. This simple fact of life was responsible for the great health scourge faced by the people of the Republic. The woman before him presented a single, if striking, example of the diversity the Republic had lost. Ursula, who he thought might well be the most beautiful Human woman he had ever seen, would never have been able to blend into a crowd in the Republic. There were folk of dusky complexion in the Republic, and no shortage of them either. The Founders had been a mixed lot racially; that was a matter of history. But Ursula's skin was almost black, not brown.

"Very pleased to meet you, ma'am," he said with a grin, speaking in the Human language, as she had done. Her accent reminded John clearly of Robert's manner of speaking. "I don't suppose you speak Leyra'an?" If the station had a translation program he did not know of it.

"I do," Ursula replied. She switched languages and said, "And you are right, we should speak in a way that all may understand."

He could feel tension rising in Wirolen as she reacted to the presence of the other woman, who by the standards of either species would be considered unusually attractive. She moved half a step past him, in a posture that John knew indicated a Leyra'an woman prepared to fend off a rival. It was all he could do not to laugh, and he wondered if Wirolen reacted as she did out of conscious jealousy or simple instinct. Instead he said, "This is Eb'shra Wirolen. I believe by the most common customs of the Commonwealth, as I understand them, you would call her my wife."

Wirolen looked up at him with a Mona Lisa smile and relaxed immediately. Her wariness regarding this Human woman all but vanished at John's description of their relationship. She stuck her right hand out in a slightly awkward imitation of the handclasp just shared by John and Ursula. "Welcome to Eb'ara Kai," she said.

"Rob mentioned your name," Ursula said, grasping Wirolen's hand. "He thought I might find you two together. In fact, he expressed the hope that I would do so." And she smiled as well, carefully, and clearly schooled in Leyra'an culture. "I am, indeed, pleased to meet you. Rob speaks *very* highly of your piloting skill, and that is no small praise, believe me."

And in that way Wirolen had, she went in the blink of an eye from seeing a potential rival to acquiring a new friend. John could see this from the way the space between them shrank as Wirolen drifted closer, into that space that Humans normally maintained around themselves. Personal space was not a concept understood by the Leyra'an to the same degree as

Humans. Ursula seemed not in the least concerned that the other woman was crowding her.

"I will download the message first thing after we are finished here," John said to Ursula. "But, ah, you did not have the station management pull us out of the line for that."

"No, indeed. We wanted to make sure you received the Human variation of the nano treatment."

"Might you have given him our version by mistake?" Wirolen asked.

"No chance of that," Ursula replied with a shake of her head. "For some reason, Rob MacGregor seemed concerned that you might actually refuse it."

John glanced briefly at Wirolen, then said, "My friend Robert is a perceptive fellow. We knew each other for only a brief time, but he knows me well enough to expect that I might be of two minds about taking this Cure."

"You will take it," Wirolen said. "Or I will refuse it as well."

"Well, we cannot have that," John said with a chuckle. "A universe without Eb'shra Wirolen would be a dull place indeed! But as it happens, I am reconciled that this gift from the Commonwealth is appropriate. I will take the treatment." And Wirolen squeezed his hand tightly.

"Yours is apparently a minority opinion in the Republic," Ursula observed. She turned a bit sideways and indicated the way they were to go, and then led them to a pair of recently vacated benches.

"I take it this means the Commonwealth has offered the same to the Republic?" John asked.

"Yes, we did," she replied. "Of course we did! I doubt the general populace of the Republic knows, though. The Trilateral Commission members from the Republic have said the offer is 'under consideration.'"

John understood by her gesture that he was to stretch out on the bench, and did so. Wirolen did the same on the bench next to his. "I cannot say I am surprised," he said, still speaking Leyra'an. "Large and sudden changes have never been readily accepted by the Republic. If there is anything larger and more sudden than being told everyone can now live indefinitely, in perfect health... Well... "

"How is it," Wirolen asked, "the gift is then given first to the Leyra'an? Will the Republic not see this as favoritism?"

"If they see it that way, it would be grossly dishonest," Ursula replied. She peered at displays that lit up in the air over her two patients. First Wirolen, and then John, were scanned, the equipment being within the tables. Only a soft hum could be heard. "We made the offer equally to both, no conditions, to *avoid* the appearance of playing favorites. There was plenty of time to consider consequences, since the offer was made a full year before the Leyra'an variant was developed. When the time came the Leyra'an said 'yes' with great enthusiasm. The Republic is in a state of paralysis by analysis. The Commonwealth finally decided that there was no reason to delay treatment of the Leyra'an because the Republic could not make a decision."

"It might force their hand," John said from his exam table. Ursula leaned over him and pressed a small patch to the side of his neck. It stayed put on its own. She did the same for Wirolen, then patted the Leyra'an woman's shoulder reassuringly. "News does travel from the Republic to the Confederation and back, through the Disputed Zone. Too many systems, too few ships in place to enforce the law against traffic across the border. The Leyra'an out there will surely talk about this, and that *will* have consequences. There are star systems in the DZ wanting to secede from the Republic and strike out on their own. Or merge with the Confederation. News of this treatment, and the realization that it has been blocked by the government, will only inflame the situation. My former government may well end up accepting the Cure in order to prevent a civil war."

"How grimly ironic," Ursula said, shaking her head and frowning. "Our gift of life and health might spark a rebellion that leads to the deaths of many. I hope you are right that they will give in, rather than risk killing their own people. And the treatment *has* been given, by the way. We are done here. If you were going to experience complications we would know by now, so you can join the celebration that I hear is even now spreading through the station."

"Done?" said Wirolen. She touched the patch stuck to her neck. "This?"

"Yes, that. We scanned for any gross irregularities in your metabolisms, and then applied the generalized treatment. Even as we speak the nanos are spreading through your system and replicating, using your bodies as sources of raw material as they adapt and tailor themselves to your individual physiologies."

"I — feel no different," John said as he sat up, not hiding his bewilderment.

Ursula shook her head and said, "Nor should you. You will experience an increase in appetite soon, but that will stabilize when the nanos have finished settling in. And there is, I am told, a feeling of increased vigor and well-being that the recently treated experience. This is presumably the result of various minor problems and irregularities being fixed as the nanos bring your bodies up to full potential. It might also merely be psychosomatic. Commonwealth citizens are born to this. We never experience it all at once, as adults, so I am not certain why the Leyra'an experience this lifting of the spirit." She shrugged and added, "Since it does no harm, it is of no matter."

"I cannot say what I expected," John said, sure that he looked as sheepish as he sounded. "Such an enormous thing, such a gift, to have it come so quietly, as if nothing unusual had happened at all!"

"Go join the party," Ursula said with a bright and toothy grin, forgetting for a moment where she was, and speaking the Human language. "If it's anything like what we saw at Serch'nach, you'll soon feel that something *truly* momentous has occurred!"

CHAPTER TWELVE

Pr'pri System
Bartram Habitat

Robert and Melep retreated to the Willow Lake, there to wait for their family, wondering if members of the Commission would join this time at all. They quietly discussed the strange confrontation they'd witnessed, as they traveled by tram car to the pub. Their usual table was waiting for them, but it was empty. Accustomed to finding members of the Trilateral Commission there ahead of them more days than not, the vacancy underscored the feeling that an important change was in motion. The unsettled feeling grew as time passed and no one appeared to join them. They kept a companionable silence as they sipped the first round of beer. Robert felt oddly conspicuous and anxious, sitting there, just the two of them. Melep nudged her chair closer to his and he put his arm around her. A Leyra'an response, and one he no longer thought about, it had become such a reflex.

After a while, Alicia arrived with Paul in his sling making happy baby noises, Vurn tucked into the crook of her left arm, and Gava'mi capering about not quite at her heels. The instant the han'anga saw where Robert sat, the Beast pelted across the flagstones and leaped, sliding across the table top with a screech of claws along the surface that raised gooseflesh. Somehow he managed not to plow through the set of heavy green and blue glass mugs waiting at the center of the table. Melep yelped and ducked away, then laughed when Gava'mi leaned from where he landed in Robert's lap and nuzzled her face.

"That was an unusual session," Alicia said, uttering a significant understatement.

"We noticed," Robert replied. "I'm thinking we may have the table to ourselves for a bit."

"Holm said he would be delayed, but not by how long," Melep said. "We had beer brought," and she held up the dark green glass pitcher that she had rescued in the nick of time from Gava'mi's arrival.

Alicia nudged a heavy glass mug from the cluster of unused glasses in the center of the table. "That'll do nicely."

"Drake was upset about something," Melep said while she poured. "I do not believe it was entirely due to the fact that he was called on to deliver the ultimatum."

"No, it had something to do with Emerson," said Robert. "Something's wrong between those two. You could see it, plain as a nova. I wonder if the word's out that Emerson has been cured of Founders'?"

"Easy enough to find out," Alicia said. She pointed to the tram line and said, "Here they all come, now."

Holm and Ersha, Ho and Sarah, and Emerson, all strolled across the turf around the end of the lake, talking and gesturing as they came. Their conversation rendered any intention to ask questions a moot point; it continued and swept up those already at the table.

"I do understand your point of view," Emerson was saying as they drew near. "And the Commonwealth is within its rights to make the choice. I'm not objecting to the exercise of your sovereign rights, much less backing my government's ridiculous demands. That they should make such a request, and then expect the Republic's sovereignty to be treated as somehow sacred, simply baffles me."

"And why now?" Sarah asked.

"I wish I knew!" Emerson wore an uncharacteristic frown.

There came a pause in which chairs were slid around on safety rails, babies were passed around to the new arrivals for proper admiration, and a han'anga was tickled and scratched while a carafe of chardonnay joined the replenished pitchers of beer. "We acquired a white wine of some sort," Emerson said as he poured himself a glass, "and shared it around the office. It was like nothing I've ever tasted from grapes grown in the Republic. We really *must* come up with an agreement on allowing the Commonwealth to send us seeds and such!"

"It's being worked up," Ho assured him. "A rather extensive inventory, I believe, and one that carries a number of wine grape varietals."

"That's good," Emerson said with a smile. "Nothing there that would do anything worse than create new business opportunities. Even Drake can't object to that!" Then, in a darker tone he added, "Not that he'll be deterred from doing so by such simple logic."

"He seemed seriously out of sorts," Sarah said.

"Drake has painted himself into a bit of a tight corner," Emerson said. "He has adopted the hardline stance of the current administration, but just in time for popular support for those policies to erode rapidly. Unfortunately for him and others like him, that very same administration has pushed some *very* unpopular ideas of late. Word is that a plan is being pushed for the pacification of the Republic's part of the DZ. There are people who have fortunes at stake, and never mind that those fortunes are not entirely based on legitimate business dealings, and they have the power to push back. The resulting political maneuvering has upset some of his career goals."

"I do wish the majority of the Republic were more like you," Melep said.

"Oh, but they *are*, my dear! The great majority of them, in fact. They're plain folks, unconcerned with agendas and idealism, just trying to get by in their lives with a bit of joy, for themselves and their children. Just like you." He smiled, and then the smile faded and he looked tired and a little sad. "The ways we pursue these goals are different, but our motives are the same."

"When Leyra'an and Humans first met, the contact was between explorers and people settling the frontier," said Ersha. "Plain folk, indeed. And they found a way to bring our two species together. The troubles began when those such as Mr. Bristol became involved."

"When business interests became involved," Emerson said. "Unexpected changes can be very bad for established business plans, a thing many find frightening. And fear causes some men to do questionable things, believing all the while in the rightness and necessity of what they do."

Robert could feel an unpleasant and quite unusual tension in their small group. Gava'mi, sensitive to the emotions of what he considered to be his pack, was alert and attentive. He frequently looked at Emerson and cocked his head, as if listening to something. There was a pause as more drink was shared about, and quieter than normal toasts were made to hope and the children.

"Drake does in fact represent clearly those who see the Way of Leyra'an, and now the Commonwealth, as a threat to our way of life," said Emerson. "They, like so many who have political power in the Republic, have built their lives around the acquisition and control of forms of wealth your life ways would render meaningless. So they resist. Of course they resist."

"It's so unnecessary," Ho said sadly, shaking his head. "You can go on with your economics. We have absolutely no interest in changing your ways! We offer what we do because we hope to enrich life in the Republic, *not* because we believe our way is better than yours. If the Republic's answer to it all is no, then so be it."

"The same is true of the Leyra'an," said Holm. "We care little about how your folk measure their lives. That is their choice, after all."

"I wish it could be so simple," Emerson replied. "But it's much too late for that. The people of the Republic have very little direct knowledge of the Commonwealth as yet, but rumors have begun to spread. Pointed questions are being asked. Your mere *existence* will be every bit as disruptive, in the long run, as this Cure you offer. We can't shut out forever the knowledge of what the Commonwealth has built, in ways very similar to the Leyra'an, ways that we persist in telling our citizens *cannot* work for Humans. And yet, they clearly do!" He held the wine glass up and gently swirled the contents. "This is why your restorative medicine is resisted. Oh, there are fools and fanatics who'd see this Cure as questioning the will of God. But most in the Republic would embrace this medicine with the same enthusiasm as the Leyra'an, given a chance. It's seen by the powers-that-be as the wedge that would open the Republic fully to the ways of the Commonwealth, the beginning of a wave of change that would end the Republic as we've known it. They see generations of work going for nothing, in the end."

"Oh, rubbish!" said Ho. "It would *not* all be for nothing. It's how your people survived, grew, and prospered for more than two hundred years!"

"Oh, I know that, my friend. I *do* know it. Convincing an entire civilization of that truth, when so many clever falsehoods are arrayed against you... Well, it's challenging, to say the least!" Emerson sighed, then after a wry smile flickered for a moment on his face, took a sip of wine. "This is *very* good, by the way. A local product?"

"More or less," said Robert. "I've tended the vines from which it was made, but they grow over on Serch'nach. The Bartram vineyards are not mature enough for a crop, yet."

"The Founders brought but a single kind of grape with them," Emerson said sadly. "They left so much of great worth behind!"

"You need only ask," said Ho. "A ship with the agricultural package could be ready to go in a matter of months."

"But therein lies the real problem," said Emerson. "How can we do that? By our most basic philosophy it should be an exchange. Trade for real. But what can we offer in exchange? Resources that you have in abundance? *Money?*" He gave a short, hard laugh. "On what do we base such an exchange?"

"Answer their gifts of Commonwealth culture with gifts from your own," Holm suggested. "Share your libraries, your ideas and philosophies. Your music and your art. I have long been a student of the Republic, and your people have done so many beautiful things! And then there are the genetic resources from the living worlds you have found. When such exchanges still took place between the Confederation and the Republic, both peoples saw great benefits."

"We do have such things," Emerson replied. "And one day I'm sure they'll figure into how we resolve this mess. But my government needs a way to control what comes to the Republic from the Commonwealth. While they wrangle over that, we talk here and I stall. I play for time, though to what end now seems unclear."

Robert stared at Emerson, something like dread gathering in him. "Emerson, what's wrong?"

Emerson sipped his wine, and closed his eyes as if savoring it with all his attention. Then he drew and released a long, deep breath. "To answer that, Robert, I must tell you a few things. First, I've come to believe through my experiences here, and by knowing all of you," and he moved his glass around in an arc that encompassed them all, "that whatever my government does, the way of life they seek to preserve is in fact doomed. The existence of the Commonwealth guarantees it, whatever your intentions. We will, eventually, be assimilated culturally by the Commonwealth, even if we maintain a separate *political* identity. This won't happen quickly, or all at once, of course. And it absolutely must be a carefully controlled process. But it *will happen!* The power of your ideas is too great, and the ideas are much too appealing to resist. Many will see these things you offer as too good to be true, and will look for the true cost, the 'catch' if you will. For my part, I no longer believe such exists. You are what you seem to be, and what you offer, you offer freely and without ill intent."

"I'm glad," said Ho, "that you have come to believe this of us."

"Well, don't be too excited about that," Emerson said. His expression was rueful. "My convictions will carry little weight. You see, I have been recalled. I leave tomorrow by way of the *Cygnet*. I will carry the Commonwealth's answer to the Republic, then my task will be done. Apparently complaints and somewhat distorted reports of my *fraternizations* have led those in power to the conclusion that I identify *too* strongly with the Commonwealth, *and* the Leyra'an. This strategy I've pursued of knowing you in order to understand the people we must deal with has turned into a most unstable orbit! My leaders don't desire such understanding. They seek only control, and don't see such a thing possible in the course I've followed. I fear that when I return home I will be dismissed and forced into retirement. I'll have little of my former influence after that."

"Oh, Emerson, I am so sorry!" Melep said, and reached out to take and hold one of his hands.

The Commonwealth and Confederation Commissioners simply sat quiet as the rest of Rost'aht expressed their sadness and disappointment; it was obvious they had already known. The reaction was contagious. Both babies began to cry and Gava'mi warbled unhappily.

"I regret that this has come to pass, and for so many reasons, not the least of which is the feeling of a job left undone," Emerson said. "But I've been a long time from my wife and family. And as it seems there is little left here for me to do, perhaps it *is* time to go home." He glanced around the table and added, "Though I'll miss all of you terribly, and pray a time may come when you are free to come and visit."

"You will always be welcome here," Ersha said gravely.

Emerson laughed suddenly and said, "I'm glad! And oh, how I wish I could bring my wife here to see this place, and meet its wonderful inhabitants!"

"Amen to that!" And Sarah raised her wine in a toast to the sentiment.

The others raised their glasses in response, but no one said a word.

"Well, my friends," said Ho, "I have a report to prepare, so I must be off." He rose to his feet, as did Emerson, who came around the table to him. "Emerson, it's been good knowing you. I hope our paths cross again, one day."

"Likewise, my friend." Emerson reached out to clasp Ho's hand. "And may the good Lord keep you well until then!"

Ho pulled him into a sudden embrace, which seemed to startle Emerson, but not alarm him. Then Ho stepped back, gave the rest of them a wave, and walked away beyond the lamplight. Robert caught a glimpse of his expression as he turned away from them and could see that he was not a happy man. His eyes glittered with tears of anger, a startling sight in the face of a man who so rarely displayed emotion. A few moments later Sarah, too, decided to retire for the evening. She kissed Emerson and said something to him Robert could not hear, then walked briskly away with tears on her face.

"So, the proceedings will be suspended until your replacement is sent," said Ersha after Emerson sat and drank a bit of wine. "Will the Republic leave Drake as senior Commissioner?"

"I don't know," Emerson replied. "The recall was not specific on the matter."

Robert looked from one to the other. There was something in the way Ersha had uttered Drake's name. "He's actually responsible for your recall," he said. "Isn't he?"

"You are a most perceptive fellow, Robert. Yes, Drake filed a scathing report on my conduct here. He complained about how much time I spend among the people to whom I was charged to represent the Republic. I have no doubt that he painted a most unflattering picture."

"Surely you'll have a chance to answer the complaint?" Alicia asked.

"Yes, I will," Emerson replied. "But the nature of the recall leads me to believe it will be no more than a formality. I won't be back as a Commissioner."

"Drake knows you received treatment here," Holm said.

"How could he not? The entire incident was rather, ah, public, after all." He sipped more wine. "Of course, all I told him was that you saved my life, not how." Emerson, when he had assured himself that none but their little clique could hear him, turned to Alicia and said, "I must ask, my dear, that you arrange to undo what was done for me. If I go back now, with your little bugs in my blood, I won't be able to defend myself from Drake's accusations. There must be no trace of Commonwealth medical technology in me, or my very *freedom* will be at stake. This must be done, even if it means my illness will return."

"It shouldn't," Alicia replied. "By now the genetic damage that caused the problem in the first place will have been repaired. If I shut down the nanos now, more than likely you will merely begin to age normally again, nothing worse. That's not a promise. We know too little about the condition we treated, and nothing at all about its ability to persist. But — are you *really* sure you want that?"

"Part of me, of course, wants to stay as I am now," he replied with a trace of a smile. "I must be honest about that. But I *will* be examined closely when I return. How will I prevent my current nature being revealed? Surely our physicians are sophisticated enough to detect these tiny devices in my blood?"

"I suppose they might well be," Alicia said. "But there's no need to worry. If a sample of your blood is drawn, the nanos will be removed from the bio-electric field of your body. They are attuned to it, and if they are removed from it they will disassemble into the raw materials from which they built themselves. It's a safety feature built into the system many years ago, when there were unanswered questions regarding the ability of these things to spread into environments for which they weren't designed. Since the nanos replicate using resources provided by your own body, there would be nothing foreign to show in the analysis to follow. Same with full body scans. Nothing unnatural to stand out and draw attention, unless the scan was programmed specifically to look for them. And since you don't have this med tech in the Republic, there is no template on which to base the scan." She frowned as she saw him shaking his head slightly. "What?"

"That's all reassuring enough, but, well, there's my wife. We've been together most of our lives. We knew each other as children." The look of fondness on his face was clear to all as he spoke. "I have no interest in living forever without her. And then to watch my own children grow old and die... " He shook his head and said, "No. That would be no way to live. Until such time as all may partake, I'd rather not."

Robert saw the wistful look on his wife's face that told him in another moment there would be tears. "Dr. Grosslin thought you might see it that way. He gave me something to pass along, just in case." Alicia pulled something tiny out of the pocket of the short jacket she wore, glanced around to make sure it was safe, and dropped it into Emerson's wine. He held the glass and stared into it, mouth drawn into a thin line, but did not immediately drink. "It's a new variation of nanomed. He called it the Worth Variation. It will restrict the role of the nanos to boosting your immune system, a guard against Founders' and its complications, nothing more. It will not alter the processes that lead to aging. You will grow old together after all." Then she raised her mug of beer and said, in Leyra'an, knowing he understood the language, "Take with you the love of our family, and find your way back to our home, for it is yours." It was a traditional Leyra'an parting wish, usually uttered by a Matriarch. "I hope you live long enough to see all those grandchildren grow up and begin families of their own!" she added in the Human language. Tears began to flow as she leaned across the table to kiss him, her loose red hair falling over him and hiding their faces. The others around the table raised their respective beverages and wished him the same.

Eyes bright with emotion, Emerson returned the salute when Alicia gave him the chance, then drank down the last of the wine in his glass. "If only the rest of the Republic could know all of you. The question of relations would swiftly be resolved. Oh, *God,* how I will miss you!"

There were tears on the man's face, but whether they were his own or had fallen there from Alicia's eyes during the kiss, Robert could not say.

CHAPTER THIRTEEN

Endmost Station
Disputed Zone

"And we now have seven mining operations extracting ores from asteroids," said the machine mind called Artie. "There are nine installations extracting gaseous raw materials from the system's Jovian-type giants. Between them they are currently able to provide sixty-three percent of the raw materials required for ongoing shipbuilding."

"Why so low?" Kester demanded. "Why not one hundred percent?" He stood with his back to the transparent bulkhead of the viewing lounge attached to Calavone's office. The glare of the system's star created a pale halo around him, rendering his form in silhouette.

Though Kester had spoken harshly, as if to an incompetent subordinate, Artie's reply was cool and unemotional. "Thirty-seven percent of total output is diverted to fabricate more mining and extraction systems, and to build the basic manufacturing infrastructure necessary to achieve established goals in the desired time frame. When that infrastructure is fully assembled, the rate of diversion will drop to zero and all resources gathered will be used to build warships."

"Okay, thanks for the summary, Artie," Calavone said from his seat near the opposite wall. Beside him were a small table, a second chair, and two empty glasses. The star-glare was centered behind Kester, leaving only a silhouette of the man, and Calavone could read nothing of the man's expression. "Now, if you'll excuse us, Commodore Kester and I need to have a private conversation."

"Of course, Jim. You know where to find me."

Calavone laughed, a bit startled, and wondered when and where the machine had picked up that idea and phrase.

"That thing gives me the shivers," Kester muttered under his breath.

Calavone smirked and said, "Curiously enough, Artie isn't all that fond of you, either, to judge by the impression he gives with the questions he's asked about you. Which may mean nothing, since I doubt he has feelings as we define them."

"Questions? What the hell kind of... ? No, never mind! I don't want to know!" Kester shuddered visibly, as if he'd just seen, or touched, something repulsive.

"Look," Calavone said. "The two of you don't need to become fast friends. You just need to work together. I need that from both of you. And toward that end, you could adopt a less insulting approach to dealing with him."

"Him? Why do you keep saying that? It's a damned machine, Jimmy!"

"Yes, well, believe it or not, this is a machine apparently capable of becoming vexed by Human behavior. You'll make my life easier if you are at least — civil, when you deal with him."

"It's a *machine*," Kester repeated. Calavone just looked at him until, finally, Kester shrugged and said, "Ah, hell, whatever you say. I'll make nice so we can get the job done. It *will* follow your orders, won't it?"

"Relax, Andy. Yes, Artie and I are on very good terms. Believe it or not, he shares our goals and concerns and is anxious to bring shipbuilding up to full capacity as soon as possible. I programmed him that way. He doesn't have a choice." Calavone waved a hand over the glasses. "Are we finished here?"

"Yes," Kester replied.

"Okay, then, I need to put in an appearance at the command center. Come on," and he rose and touched the wall briefly to open the door. He heard Kester come up from behind and follow him through. "Things seem to be coming along. Past the break-even point our capacity to build ships could increase exponentially, if we weren't holding Artie back."

"You know, that sort of gives me the creeps, as well," Kester said. They walked side-by-side down a short, brightly lit but rather drab corridor that skirted the office complex, a direct route to the lifts. A frown darkened his face. "It's not natural!"

"If we stick with what's 'natural,'" said Calavone, "the Commonwealth will swallow us whole. We need a way to make the Republic unpalatable to them." He glanced at his friend as they walked the corridor. "Artie can do that for us."

"Fine," Kester said, obviously not pleased. "I'll give him a fecken medal when it's done."

"Really?" Calavone laughed out loud. The lift capsule opened, then closed when they were inside. "Where will you pin it?"

"Somewhere that hurts, if I can find the right spot."

And Calavone laughed again. "See? You really *are* starting to think of Artie as a person. I told you that would be hard to resist!" The capsule began to move. It was a very short trip.

"That was sarcasm, Jimmy. It's a *machine*. I don't think of it any other way."

They left the capsule and entered the control center by way of another short corridor. The main display was dominated by a cluster of machines boring into and excavating a roughly-cratered asteroid. The haze of dust now in orbit around the rock reduced the level of detail to be seen. Calavone noted the increased depth of the great pit in which machines moved, gnawing away at the rock. Their point of view was just slightly off-set from straight up over the scene. Off to the side was a complex of metal frames that kept a variety of blocky-looking extraction and processing systems locked in place. Fat tubes housed conveyors that took crushed rock from the borers to the processors. The processors themselves fired off a steady stream of ingots that flew to the fabrication systems elsewhere, which were busy building more mining and shipyard facilities, and the first ships of the new fleet. There was no true scale in the image, but Calavone knew from first-hand visits that everything he saw existed on a gigantic scale, and that the ingots of iron, magnesium, and aluminum — among other resources — were the size of standard shuttles.

It was only *one* of the systems Artie had built for them.

A self-replicating system, and it almost seemed alive. Machine life. Calavone could not help admiring it all, even as it made him a bit uneasy. It truly was not the way the Republic should work. He could easily imagine the complete economic chaos that would follow the introduction of such technology. It was not a thing he intended to allow.

"That's kind of creepy, too, if you want my honest opinion," Kester said with a wave of his hand toward the display area. "Those things look like they're eating that rock!"

"That's exactly what they are doing, and at an ever increasing rate, too." Calavone turned part way around to talk to his friend while keeping an eye on the display. "Easy to see how such things could absolutely wreck the Republic, isn't it? No way we could ever turn this stuff loose for people to use in a business-as-usual way. Might as well hand everything over to the Commonwealth and be done with it."

"And yet we're going to use it in our *just cause*." Kester continued to stare at the display. "So how do we reconcile it to the beliefs we defend, when all is said and done? We're going to take over and prevent this sort of tech from infesting the Republic and undoing what we've built, by using that same tech to arm ourselves. That's going to prompt some awkward questions."

"Trust me to have given the matter some thought." Calavone led Kester to the raised back portion of the command center, waved off the officer of the watch, and sat behind the array of instruments. Touching a spot on the board, he brought the privacy screen up, and the sounds from the room around them became muffled. Kester stood before him at parade rest, and Calavone did not doubt for a moment it was out of habit and not deference. "We're going to flat out lie about where our ships come from. We'll hint at a secret facility out in the deep dark, crewed by dedicated men and women, working in a way that really sets an example."

"You're joking."

Calavone shook his head. "Dead serious. Artie is even developing video proof of the work being done."

"I'll be damned!" was all Kester said.

"So some will surely believe, when all is said and done," Calavone said quietly. "Hell, they believe that of you, at least, already. It won't matter. In a matter of months we'll be ready to move, and then people will see us both in a very different way."

"Months?" Kester asked, eyebrows raised.

"And that's if I apply the breaking thrusters, so to speak," Calavone replied. "If I gave Artie free reign instead of a specific target, we could replicate the RDF fleet in less than eighteen months."

"I hear what you're saying," Kester replied, and he looked stricken. "But... "

"Just can't quite stabilize the orbit, eh?" Calavone stood and briefly put a hand on his friend's shoulder. "I hear myself saying it, but believing it in my gut is another matter entirely."

"How do we crew these ships we're building?" Kester asked.

"I have enough people here to create a skeleton crew for the strike force we have in mind. I'm also using my network to quietly bring in more from elsewhere." He caught Kester's concerned look and said, "Yes, that's a risk and I know it. But crew with Fleet experience is the one thing Artie and his new flock can't build for us."

"I see your point," Kester replied. "And I see no way around it. I just hope those people of yours out there are careful! We're all for the gallows if this operation is revealed before we're ready."

"This network has served us since my father's days. I trust it. I must. This could go badly for us in so many ways," Calavone said quietly. "But we're certainly lost if we don't try!"

"That I can understand all too easily!" Kester replied.

Calavone was silent for a moment, then said, "Speaking of the network, word came just a bit ago that the government has recalled one of the members of the negotiating team sent to Pr'pri system. Emerson Worth, in fact. Seems he's been a bit too friendly with the other sides. They'll likely replace him with a well-connected hardliner."

"Worth was always a bit soft-hearted," Kester said. "Or soft-headed."

"That's not a man you should underestimate, my friend," Calavone said. "He was instrumental in the effort to halt my father's insurrection and he's very popular, especially with folks in or near the DZ. If the government doesn't handle him carefully, they'll shoot themselves in the head, for sure!"

"If you say so. Now, what has this to do with us at the moment?" Kester asked.

"His departure was apparently precipitated by a formal protest lodged by the Republic. Seems the Commonwealth has created a version of their longevity treatment that works on the Leyra'an. The concern is that they will go ahead and give it to the scalies even though the Republic hasn't yet decided how to approach using the technology. Not that the government would ever make such a thing *freely* available." Calavone shook his head. "Seems the Republic has demanded that the Commonwealth cut itself off from the Leyra'an until the Republic says it's ready."

"And how has the Commonwealth responded?" Kester asked.

"Don't know, yet. My contact is an aide to the regional governor out that way, and her last report covered only the demand being sent to Pr'pri, and that Worth's recall went out with it. We won't know how the Commonwealth responded for several weeks, at least."

"Uncommonly hard line, even for the current government. To judge by what the network has brought to light, they've been weaseling their way through negotiations without drawing *any* sort of line, until now." Kester looked thoughtful. "I wonder if the Commonwealth would really share that stuff with the scalies now, under the circumstances."

"I wouldn't be at all surprised," Calavone replied. "In fact, I'd be surprised if they have not already begun doing so. The only thing that might hold them back would be a desire to treat both the Republic and the Confederation equally, and the Republic is making that impossible."

"It would be in their best interest to wait," Kester said with conviction.

"I wonder if they'll see it that way, and if so, for how long?" Calavone asked. "Did you review that analysis of Commonwealth belief systems?" When Kester shook his head by way of reply, Calavone said, "It would be a good idea to catch up on that stuff. They really don't work the way we do, or as much like the Leyra'an as it might seem, at first. Most of them follow some form of something called Gaianism — no idea if I'm pronouncing it right — which is some sort of mother goddess worship with its roots in pagan traditions of Old Earth. They express a profound reverence and respect for life, and see their purpose, their entire reason for being, as bringing life into lifeless space, what they call the Void. They don't even kill livestock for food, cultivating animal protein artificially and raising animals themselves for nonlethal uses. I'd be willing to bet they're really fond of pets, into the bargain. And they have an absolute horror of anything that brings any sentient being to an untimely end."

"I think I see where this is going," Kester said. "You're thinking they won't withhold the treatment from the Leyra'an if the Republic refuses it?"

"It's hard to be sure," Calavone replied. "We have a wealth of technological information direct from your salvage. Unfortunately, there's not a lot of cultural information, and most of what I know has come by way of the agent we have working in Pr'pri system. But, yes, my gut feeling is they won't be able to stand by and know that Leyra'an are dying of what the Commonwealth sees as a preventable condition, namely old age. The Republic's reluctance to open themselves to such technology is something their beliefs can't touch, no matter how much the consequences bother them."

"If they do that, the Disputed Zone will be a much bigger problem," said Kester. "Those systems are in communication with the Confederation. They'll find out."

"And they'll be far less disposed to support the central government than they are now, once they know what they're missing." Calavone paused for a moment, then added, "That's a matter to which I must give some thought."

"Can it wait until after lunch?" Kester asked.

Calavone realized he had stopped talking, and that his friend remained there before him. "Yes, of course it can," he said, shaking his head to refocus on reality, and then leading his friend out of the command center.

CHAPTER FOURTEEN

Eb'ara Kai Station
Confederation of Clans

Ursula's prediction of the station-wide celebration turned out to be an understatement, and John was forever after convinced he survived only through the grace of the Cure. He joined in with a host of others when the time came for the post-celebration restoration of the station. "Back home," he said to Wirolen, as they gathered broken cups and plates from a small park, "this would have been called a riot, a matter for law enforcement."

"I imagine it *would* disrupt the usual order of things," she replied mildly, still more than a little hung over.

"Business-as-usual would have been disrupted," John agreed. "And likely at great cost. There would have been recriminations. Blame would be assigned. People arrested."

"I like our way better," she said with a glance up at him. "We need only hand out brooms!"

"It is difficult not to think of those most recently lost," he said as he dumped a collection of debris into a nearby waste bin. "Eb'shra Mosin. How will his mother feel about all of this when life settles back into its normal routine?"

"He is gone," was Wirolen's simple reply. "It is a sadness that some, like my cousin, are so *recently* lost, but . . . They are gone." She raised her hands, palms out toward him in the characteristic shrug of a Leyra'an who means to say 'what is to be done?' "They will not be forgotten, of course, not while those touched by their lives live on and remember," she added. "And now, of course, they will be remembered far longer."

"Is it really so easy?" he asked.

She crossed the small distance between them in slow steps, took his hands in hers, and met his gaze. "No, *sip'ya'a*. It is *not* so easy."

John leaned down and touched his forehead to hers. Then he lightly kissed her forehead, knowing she had come to accept this Human style of touch. "All the more reason to find an end to the war," he replied quietly. Then he smiled a Leyra'an smile and slowly shook his head. "I don't wonder, now, why there's so little of what my people call mental illness among the Leyra'an," he said in his own language. "Unlike Humans, your people know what to carry, and what to let go."

"Yes," she said. Wirolen looked up into his eyes, and hers were amber gold and glittering. "Acceptance is the heart of the Way," she said quietly. "Sometimes what you must accept is the sad truth that a life has ended. Perhaps one day you will *feel* this, as I do, and not merely understand the words."

"I might need to live among the Leyra'an for a very long time," John said in her tongue, "for that to happen."

She smiled a little and said, "That can be arranged."

In the days that followed, the Cure affected him as John had been led to expect. After a brief episode of mild fever his appetite increased, while at the same time he found his senses of taste and smell more acute than before. Food and drink tasted better, something he was told was an illusion, though he didn't agree. Nor did the Leyra'an, from what he saw and heard around him. After that, as days added into weeks, John felt a general sense of well-being, the result of numerous drains on metabolic energy being eliminated as the nanos did the work of repairing the wear and tear of his thirty-seven years of life, and then improving the overall efficiency of his metabolism. He read the technical explanation for why he felt as he did, but soon forgot the details. It didn't matter. Whatever the exact explanation, he felt *good.*

With this new sense of well-being, John reapplied himself to his studies of the Leyra'an and their ways, a task he found much easier to manage. He was more clear-minded, and had a better memory than before, as the nanos also set his central nervous system to working at a higher rate of efficiency. He found himself comprehending more things, more quickly, and making connections between ideas at a rate he might not have thought possible prior to his treatment. And he watched as the Leyra'an sorted through their own reactions to the Cure.

It was gratifying in the extreme to watch the effects take hold of the Matriarch. The Matriarch, being Wirolen's grandmother, lived in the same complex as Wirolen and John and the rest of their large, extended family. He encountered her on a regular basis, and frequently spoke with her at evening meals. The first change he noticed was simply an increase in laughter, as she reacted with delight to the sensation of the weight of years lifting from her. The nanos took stock, then set to work repairing the damage of merely living to the age she had. Her appetite became prodigious, something about which she made jokes. She stood taller in a few days and in a week the arthritic limp he associated with the old woman was gone. The ornate cane was not abandoned, however, as she had long since found it useful to command the attention of the young and irreverent. She flirted with old lovers and younger men, and even made a blatant and embarrassing pass at John, much to the outrage of Wirolen. But it was almost immediately apparent, to John's immense relief, that she had done so to tease her granddaughter.

As the weeks passed, the changes grew more obvious. The tautness of the skin on her hands and face relaxed as muscle mass was regained. Patches of lost scales regrew, and everywhere her scales were gradually replaced with newer and glossier ones. Her hair turned dark at the roots and thickened. She walked with a lighter, more confident step, and stood more fully upright. Weeks became months and the extremely elderly woman John had first met was transformed into someone younger and more vital. John began to understand the stories he had been told about the Matriarch, of how she was much sought after and often courted, though seldom fully won. And John had no problem, now, believing those tales, as she changed from a bent and wizened creature, leaning over a cane, to a woman tall, robust, wide-shouldered and well-endowed, with dark amber eyes in an expressive face that left little doubt regarding her moods, and her desires.

The effects on people around his age, and presumably Wirolen's, was more subtle at times, but could be spotted. In his lover's case, it was not just an appetite for food and drink alone that increased significantly, and John was grateful to have received the Human variant of the Cure. Wirolen might well have injured him, otherwise.

It broke his heart to think of his own people being denied this great gift, because a few were concerned with what such a great change might cost them. It also made him angry.

"Your people will know this gift," Wirolen said one night, in response to his anger. "It is inevitable. Soon they will know *of* it. How can it be withheld, then, when so many will demand it? In the end, those who rule the Republic will give in. They will simply have no choice."

"I hope you are right, *sip'ya*," John replied. And thought immediately of the border systems, the Disputed Zone and how easily news from the Confederation leaked across as the "deezees" made their way from one side of the porous border to the other. "Yes, you almost certainly are. The Republic can control information flow from the Commonwealth. There's only one point of contact. But the Disputed Zone systems along the border are another matter, especially the ones where Secessionist sympathies are strong. People there will find out about the Cure, and that it was originally applied to Humans."

"The Republic would need to fully control those systems and stop the illicit traffic into and back from the Confederation," Wirolen said. "I cannot help wondering why they have not yet done so."

John shrugged, staring up at the ceiling of their bedroom. It was not fully dark; no Leyra'an place ever was, coming as they did from a world with multiple moons. "The expense of shipbuilding and fleet maintenance is part of it, I suppose. That and a certain lack of political will. Deploying the Fleet against otherwise law-abiding Republic citizens would not be popular. Might even trigger the sort of large scale unrest my government is trying to avoid. But mostly the situation persists because some very powerful people acquire a great deal of wealth by way of illicit trade with the Confederation. That wealth has great influence on the politics of the Republic."

"I do not see how any good can come of it, then," Wirolen said, sounding and looking puzzled and sad.

"Not in the short term," John said. "But maybe someday. The Cure will become known to my people because of news from the DZ, and just as inevitably the Cure will come to the Republic. It will be socially and economically disruptive, no doubt, but Humans are resourceful people, my love. We'll adapt. And we'll thrive."

"As soon as everyone has the Cure," said Wirolen, "You won't be able to *help* but thrive!"

CHAPTER FIFTEEN

Pr'pri System
Bartram Habitat

In the immediate aftermath of Emerson's recall, family Rost'aht took to having evening meals together at home. The usual gaiety of the Willow Lake was too much at odds with their collective mood. Emerson had become a part of them, something more than a friend of the family. He had opened himself to them so freely, and in so doing had drawn them out with so little effort. Robert took comfort in the knowledge that Emerson would soon be among the people he loved most in the universe. It was impossible to hold a desire to go home against the man; Robert remembered all too keenly his voyage aboard the *Han'anga*, cut off from Alicia.

With the adaptation of nanomed tech to Leyra'an physiology completed, Alicia spent her time reviewing Leyra'an genomics, which she did at home while watching over the two children and one steadily more independent han'anga. Using the wealth of experience the previous project provided, and as safe from Artificial scrutiny as could be contrived, she began a detailed examination of the code that made up the Leyra'an.

Robert silently approved of the renewed effort. As unsettling as the great mystery was, it gave Alicia an additional focus that kept her mind away from the darkness that had invaded it. Between the children and her work, she seemed almost normal.

They still slept with a light on.

"What are you hoping to find?" Robert asked on an evening when she mentioned the progress she was making.

They were all home together, the evening meal was done, and she sat beside him in the center of a Leyra'an-style disk chair. "I'm not looking for a particular *thing*, exactly. I'm studying their genome, examining the commonalities with the Human counterpart, and trying to identify the other species from Leyra'ach that were used to build the original template. I'm coming around to the idea that there was more than one. I suppose you could say I'm taking an inventory. I'm hoping that such familiarity will give me some idea of what I *should* be looking for."

"The first step in learning," said Holm from where he lounged in an old-style wing chair. "Finding out what questions to ask."

"Yes," Alicia said with a nod. She shifted little Paul to a more comfortable position, and settled back into the generous padding of the chair. "I need to know what is Human, what comes from the Leyra'an home world, and what materials fit neither point of origin. Some of those could be constructs, designed to make the disparate bits work together. There's sure to be a *lot* of constructs. But if any of them are naturally evolved sequences that *don't* match worlds in either the Commonwealth or the Confederation, it might give me something in the way of a direction to look."

"Direction?" Robert asked.

"Where did the engineers come from?" she asked. "The origin of materials used, if I can identify enough of it, might give a clue as to where in the Void they live. That's really what it's all about. Who created the Leyra'an? If we can find the engineers, we might have a chance to figure out why they did this." She looked around the room at her kin. Holm relaxed in his chair, annotating committee reports that drifted in the air before him, and Melep was playing with little Vurn on a mat. A well and thoroughly fed Paul formed a warm lump between Robert and his wife, sound asleep. "There's at least one other intelligent species out there," she said. "They've been around a lot longer than we have. They must have been. Imagine what we might learn from them, if we can find them!"

"Assuming they still exist," Robert added.

"Our creators," Holm said softly, peering at her through the shimmering projection before him. "Assuming that Alicia is correct in her original analysis, and I confess my doubts remain, imagine it! These beings are not gods and goddesses of mythology, not spiritual beliefs taken too literally. They are, or were, as real as *we* are. If they still exist out there, we could do a thing unimaginable!"

"Meet your makers?" Robert suggested.

"Exactly!"

Robert fought back a smile as he made a mental note to explain the ancient reference to his brother, at another time. "Whatever would we say to them?" he wondered aloud.

With a nod toward the other half of their family, Alicia said, "Thank you. For starters, at least."

"Sister, I've meant to ask," said Melep. "The Human genome shows none of these 'markers' of which you have spoken?"

"None," Alicia replied, shaking her head. "We are the product of completely natural evolution, as far as I can tell. So are the fossil species from which your people believe the Leyra'an descended. Because of that, I have a general idea of when the work was done."

"That's something, I suppose," Robert said.

"So long ago," Melep said. Vurn, no longer the center of her attention, became fretful. She cuddled and spoke softly to him, and as was so often the case with Leyra'an infants, he settled down quickly. "I've been considering how best to open the Confederation's resources to you," she said when the child started to nurse. "To do so without the Commonwealth Artificials knowing what you are doing could be tricky."

"That's an understatement," Robert said. "Their presence is felt anywhere the Commonwealth expands. I'm not sure how you would get away from that. But then, it never occurred to me we would ever need to try!"

"They have no presence here," Melep said.

"That's true," Alicia replied. "But with the massive data load passing through the system, the *Newcomb* shipmind and the library annex bookmind would handle all communications. We'd be a sort of bottleneck, here in Pr'pri, if we didn't put them in charge of such things. If I have data sent here, there's nothing to stop the Artificials from altering it in a way to suit their purpose." She started twirling a strand of her hair between the fingers of her right hand, eyes unfocused as she considered possibilities.

Robert knew that look, and by then the others recognized it as well. Pieces of a puzzle were coming together in the mind of their resident scientist. Silence and patience were the best help they could give. "I believe we need your uncle's assistance to do this thing," she said after a pause of several minutes.

"He does have access to high-level people and resources," Melep replied thoughtfully. "But how might he help?"

"I need the input of someone intimately familiar with such resources. He can get me in touch with such people." Alicia shrugged, a Human gesture, the rise and fall of shoulders. "If anyone is clever enough to do that without alerting the Artificials, it's Kr'nai Ersha!"

"You've been so reluctant to speak of this before," Robert said in surprise. "Is it wise to alter that policy now?"

"I'm still reluctant," she confessed. "But I've hit a wall, and I believe Ersha's knowledge and experience may help."

"Should we gang up on him?" Robert asked.

Alicia thought for a moment, then nodded and said, "Yes. It might sound a bit less daft if it comes from all of us. And we might as well do it sooner, rather than later."

"I will arrange something that allows us to meet him in private," Holm said.

"Assuming you can persuade him to step away from his Commission work for an hour or two," Melep said with a short laugh.

"Leave that to me," Holm replied.

Now it was the Human infant's turn to grow restive, which he rarely did after feeding. Robert lifted him up and let him sprawl across his chest, one hand holding the boy in place. The little one's fists clenched his father's shirt and in a moment Paul was sound asleep.

"You would think him a Leyra'an child, the way he craves the nearness of others," said Melep.

"He is surrounded by good influences," Robert said, with a fond smile. He gave little thought for whether he smiled as a Human or otherwise; in their little group a smile was just a smile.

"Will you need the Commonwealth's genomics database for proper comparisons?" Holm asked suddenly.

"Sooner or later, yes, I'll need to tap that source, though how I'll use it without interference is a mystery." She shook her head, absent-mindedly twisting her hair around her finger again. "I'd need to find someplace to download it that lacks an Artificial. That's not likely to happen!"

"That's a rather large database, isn't it?" Robert asked.

"Only the astrophysical database is larger," Alicia replied. Then she sighed and closed her eyes. "Assuming I could get such a copy, making the number of comparisons necessary will be slow and damned tedious without an Artificial, but I don't dare involve them! Not until I know why they're suppressing knowledge of Leyra'an origins."

"We've been through some things," Robert said quietly, stroking her hair. "But none of it worries me nearly as much as that last bit."

"The Library Annex," Holm said. "The Commonwealth has prepared one and will soon send it across from Eriola. Given the long system transit necessary, it will be a few weeks before it arrives. When it does, the Republic intends to establish a facility here to study its contents."

"I've seen those," Robert said. "They're standard equipment when a new system is settled." He laughed and added, "If you think a probeship was big, wait 'til you see an Annex!"

"I remain puzzled by that," Melep said. "When it was discussed in the TC, it was made plain these things are managed by an Artificial. Aren't those illegal in the Republic?"

"They are, indeed, which is why acceptance by the Republic may at first seem surprising," Holm replied. "But the Annex will not be going into the Republic. It will stay here, in Pr'pri system, and teams from the Republic will come to study what it contains from a safe distance."

"Safe distance?" Alicia asked.

"They will make inquiries, and the Commonwealth techs will retrieve the data," Holm replied. "They will then convert it to an ancient analog format and give it to their counterparts from the Republic, who will presumably convert it back into something digital. To put it as gently as possible, this is seen as a long-term project."

"They're going to do with the Annex what they're doing with communications?" Robert asked, letting his disbelief show. "They're going to print it out?"

"For all practical purposes, yes," Holm replied.

"Long term," Alicia repeated, shaking her head. "Mother of Life! Generational would be more accurate! Scholars from the Republic will grow old and die while that work goes on. This is insane — do they really comprehend what they're getting into?"

"I am sure they *think* they do," Holm with a quick, toothy grin. "We shall see."

"How does this matter, in the current context?" Robert asked, a little lost in the apparent change of subject.

"They will surely download the genomics database," Holm said. "Considering how Founders' disease troubles them, it will likely be a high priority."

"I wonder if they would find my assistance of use?" Alicia said quietly.

"I shall inquire upon your behalf," Holm said.

"Aren't you concerned that the Annex librarian might alter output in a way to impede your search?" Robert asked.

Alicia shook her head and said, "No, I'm not. The sort of material they would need to excise would leave huge gaps in data well known to millions of researchers, myself included. They would need to be more subtle than that. And they have been, in the way they alter research results to make them seem in keeping with the existing record."

"They'll know you're taking that 'inventory,'" Robert said.

"And they are surely smart enough to know why," Alicia conceded. "But I don't expect a problem. I'd be assisting in the interpretation of data, and would surely be a part of a team. If material is omitted by the Artificial running the Annex, there's a chance someone would notice the gap. That would draw exactly the wrong sort of attention. I'll get the comparative data I need. I'm betting they'll stick to altering lab results and steering theory development."

"Hell of a bet," Robert said. "They're a very clever lot."

"If they're that clever, my love, I've already failed. I can't go forward with such an assumption."

Holm's head lowered until his chin neared his chest, the Leyra'an equivalent of a headshake. "I fail to see how they can believe the matter can be concealed indefinitely," he said as he looked up. "Surely you cannot be the only one to see the unlikelihood of so many similarities?"

"My colleagues are being guided to the same conclusion your people came to more than fifty years ago. That's why I mentioned the development of theory. They have no reason to suspect interference from the Artificials, with whom they have worked as friends and colleagues all their lives. If the calculations of the Artificials can be made to seem plausible, Humans will accept them." She paused a moment, then said, "Now if they'd seen the raw data I gathered that first time, they would react as I have. But that can't happen now."

"Curious," said Melep, "that it ever happened at all."

"Yes," said Alicia. "But if I was the first Survey scientist to uncover the nature of the Leyra'an, my results may have triggered the protocol that set up the concealment."

"Something we need to keep in mind is that this business of concealment surely did not end with the destruction of the *William Bartram.*" Robert looked at his wife as he spoke. "Our shipmind was in contact with the *Newcomb* and the *Herschel* until we made the nodal transit away from Pr'pri the day of the attack. Your initial results were almost certainly communicated to them."

"Way ahead of you, Rob," she said. "That's why I'm not working on this even here, in an experimental sense. I have to wait until we can come up with a more thorough way to work free of any influence from an Artificial."

"Do you think they will try to stop us?" Melep asked in alarm. "I mean, *really* stop us?"

"Not by doing anything overtly dangerous," Robert replied slowly. "If they were willing to go that far, I doubt we would be having this conversation."

"You're probably right," Alicia said. "All I can do is proceed and deal with the Artificials when and if they react to my efforts. It's best to plan for what's likely, and not for what's merely possible. And when I've done what can be done in that regard, that's when I'll need Ersha's help with the Leyra'an side of things."

"Might need to travel a ways into the Confederation," Robert said.

"We might," said Alicia, and then she shook her head. "That's a node I'll transit when I come to it."

"I wonder what the Artificials hope to accomplish?" Melep asked. "This is an intimidating mystery, no doubt, especially to one of my species. But surely such a great challenge is worthy of the attention of a civilization such as the Commonwealth? What could be gained by *not* pursuing the question?"

"I can't imagine," Robert said. "That's why it worries me. In all the history of the Commonwealth, they've never done such a thing." He almost added the words *that anyone knows of,* but saw no purpose in going down the path of paranoia. "What could they possibly be hiding?"

"Might we be making an incorrect assumption here?" Holm asked suddenly. He sat forward and banished the display from the air before him. "Regarding the alleged motives of the Artificials?"

"What do you mean?" Robert asked.

"What if they are as surprised by this discovery as you were?" Holm asked in response. Then he looked at Alicia. "There was an Artificial involved in your initial research, looking over your shoulder, so to speak, but there was no interference at that point. If they knew of us and our origins already, you would not have found what you did. The shipmind of the *William Bartram* must have been every bit as surprised as you were."

"Gaia!" Alicia's eyes opened wide. "Damn, now why didn't that occur to me?"

"You were too close to have the proper perspective," Holm said with a Leyra'an shrug. "I would suggest that we consider an alternative interpretation. Are the Artificials really trying to *conceal* the origins of the Leyra'an? Or are they trying to control the manner in which it is revealed? Consider how Melep and I reacted when it was explained to us, then imagine how such a thing might affect the population of the Confederation as a whole."

"And how that might alter relations between the Leyra'an and Humanity," Robert said. "It could be catastrophic!"

"It likely would be," Holm said gravely.

There was a long moment during which none of them spoke. Little Vurn fussed half-heartedly, and there was a brief flurry of claws on scales as Gava'mi attacked an itch. "Mother of Life," Alicia whispered. "They might be trying to buy time while they figure out what to do with this."

For a moment Robert expected Alicia to declare that the project was over, that too much was at stake.

"We'll need to be extra careful to keep this quiet, then," Alicia said.

I should have known better, he thought to himself, even as he nodded in agreement.

CHAPTER SIXTEEN

Endmost System
Disputed Zone

"This has been verified?" Kester demanded. "Beyond reasonable doubt?"

"Yes," Calavone replied patiently. He stood abruptly from his seat in the observation lounge and strode to the vast expanse of transparent metal that looked out on the distant stars beyond Endmost. Calavone could pick out, from among the brighter ones, the DZ systems nearest Endmost. Hidden in plain sight was the way he'd come to think of their location. "The government gave the Commonwealth an ultimatum, and the Commonwealth has called their bluff. Now the Commonwealth is giving the Leyra'an the longevity treatment rather than waiting for a three-way agreement. Artie had it right from the beginning. They were working out a Leyra'an version all along."

"So the Commonwealth shows its true colors," Kester said. "It's the way I said it was."

Calavone sighed and turned his back to the stars and leaned against the chilly window. "They offered equal treatment to both sides, which is exactly what they *should* have done if they were *not* taking sides. Simply accepting the offer would've been awkward for the Republic, but instead of showing an ounce of creativity and buying more time, they drew a hard line. That was a huge mistake. They should've taken what was offered in order to maintain parity, even if it was *not* made available to the general populace." He turned again and placed his right hand against the broad window and peered out. "By making an unreasonable demand of a fellow sovereign state, they untied the Commonwealth's hands, leaving them free to pursue relations with the Leyra'an as they see fit, without concern for what we think of it. And to be absolutely honest about it, Andy, they're within their rights! Politicians from a state that calls itself *the* Republic damn well ought to know better!"

"We're their long lost cousins, who just happen to be the only remnant of Humanity left following the right path for human beings." Kester's irritation was obvious. "They should have joined *us*, they should have joined with their kin against the threat posed by the Leyra'an."

"You're being unrealistic. God, how can you not see that? You saw the reports about that first bunch, the survivors of that ship they found around Alconese Five. An alliance of the sort you mean was *never* possible with the Commonwealth! The beliefs we hold dear are ancient history for them. Probably *unknown* to most of them. The only connection we have is biological." He made a fist and gave the window a half-hearted thump. The impact made almost no sound. "That's not going to be enough."

"What else could they have done?" Kester demanded. "They had to draw a line somewhere."

"No, they didn't! At least, not in a way so boldly visible. The Republic should have accepted this medical technology, even if they lied about distribution. That might have bought time enough to understand Commonwealth culture and make realistic plans about how to deal with it, while preventing the Leyra'an from gaining an advantage." He remained facing the window and struck it harder in his frustration. "They had the right man on hand for that job, too, in Worth. I have my problems with him, which is an understatement. But for the task of holding off the Commonwealth while finding out what we need to know, he was a good choice."

The reflection Calavone could see of Kester in the window made a dismissive gesture with one hand. "Doesn't matter, now. We're going to make it all a moot point anyway."

"Oh, but it does matter!" Calavone said. He turned to look at the other man. "First, word of the treatments being given to the Leyra'an will leak into the DZ. Only a matter of time before the Human version follows, there being a fair number of Humans living in the Confederation in that region. Do you think the Commonwealth will overlook them? When that treatment is available to the deezees, our leverage evaporates."

"So, what now?" Kester said after a moment.

Calavone made no immediate answer. He turned away and leaned his forehead against the clear wall, feeling a ghost of the chill of deep space seep into his skin. The data from a dozen relevant intelligence reports sorted themselves in his mind as he considered the ins and outs of potential responses to the situation. "We can be sure that the Commonwealth is going to pursue their relationship with the Leyra'an," he said at last. "They'll send crews into the Confederation both to distribute this med tech and to train the Leyra'an."

"The Leyra'an probably have it by now, if that's true, considering the delay we experience getting news here." Kester got up and joined Calavone at the window. The lights had been dimmed enough that what lay beyond was easily seen, and Calavone was sure that Kester saw not the distant stars, but the nearby brace of warships taking shape, ships of the same class as the *Vengeance*. Beyond that, flares of light marked the site of self-replicated robotic systems. "That means the border systems will know of it. Soon."

"Good point," Calavone said. "When the Secessionists get that news, and find out that the Republic refused that same offering, the whole DZ situation will blow wide open. The government won't have any choice left regarding increasing fleet strength there. And if they do that, we're done. No matter what we can build out here, we won't be able to take control of the DZ after the Republic does so. Not without fighting our way from system to system. That's not a war we can win without being seen as the bad guys."

"The plan has always been to get in first, to prevent that exact scenario," Kester said. "So, how long before we can do it?" He gave a nod toward the view beyond.

"At the rate things are moving along, just a few months more," Calavone replied. "We still need to build the bulk of the fleet in order to send workable task forces out to strategic systems in the DZ. In addition to that, we need to have the support ships ready to keep lines of communication open. That's the easy part, at the rate Artie is moving things along. But Artie estimates that the Commonwealth will be in the Leyra'an side of the DZ before then!"

"Somehow we need to buy back the time the government hardliners cost us," Kester said.

"Yes, we do. But that's easily said." At that, Calavone fell silent, gazing out at the stars, lost in thought for several minutes. "We need to give people a reason to doubt the Commonwealth, some reason to doubt the story when they hear it. Since it will be news of potent medical technology that arouses ire in the DZ, that's probably the right angle to use in our counterattack. Fighting fire with fire."

"Part of that made sense," Kester said. "What is it you have in mind?"

"Oh, sorry, Andy. Thinking out loud again. Given the news that's going to cross the border, how surprised will the deezees be if medical crews from the Commonwealth start showing up?"

"You think they might... ?"

"No, I don't. But the deezees don't have the information we have. So if people show up *claiming* to be medics from the Commonwealth, there's a good chance it would be taken at face value." Calavone found himself grinning. It always felt very good when the pieces of an idea came together to form a plan. "Medics from the Commonwealth, slipping into Republic space to save the people from their government's neglect. I'd be willing to bet most people would buy it."

"Maybe they would," Kester said. He looked flat out puzzled. "But what possible purpose would that serve?"

"Well, just suppose that these altruistic souls really do dispense something of a medical nature? Something far less than benign?"

Kester stared at him for a long moment, face devoid of expression. "You know, you are in your way as creepy as that thinking machine of yours."

"Could explain why Artie and I have such a healthy rapport." He smiled, but the look on Kester's face made it plain his friend was anything but amused.

CHAPTER SEVENTEEN

Pr'pri System
Bartram Habitat

Robert found the message from Emerson shortly after the *Cygnet* made its nodal transition back into the Republic. An hour after the ship was gone, the message appeared in the house system, alerting him with a soft chime when the system found him on the premises. Robert was more than a bit surprised that Emerson wanted his note seen only after he was gone.

"Robert, just before I packed up for my return home I finally got around to calling up recordings of you playing the bagpipes," the image of Emerson said. "Alicia told me how to find them. The music I've reviewed so far, and I must say the catalog is impressively large, amazes me. It saddens me deeply that you have given up performing. We have a few pipers in the Republic, but those I've heard have nothing of your talent. Of course, you've been practicing on the instrument longer than most of them have spent time breathing, so don't take that as unfair criticism of pipers in the Republic! I listened to your solo work, and material recorded aboard the *William Bartram* when you performed with all the friends you lost there." Emerson looked down and to one side a bit, as if for a moment self-conscious. "Now I understand why your son is named Paul."

Robert paused the message, and Emerson's image froze just as he looked up again and his mouth opened to say more. The words Emerson spoke conjured memories, ordinary memories from the part of his brain he was born with. Paul Soo playing the fiddle as he hopped and bounced around Robert on the stage, a manic gleam in his dark, almond-shaped eyes, the fiddle and bow seeming tiny things in his large, long-fingered hands. All elbows and knees and slim limbs that looked so ungainly, but added up to the picture of grace on the stage. Grief welled up as thick and hot as if he had just found out Paul and Judy and Eb'shra Vurn were all dead. He had long since thought he was done with tears in the matter. Robert discovered he was quite wrong about that.

"Dammit, Emerson," he whispered. He sat on the edge of the nearest disc chair and leaned forward, face in his hands.

And then, when he caught his breath some time later, he resumed the message.

"The joy I see in you, and them, as the music is played is nothing less than inspiring. I can see it in your eyes and in the way your fingers fly as they work the pipes. I can hear it in the music itself. Because these things are so plain to see and hear, I can understand why the loss of those people would make it difficult to play the pipes for yourself and others. That music was part of something that exceeded the sum of its parts, and with the rest of those parts missing, the pipes surely sound like a mockery of what once was. But I believe you will never be fully healed of your grief if you forever deny yourself this part of your old life.

"I'm saying all of this to urge you to begin again. Bring the music back, my friend! The other Bartram survivors will all gain a measure of healing when you do so. Not an evening did I pass in your company without one of your former shipmates asking if you would play that night. They *need* you to do this, Robert. And you need it as well. Look into your own heart if you think I'm wrong. Do you not hear the pipes playing there?

"Take care of yourself, my dear friend, and take care of those people you love most. They are very dear to me as well. Until, God willing, we meet again."

The recording ended and Robert sat there for a very long time. He was alone in the Rost'aht residence, except for the Beast. Gava'mi climbed into the disc chair with him, warbling in a way that Robert knew meant he was uncertain of what might be wrong. "Sorry about that, Beast. Didn't mean to upset you." He put an arm around Gava'mi and sat quietly for a moment, rubbing his knuckles under the animal's broad chin. They were tactile creatures, much like the Leyra'an who had domesticated them and now carried han'angas out to the stars. Gava'mi gazed up at him, ears erect and crest spines lowered, offering his fosterer comfort as much as he received it.

You may be right, Emerson, Robert thought. *But, Gaia, it still hurts to even think of it.* He hadn't even listened to any of the recordings Emerson mentioned, not since his return to Serch'nach. It suddenly seemed a long time ago, as if it were a story he had heard about someone else.

Robert was seized by a strange restlessness, almost a feeling of impatience. He gave the Beast a pat, stood up from the cushions of the disc chair and headed for the suite of rooms he and Alicia shared. He stood in front of the cabinet in which he knew the pipes were stored. He could picture his hand going to the latch, opening the door, and reaching inside. He did nothing but stand there, an odd tightness gripping his throat and chest.

Then his hand seemed to move of its own volition, reaching for and turning the latch, and then pulling from the space in the wall the case containing the Highland pipes he had played most often. The very set that journeyed with him aboard the warship *Han'anga*, played so often during that frightful voyage to keep the morale of his shipmates from sinking into despair. There was so much darkness in that time, so much death, and in that shared trial he had become one of them. Their love of his music had opened their hearts to him, and the Leyra'an being what they were, they had drawn him in. *Mora'na* was their word, and it meant shipmate, a bond almost as strong as family.

Robert didn't take the pipes from the case. He sat on the edge of the bed and held it in his lap, with Gava'mi pressed against his side, still sensing Robert's distress. "What do I do, Beast? He's right, I can't go on without this, not forever. But look at me! I can't even open the case!" And yet, that was all it would take, an open case. It would never again be the way it was, that was impossible, but it would *be!* But that first step, flipping the shiny chrome latches on the wooden box, remained untaken. His hands trembled and his fingers felt oddly numb.

The restlessness gripped him again and he got up to stride briskly back into the family room. He realized when he paused there that he carried the pipes with him, and though he turned to take them back to the bedroom cabinet, did not take the next step. Gava'mi circled his feet once, then sat with his short, broad tail flopped over Robert's shoes, gazing up at him. "See, this is how you get stepped on," Robert admonished as he slid his feet to keep the tail out of harm's way.

There was a table along one wall of the room bearing a clutter of odds and ends. Robert cleared some space and set the case on the table. Moving with quick, abrupt motions, he finally opened it. The stasis field crackled as he disrupted it by lifting the pipes up from the case. Gava'mi watched closely, from time to time opening his mouth in a wide yawn that revealed sharp, white, slightly curved teeth.

"Well, here it is," he said. Such was the nature of the stasis case that the pipes were in the same condition as when he had packed them — how long ago? Could it really have added up to years already? The state of preservation meant he could put his breath into them and tune them up without further ado. And he did so.

The drone as the pipes were readied brought Gava'mi's head up, eyes wide and wary. The first notes Robert played had an immediate and dramatic effect on the Beast. He let out a loud, querulous cry and scooted backwards until he hit the base of one of the room's two disc chairs. His eyes were wide and black, his ears were up, and his crest bristled in all its colors in alarm.

"Oh, if you liked that, you're going to love this," Robert said, and he played a few more notes.

Gava'mi whirled and bolted, colliding head-on with the disc chair, frantically scrambling into and then over the back of it. The chair tipped as he traversed it, dumping the terrified animal and burying him with cushions. The Beast let out a pathetic cry and fought briefly with the cushions before he tore himself free, then raced from the room and out into the ground floor patio. Robert stopped playing at once, mostly because he couldn't play the pipes and laugh at the same time. When he managed to contain himself, Robert called out to the han'anga, but there was no sign of Gava'mi.

"Gaia," Robert muttered, not at all encouraged by the reaction. "Sorry, Emerson, but it would seem I face an unforeseen difficulty." He put the pipes on the table and made his way as quickly into the garden patio as he could, hoping Gava'mi was not so panicked that he had simply kept running out into the habitat.

Outside, after some searching, Robert found Gava'mi hiding under an unused cast resin flower pot of considerable size and weight. He wondered how the Beast had managed the trick of inverting the thing to cover himself, and was sorry he had not seen the maneuver, as it must surely have been an impressive effort. It was not an entirely effective hiding place, since the han'anga's tail was sticking out. "Gava'mi," Robert said gently. "Come on, boyo, I know you're in there." He nudged the tip of the tail, and the tail flicked out of sight into the pot. "Come on, boyo, I put the evil noisy thing away. It's safe. Come on out." He repeated variations on that theme several times, keeping his voice calm and quiet. From inside the pot he finally heard a soft warbling call, the sound a han'anga made when it lost track of its pack. "Hey, I'm right here, Gava'mi. I'm right here."

The pot rocked, then tipped back a bit, and a scaly muzzle poked out. Robert held his hand down and the Beast snuffled it. In a moment, wide, frightened eyes followed the muzzle, and Robert offered words of encouragement and a light touch of one finger to the side of the Beast's face. With that Gava'mi crept out from under the pot, which Robert caught as it tipped and then set upright. Though he had become a bit large to handle, Robert bent and scooped him up, holding the shivering and altogether pathetic creature. He murmured apologies and carried Gava'mi back into the family room, placing him in the other disc chair. From there the han'anga watched as Robert restored order to the room.

"Think we need to trim your claws again, Beastie," he said. The cushions from the flipped chair would need to be replaced.

When that was done he carefully packed the pipes back into the case, but left them on the sideboard. He joined the Beast in the chair and hugged him to his chest. "Better now?" Robert asked. Gava'mi butted the top of his head against Robert's chin. "That's better. You know, Beast, you've become a problem. I'm finally prodded in a way that gets me back to something I really should never have given up, and now I have a scaredy cat han'anga puppy on my hands!" Another head butt. "Yeah, I can tell you're just full of remorse." Gava'mi sprawled across his lap with a sigh, and Robert leaned back into the chair, right arm draped loosely over the han'anga, with Gava'mi's chin propped on his left arm.

After a while, Robert called up the house system and asked for the music library. With voice commands, being thoroughly pinned by a dozing han'anga, he scrolled through the listing, seeking certain old Celtic and Celtic Revival pieces he thought might suit his situation. Han'angas being marvelously adaptable and intelligent creatures, Robert was sure he could get Gava'mi past his initial fear. It was likely to take time and patience. Although a wide variety of music was often played in the house of Rost'aht, bagpipes were not on the playlists. Gava'mi had never heard such sounds before. And Robert being the only piper in Bartram, no such sounds were heard at the Willow Lake, either. It would be necessary to train the han'anga to accept such music as normal, and recorded music seemed a safe way to begin.

Mindful of the claws of his scaly companion, and most unwilling that his lap should suffer the fate of the cushions of the other chair, which really were decidedly worse for the wear, he started a piece by a band he had heard in his youth. Old memories, there, nothing that overlapped the events that caused him so much grief. He set the volume very low, then started talking calmly to the beast, telling him how smart and brave he was. Gava'mi remained relaxed until the pipes made their presence known in a particular set. His head came up; he tensed for flight or fight, teeth bared, crest bristling dangerously close to Robert's face. Gava'mi hissed and looked around for the source of the frightful sounds.

"Hey, Beast," Robert said. "Hey, you beastly beast. There's my brave boyo... " And all the while patting him on the back and hip, thumping him firmly as the Beast preferred. "It's just music. Strange music to your ears, but only music." Gava'mi turned to look at him, eyes glittering, body language undecided. Robert puffed air in the han'anga's face and was promptly nuzzled and head-butted. "There you go, my lad. It's okay."

And it no doubt would be, until it came time to practice for real. But that was a problem for another day, and though Robert felt the time really had come, he saw no reason to hurry. So they sat through the afternoon together, listening to music, with varying amounts of pipes involved and at various volumes. Gava'mi would flinch and leap up when particularly exuberant bagpipe solos were played by the house system, then regard his fosterer with great interest when no such reaction came from him. It sounded dangerous, but the person the Beast trusted most in all the universe seemed unconcerned, and after a while Gava'mi stopped flinching.

Shortly before Alicia and Melep were due to return home for the evening, Robert switched to the household's usual mix of quiet Leyra'an evensong. Alicia came home first, of necessity greeting the eager Beast first and then Robert. He saw her eyes pick out the pipes on the sideboard. Speaking in carefully casual tones, she said, "Got a little practice in today?"

"Tried to," Robert replied. "The Beast was not amused."

"Is that what happened to the cushions?"

"Well, yes. He was on his way out to the garden patio and the, uh, chair got in his way." Robert glanced at the chair in question and its torn cushions. "That was the only casualty."

"You must really be out of practice, then. The effect is usually general devastation."

It was the sort of teasing banter about the playing of the pipes that had sprinkled their conversations almost since the day they met. Absent for so long, hearing such words brought a huge lump to his throat, and Robert found he could not respond. Alicia came forward and took his hands in hers, and they stood with their foreheads touching, in the Leyra'an way. Little Paul was tucked between them in his sling, making happy baby noises, waving pudgy arms and legs. Neither of them spoke for a long time, and then Alicia kissed him and stepped back without releasing his hands. "I guess you probably shouldn't practice here."

"I was thinking of out at the vineyards, after the crew is gone for the day. In the meantime, I've been playing music on the system, trying to get the Beast accustomed to the new sound."

"Good ideas," she said, nodding. A gleam came into her eyes. "Get him used to it, so he doesn't jump into the lake and drown himself the first time you perform."

Robert raised an eyebrow and said, "Actually, he's a strong swimmer."

"I didn't mean it would be accidental," she replied patiently.

The tale of the afternoon's adventure was repeated when Melep and Holm arrived, to the delight of each. Their evening meal was taken at home and techniques for the habituation of young han'angas were debated, discussed, and all eliminated in favor of a slow, patient approach.

"He has hiding places in and around the vineyard," Robert said. "He'll know he has safe havens. That seems to have emboldened him when past events have surprised him."

"Something else has frightened him this much?" Holm asked.

"You've forgotten the incident involving the test of the high pressure misting system?" Robert asked. He and the vineyard crew learned something about the sharpness of han'anga teeth that day, with results that were not to the liking of Gava'mi.

"Oh, yes!" Holm replied. "Well, he *is* a han'anga, after all."

The aforementioned han'anga, on his back in the disc chair with the torn cushions, followed the conversation, looking from face to face. That he did so upside down damaged the illusion that he understood the words. From the low-walled crib near the sideboard, one of the little ones could be heard fussing. Gava'mi was on the floor in an instant, first peering into the pen to check the children, then snuffling around the outside until he seemed assured it was just a cranky baby, and that the youngest members of his pack were in no danger. Having done so, he hopped back into the chair and promptly rolled over onto his back again.

"If we lived in ancient times," Holm said, "those would be well-warded children."

Robert smiled and said, "He's a pain in the butt, from time to time. But I don't regret adopting him." He looked at Gava'mi as he spoke, and the han'anga warbled happily.

CHAPTER EIGHTEEN

Eb'ara Kai Station
Confederation of Clans

John adjusted the *es'ava* across his chest as he walked, and made a determined effort not to let his anxiety show. He and the Matriarch were hardly strangers to one another, residing as they did in the same family complex managed by Eb'shra Vil and Wirolen's other numerous relations. Their interactions had gone from cordial to fairly easy-going, as John had passed from being an honored guest to someone treated like a member of the family. They sat together on a regular basis when she chose to dine with immediate family, during which meals she sometimes teased Wirolen with threats of stealing him from her. He could not imagine what would prompt a *formal* summons, a command that specifically *excluded* Wirolen.

Wirolen had always been there to guide him away from foolish mistakes. To answer such an important call without her was a bit intimidating. He had come a long way in understanding how to behave in a civilized Leyra'an way. He spoke the language very well, and rarely made mistakes that gave offense. In any case, the

Matriarch spoke the Human language with equal facility, so there was that as a fallback. John doubted he would make an utter fool of himself. Still, it was a bit unsettling to ponder what possible motives might be behind such a summons.

"Did she give you any idea of what this was about?" he asked the man on his left. The same pair of bodyguards escorted him who had done so the day of the official audience. The difference was that he now knew them by name and thought of Eb'shra Arka and Eb'shra Lelan as friends.

"She told us only to bring you to her," Lelan replied.

"That she sent us and not a message *does* imply a matter of some importance," Arka added. "But if there was something *wrong*, rumor would have reached us."

"Well, that does reassure," John conceded. They made their way briskly from the lift station and down the concourse of the main torus. The warm, bright place, with its profusion of trees and flowering vines, was by now familiar to John. "I do hope I have not given some offense, somewhere, that has put the Matriarch in an awkward situation."

"We would know of it, were *that* the case," Arka replied. "Wirolen would have been told, and you would have been quietly corrected. Indeed, this has gone on since your arrival."

"Did you not know?" Lelan asked.

"I suspected," John replied, though he did recall several instances in which he had been spared embarrassment only because Wirolen was so fast on her feet, and so well known. "It is good to know for sure."

"It was by order of the Matriarch, to honor our lost cousin," Arka said with a glance at John. "Now it is done for *your* sake. You have many friends here, John Knowles!"

That made him feel better.

They arrived at the now familiar dome of the council chambers, and he was led inside, then off to the right. The center of the dome, where the Matriarch made herself publicly available on a regular basis, was unoccupied. He was led out into one of the open-air side complexes and up several turns of a spiral staircase, to a floor screened on three sides with light, movable wall panels. The office, with its profusion of flowering plants in black hydro trays, opened out onto the broad, brightly lit promenade of the main torus. The noise of a busy Leyra'an city in space drifted up from below, but remained below the level that might have impaired conversation.

The Matriarch sat behind a wide, black desk, before which three high-backed chairs had been drawn. She little resembled the wizened creature he had first known. Her hair had almost been restored to the jet black mane of her youth, with here and there a streak of white still showing. John wondered what it must feel like to experience such age, and then feel the weight of years fall away. The giddiness of the elderly Leyra'an in Wirolen's immediate family was easy to understand, though the cause remained hard to imagine for one who lacked the experience of old age to begin with. The Matriarch, dressed in dark brown and black as a sign of her station, greeted him with a smile. The only color she wore was the *es'ava* that passed diagonally over her breasts. She waved him forward as he bowed and his escort faded away back down the stairs.

John faced the Matriarch and said in Leyra'an, "Matriarch, I have come. How may I be of service?"

"Be comfortable, John Knowles," she replied, and pointed at one of the chairs.

It was the one that remained unoccupied. In the other two were men he did not know, Leyra'an with that elderly-but-not-old look of those who had only recently received the Cure, and for whom full restoration was a work in progress. John bowed to them, and when they nodded acknowledgment, took the offered chair. They were dressed in warm browns and dark green, in tunics, trousers and boots, typical of Leyra'an men of mature years. Neither wore sashes of family colors he recognized. One bore on his *es'ava* a number of military honors. From his own prior training as an officer of the RDF, John knew he was looking at the Leyra'an equivalent of a full fleet admiral. The other had but a single badge clipped to his sash, the sign of the Watchful Eye used by those employed by the intelligence analysts of the Confederation.

"Your knowledge of the Leyra'an tongue is much improved, young man," she said with a classic Leyra'an smile. For not the first time, John was reminded of the ancient work of art known as the Mona Lisa.

"Thank you, Matriarch," John replied. "I have had most excellent teachers."

"For all that," she replied, "these worthy gentlemen speak the Human language perfectly. To avoid possible confusion, we will use the language of your birth."

John rose and bowed to the three of them. "I am honored by your courtesy," he said in Leyra'an, and then sat back down.

"Here you see Lor'prai Pilip, Admiral of the Ipna Fleet," said the Matriarch, in the Human language, with a gesture to indicate the more decorated of the two men. "And with him is For'long Fria, of the Confederation's information analysis service. They have come seeking your assistance."

For a moment, John was nonplussed. "*My* assistance?" He could not help the response, but recovered quickly and added, "Forgive me, Matriarch. Of course, I'm ready to help if I can."

"Rest assured," said the Admiral, placing a hand over his heart, "we are not here to ask help that might put citizens of the Republic at risk. Far from it, in fact."

"That's much appreciated," John said. The possibility that what he knew might be used to give the Leyra'an leverage in the current stalemate was something that had worried him from the beginning of his adventure. These fears had faded as he learned that the Leyra'an were, contrary to the Republic's propaganda, an honorable people.

"There is something going on in the Disputed Zone systems controlled by the Republic," said For'long Fria. "Our contacts, where we are still able to maintain such, report that anti-government sentiments are growing, due to word that the Humans of the Commonwealth can give the gift of long life. The Republic has denied that this is so, but... "

"Word has leaked from the Confederation of the Cure," John concluded with a faint nod. "I expected as much."

"Humans in the Confederation are being treated as you have been," said the Admiral. "And those who are able to travel back and forth across the border have surely displayed the effects. I speak of the eldest of them, of course. The rumors of this thing being real, and of the Republic's false denials, are spreading as fast as real space allows. With them, there surely spreads unrest."

"Of that, sir, there should be no doubt," said John.

"We are, of course, interested in monitoring events in that region as they develop, to prevent unfortunate consequences due to the rather porous nature of the border zone," said For'long Fria. "We wish to keep a more *effective* watch on the situation, and to do so we are assembling a team we hope will have the necessary knowledge to properly interpret the information we gather. Because of your background in military intelligence, and the fact that you grew up in the Republic, we would greatly value your participation."

"My background in military intelligence?" John felt his heart skip a beat, but maintained his outward composure. He knew, though, that even a crude monitor, should one be present in the office, recorded a spike in heart rate and body temperature.

A flicker of teeth showed in Fria's smile. "Are you curious how we know this?"

Tactics of denial sorted themselves out in his mind for a moment, then John decided to surrender to the inevitable. "You'd be a fool to reveal such a thing." And revealed a hint of teeth in his own smile.

Fria rose to his feet for a moment, and bowed to John. In the Leyra'an way, the gesture acknowledged that nothing more need be said of the matter.

"Excellent!" said the Matriarch with a hint of laughter in her voice. "You two were clearly meant to be friends!"

"Should you accept," said the Admiral, as if the exchange had not taken place, "you will always have the option of stepping aside, should it seem you are about to betray the best interests of your own people. We ask for no secrets you might hold."

"Nothing that would give you any military advantage?" John asked, and he could not help the sarcasm in his voice.

"Do we need such?" the Admiral responded calmly.

John knew very well what the man meant. Leyra'an technology was the equal of the Republic, and their numbers were far greater. The stalemate existed for a good reason. The Leyra'an had always fought a defensive war, blocking the Republic's advances, and then rolling them back from Confederation territory. They had never *once* invaded territory originally of the Republic.

"We simply wish to know what is happening, and why, so that our own decisions do not create problems of their own," the Admiral went on to say. "We would *greatly* value your perspective on what is happening."

John's first thought was to decline. His path had led him away from war, and he found himself profoundly reluctant to return to such matters. Of course, his goal was to help bridge the gap between the Leyra'an and the Humans of the Republic. He could not ignore the possibility that being a part of this effort might facilitate this goal. "An interpretation of events and their meaning?" he asked, to be sure. "There being no small number of Human residents within the Confederation, I can't help wondering how my perspective would be of particular value."

"There are indeed many Humans among us," Fria replied. "But none have experience in the analysis of intelligence data. That we are aware of," he finished with another brief flash of pointed teeth.

"We fear the Republic might be about to launch a violent suppression of dissent in the Disputed Zone," Pilip said. "If that is to happen, our forces need to be ready to prevent the conflict from spreading to our side of the zone. Advance warning would be helpful, and might save many lives. We believe your experience offers the best chance of providing such."

"And you are willing to trust me? Knowing of my past duties?"

Fria nodded toward the Matriarch and said, "The Matriarch of Eb'shra trusts you, John Knowles. That is enough."

John rose and bowed low to her, and received a nod in acknowledgment.

"With it understood that there are lines I will not cross," he replied, "I'd be happy to help as much as I can."

The two Leyra'an exchanged glances and then looked at the Matriarch, who nodded in agreement.

"Thank you," said Pilip, and bowed where he sat, a slow nod of the head and shoulders. "May this joint effort spare many lives. We will depart when you are ready."

"That should take very little time, as such things go," John replied. "I travel light."

The Matriarch touched a spot on her desk as the Admiral spoke, and a moment later a young woman dressed in a long, dark blue skirt and a cinnamon blouse appeared bearing a tray with a tall bottle and four cups. The bottle contained *bosh'sh*, the Leyra'an beverage of choice for any occasion that warranted a toast. Among the Leyra'an, John now understood, just about any agreement beyond where to have the midday meal could qualify. And sometimes even those agreements were indeed saluted, after the fact. He did not hesitate to take his cup after the Matriarch's aide had filled them and passed them around. "To peace between our peoples," the Matriarch said. Then, lowering the cup after taking a drink, she added, "Eb'shra Wirolen is free to accompany you, should she so desire."

The slight narrowing of her eyes and turn of one corner of her mouth spoke of amusement, and John realized he was being teased. He nodded his head politely toward her and said, "It is, as always, her choice."

"This I know," said the Matriarch, switching back to her native tongue. She raised her cup again, but before drinking, met his eyes and said seriously, "Her choices speak well of her character."

Unsure of what to say to that, although it sounded like a compliment aimed at the two of them, John merely saluted the Matriarch with his cup.

"Gentlemen," she said, after tossing back the rest of the drink, "let us take this elsewhere. I am hungry! And you," she said to John, "If you would be so kind as to summon my granddaughter to join us?"

"Right away, Matriarch," John said with a bow, the three of them having risen to their feet before her. He was, as it happened, more than ready to eat, and had no doubt the others felt the same. The cup of *bosh'sh* burned brightly in his empty stomach, and was going straight to his head. And of course, the Cure was still working its energy-intensive miracle.

CHAPTER NINETEEN

Pr'pri System
Bartram Habitat

Holm's speculation regarding the motives of the Artificials was very much on Robert's mind when he met Alicia at her lab. The idea that the shipminds in Pr'pri system had looked at her data and had been so shocked that they buried her results, was disturbing. And he could guess what the calculations of the Artificials had revealed; they had all come to the same conclusion before the evening was done.

Somewhere out there, hidden in the great Void, were beings who could create other intelligent species, and in a way that seemed to defy both time and space. They had used, Alicia said, modern Human DNA, ages before such Humans walked the Earth. The implications of *that* aspect, all by itself, were staggering. But what would happen if, in spite of seeming impossibility and Holm's careful doubts, Alicia were proven correct? What would the consequences of such knowledge be for Leyra'an civilization?

Having seen the reaction of only a pair of Leyra'an to the idea — and Holm's distress was still very clear in his memory — he could well imagine the impact such a revelation would have on both species.

Were the Artificials trying to protect the Leyra'an? Given such a possibility, it suddenly made sense that the Artificials would do a thing that was, to the best of Robert's knowledge, unprecedented.

He came to the end of that train of thought, with its unanswerable question, as he reached the entry to Alicia's lab complex. Passing through it, he greeted and was greeted by a variety of folk working on projects at desks and lab benches. He knew the place well enough to safely navigate the maze of work stations and equipment and soon came upon Alicia with a pair of Leyra'an, a man and a woman, the three of them peering at a long bank of equipment on a black-topped bench. Lights rippled across the center, and out in front a screen was projected, scrolling data that Robert had no hope of rendering sensible. They spoke together in low tones as they examined whatever so captivated their attention.

"A truly impressive light show," Robert said. All three of them were startled, and her colleagues glared at him. "Sorry," he said. And to Alicia, "You were expecting me, remember? Lunch?"

"I hadn't forgotten," she replied, a bit defensively.

"Thought never crossed my mind," he replied, the very picture of innocence. To the acerbic look the comment brought he said, "Kr'nai Ersha will be waiting."

"You should go," the Leyra'an woman said with a laugh. "We can take care of this."

"Okay, thanks," Alicia said as she stepped away with visible reluctance. "Post the final result to me, if you would."

"Of course."

After strapping the carrier holding Paul to Robert's back, they worked their way out of the lab complex, making three stops as Alicia double-checked works in progress. Robert waited patiently through the lengthy departure. Knowing how she worked, he had in fact come for her with a generous amount of time to spare. "Ready for this?" he asked as they finally made it to the outer corridor.

"No, not really," she confessed. "But then, how could I be? I'm about to reveal something to a dear friend who is likely to find the news deeply unsettling. You remember how badly rattled Holm and Melep were."

Robert nodded in silent agreement and held out his hand to her, and she took it, holding tight as they headed toward the nearest lift station. They spoke of casual things as they made their way to Kr'nai Ersha's favorite traditional Leyra'an restaurant. It was also a location at which he had the sort of connections that guaranteed privacy. The trip took them to the far end of the habitat, about as long a journey in a tube capsule as was possible in Bartram. They were the only occupants of the brightly painted pod that whisked them to their destination. The convention of the Leyra'an with regards to such transport systems had been adopted by the Bartram survivors, and each pod had its own character, no two being the same. Sometimes Robert found the pods he used pleasantly amusing or relaxing. Now and then he just wanted to close his eyes; this was such a journey, trapped in a pod with a garish blue and orange color scheme, so of course it was a long one.

The open-air restaurant was quiet at that time of day, a place of white tables and chairs, and potted plants. Robert was by then so adapted to matters Leyra'an, and these styles were so tightly interwoven with Human ways in the habitat, that he usually took no note of it. But now he noted every detail as adrenaline leaked into his blood and he shared Alicia's anxiety over how to tell Kr'nai Ersha, one of the great leaders of his people, that the Leyra'an were an artificial species.

Kr'nai Ersha, who awaited them at the entrance, looked much as he had when Robert first saw his face in the recording through which First Contact was made. He was not very tall for a Leyra'an, and more broad-shouldered than most. The only family resemblance to Melep would have been the colors of the *es'ava* he wore, but those colors had been replaced when she married Rost'aht Holm. He stood up from the bench he occupied and greeted them warmly, laying a hand to each Human's right cheek, then accepting the Human-style embrace. "Welcome, dear friends," he said, using the Human language, which he did by habit, sprinkling his speech with Leyra'an words for which no precise translations existed, or he thought better served his purpose. This mixing of words was now commonplace, as more people became equally conversant in both languages. "You look as lovely as ever," he said to Alicia, who replied with a simple word of thanks. After a glance over Robert's shoulder at the soundly sleeping Paul, he said, "And you, shipmate? How are the vines? And I hear you are playing the pipes again?"

"The vines are growing well, and yes, I am practicing again." He gave Alicia a look and pre-empted the comment he was sure would come. "To the horror of one han'anga pup."

"Gava'mi objects?" Ersha asked, an upward quirk of one side of his mouth showing his amusement.

"Cushions suffered a tragic fate," Alicia said.

"That sounds like a story to hear!"

And so as they entered the restaurant Robert recounted the tale of the Beast's reaction to the sound of bagpipes, and the destruction of cushions that followed. Ersha laughed as the event was described to him. "So, I'm not planning a concert anytime soon. I'm a bit rusty... " Robert said at the end.

"How can you tell?" Alicia asked.

"... and practice will be a unique challenge all its own," he finished.

"Do not worry about Gava'mi," Ersha said as he ushered them to a wrought iron table surrounded by five chairs of similar style, with cushioned seats and backs. They occupied three, with Alicia on Ersha's right hand, and Robert on his left. "His kind are quite intelligent, as well as adaptable, and he is a very bright boy."

"I've always thought so," Robert admitted.

"So life takes a step closer to what you once knew," Ersha said, looking pleased. "I am very glad to hear that, par'adnan." Nephew, it would have been in the Human tongue. He had taken to addressing them as niece and nephew, even though by Leyra'an traditions they weren't, quite. Legally, they were bound to Rost'aht, not Kr'nai. "I was for a time concerned."

"Me, too," Robert replied quietly, and he reached over to clasp the man's hand for a moment, a very Leyra'an gesture. Ersha knew better than most the toll the voyage of the *Han'anga* had taken on Robert. Ersha had been there. Both men had watched friends die.

"Melep is to be here as well, is she not?" Ersha asked.

"She should be here soon, and Holm with her, as soon as they can be spared," Alicia replied. She gave Robert that irked look she had worn back in the lab and added, "We're a bit early."

They spoke of light matters and sipped *a'boshna*, the lightweight version of the stronger beverage *bosh'sh*. It was not long before Melep and Holm arrived. The baby carrier seemed a tiny thing, perched on Holm's broad shoulders. Vurn's small head turned this way and that, his tiny face goggle-eyed. They greeted Ersha and joined them at the table.

"Melep said you had a matter of some urgency to discuss, something in which I might be of assistance?" Ersha said as the new arrivals settled into their chairs. Extra chairs were dragged into place to hold baby carriers.

"I have need of resources only the Confederation can provide," Alicia said, starting out simply. "And the material I need isn't available here in Pr'pri."

"Indeed?" was the mild response. A server came to the table and they let Ersha order the midday meal, and request a second decanter of *a'boshna*. Ersha topped off their cups, then raised his own and said, "To Robert's most excellent vines." And they drank. "I have what you Humans would call a gut feeling," Ersha said over the top of his cup. "You are not simply consumed of a sudden by wanderlust, are you, *par'erdnan?*"

"No, *par'aman*," she replied. She sipped her drink, then set it deliberately on the table. "I need data that will help me answer a question. A very important question. That data can't be brought to me by the usual means."

"I do not understand what you mean," Ersha said with a frown.

"We need to bypass the normal lines of communication," Holm said when Alicia didn't answer right away. "The information would need to be stored in isolation and brought here, without passing through Commonwealth ships or facilities."

Ersha was silent for a moment, then said, "That would take some arranging. The shipmind of the *Simon Newcomb* has been instrumental in making efficient data transfer possible. I wonder at times how we managed all this before you brought the Artificials to us. Taking it out of the loop... There would be questions asked. What reason am I to give for this request?" He looked from Holm to Alicia.

Alicia looked down and started rotating her cup where it sat on the white table top. Once again, she made no response.

"You can't tell anyone why the data needs to be hand-carried," Robert said quietly, giving Alicia a long look. "In fact, it probably wouldn't be a good idea to tell anyone except the couriers that we were doing this."

Ersha's brows twitched as he looked from Robert back to Alicia. "In that case, I truly *must* know what is going on, if I am to fabricate a believable excuse on your behalf."

"Yes," Alicia replied at last. "You need to know." She raised the cup, drained it, and refilled it, leaving the men and Melep to fend for themselves. "You're aware of the incredible degree of similarity between Leyra'an and Human physiology."

"Ah, you seek to unravel *that* riddle?"

"No," she said. "I already *know* why we are so alike. Unfortunately, the explanation begs a different question. A much bigger one."

"I am bewildered," Ersha admitted.

"Shortly before the attack on the *Han'anga* and the *Bartram*, I ran a comparative analysis of our respective genomes," Alicia said. "I found the well-known similarities. But using the Commonwealth's more precise techniques, which are built around our science of genetic engineering, I found... well, I found something amazing and, frankly, alarming." She met Ersha's gaze and held it.

"There is, spliced into the genes of the Leyra'an species, material from the Human genome. A rather large amount of material."

"How... " and he paused, then muttered something in Leyra'an that Robert did not catch. "How can that *possibly* be right?"

"I found, in my analysis, unmistakable markers of tampering, of wholesale splicing to construct what my people call a chimera, a life form constructed from the genes of more than one species."

Robert watched as Ersha's expression became one of blank disbelief, as if he had for a moment stopped hearing what she said.

"No," Ersha said. "This makes no sense, *par'erdnan*. And forgive me, I do not mean to accuse you of being false with me. I can see no reason why you would do such a thing. But what you say flies in the face of everything I know of our evolutionary history. Meaning *my* species, of course."

"How familiar are you with the fossil record of your home world?" Alicia asked quietly.

Ersha raised his hands before him in the standard Leyra'an shrug. "I am no student of such matters," he admitted.

"There is a gap," Melep said. "When Alicia first told Holm and me of this matter, it was mentioned. We checked the archive. On one side of the gap lived the species long considered a precursor to our own. On the other side... *us*."

"From the data I gathered," said Alicia, "It appears that this ancestral species was altered, mostly by adding Human DNA. It was done sometime during the time represented by the gap in the fossil record. The result was the Leyra'an species, and the techniques by which this was done were very sophisticated."

"Done?" Ersha echoed. "Done by whom?"

"I don't know, *par'aman*," she said, reaching up to push a lock of red hair away from her eyes.

Ersha looked around at the three of them, and finally said to Melep, "You and Holm *believe* this?"

"We believe our sister has discovered something amazing. We are not completely sure of her conclusions," she added awkwardly. Alicia reached over to take her hand. "They are difficult to accept. But we trust in her, and her skills. We mean to help her find the answers she seeks."

"And you?" he asked Robert.

"As insane as it all sounds," he replied, "I know Alicia. She would not share this with us unless absolutely sure of what she found."

Ersha sighed and took a long drink of *a'boshna*, then peered intently into the half-empty glass. Robert looked at Alicia, who shrugged her shoulders a little. He found that Holm and Melep were studying the table. Even the children remained quieter than usual. No one made an effort to prompt or nudge Ersha. He drank again and set the glass down. "I do not believe that this can be true." He looked around at them all, then directed his gaze to Alicia. "But like the rest of you, I do not believe Alicia would voice such a conclusion without good reason. There is a mystery here to unravel, and I will help if I can. What is it you hope I can do to aid in its resolution?"

"At the time I discovered all of this, I only had that part of the database you'd shared with the shipmind of the *William Bartram*," Alicia replied. "It contained overviews, but no raw data. I need such data. And I need to study the genomes of other species from Leyra'ach, and perhaps from other worlds within the Confederation. There may be elements of species from those worlds within the Leyra'an genome. The sources of such things may give me clues regarding the identity of these engineers."

"If that is so, why the need to transfer data in such a difficult matter? The data you require can be summoned from the Archives, easily enough, and sent here." He gave her a long, hard look. "There is, unbelievably, more to this matter than you have told me."

When she did not reply immediately, Melep said. "*Par'aman*, her original work was lost with the *Bartram*, and in her effort to replicate it aboard a probeship, she found that her results were tampered with. To conceal the markers of genetic reconstruction."

"Someone is hiding the truth?" Ersha demanded. "But who would be able to... Ah! The Artificials! But what would possibly motivate them to do so?"

"There's no way to know for certain," Alicia replied. "At least, not until I can confront one of them with results and demand an accounting."

"It is possible," said Robert, "that they're trying to delay the open discovery and discussion of the matter. The Artificials seem like us in many ways, but they have a very different perspective on events. They see further, and make connections sooner, than Humans. That ability has saved the Commonwealth from danger several times."

"There might be a danger to us in this?" Ersha asked.

"To the Leyra'an," Alicia replied. "That's our best guess. Consider how you felt when I explained the matter to you. Imagine that reaction duplicated many billions of times, especially if I can prove the matter beyond reasonable doubt."

"I see your point," Ersha said quietly.

"If we are right about this," said Melep, "there is reassurance to be found. There would be nothing malicious in what the Artificials have done."

"Best of intentions," Alicia said softly, shaking her head. "Either way, they've made it impossible for me to pursue the matter."

"Should you?" Ersha asked. "Pursue the matter, I mean. Or should you trust that the Artificials know best?"

"I can't do that, knowing what I know now," Alicia replied, shaking her head. "Could you?"

"No," Ersha replied with a sigh. "I suppose not. So, why not reveal what you do know? Force the issue now? I realize the data exists only in your memory hoard, but would that not count? Your people put great faith in those artificial organs in your heads."

Alicia shook her head, then pushed the unruly lock of hair aside again. "The contents of enhanced memory do not constitute proof, *par'aman*. I could easily fabricate such data and imprint it, and then make up any story that suited. It's been done before, you see. No, what I have in my head will guide us, but I can't use it to convince any of my colleagues. They would try to replicate my findings, see what the Artificials wanted them to see, and that would be the end of me as a scientist."

Ersha nodded, then said, "We are not bound by the decisions of your Artificials, so I will see what I can do. My heart says that you are all telling me a truth, as you understand it. So I will find a way to make what you need possible, if it is possible at all. But... One other thing I must ask. Why not travel into the Confederation and do your work there, beyond reach of the Artificials? It might be more easily arranged."

Robert watched as his wife's grip on the cup tightened, and her knuckles turned white. Her normally fair complexion went a shade paler, then color flushed her face and a quick shiver passed through her. He was about to put a hand on her arm when she stammered something that never quite resolved into words. Alicia closed her eyes, took a slow breath to calm herself, and said very carefully, "I can't go anywhere away from here. I just... Paul is too young."

"Ah, I see," said Ersha. He sounded understanding, but the frown that twitched for a moment across his brows said otherwise. He could not resist a glance at the still sleeping Human child.

Her excuse was an empty one. Robert knew this, and didn't doubt Ersha knew it as well. On Robert's left, Holm and Melep exchanged a quick look of concern.

Ersha drained his cup, then filled it and topped off the others. He gave the server the sign that their discussion was done, and that it was now time for food. "This is no small thing you ask."

"Of this, *par'aman*, we are well aware," Melep replied.

"Well, I have somewhat fewer connections, these days, than was once the case. But I will try. For I agree with Alicia. No matter what the Artificials are trying to do, we must have the truth of this matter!"

CHAPTER TWENTY

Tak'ak Na Station
Confederation of Clans

John waved his hand through the green-framed, green-lettered display to banish it, dismissing yet another report that added to his rapidly growing puzzlement and concern. "Whatever is going on out there, no good can come of it," he said in Leyra'an.

The others in the room, Wirolen, Fria, and the Admiral, looked up at him from their own work stations. "You think we can trust the unofficial reports of fleet activity?" Fria asked.

"I think so," John replied. "Especially since so many elements of the Fleet are so blatant about the fact that their activities do not match the RDF cover story."

"It helps greatly that you can spot the planted disinformation so quickly," Fria said. "That has made a significant difference."

"Helps that I used to write the stuff," John replied, thinking of two years spent as a junior officer in the RDF intelligence service. "The government is letting it be known that tolerance for separatist sentiments is at an end, and is making bold threats even as public sentiment against direct action grows." He leaned back and lifted his mug of steaming *mi'pat* from the gray metal desk. "The Fleet is gathering, but not in a location that makes any strategic sense if a zero tolerance policy is about to be put in place. Probably a moot point in any case. In my opinion, fleet strength isn't up to the challenge, even if the public were willing to support what amounts to a civil war. After that last offensive... Well, the RDF paid a stiff price when the Confederation reclaimed the systems that fell to Kester. They would be spread pretty thin trying to stay on top of border security *and* the ever stronger secessionist movement. Instead, most of them are gathering in a single system and calling it an 'exercise.'"

"They are not deployed for an offensive against the Confederation, either," Fria said. "They are not actually within the DZ."

"Odd, indeed," said the Admiral. "Your government says one thing, the Fleet's movements seem to suggest another."

John put down his mug and sat up straight, appalled by what had just crossed his mind. "I'll be damned!" he said in Human. Switching languages he said, "This may be a mutiny!"

"Are you serious?" the Admiral asked.

"Yes, sir," John replied. "Consider what we know. The news we have out of the Republic clearly indicates a deepening divide between the hardline, anti-Leyra'an government and the general public. Rumor of the effects of Commonwealth medical miracles has spread into the Republic along the DZ, inflaming Secessionist sentiments there. The government has been making threats. The RDF Fleet considers itself a servant of the *civilian* population. They are sworn to protect and serve the citizens of the Republic. They will be very reluctant to take action against citizens of the Republic without better cause than currently exists, but that is almost certainly what they have been ordered to do." John looked around at the others in the room. "I believe the RDF Fleet may have withdrawn its support of the government. They may have retreated to their current location rather than wage war on their own people."

"For what purpose might they have chosen their current location?" the Admiral asked.

"As good a place to stand fast as any, I would think," said Fria.

"I think I see what the Admiral means," John said. "The Fleet would mutiny to protect the people, not necessarily out of a desire for peace with the Confederation. I think the Fleet may be abandoning the DZ, pulling the line back to a zone of systems in which the Leyra'an have had no recent contact." He flicked a finger at an icon in his display area and a map unfolded in the space between the circle of desks. They occupied a quartet of desks on one side of the circle. A lumpy area lit pale red stretched across the center, and to one side of it a star system blinked in yellow. "Look where they are in relation to the DZ. Pay special attention to the nodal network in the region."

"Perfectly positioned to draw a new boundary that excludes the troublesome systems. I see that now. But what would such a move accomplish?" Fria asked. His brows were puckered, the look of a puzzled and perhaps skeptical Leyra'an.

"It would cut their losses," John explained. "The new border would exclude the Secessionist movement, rather than suppress it. They can draw, and support, the new line with the ships available, because they will not be in hostile space. It would take several years of shipbuilding to bring the Fleet up to a strength that allowed them to simply invest all of the DZ, and make resistance nearly impossible through sheer force of numbers. The Secessionists will make their move long before then."

"Your way of doing things so often works against you," said Fria. "We could build such a fleet in a matter of months."

John nodded. "I know. RDF intel came to the realization years ago that you could literally bury us in ships, if you wanted to. That you have never done so is part of what erodes support for the war."

"We have never desired mastery of the Republic," Fria said. "We could, as you say, build a fleet to overwhelm any defenses you could muster, but what would be accomplished? Enforcement of our way on others? You are not like us. We can accept that. It would be a violation of the Way of Leyra'an to do otherwise. So we build ships enough to prevent deep or permanent incursions."

"Now that I have come to know the Leyra'an, I believe that," John said quietly. "So, it seems the hardliners are running out of options." He poked a finger into his display and the system housing the RDF Fleet flashed twice. "My feeling is the Fleet has gathered here instead of deploying in order to send a message to the government."

"The message being, 'Find another option,'" said the Admiral.

"And they are pointing out the best option that exists at this time." John stared at the map as he raised the mug and took a sip.

"Your government cannot simply order them back in?" Wirolen asked.

"They will, if they have not done so by now," John replied. "If I am correct about the mutiny, the Fleet will hold its position."

"Might current Fleet activity be a reflection of concern over the Commonwealth's relationship with the Republic?" Fria asked. He was scanning a report and frowning as he spoke.

"I would not think so, there being no Commonwealth presence in the DZ," John replied. Noting Fria's expression, he added, "Why do you ask?"

"This," Fria said.

The display in the air before John reconfigured itself to show a set of new documents. It blinked out briefly and reappeared, translated so he could read it. He took his time and did so carefully. Then he said, in the Human language, "Damn! This can't be right!"

"I agree," said Fria, answering in kind. "I do not believe the Commonwealth is any more inclined to meddle in the affairs of the Republic than we are."

"And if the Republic had suddenly decided to embrace the Cure, we'd know about it." John paused to calm himself and returned to using Leyra'an. "The information services would be hurrying word of it from one side of the Republic to the other. Nothing else would be discussed!" John dismissed the screen with the flick of one finger. "And the distribution would begin in the Core Systems, *not* in the DZ. This makes no sense at all!" John said. "How reliable is this source?"

"It has been of great use in the past." Fria was calling up and flicking away screens in a quick search of unviewed reports as he replied. "Ah! Here is another. And a third!" The same displays were appearing for John, Wirolen, and the Admiral. "Notice something about the three locations?"

"Far end of the DZ from Pr'pri system," John said with a nod. He touched something on his desk and the 3D map of space reappeared. Three of the systems labeled as territory of the Republic were suffused with a pale yellow glow, with a bright blue tint marking Confederation systems interspersed between them. "Can we see which systems in the Confederation have received the Cure?"

Fria touched something on his desk's pad and a succession of systems turned green, starting from those with direct nodal access to Pr'pri. The procession stopped well short of the portion of the map having a yellow tint. "Whoever does this thing is *not* from the Commonwealth," Fria said.

"They claim to have the Cure," said Wirolen, having read a synopsis of the first report. "They say they *are* from the Commonwealth!"

"What in God's name is going on out there?" John said to himself in Human.

"To make sense of it, we need an agent in the DZ, in one of the more loosely controlled systems claimed by the Republic." Fria did not quite look at John. "Sending someone with the proper perspective would be safer than trying to get messages to those already in place."

"That's a bit more than I expected to undertake, coming here," John pointed out.

"That means 'no'?" Fria asked.

"Not what I said," John replied. He thought for a moment, then said, "I've got the necessary experience, and can find my way around in the DZ easily enough. If you're willing to trust me, knowing my background as you do… "

"You are trusted, John Knowles," the Admiral said with a little half bow from where he sat.

"I will do it," John said, in Leyra'an.

Wirolen was not at all pleased with the idea of John slipping into the Republic, not pleased at all, and she was not shy about expressing her displeasure, with all the eloquence of her native tongue. Of course, there was little shyness in the woman to begin with, so John wasn't surprised by her reaction. They gave her a few moments to express that displeasure, then John sought to answer her concerns.

"Yes, there is a risk," he admitted in the end. "But For'long Fria is correct. This would be the best way to understand what we've been reading. And we need to understand! Whatever is happening out there now could create a dangerous situation on both sides of the border, and create trouble for the Commonwealth as well. We need a direct look."

"And *you* must be the one to take this look?" Wirolen asked. Her voice held an angry edge to it.

"It is a thing I believe I must do," John said patiently. He met and held her gaze with his.

Wirolen did not flinch, but kept her beautiful amber eyes locked on his as she gave him a smile that showed teeth. "Then I will be your pilot!" she said firmly.

"What? Are you out of your mind?" John demanded.

"I am at least as sane as you," she replied, eyes narrowed slightly in anger. "And as well-informed. Crossers of both species exist in the nearest systems. Relationships between our species are frequent, so no one would question our traveling together."

"They would not question it," Fria said, "though some will envy it."

"That does not help me," John said, while Wirolen gave Fria a smug look.

"Wirolen's point is well taken," said the Admiral. "She is also a highly rated pilot, one of our best, with full combat training. I believe you would make an effective team."

"We will need an appropriate ship, perhaps of the sort that is often used by those involved in the illicit transfer of goods." Wirolen swept her finger through her display, which from where John sat looked like a disk of green mist seen edgewise. "The faster *Mori'na* transports are often used by our people out there. I am trained on those flight systems."

Reluctant as John was to see Wirolen even remotely in harm's way, he could find few reasonable arguments against what they were suggesting. He knew as well as they that, in the realm of overlapping systems called the DZ, any system claimed by the Republic was accessible by one or more of those claimed by the Leyra'an. The constant flow of illicit goods guaranteed that Human populations there were accustomed to seeing ships from both sides come and go. "All right, then, which system do we take on?"

Fria studied the map, and suddenly one system lit up bright gold and flashed several times. "This one," he said. "We have no reports yet of so-called Commonwealth missions there, but there is a report from a system with direct nodal access."

"Good chance this will be next on the list," John said.

"It also has nodal access to Leyra'an space, and the Commonwealth by way of Pr'pri," Wirolen pointed out. "Multiple routes to safety."

"There *will* be a garrison, System Guard it's called, even if there's no regular fleet presence," John cautioned.

"You should already know the answer to that concern," Fria replied with a laugh. "Your RDF colleagues out there are a clan corrupted. They know Leyra'an are in the system, but because Republic citizens are making a profit — correct word? — on illicit trade from the Confederation, they take their — payoffs?" John nodded a second time. "They take their payoffs and look the other way." He tilted his head, and his forehead twitched in puzzlement. "These things are surely known to you?"

"We know about it," John replied. "Commodore Kester, my last commanding officer, would practically foam at the mouth when the subject came up." He laughed quietly and added, "I always thought it proved how far up the corruption went, the fact that he was never assigned a permanent command in the DZ. He would have closed off all the crossings, and there are highly placed individuals who would think nothing of wrecking his career to prevent that!" He rubbed his chin, staring at the far wall as he thought things through. "A common motive for Humans crossing over has much to do with keeping families in touch," John said. "That won't work for me, since my few living relatives are on the far side of the Republic. Too easy to trip over that sort of deception. Smuggling would be the best cover."

"We will provide you with a cargo that suits the reason for your journey, and serve as a resource for acquiring fuel and other supplies," Fria said. "Younger members of our Human population also sometimes go there just for the sake of going. I would suggest including an element of that in your cover story." He closed his eyes and lowered his head, almost chin to chest, for a moment lost in thought. "Yes, lovers off on an adventure, chasing rumors of people from the Commonwealth, a place you hope to visit if you can make connections with Commonwealth citizens alleged to be in the DZ. And of course you have material to trade in order to make your way."

"One thing I don't have much of a sense for," John said carefully, "from the intel I've seen. How exactly do folks in the DZ view interspecies relationships?"

"From what our agents have relayed, and regrettably we haven't really made much of an effort to gather such cultural information, it is generally well tolerated," Fria replied. "I have no doubt you will garner some hard stares, and maybe a short comment or two, but I doubt there will be anything worse than harsh language." He gave John a look of appraisal. "To be honest, my friend, if I were a Human, I would not risk a confrontation with you."

"You could pretend to be merely a passenger on *my* ship," said Wirolen.

"No," John said firmly.

"Then we will travel together, and allow others to form their own conclusions."

"We shall bow to the lady's wisdom," said Fria, giving John a quick look, both eyes blinking in a Leyra'an wink. "And seem, thereby, more wise ourselves."

CHAPTER TWENTY-ONE

Pr'pri System
Bartram Habitat

Robert held the pipes in the crook of one arm as he sat alone. The stone seat on its small hill overlooked the long rows of *boshna'ti* vines that swept gently up out of sight into the hazy habitat air. The vines had brown bark with streaks of red showing through, marks of new wood as the vines added to their mass through expansive growth. Fern-like leaves waved in the gentle breeze designed to blow through that part of the habitat, mimicking the conditions the vines had known on faraway Leyra'ach. The leaves were dark green, and both white flower clusters and fruit in varying degrees of red ripeness were visible, scattered thickly through the feathery growth. Nothing could be seen of the support structures except the bases of posts.

Behind him, also sweeping up the broad curve of the habitat, grew grape vines, wine grapes bred for millennia to provide a uniform and convenient harvest. The Leyra'an did not work that way. They accepted it as a given that the vines knew what they were doing, and that fruit would be ripe and ready to pick when the time came. Acceptance, as he had so often been told, was the heart of the Way.

Acceptance.

There was something of that concept in the Gaian tradition in which Robert had been raised, often expressed in the form of an ancient prayer. *Mother, grant me the serenity to accept what cannot be changed, the courage to change what I must, and the wisdom to see the difference.*

As if he needed more proof that Humanity and the Leyra'an were nearly the same species.

On Leyra'ach a vine warden would sit on the traditional stone seat with a pack of *han'angas* at his feet, watching for vermin and pests seeking to raid the vines. In the habitat, of course, there was need for neither a vine warden nor a set of *han'angas* tethered to the stone. The stone and its hillock were built because, as Holm explained, this was how a proper *boshna'ti* vineyard should look. As for *han'angas*, there would be just one in this vineyard, who at that moment was snuffling around somewhere among the vines.

Robert shifted the pipes back up over his shoulder and filled them with his breath.

Acceptance, he thought to himself as the pipes began to drone. He remembered gentle Paul Soo, the fiddler in the Willow Lake band, and Judy with the bodhran. Captain Moresh was dancing, and the crew around them clapped hands as they kept time. He could not play without seeing these things in his mind's eye.

Serenity to accept what I cannot change...

The memories were painful, but they felt necessary. Sequestration of these memories was not an option; he would let them live in his mind, and not crowded into a closed corner of his memory hoard. The music was a part of the life he wanted young Paul and Vurn to know, a connection of sorts to the men for whom they were named. But when he played the sort of tunes for which the Willow Lake band had been known, the lively jigs and reels that sent people of both species to their feet and dancing, the music still felt hollow, and nothing at all like a tribute. So instead, when he practiced, more melancholy music suited him, songs that came from the deep past and were born in misty twilights and gray dawns of a land that no longer existed. Such was the tune he played then.

"You played that one aboard the *Han'anga*," Melep said from behind. "The day we released the souls of those we lost."

Robert had just finished and had not been aware of her approach, but wasn't surprised by her appearance.

"Yes," he replied. "I did."

"You played other things, back then." She stepped around into view, dressed casually in red and brown, pants and snug blouse with *es'ava*; curiously enough the colors coordinated with the vines. Without so much as a by-your-leave, she used the short, carved steps to come and sit beside him. It was a tight fit, and Robert found himself with the pipes over one shoulder, and the other arm around Melep to make sure she didn't fall off. To a Leyra'an it wouldn't seem crowded at all. "Songs that made us dance and forget, for a moment."

"I don't play them often now because they make *me* remember," he replied. "And, well, they also frighten Gava'mi."

"I am glad you put it in that order," she said with a quiet laugh.

Robert held her closer and she put her head on his shoulder. Their closeness brought its own sharp memories, of leaning on each other in much the same way during the days when they wondered whether they would live or die. She sought comfort while he wondered if his wife was dead, with neither of them really finding what was needed until all was said and done.

"I'll play the others," Robert said quietly, hugging her to him. "I will. Someday. Afraid I'll have to work my way up to it, though."

"*Yia*," she replied. "This is but one step forward. We all know that."

Gava'mi chose that moment to emerge, saw Melep and raced over to leap up and down and around the base of the stone seat, warbling and chuckling delightedly.

Almost as quickly he vanished, darting away behind them and out of sight. "Silly boy," Melep said.

"You didn't come here to request a tune," Robert said.

"No. I need to talk to you about Alicia." Robert felt her move and looked down to see wide amber eyes gazing at him. "Does she still have the dark dreams?"

"Yes," Robert replied. "Not every night, the way she did after that incident in the *William Bartram*. But she has them."

"We are afraid for her," Melep said. "She sometimes seems so fragile, since that day in the dead ship."

"Me, too," Robert said. "But family is keeping her grounded. Our *child* is keeping her grounded. There will be problems because of what happened to her, no doubt. But if we support her, she will recover."

"We *will* be there for her," Melep asserted firmly. "Holm said it, that day as we flew to the wreck. We are with you, as family should be."

"I know that, *eli'sana,*" he said, hugging her to him. "We both do."

She sighed again, then said, "I can hardly blame her. After what happened with the *Han'anga...* " He felt her shudder slightly. "I have no desire to travel again, at all!"

"Alicia said much the same, the night after we spoke to Ersha," Robert said. "She wants the answer, but she can't bear the thought of leaving home."

"It must be very difficult for her."

"Well, yes, it is," Robert said. "But this mystery has been there for millennia, and she knows it. On such a scale, even if we wait until the boys and their eventual sibs-to-come have grown up and given us grandchildren, we will have waited less than a moment."

Melep laughed quietly, then said, "Yours is such a very different perspective. You have three times my years, and grew up never having to worry about having enough time." She looked up at him again, their faces so close he had trouble focusing on her eyes. "What you think of as a small part of your life is, to me, a life age!"

"No," Robert said. "Not anymore."

"It is not easy to adjust one's thinking on the matter," she said with another quiet laugh.

Courage to change what I must...

Robert slipped off the stone seat and, after setting the pipes in the space he had occupied, reached up to help Melep down, setting her lightly on the ground. "I know something about what that can take," he said as they faced each other for a moment. "Accepting that everything about your life has changed, and there's no going back. It's hard, even when some of the new things are worth celebrating." He turned and stepped toward the *boshna'ti* vineyard. "Come on. I want to check something before we go home."

Melep reached out and took his hand, but tugged him back to her and reached up to bring his head down close to hers. Robert, knowing what she was about, obliged and pressed his forehead to hers. It was, for the Leyra'an, a kiss. Then she followed him into the vines, with Gava'mi suddenly scampering up from the rear as if afraid he would be left behind.

With his sister-in-law beside him, Robert walked slowly down the nearest row of vines, assessing the need for harvest. He popped a round berry from a bright red cluster and rolled it across his palm, sniffing it, then biting into it. The harsh, bitter tang told him there were berries indeed ready to pick, something the scanners had doubtless already recorded. Then he spit it out. No one of either species could tolerate the taste of unfermented *boshna'ti*.

Gava'mi darted to where Robert had tossed the berry. "Silly boy! You won't like it," he said. But the han'anga snatched it up and chewed all the same, just as he had done the time before. And just as before he quickly coughed it up, and stood there gagging. "I warned you!"

Robert went to a convenient hose bib and turned on the water. Gava'mi drank eagerly, purging the taste from his mouth. And Robert wondered that the vines on Leyra'ach ever had any pests at all.

CHAPTER TWENTY-TWO

Webster Two
Disputed Zone

Three stellar systems were used to travel to their destination, but at each stop their navigation records told a tale of a different route altogether. Their true point of origin was thus thoroughly concealed. They spent a few days at stations near the nodes they used, trading and building credibility for their cover story, and adapting Wirolen's tastes to Human cuisine. Fortunately she was as open-minded in her eating habits as she was in other matters. Their final stop at Webster brought them through the node and into a heavy traffic zone. Their small ship's automated beacon told yet another clever lie as they let local traffic control take them in. Everything in the *Eli'ahtna's* log reflected their story of a young couple on a jaunt, doing a little trading along the way to meet expenses.

Traffic control brought them in to a safe dock at the primary station for the node, which was unimaginatively named Webster Alpha. They cleared customs and were welcomed aboard perfunctorily. Of Wirolen's presence no comment was made. Leyra'an frequently served as crew aboard runner ships. They took Human names — Wirolen had spent hours deciding on the name Patricia — and were both logged in as Human visitors. Security here was, John knew, a joke. But it was an enormously lucrative joke, and so the punch line rolled on, with John crossing the right palms and seeing a vaguely pretty face assigned to the logs under Wirolen's assumed name. That Wirolen traveled alone with a Human male led to certain assumptions, which her body language around John surely encouraged, but those assumptions worked in their favor. Apparently the Humans of Webster Alpha included men of eclectic tastes; Wirolen drew several appreciative glances and a few admiring stares. She carried herself as if this were only to be expected.

They traveled from the usual cold brightness of the null-g docks inward to the spindle, then to the main torus of the station. Wirolen reacted to the typical style and appearance of a Republic-built station as she had done the other three, with studied disinterest that concealed distaste. This station, like the others, was very different from its counterparts in the Confederation. They left the lift tube and stepped out onto a broad, bare gray concourse that ran off on either hand, then curved up and out of sight behind the station's horizons. On each side of the concourse were rows of buildings: stacked cubes of residences and strips of shops, service vendors, and restaurants. Around each residential block were kitchen gardens, a legal responsibility of Republic citizens. Baskets of flowers were suspended on hooks attached to vertical surfaces, and trees rose from stone boxes, the rims of which doubled as benches. A single line of trees, which John thought might be maples, ran the center of the concourse, marching away into the distant curve of the torus. The star of the system was a blue-white giant, and for all that it burned a comfortable distance away, the light directed from it by mirrors into the transparent ceiling of the station was very bright. From the angle of the mirrors, he knew it was approaching mid-day.

"It is so bare!" Wirolen said, just loud enough to be heard over the bustle of people and business around them. "Why are these places always so barren?"

"Does seem so," John said. "And compared with the way your people arrange things, it really does look in need of a good gardener." He laughed and added, "Before I lived among the Leyra'an, this place would've seemed a lush oasis after months of tour on a warship. Guess it's all relative."

"I would think living so near my people would have had a kinder influence on Human tastes!"

"Costs money to do things, *sip'ya,*" he said, taking her arm. "That includes planting flowers. This place is much better appointed than most, probably because of the wealth flowing through here."

"Money," she muttered. "Cost." Then she switched to Leyra'an and said, "Your people are insane!"

"I find it ever harder to argue that point," John replied in kind. "But this is the way we have always lived. Most people cannot even see it to question it; there's simply no other frame of reference. And we should *not* assume we can speak privately to one another in the Leyra'an tongue."

"Quite right," she replied. Holding his arm more tightly, she asked, "Now that we are here, how do we begin?"

"We begin by taking a stroll down the main concourse, to see what sort of establishments this sector has to offer." And John started walking. People passed back and forth, and across their path. The great majority were Human, singles, couples and small, talkative groups. Workers of all sorts were headed out on lunch breaks. There were Leyra'an among them, usually parts of small groups of Humans, and most of the Leyra'an were male, dressed Leyra'an style with the traditional, colorful clan sashes across their chests. The Leyra'an seemed fully accepted in these groups. Of security officers, either stationer security or RDF, there was no sign. "Watch for a spot that seems to draw more Leyra'an than others. We'd fit into such a place a bit more easily."

And so they strolled, and met looks directed their way with polite nods. When they reached the end of the sector, marked by the great ring of a section seal, they switched sides and walked casually back the other way. One place, flanked by a bakery on one side and a purveyor of wines and beers on the other, seemed very busy, popular, and the preferred establishment of groups that included Leyra'an.

"I think this will do," John said. There were tables outside, shaded by potted palms with long, slim trunks, but John ignored the exterior seating and led her inside. A young, fair-haired woman met them at the door, made sure it would be just the two of them, and led them to a round, simulated wood table with a candle in the center. She waved a hand in the air and the menu appeared before them.

"Take your time," she said with a smile. "Order when you're ready."

Wirolen looked around and smiled. "I rather like this place," she said. "It is nice."

"It should be," John said with a glance at the menu's prices. He didn't quite wince, as he and Wirolen had been provided with generous resources. And he had to laugh at himself that he suddenly found the concept of *paying* for food a strange one. "This place is what they call 'old school.'"

"Old school?"

"Live servers, instead of an automated menu."

"Ah," said Wirolen, though she seemed not entirely sure of it all.

In a sudden moment of clarity John understood something. He firmly believed he was following a path ordained by his Creator, and would follow it to the end, to whatever end that might be. But he knew in that moment, and quite suddenly, that journey's end wouldn't take him back into the Republic. The Republic was no longer his home. He stared at the prices on the menu, which now seemed both very familiar and terribly strange all at once, and was shaken by the realization. The truth of it had been there before him all along, but for some reason his mind chose that moment to register it as a fact.

A warm, firm hand closed around his. "What is wrong, *sip'ya'a?*" she asked softly.

John managed a weak smile and said, "I've just discovered a new truth behind the very old saying, *you can't go home again.*" To the puzzled twitch of her fine-scaled brow he said, "Don't worry about it, *sip'ya.* I'll explain later."

It was indeed an old-fashioned establishment. Instead of drawing their fingers through items on the menu, they waited for the young woman to work her way back to their table to take their order. "Hello, there," she said with a bright smile. "I'm Eliza. You're new here, aren't you?" She did not specify new to the establishment or new to the station.

"Just arrived this morning, station time," John replied. He read off their order.

"Good choices," Eliza said. "So, here to trade?"

Well, that certainly didn't take long, he thought. "We have a few things," he replied. "Nothing major, really, just the sort of things that keep you fueled and aired while traveling."

"Ah, playing tourist, then."

John nodded and smiled at her. "Following stories and rumors. Been hearing some wild tales, these days."

"Oh, yeah?"

"Something about people from Old Earth showing up," John said. "Working miracles, curing diseases, that sort of thing. Second Coming kind of stuff. I'd have laughed it all off, but the stories are kind of persistent."

"And consistent in their details," Wirolen put in.

And the server grinned at them. "That's 'cause it's all true!"

John just stared at her, and did not need to feign the reaction. "You're joking!"

"No, I'm not! There's a ship docked here from something called the 'Commonwealth,'" she replied with a grin, clearly enjoying her status as one in the know. "We've been hearing news of such goings on for a while now, but they're just now getting out here." She gave a sharp, sarcastic laugh and added, "With all the rabble-rousing and secession talk, I guess we just weren't much of a priority for a while."

"We saw a ship we sort of wondered about at dock, as we came in," John said. "Didn't recognize the design."

"Word is this Commonwealth has met up with the Leyra'an, too," Eliza said. "Same deal they have for Humans."

"What is this 'deal'?" Wirolen asked.

"Well, seems this Commonwealth is way ahead of us, in a lot of ways. They can cure anything, they say. You can get a treatment from them that keeps you from growing old, if you can believe that! Figured I had nothing to lose, so I went upper deck and got the shot." She shoved up the sleeve of her white blouse and revealed a faint, round, pink spot. A voice called out, and she looked aside. "'Scuse me, folks. Someone's getting impatient. Be back with your lunch soon!" And bustled off.

Wirolen stared at John for a moment, then scooted her chair around to his and appeared to cuddle up. Whispering in his ear she said, "We are rather far from the locations of the first reports. Is it possible news of a change in relations got out here before we heard of it? Could the Commonwealth be here?"

"No," John replied firmly. "The Republic will eventually accept the Cure and distribute it, but only after the process has been replicated and licensed to a few fortunate pharmaceutical firms. There's no way in hell they'd just let the Commonwealth in to distribute things like this for free. Besides, did you see the mark on her arm?"

"Ah, yes!" Wirolen said. "Our treatments left no marks. Not the Commonwealth, then."

John leaned the side of his head against hers to maintain the picture of an affectionate couple out for a bite to eat. "We need to have a look at this upper deck facility for ourselves."

"But *after* lunch," Wirolen insisted as the server returned with food and drink. "After lunch."

"Your lady has a healthy appetite," Eliza said.

"I am a *creature* of appetite," Wirolen said with a malicious laugh and a glance at John.

"Well, honey, aren't we all?" And she burst out laughing, patted Wirolen on the shoulder, and went away, unfazed by the teeth that flashed as Wirolen smiled.

"I *like* her," Wirolen remarked.

"Just a gut feeling," said John, "But I have the feeling the two of you have a lot in common."

She grinned at him, allowing the pointed tips of her teeth to show.

And John just laughed quietly. "Since you've established a rapport, maybe you could ask her *where* in upper decks territory the, ah, *Commonwealth* is to be found?"

The meal brought to them was a selection of dishes dominated by meat, in keeping with normal Leyra'an habits. "Can I do anything else for you?" Eliza asked when she circled back to check up on them.

"We would be most interested in knowing where in upper decks the Commonwealth has set up," Wirolen asked.

"Section four, about halfway around from here, anti-spinward." She laughed and added, "Just get into that neighborhood and follow the crowd. You won't be able to miss them!"

"How long have they been here?" John asked.

"Arrived the day before yesterday. They're sayin' they won't be leaving until everyone gets the treatment, so don't worry about missing out." Eliza grinned. "Really nice people, too, giving it away free like that."

"For free?" John put all the surprise he could muster into the question, knowing it would be a perfectly natural response coming from a citizen of the Republic.

"Yep! There's a couple of official types from the government traveling with them to make sure we all know things are being done right and proper."

"How does it feel?" Wirolen asked.

"You know, right off the bat I felt like I'd had a stiff shot of whiskey. That faded in a few hours. Right now, I don't feel any different at all, but they said I'd sort of be up and down while the medicine gets to work. Then I'll feel like a new woman." She laughed and leaned toward Wirolen. "Hope they're right, 'cause I've got a date tonight!" They made eye contact, Wirolen laughed knowingly, and Eliza hustled off to handle a call.

They put other matters aside and ate. Wirolen was particularly pleased with the sausage dish they ordered, although the pasta over which it was served went down slower. The pitcher of beer brought a look of disdain. "Does no one in the Republic know how to brew beer?"

"Careful, *sip'ya*. Where would you have acquired expertise in beer drinking?" John, having never tasted beer anywhere but the Republic, found the brew quite acceptable. In fact, he missed beer so much that he'd found himself in search of it at each stop they made.

Wirolen started to say something and caught herself. He did not doubt she was about to extol the virtues of Commonwealth beer, tasted during the times she had visited the probeship on which Robert MacGregor served. Such a comment, overheard by the wrong people, would have been very awkward to explain.

With their meal completed, they took a tour of the main torus, by way of the tram that ran above the concourse and inside the boot of the torus ring. The previous stations had used trams run down inside the concourse, not up on the rim. Wirolen found the whole thing delightful. Partway around they saw a long line of people queued up along the railings of the upper decks balcony. "She was quite right," he said to Wirolen as they passed the long crowd of waiting Humans. "Can't miss it."

"Do we investigate the possibilities today?" she asked.

The tram slid quickly on, finally passing the head of the line and the office complex into which the line fed. "No, let's figure out where to spend the night. Might have a shorter wait if we get there first thing in the morning."

"Perhaps we could stay someplace nice, tonight?" Wirolen said. She slid as close to him on the seat as she could without crawling into his lap.

CHAPTER TWENTY-THREE

Endmost System
Disputed Zone

Calavone programmed the shuttle to run a course that followed a line across the midsections of the completed cruisers, and cleared the compartment canopy to full transparency. Featureless gray metal, dull even in the bright light of the system's hot white star, passed in silent review over their heads, ship after ship after ship. A glance one way down the length of each revealed drive pods and polygonal matrix engines. A look the other way showed the ship ending in the bluntly rounded prow of a cruiser class RDF ship, the all-purpose warship of the Fleet. Of course, these ships were only RDF in design, not manufacture. They belonged to Endmost. They belonged to James Calavone.

He wondered if Kester understood this. He could hear the man counting the ships as they flew along — he was well into the 'teens, and they weren't quite halfway down the line. Kester was rigid in his seat, gazing up at the new and swiftly growing fleet with eager eyes. Kester's scruples regarding the methods used to build these ships could be seen to fade as he watched them pass by in silent review. There was something in his friend's expression that reminded Calavone of a greedy child being told to take all the toys he could carry. After a considerable amount of time they came to the end of the review, and there before them were the next ships in production, partly covered with dull metal plating but mostly open mazes of frameworks and ducts, naked to the hard vacuum of space. The partial skeletons of two more could be seen not far off. The automated assembly systems surrounded the ships in progress, each a huge cocoon of bright metal meshwork studded with articulated robotic arms, all of which cast surreal shadows on the enclosed ships. Smaller robotic devices cruised within each cocoon, and inside the ships as well, and the sparks of welders burned like blue-white suns seen light years away. It was all done, of course, with inhuman speed and accuracy.

"Looking good," Kester said. He looked at Calavone and grinned. "Looking *damned* good!"

"Properly deployed, with the usual flotilla of gunboats and weapons stations hauled along — and we'll review that construction site tomorrow — these cruisers will be able to control the necessary systems," Calavone said. "Because of the way the nodes are distributed, we need to nail down eight of them in particular to control the DZ, or so says Artie." Calavone touched the board in front of him and a small map of the DZ unfolded between them, with eight small regions shaded soft amber within the mosaic of star systems.

"What of the overlapping Leyra'an systems?" Kester asked.

"So long as the Leyra'an sit tight, we'll leave those alone for the time being," Calavone replied.

"And if they don't?" Kester asked.

"If they don't, we're dead," Calavone replied. "We can't take on the Confederation and the Republic at the same time." Then, because he knew how Kester's mind worked, he added, "We aren't building for an offensive operation at the moment. The idea is to control this stretch of the Republic, here," and a string of systems on the Republic's side of the DZ turned blue. It was a set of ten contiguous systems within the Republic proper, through which all traffic in or out of the DZ passed. "If we focus on that and leave Leyra'an territory alone, they'll have no reason to become involved. We can only hope they see it that way. They've been content in the past with just recovering lost systems."

"That's true," Kester said. He sounded reluctant to admit it.

"So, along with the eight DZ systems, this region becomes a shield against Leyra'an influence. We'll be the arm holding that shield, our credibility having first been created when we rush in to aid the victims of the Commonwealth-Confederation 'conspiracy.'" He found himself grinning and added, "This will all, of course, be *very* inconvenient to certain business interests."

"Is this all working out fast enough?" Kester waved his right hand outward, toward the shipyard that seemed to hang over their heads. "I mean, you've already got people delivering our little surprise to the deezees."

Calavone laughed and prodded Kester's shoulder playfully. "Trust Artie. He's got the numbers. We're on schedule. We even have the defenses of Endmost upgraded, as planned."

"We might need that," Kester said. "More than likely the government or the Admiralty will see through your little plot, even if plain folks are fooled. They may not be in a mood to negotiate."

"True," said Calavone with a nod. "At least in the beginning, the government of the Republic *itself* will be the most realistic threat. I truly hope and pray that we don't end up fighting the RDF, but I'd be surprised if they don't come calling after we tip our hand. But either way, the only way to roll the dice involves a risk of detection. If this works, of course, being hidden away will offer no further advantage."

Kester nodded thoughtfully, then said, "Recruitment is going well, I hear."

"As well as we could hope, considering how extremely careful we need to be," Calavone replied. "We'll have the crews we need, though, these ships being somewhat more automated than their counterparts."

With their review completed, the autopilot turned them toward the station, far enough away that its rings were just discernible as such. Motes of light moved toward and away from the station as system traffic dealt with the general business of Endmost. A larger object slowly approached the docking pole of the station. Calavone knew it to be a transport bringing in the most recent batch of recruits.

"Speaking of conspiracies, how's the plot thickening, yonder?" and Kester waved toward the nearby node. "Are people buying into it?"

"Reports are sort of sketchy just now," Calavone replied. "And the full effects of our little gift are not yet being felt. I'm confident they will be more than eager to be liberated, by the time we're ready."

"What are the expected casualties?" Kester asked.

"Hard to predict," Calavone replied. "The bug was not designed to be lethal to Humans, though the symptoms *are* rather dramatic. The danger is that it might interact with those who actually have Founders', or are on the brink of developing it." He laughed briefly, then added, "Might actually scare some people to death, now that I think of it. The Leyra'an, however, will not fare so well."

"Really?"

"Oh, they won't get the disease. They'll get a shot of saline and be told it's the counterpart to the Human med. The *Humans* will get sick. The Leyra'an will be *conspicuously* unaffected. Combine that with the rumors we'll plant regarding alleged Commonwealth-Leyra'an collusion, and fevered imaginations ought to do the rest. And they *will* be feverish, no doubt about that!"

"That ought to clear the DZ systems of illegal visitors," Kester said. "And then we come in to save the day."

"In the proverbial nick of time," Calavone said with a grin and a nod. "And in so doing discredit not only our enemies, but the current regime. That should give us the leverage to hold the border systems, and give us an opening with those immediately inward, as well."

"You'll end up with the power base your father missed assembling."

"Yes," Calavone replied quietly. "We'll avenge him and the others, and accomplish what they could not. In the long run, the Republic will be in a stronger, more secure state. The fools currently in charge have suffered a failure of nerve when it comes to dealing with the scalies, and now the Commonwealth is in the frame. We need to assert the power and privilege of the Republic right now, and in no uncertain terms, or we will fade away and be assimilated by the Commonwealth. All that we've built will be for *nothing*."

"I need no convincing," Kester told him with a laugh.

"Think of it as a rehearsal," Calavone said. "For when I'm called upon to justify what we've done out here."

"They won't be giving you any medals for it, you know."

Calavone shook his head and said, "That's for sure. But in the long run, we'll be remembered as heroes." He looked out the canopy and said, more quietly, "We *will* be heroes."

There was a long, thoughtful silence in the cabin. The canopy was still clear, and the stars of the galaxy were easily seen. At last, Kester said, "The eighth system we've targeted, what's the name... Webster? It has direct access to Pr'pri." He turned in his seat. "Taking that one gives us short-term control of contact between the Commonwealth and the Republic, which could be very useful. It's also the site most likely to see a military response from the RDF. They won't simply surrender that access to us."

"I agree," said Calavone. "That's why I want you to take *Vengeance*, and a sizeable portion of the fleet out there. If it looks like an expensive fight, they may be willing to talk first. Once we've got them talking, time is on our side." He leaned forward and tapped a key, calling up data on a flat panel. "Yes, it's called Webster. I believe our people are there by now." Calavone hooked his thumbs, chest high, into the harness holding him to his seat. "Now we focus our efforts on getting the volunteers up to speed. We aren't far off from launching the campaign."

"Can't get started soon enough," Kester said half to himself.

"You know, that far into the DZ it's possible you'll run into folks from the Commonwealth. You *do* realize you need to treat them as noncombatants?"

"Jim, come on," and Kester held up his hands as if to forestall further comment. "I freely admit to screwing it up, that other time. I'm keeping Commonwealth ships and personnel out of the targeting system, whatever the hell else happens. If we find anyone, I will personally see to it they are protected from whatever might be going on."

"Good," said Calavone. "Ah, never mind me! I'm trying to keep track of so much shit these days, I'm automatically worried about anything that comes to mind."

"Nothing to apologize for, Jim," Kester said.

"After you have Webster, and only then," Calavone said, "we'll send a mission in to Pr'pri system. I'll have someone on your staff prepared to deal with that Trilateral Commission and offer the Commonwealth proper assurances regarding our intentions."

"You don't want me to go ahead and make contact?" Kester asked with one eyebrow raised.

Calavone turned from the boards to stare at Kester, who looked back at him with a bland lack of expression. "You're joking, right? Andy, you show up in Pr'pri system and this whole thing blows up in our faces! There will be people there from all three civilizations, and you're a wanted criminal in at least two of them."

"You know, it's not like I've forgotten recent history," Kester said, frowning angrily. "But Pr'pri... Oh, hell, you're probably right. As usual."

"I have no doubt about it. I need you running the fleet, but I need you to stay out of sight for the time being. I hope you understand why I'm requiring that of you," Calavone added. "It's not meant as an insult, or anything like that. Just a practical matter."

"Sure, Jim, I get it. Not to worry, okay?"

Calavone gave a short, hard laugh and said, "Who's worried?"

He realized just then that he *was* worried, but could not quite spot the source of his anxiety.

CHAPTER TWENTY-FOUR

Pr'pri System
Bartram Habitat

At long last the *Cygnet* returned from the Republic, and while it didn't bring Emerson's replacement, it did *not* return empty of consequences. Within hours of the ship's arrival, Drake Bristol called for an immediate emergency session of the Commission. He demanded that it be held behind closed doors, but the agreed-upon protocols did not allow for such a thing, however much he protested the announcement of the meeting. That the demand was made all the same was soon known outside the Trilateral Commission offices, and aroused both curiosity and rumor-mongering.

Family Rost'aht, minus Holm, elected to follow the special session over the net, and settled in for a holographic experience of the meeting. They gathered in the family room and let the projection system surround them. Gava'mi, who had by then experienced a holographic display, paid the entire affair no mind, and slept through it on a pile of tape-repaired cushions. Once the projection was up it was easy to forget they were not actually present. Holm, as a member of the Leyra'an delegation, attended the meeting physically. It was a single channel transfer, and no one in the chamber or gallery would be aware of the family's regard. Alicia requested stats, and amber letters and numbers glowed in the air to the left, showing among other things attendance, real and virtual. From the numbers that rapidly flickered to high orders of magnitude on the counter, everyone within the real-time broadcast limit was logged on to witness the meeting. The meeting would indeed be anything *but* secret.

Robert, Alicia, and Melep were crowded together in the larger of the two disc chairs. The two infants, recently fed, were mercifully sound asleep. The holosystem gave them a perspective from just above the floor-level seats. Melep had tucked herself as close to Alicia's left side as she could, with an arm around the Human woman's shoulders, fingers playing absently with a lock of Alicia's red hair. Robert knew this for a sign of anxiety on Melep's part. Alicia was as close to Robert as she could be, and clutched one of his hands tightly in hers. Their family room was replaced by a space in which people of both species milled about, seeking seats in haste as the chairman attempted to call the meeting to order.

"Please, find seats and settle down immediately," Yu Sei Ho said from his position at the bend of the negotiation table, facing the auditorium. Beside him sat Sarah, looking grave and anxious, dark eyes flashing, first at the crowd, then to Drake Bristol, and then back again. To the right of the Commonwealth delegation sat the Leyra'an, represented by Rost'aht Holm and Kr'nai Ersha. To the left of the chairman's position there was only Drake Bristol, who appeared pale and drawn, as if short on sleep, deeply anxious, or both. Clearly short of patience, Ho suddenly added, "The sergeant-at-arms will remove anyone still standing two minutes from now!"

The role of sergeant-at-arms, an archaic convention resurrected by the Republic, was on this occasion filled by a very large male Leyra'an. He bared his teeth at the invocation of his position. A full minute of Yu Sei Ho's final warning remained when the last audience member landed in a seat.

"Mr. Bristol," said Ho, "I yield the floor to you."

And Drake rose to his feet, jaw set and eyes glaring. He was not as shrill as he had been during the last session, but was every bit as abrupt as Robert had come to expect, and clearly angry.

"First of all, I must protest for the record the open and public nature of this meeting. It simply is not appropriate for the situation."

"Protest noted," Ho replied. "But as you well know, the Republic agreed to open meetings without exception. Your request to close the meeting is, itself, inappropriate."

Drake just stared at Ho for a moment, then said flatly, "I have been instructed to demand the immediate removal of Commonwealth vessels, involved in the unauthorized distribution of medical services, from the Republic's colonies along the common border with the Leyra'an Confederation of Clans. These ships, their crews and their activities, are a violation of the Republic's sovereignty. It will not be tolerated!"

For a moment there was hardly a sound in the hall as the other four Commissioners sat upright and stared at Drake in shocked bewilderment. Sarah's mouth literally fell open in surprise.

"There's no way that's true," Alicia muttered, shaking her head. "It can't be! The Commonwealth wouldn't pursue such a policy!"

"There are no ships from the Commonwealth operating in the Disputed Zone." Ho spoke flatly, in a tone that brooked no argument. "No ship of the Commonwealth is authorized to enter the Republic without its consent."

"Indeed," said Kr'nai Ersha, "they could hardly do such a thing and keep it secret, since the only known lines of traffic from the Commonwealth to the Republic run through this system."

"Other routes may have been discovered," Drake said. "We're all mapping new systems out here, seeking to understand where our respective territories connect.

Perhaps the Commonwealth has discovered a viable route."

"If that were so, we would know of it," Ho replied.

"You're sure of that?" Drake said with a trace of sarcasm. "Your government has never lied to you?"

"Never," said Ho. "Not since the establishment of space-born civilization. Of course, we don't have a government the way you mean, but that's beside the point. A decision to take such an action would literally take a year to be discussed between the nearest relevant system councils. Most of them don't even know yet that the Republic has demanded that we cut off our relationship with the Confederation."

"You're assuming the incursions weren't already planned long before any of the events to which you refer," Drake countered.

"Yes," Ho replied calmly, but with a look of growing anger on his face. "I am. And I am completely comfortable with that assumption."

Clearly exasperated, Drake changed tactics. "I'd be interested in hearing what you intend to do about this?"

"*Do* about it? Well, first I will spread the word to the neighboring systems and ask if any of them have noticed any unusual traffic. A moot point, since we have not yet mapped vectors leading from the Commonwealth into the Republic, that I'm aware of. An investigation *will* be made to determine whether or not over-zealous Commonwealth citizens are behind this, though I very much doubt this is the case. Beyond that, there's not much we *can* do from here."

"If you could give us permission to send a ship into the DZ..." Sarah started to say.

"I have no such authority," Drake replied. "I can only demand that these incursions be halted immediately." The shade of red that crept into Drake's features did not seem, to Robert, to be a healthy color.

"You'll need to direct your demand to those responsible, whoever they are," Sarah replied. "But *we* don't know who is behind these 'incursions.' Truly, Drake, we *don't* know what this is about, or who is behind it all. There's nothing we, or any Commonwealth official, can do."

"A question, if I may," Holm said. Until that moment he had directed his eyes down to the desk, where a faint glimmer indicated a data display kept discreetly horizontal.

"Please, feel free," Ho replied with a wave of his hand. He looked and sounded annoyed by it all.

"What makes you certain the Commonwealth is responsible for these incursions?" Holm asked.

"Do you doubt my word?" Drake demanded.

"I am doubtful of the information you were given," Holm replied mildly. He touched something on the pad before him and the image of a spaceship appeared in the air, as real-seeming as a solid model. "I have taken the scans of the offending ships that you provided as evidence and run a comparison with the Commonwealth record. The ships are all of this class, and are in appearance nearly identical to the heavy courier and transport vessels used by the Commonwealth. These are the very ships currently in use within the Confederation by Human medical crews. But the energy signatures of their engines do not match. Their propulsion systems most closely match those used by the Republic."

There was another loud murmur from the onlookers, and Yu Sei Ho warned them with a hard look.

"Are you sure of this, Holm?" Ersha asked.

"As sure as I can be, with such a cursory analysis," Holm replied with a shrug. "But based on that analysis I would say there is very little chance that these ships were built by the Commonwealth."

"Could this be something perpetrated by Humans living in the Confederation?" Ho asked Ersha quickly, before Drake could explode about the obvious inference.

"Unlikely," Ersha said. "But I cannot say it is impossible. Elements of our Human population have been known to provoke incidents in the border region, some of them resulting in serious consequences. But I have never heard of anything remotely this sophisticated or on such a large scale."

"Has the Republic confronted any of the people directly involved?" Holm asked.

"Not to the best of my knowledge," Drake replied. His face was returning to its normal pallor. "We are attempting to do so."

"Good," said Ho, with more than a trace of sarcasm this time. "We will investigate the matter from our respective sides, as well. May I suggest that the Republic share the results of their inquiry? It might help us determine the most useful approach to dealing with this bizarre situation."

"I will pass your suggestion along." The usual response to anything that suggested the Republic share data.

Robert's impression was that Drake had come to the meeting ready to roar, convinced of Commonwealth guilt and expecting the other delegates to stagger back under the weight of guilty consciences. No one reacted the way he expected, and then Holm had pointed out something that should have been obvious to those in the Republic responsible for Drake's evidence. Someone, Robert suspected, had been in too much of a hurry to do an obvious analysis. Now Drake was adrift. Sweat stood out on his brow, and his ruddy flush was replaced by an unhealthy pallor. There were words back and forth after that point, including the suggestion that this incident showed the need for better communication with the Republic.

"At the very least," said Ho, "we need to resume regular sessions. The sooner Mr. Worth's replacement comes... "

"I *am* his replacement," Drake said. "And in view of the current situation I have been instructed to resume the normal meeting schedule on my own, rather than wait for the selection process to be completed."

"Well," said Ho. "That's something of a relief. Thank you."

And with that the emergency meeting was adjourned and Drake turned on his heel, stalking away and beyond range of the pickup. The projection cut out and their family room and its furnishings reappeared.

"Who could possibly be responsible for this?" Melep wondered aloud. "I truly do not believe, not even for a moment, that the Commonwealth would do such a thing!"

"No," said Robert. "The Commonwealth is *not* behind this. I think Ho may be on to something, though. The evidence certainly does implicate the expatriate Humans."

"Whoever is doing this," Alicia replied, "has gone to considerable trouble to make it *look* like it's the Commonwealth." She frowned and added, "Gaia, I sure hope Holm's analysis holds up! If those *are* ships from the Commonwealth, we've got trouble coming!"

"I wish Emerson had brought the news," said Melep. Little Vurn fussed a bit and she hugged him closer. "There would have been a *discussion* of the situation, not a set of angry accusations. That Drake Bristol — can you imagine him getting along with us the way dear Emerson did?"

"Not quickly," Alicia replied. "He's afraid, you know. Most of them are. So afraid of the changes coming their way."

"You are likely right," Melep replied. "Whether the changes are for better or worse, it will be a strange and frightful thing for the Republic. And fear so often leads to questionable deeds."

Robert looked at the children, both of whom he thought of as his sons, and considered the universe into which they had been born. "Something isn't adding up," he muttered. "I don't think the Republic is putting us on with this, and yet I can't bring myself to believe either the Commonwealth or the Confederation is behind it. I wonder if those people... What did Emerson call that faction in the DZ? The ones who wanted to break away?"

"Secessionists," Alicia said. "Pretty sure that's the word he used."

"What if these people are up to something? Maybe with help from Humans in the Confederation?" He looked from his wife to his sister-in-law. "They've been a problem for both sides for years. And according to

Emerson, it's recently gotten worse. This might be part of a plot to break away from the Republic."

"I suppose they could have gotten exterior ship design specs from data already given to the Leyra'an," Alicia said. "But that doesn't make sense, either. The way things work in the Republic... Well, how *did* they build these ships so quickly?"

"The Confederation and the Commonwealth could pull that off," Robert said. "Not the Republic."

"It would take a much smaller effort to alter existing ships to *look* like Commonwealth designs," said Melep.

"That would explain the power emission signatures," Alicia said. She hugged Paul to her breast, looking alarmed. "Imagine all of this blowing up on us, because of a small group of fanatics!"

"Let's hope cooler heads than Drake's prevail," Robert said.

CHAPTER TWENTY-FIVE

Webster System
Disputed Zone

They found a hotel to their liking and checked in, then spent the hours before the station's night cycle strolling and taking in the sights of an unfamiliar place. That night they spent locked in a small but comfortable room, shutting out the strangeness and risk of their mission and simply being together, a thing Wirolen made very easy to do.

After breakfast, at the same restaurant but with a surly male server who seemed utterly resistant to Wirolen's charms, they went to the first level of the upper decks running along the wall of the torus, and found that an enormous crowd had already lined up for entrance to the hastily arranged clinic, set in a long row of bare, beige offices with only token shrubs and flowers flanking the doors for decoration. From the looks of the citizens queued up for the treatment, many holding blankets and pillows, no small number had held their place in line by spending the night and sleeping on the deck. John and Wirolen were somewhat and deliberately overdressed, John in a dark blue, expensively tailored suit, with a pale blue shirt open at the neck. The style was considered uncouth in the Republic. Wirolen's skirt was short enough and blouse tight enough to be just a touch provocative. Gold bands glittered on her arms as she clung to John. He was the picture of a young man, well-to-do and with perhaps a bit more money than sense, flaunting a forbidden relationship. A man not to be taken too seriously. The ruse seemed to work, for the only second glances they received were from men who did double-takes as Wirolen passed by.

Arm-in-arm they strolled, and did so for quite a few minutes, the line already being very long, and obviously growing longer. Every sort of person imaginable on a Republic station was to be seen. John found himself wondering, at first facetiously, what percentage of the way around the torus the line of eager Humans stretched. As he and Wirolen continued to walk along, however, it ceased to be a joke. The quiet of the previous afternoon was suddenly clear to him. A substantial percentage of the station's population stood in that line, anxious for their chance at what was reputed to be an indefinite life span, lived in perfect health. The crowd was quite animated, but very well behaved. Folk who needed to leave the line for a restroom facility found their spots held by their neighbors, and vendors drawn to the scene cruised the line selling refreshments.

Snatches of conversation drifted to their ears as they strolled by, the most that could be gleaned from the sound of so many voices speaking all at once. Semi-informed speculations on how the largess of the Commonwealth would change the economic state of the Republic were most common, mixed with expressions of hope that the new med tech would eliminate the dreaded Founders' disease, the great multi-faceted health scourge of the Republic. John found himself gritting his teeth in rising anger, knowing as he did that the Commonwealth's medical technology *would* do so. These people were doomed to disappointment, but he dared not warn them. He had nothing to offer as proof that would not lead to the arrest of himself and Wirolen.

"They call it 'Treatment' and not 'Cure,'" Wirolen breathed into his ear, speaking softly in Leyra'an.

"I hear it," John replied quietly. "Another sign things are not as they seem."

Anyone who noticed the exchange would have seen a young Leyra'an woman playing affectionately with a Human male. Some who did so frowned in disapproval. But most, when caught looking, merely nodded slightly, with here and there a Human male acknowledging John's apparent good fortune with a smile or a wink. He played his role, grinning and winking back at them, or simply looking smug, well aware of the reputation Leyra'an women had for being of a passionate nature.

They think I'm a lucky man, he thought, and drew Wirolen a bit closer, which elicited the Mona Lisa smile that always raised his blood pressure. *They have no idea.*

At last they came to the head of the line, where the stream of excited people vanished one by one through the double glass doors of an ordinary-looking office suite. John looked more closely and realized that the suite was actually a public clinic. It made perfect sense, that the station's medical staff would be monitoring the process. Those on the way out were, if anything, more excited than those waiting to get in. In fact, they seemed nearly euphoric, almost as if...

"Whatever they are receiving in there, they certainly are enjoying it," Wirolen observed. "John, look at their eyes! They are drunk!"

"Yes," John replied. The behavior of the recipients in no way matched that of the Leyra'an or of the lone Human example he himself represented. He was absolutely convinced now that some sort of fraud was being spread through the Disputed Zone. He steered Wirolen just so, into the path of two giggly women who held to each other as if to maintain balance. There was a brief, tangled collision, with Wirolen clutching at one of the pair to keep her from tumbling to the concrete pavement. "Whoa! Terribly sorry, ladies," John said. "Wasn't paying enough attention. Sorry for that."

"S'okay!" one said. "We'll just heal up them bruises, quick as a wink!"

"They shoot you yet?" the other asked, and then burst out laughing.

"Not yet," John said as he reclaimed Wirolen's arm. "Soon, though. Thought I'd wait until the crowd thinned a bit."

"You'll love it when you do. Don't know how long this feeling lasts, but — damn!"

And giggling like young girls, the two middle-aged women staggered away.

"John," said Wirolen. "I do *not* like the way this feels."

"Neither do I, *sip'ya*," John replied as he watched the women depart. "This is all wrong. Bears no resemblance to what we saw when the Commonwealth came to your home system."

"Who is doing this?" she asked. "And *why* are they doing it?"

"First guess would be some charlatan trying to run a scam, but we've heard stories like this from elsewhere, in multiple systems. Something on that scale doesn't fit a scam. And apparently no one is being charged for this alleged service."

"That works with the fiction that the Commonwealth is here." Wirolen glanced back over her shoulder to where the line of people vanished through the double glass doors. "They are no more interested in the markers your people count than my people are."

"And that leaves the answer to the question of who is doing this dangling out of reach," said John.

"Do you still mean to join the line?" Wirolen asked.

"Not without knowing what it is they're shooting into people," John replied.

"The Cure you carry would not protect you?"

John stopped so abruptly that he swung her around to face him. "I don't know for sure, but it's a good bet it will. Didn't Ursula say it augmented the liver's ability to deal with toxins?"

"I don't recall specifically," Wirolen admitted, "but her list certainly was comprehensive."

He looked back at the line for a moment, then nodded. "Let's go back and find the end of it, then."

"Uh, *sip'ya'a*, I did not mean literally join *that* line. Folk at its end will surely not see the inside of the clinic this day."

John laughed and drew her close for a moment. "You need to stay with me forever, my dear, or I will surely miss all the obvious answers."

"You would also most likely starve to death, since you obviously cannot tell time!"

And so, in a little while, they found themselves back at the restaurant from the day before, seated outside this time at a round, metal, mesh-topped table. The server from the day before came out and greeted them with a faint smile.

"Has business picked back up, Eliza?" John asked.

"Not really, no. Why do you ask?"

"You look a little tired," he explained. "So I thought things had gotten busier."

"It's that Commonwealth medicine," Eliza replied. Strands of pale hair drifted around her face, escapees from the pony tail that held the rest in check. "Got me so high that I had trouble sleeping. I have the feeling I'll sleep like the dead, tonight, though."

"Ah, so there *are* some side effects, then," said John.

"Well, they did warn me, so it didn't come as a surprise. Said I'd feel a bit giddy at first, like I'd been drinking too much, and then a bit edgy. After that, back to business as usual, except that I'll never be sick again." She tilted her head and asked, "So, you haven't been there, yet?"

"Been there," John replied. "Didn't like the looks of the line. Must have been half the station population up there!"

"This business has pretty much shut down the station! I mean, look at this place!" The server waved her hand around at the deserted tables. "We're usually running our butts off trying to keep up, this time of day. But right now, everyone is on the upper decks, trying to get their dose. And it's a good thing folks are behaving, 'cause station management can't round up enough Security to do traffic control!"

"Any idea how long they plan to stay station side?" John asked.

"They didn't say exactly," she replied. "Something about staying as long as it took. They are also training staff here so we can manage the rest of the system's population without them."

"Does this, um, stuff cure Founders'?" asked John, trying to sound as if he feared what the answer would be.

She nodded, eyes becoming a bit teary. "Yes," she said. "Too late for my mother, but no one else will go that way!" When Wirolen reached up to put a hand on the woman's forearm, the server patted the scaled hand and forced a smile. "Now, what'll it be today?"

It turned out to be another round of sausage dishes. The server went off into the restaurant proper, though not quite as briskly as the day before.

"Whoever is doing this does know something about the real thing," Wirolen said.

"Just enough to fool anyone who has heard rumors of what's happening in the Confederation," John replied with a nod. "It'll be interesting to get up there and see things for myself."

"You *will* back out if there's a risk?" Wirolen asked.

And he nodded firmly. "Yes. Count on it. I trust the Commonwealth, but I very much doubt they saw this coming when they designed the Cure."

"Good," she said quietly. Wirolen glanced around, then spoke very softly in her own language, stroking his arm to give the appearance of an affectionate moment, when her words were anything but. "John, what if the *Republic* is doing this?" she asked. "They resist the changes that would be brought by what the Commonwealth wishes to share, especially the Cure. But the Cure would be such a blessing, that soon it will be demanded. What if your government seeks a way to discredit the Commonwealth... ?"

"That thought has plagued me ever since we got here," he said softly. "Because you're right. There are elements in the Republic who would do this much, and worse. If that's the case, well, God save us! What are they *really* giving these people?"

"And what will it do to them, in the end?" Wirolen said. For just a moment the tips of her teeth could be seen.

CHAPTER TWENTY-SIX

Pr'pri System
Bartram Habitat

"We need direct access to the situation," Holm told them a few days later, as they leaned back in their chairs following their evening meal. They had chosen to dine outside, on the upper garden patio. The elf lights gleamed softly around them. Out in the deep twilight of the habitat, clusters of tiny lights, like faint stars, marked other residences. Their inverted world was quiet and peaceful. "But rather than escort a team from the Commonwealth into the border region to see what is happening, the people here from the Republic have yet again deferred the matter to higher authority."

"Your analysis of the ships held up," Robert guessed.

"*Yia,*" Holm replied. "They are now blaming the problem on dissidents living in the DZ, and calling it an internal matter. With none-too-vague hints of Leyra'an collusion."

"It's as Emerson said," Alicia muttered. "They'll hold us out as long as possible, any way they can, no matter *what* is happening."

Holm sighed and ducked his head toward his chest, as if weary. "They cannot go on that way forever," he said in a low voice. "News of the gift you have given the Leyra'an has surely traveled into the DZ by now. No matter what is happening there at the moment, the truth of the Cure will one day be known. And then the DZ will explode!"

"I've never gotten around to looking up why that is," Alicia said. "Why is such traffic allowed, while the two realms are in conflict?"

"From our side, it is a lack of desire to inhibit contact. We have nothing against the people of the Republic, just those who govern that realm, who have turned us into make-believe monsters. From their side, it's a matter of logistics and corruption." Holm leaned forward and retrieved his mug of ale, then relaxed again. "Maintenance of their fleet puts a significant strain on that contrived system of wealth of theirs. That limits the number of ships available for patrol. Complicating the matter further, the boundary is no simple line. The Confederation and Republic expanded into each other before contact was made. There are eleven systems I know of that were settled by the Republic well within the general sphere of Confederation space, and seven by my people inside what is technically the Republic. There are many more systems and dark masses mapped but as yet unsettled or otherwise used. This all adds up to making control of the area costly, as the Republic measures such things."

"You mentioned corruption?" Robert asked.

"Yes, and here is the part that puzzles most of my folk, and perhaps yours as well," Holm replied. "Humans travel from the disputed region and acquire goods from the Leyra'an. All manner of things, from foods and beverages to works of art. It is a violation of Republic law to own, much less traffic in Leyra'an goods. For some reason this restriction endows such items with enormous value, by their standards. Those who smuggle such are well rewarded, and in turn reward authorities who might otherwise enforce the ban, but choose not to." He raised his hands, palms out, in a Leyra'an shrug. "Please, do not ask me to explain why they do as they do."

"Isn't it counterproductive to allow this?" Robert asked. "Doesn't it exacerbate the situation?"

"That point has been made, many times," Melep admitted. "But the counter-argument is very strong. The more contact we have with the Republic, the more obvious it is that we are not monsters after all. The hope is that this understanding will reduce support for the war."

"It may be working, since support for the war appears to be slipping away," Holm added. "But there has been an unintended consequence. Most of the Disputed Zone systems welcome the Leyra'an, and a movement to withdraw from the Republic and establish a new state, one that can work openly with the Confederation, now exists."

"John told me the Republic has suffered civil strife in the past," Robert said. "He feared it was about to happen again. The Republic at war with itself. Civil war, he called it."

"It has been slow to come because we've let it be known the Confederation will play no part in such a thing," Holm said. "We will not aid those who would break away. If it becomes a conflict, we will stand aside and let the people of the Republic find their own path to a resolution."

"Since we will not intervene, these rebellious Humans are left with few military resources," Melep said. "Holm is likely right about it. We may have prevented a civil war by refusing to take the side of the Secessionists, as they are called."

"I do hope your friend John is wrong about all of that," Alicia said. She wrapped her arms around herself as if shivering. "A civil war sounds — ugly."

"We had only just begun to know Humanity at the time the internal strife occurred," said Holm. "No Leyra'an witnessed any of it unfold. But the tales we were told of those dark days are grim stories indeed!"

"The people of the Republic have many things to be proud of," said Melep. "That episode is not one of them."

"So, the region between the Republic and the Confederation is volatile. Reports indicate much unrest," said Holm. "Even Emerson admitted that control of the Republic's systems in the Disputed Zone hangs by a slender wire."

"And now, from that same region of space we get a story of illicit intervention by the Commonwealth," Alicia said. She deliberately kept her voice low, to avoid disturbing sleeping infants, in their crib nearby. "And that just can't be."

"I agree," said Holm. "And the initial reports brought to us by Drake Bristol make it difficult to believe this is a fabrication on the part of the government of the Republic. The idea that people in the DZ are responsible looks stronger as each day passes."

"Do the Leyra'an who travel to and from the border zone tell the same story?" Robert asked.

"An inquiry has been made," Holm said. "It is, of course, too soon for a response. That will take at least another week."

Melep gazed with bright Leyra'an eyes to where the babies slept soundly together, small arms around each other. Vurn rolled away from his brother and began to fuss. Melep went to the crib and lifted him to her breast. "We brought them into this life with a wish for peace. Was that too much to ask?"

"This all *is* worrisome," Holm agreed. "But do not give up hope on that wish, yet, *sip'ya!*"

"No," said Robert. "No, it isn't hopeless. Consider that the Republic came to us and shared this, albeit as an accusation. But they brought it to the Commission before taking direct action. At least *some* willingness to try to work with us has developed. And that's got to count for something!"

"They wanted to provoke a response, to better measure our honesty," Holm said, in quiet disagreement. "*Believe* that the session recording has been analyzed for voice stresses, with every gesture and facial muscle movement taken into account! The response did not provide the easy answer they sought, I am sure, which leaves them few alternatives. This will surely bring their situation in the DZ to a breaking point. The Republic's fleet is almost certainly being readied, as we speak, for the pacification of their border systems. The current regime will not allow those systems to break away!"

"Whoever is responsible, they've provided an excuse for military action," Alicia said. "I wonder... Might it be the Republic itself behind this after all? Maybe some faction using the dissent in the DZ?"

"A manufactured crisis?" Robert asked.

"Why not?" Alicia replied. "Their government, as Emerson told us, is as divided as their people. It seems reasonable to me that one faction might try to force the issue."

"'Reasonable' is not a word I would use for it," Melep said.

"No argument," Alicia replied.

"Someone or something associated with the Republic, probably from within the DZ, will surely turn out to be the answer," Holm said. "I would, as Emerson so often put it, bet on that."

"So, now all we can do is wait?" Robert asked.

"That, and increase our military presence in the Confederation's part of the DZ," Holm replied. "Acceptance is the heart of the Way, and in this case, we must accept the necessity of waiting. But we will wait carefully."

A soft tone chimed, announcing a visitor at their door, downstairs. "Are we expecting someone?" Alicia asked. The answers were shrugs and a quiet "No" from Holm. So Alicia called up the house system to see who was at the door. An image appeared over the table, revealing their visitor. Drake Bristol stood there, looking pale and nervous.

"Mr. Bristol," Alicia said, more in surprise than seeking confirmation.

"Yes, ma'am," came a quietly tentative reply. "Forgive the intrusion, but if this is a bad time... ?"

"Not at all," Alicia said. "We're upstairs and outside. Just take the stairway to your left and you'll find us." And moments later the man appeared, in the flesh. They all rose to welcome him.

"Drake," Holm said, standing with the rest of them and bowing, the simple courtesy of a Leyra'an householder to a visitor. "Be at home among us."

"Um, thanks. Thank you," Drake replied, and took the chair offered to him. He perched there on the edge of the seat, hands on his knees, back rigid, obviously very ill at ease. "I imagine you folks are, um, surprised to see me here?"

"That would be an understatement," Holm replied gently. "But that does not make you unwelcome. Please, be at ease, and tell us why you have come."

Drake looked around at them all, made a visible effort not to stare when he realized Melep was nursing little Vurn, and turned to look elsewhere, down and to one side. That put him face to face with an inquisitive han'anga, who warbled happily, a sound that clearly did not reduce Drake's stress levels. "What in God's name is that?" he blurted.

"Family pet," Robert replied with a light laugh. "A han'anga. He just assumes that anyone who comes in here is a new friend to play with." Seeing how ill at ease the Beast made the man, especially when Gava'mi sat up and placed a taloned forepaw gently on Drake's thigh, Robert said quietly in Leyra'an, "*Gava'mi, ets ets, no'eh prioha.*" Gava'mi looked from master to visitor and back, then ambled into the other room and leaped into his pile of cushions, from which he watched the unexpected visit unfold.

Drake drew a deep breath as if to steady himself, grimaced, and then said bluntly, "Emerson says you cured him of Founders' disease." He looked straight at Holm.

"That was not my doing," Holm replied. "Our friends from the Commonwealth assisted his recovery."

"Is Emerson well?" Alicia asked, obviously concerned.

"Yes, ma'am, he's fine. Or he was, last I saw of him. I have no reason to believe otherwise." He sighed and looked at the floor. "I have Founders'. The blood form." He paused, then added quietly, "Stage five."

"How many stages are there?" Robert asked, frowning.

"Five." Drake was more uncomfortable by the moment. "Seems the younger you are when the blood form develops, the quicker you, uh — decline. I thought I was just working too hard, running myself down, but... " And he trailed off with a shrug.

"How long ago were you diagnosed?" Alicia asked.

"Less than a week," Drake replied. "I had a fainting spell, and now I keep getting dizzy, among other things. The ship's surgeon ran a diagnostic, gave me the bad news." He finally looked up. "Accepting medical treatment from the Commonwealth isn't allowed, you know."

"So we have heard," Melep said gently.

"Um, yes, well... Let's say my perspective on that matter has been changed." His gaze shifted down and locked on the tiled floor.

"How is it they let you loose long enough to seek us out?" Robert asked.

"The surgeon said he's tired of people dying of Founders' when he knows there's a cure. He, ah, well... He filed a fake report and suggested that I use my Commonwealth contacts to get help."

"And you are hoping to be cured before anyone finds out?" Holm asked.

"Yes, sir," Drake replied quietly. "If you people are willing to risk helping me."

"There is no risk on our part," Alicia said. "I can arrange treatment. It'll reset your immune system and restore current genetic abnormalities without changing the rate at which you age. There will be no evidence that you were ever ill. Could probably do it within the hour, in fact. That way you won't have to risk a second unauthorized visit."

"Is that what you did for Emerson?" Drake asked. No one replied, and after an awkward moment of silence, he smiled ruefully and muttered, "Right. Forget I asked."

"I'll set things up," Alicia said, and quietly opened a com link.

"And I will log your visit here as a semi-official diplomatic overture," said Holm. "Those have been common enough in the past, and under the current circumstances it will seem quite plausible. It should provide a convenient excuse, if this foray is questioned."

Drake looked up, obviously puzzled and, to Robert's eyes at least, a trifle suspicious. "You would do that? For an enemy?"

No one spoke for a moment, then Holm said gently, "I am not your enemy, Drake. You have no enemies in this room. No one from the Republic does."

"Done," said Alicia. "If we leave now we should reach the clinic at about the same time as my colleagues."

"Let's use the downstairs access to the lifts," Robert said. "Probably wouldn't be a good idea to be seen taking the tram over to the clinic."

Drake put his hand over his mouth and closed his eyes, and for a moment Robert thought the man was about to cry. Then he drew himself up, nodded, and rose to follow Alicia and Robert into the house and downstairs, safely out of sight.

CHAPTER TWENTY-SEVEN

Webster System
Leyra'an-Republic Disputed Zone

John and Wirolen attended to the refueling and
resupply of the *Eli'ahtna*, then played tourist for a few
days, killing time while waiting out the persistent line of
stationers. Nothing they did was out of the ordinary for
casual visitors to a station on the Republic's frontier.
John watched with interest the interactions between
Humans and Leyra'an, and noted how rarely anything
like friction took place between the two species. They
overheard bold talk of breaking free from the Republic,
on the concourse and in restaurants and bars. The story
going around, based unfortunately on the truth as John
knew it, was that the Republic had initially balked at
accepting Commonwealth med tech, including the
nanomed that could reverse and even prevent Founders'
disease in its many manifestations. The deezees seemed
to believe the story easily enough, and were quick to
express righteous indignation.

They saw bright red graffiti, the letter S for Secession,
being scrubbed from walls and lift tubes on a daily basis.
One such removal was in progress as they walked

casually away from a set of shops, in which Wirolen had once again tried to grasp the concept of buying things with money. "You are troubled, *sip'ya'a*," Wirolen said after watching him observe the cleanup. Since most residents of the station did so, they spoke a mix of the Human and Leyra'an languages.

"*Et na, seth'a piata, nia,*" he replied. *I fear dark times are ahead.*

Wirolen ran her hand up and down inside his arm as they walked, then clasped his hand tightly. "That may well be, *sip'ya'a*, and there will be nothing we can do to prevent it."

"No, there won't," he said with a sigh. Then, trying for a lighter tone, he added, "Soon we will be home, doing what little we can by providing others the information they will need to keep this mess out of the Confederation. It will have to be enough."

"Do you really think of it that way?" Wirolen asked. She pointedly did not look at him as she spoke.

"That it'll be enough? No, not really, but... "

"I meant the part about going *home,*" she said, glancing up at him for just a moment. "Do you really see Eb'ara Kai as *home?*" Her voice dropped in a way that, to Human ears, was suggestive of shyness.

"*Eh'fara nar mo,*" John replied, squeezing her hand in his. "Home is where we are together."

"*Aza had'na.*" *I am content*, she said.

The sound of business and conversation along the busy concourse had been rising in volume as they spoke, and in that quietly sentimental moment they shared, it became intrusive. Somewhere nearby voices were raised. As they paused and listened more carefully, it was obvious concern and even alarm were being expressed. Passers-by were gravitating toward something anti-spinward of where they stood. "There's a public news terminal over that way, I think," John said. "Let's follow along and see if this is a reaction to a report."

It was not far, and what they found was a holographic newscast being looped over and over, a well-dressed young woman at a low desk, calmly assuring the public that, while the Commonwealth had departed, they had first trained station medical staff, and left sufficient supplies to finish treating all residents. As people arrived in waves, and departed in small groups, comments changed from, "They've left?" to "I hope they left enough," and many variations on those themes. To the question of *why* the Commonwealth mission had pulled out so soon, and so suddenly, no answer was forthcoming, but the buzz of conversation quickly passed from alarm to the sort of puzzled speculation that would keep conversations alive in bars and restaurants through the night.

"Looks like I blew my chance to do that bit of recon," John said to Wirolen as soon as they were far enough away from the terminal to avoid being easily overheard.

"So it seems. John, this feels even less right than before, if that is possible."

"It has the feel of a plot moving forward, doesn't it?"

"We should leave, too," Wirolen said.

"Our flight plan is for departure forty-eight hours from now," John replied. "Changing that right now might look suspicious to the station master's office, with the alleged Commonwealthers moving out in such a hurry."

"*Yia,*" she said, seeming a bit reluctant.

John nodded and said, "Can't say I blame you. But out here in the DZ, calling attention to yourself by doing something unexpected is a very bad policy."

"Well, if we are to behave normally, let us do something normal, like having dinner."

"The usual place?"

"*Yia.*"

It was halfway around the station from there, so they found their way to a tube station and caught the first capsule passing in the spinward direction. The capsule was moderately crowded, a mix of folk coming home from the day cycle work shift. Some were still a bit high on the medicine dispensed by the recently departed medical team; others were discussing the lack of reason given by the Commonwealth for their sudden departure. Mixed in were people who seemed weary, as if the day had been long. Wirolen was the only Leyra'an aboard, and attracted some attention. A dark-haired man, graying at the temples, surrendered his seat to her, and attached himself to a handhold, giving John a nod when the two made eye contact.

John almost did a double-take, and barely restrained himself. The courteous gentleman had an odd combination of flushed cheeks set against an overall pallor, and sweat beaded his nose and forehead. And there was a small but angry-looking red welt on his neck just below the right ear. He glanced down at Wirolen, but if she had taken note of the man's obviously feverish condition, she gave no sign. And the gentleman in question left the tube capsule at the next stop.

Two stops later, one stop before their own, a woman boarded with two pre-teen girls in tow. The woman seemed out of sorts and spoke sharply to one of the girls, then pressed her hand to her left temple, as if plagued by a headache. For some reason, this too caused John a feeling of concern, though he was damned if he could put a finger to what troubled him.

Came their stop, and they found themselves back on the concourse, in the same strip of shops, offices, and eateries they had found the day of their arrival. Wirolen wrapped her arm around him, as was her habit when they strolled anywhere. The outside tables were all taken, so they strolled through the door, and found themselves greeted by the same waitress. Once again, Eliza looked and sounded tired.

"Not sleeping any better?" John asked as she led them to the same table they had used on several visits.

"It's that obvious?" she replied. She scratched absently at the back of her head, and then did it again. "But I've been sort of off the mark for a day or so, now. Must be that medicine taking hold. They said I'd go way up, then sort of drop a bit before things sorted out."

"*Ahs'ah impris!*" Wirolen gasped, and caught at Eliza's arm from where she now sat. "What happened to your elbow?"

"I... I don't have any idea," Eliza said, looking with wide eyes to where Wirolen indicated. "You'd think I'd have felt that, if I banged into something!"

"It almost looks like a burn," John said, examining the ugly red lesion.

Even as it came to him that it looked just like the welt on their fellow tube passenger's neck, and that Eliza looked a touch feverish, the woman scratched her head again. Her hand came away red with her blood on her fingertips. "What?" she gasped, gaping at her hand. "What? What?"

John came to his feet and stepped around behind her. "Hold still and let me see," he said. "And calm down." Her hands were shaking. Wirolen picked up a napkin and wiped the blood from the girl's fingers, removing the visual stimulus that so clearly upset her. "Do you feel any pain back here?" he asked, searching through hair dampened by perspiration and a small amount of blood.

"N... No," she stammered. "It itches. A lot."

Just at her hairline John found an ugly, bleeding sore, sunken in the center. "You should get to medical, right now."

"Is it Founders'?" She turned to look at him, blue eyes round and fearful. "Do I have Founders'?"

"No," John said firmly, knowing it might calm her even as he cast about for a way to motivate her to seek help without simply giving her something else to fear. Before he could go further an elderly man in a pale green suit and a white shirt joined them.

"What's going on here?" he demanded, frowning.

"I think I'm sick, boss. I think I need to see a doctor."

"Let me see," he said gruffly. He looked where John indicated and shuddered. "Yes, okay, why don't you take off and... "

Someone outside screamed, a high, thin wailing. And then kept screaming.

Somehow, Wirolen was out the door ahead of him, even though she was seated when the outcry arose. John followed, the server — hand to the back of her head — and her employer trailing along behind. A crowd had gathered around one of the outside tables, near which a young man lay on the ground, shivering and twitching. A girl knelt by his head, now gasping and crying instead of screaming. Wirolen dropped down beside her and asked,

"What happened to him? What did you see?" She shook the girl hard and said, *"Answer!"*

"He wasn't feeling well. Said he felt hot. Then he started yelling that it hurt and he fell down! And look at him! Look at his face! Oh, God, please, help us!"

John looked, and muttered "God save us!" a prayer to match that of the young woman. People around them were already drawing back and turning away, too unsettled by what they saw to remain nearby. The man's face should have been fair-skinned, to judge by the pale color of his hair, but instead was a pasty gray with a sickly blue tint. His face and arms were sprinkled with small lesions that oozed blood, and were spreading and opening even as they watched. Sweat soaked his clothing, and he gasped for breath as he lay trembling on the green concrete of the concourse.

Around them, mixed in the buzz of conversation, were exclamations of fear as people saw that they had welts on their hands and arms similar to, if not yet as frightful as those of the young man on the ground. The young victim of the bizarre plague that seemed to be spreading through Webster Station opened his eyes, coughed, and gasped out the word, "Help... "

"Easy, lad. I know it's hard, but you need to calm down," John said sternly. "The good people around you are praying for you, and help is on the way." He glanced up at the proprietor, who nodded vigorously. The young man's companion had by then collapsed into Wirolen's arms, clinging to her, eyes wide but unfocused. Wirolen spoke softly to her, as if comforting a child awakened from a bad dream.

And help did arrive then, a med cart that rolled to a hard stop nearby. Four men in white uniforms hustled over, gruffly ordering the crowd back and out of the way. They set to work on the victim immediately, checking his signs with a hand-held scanner and then hoisting the victim onto the back of the cart, strapped to a stretcher. There was another person strapped down there as well.

"What's going on?" John asked the ranking officer of the med crew.

"Wish to hell I knew," the white-clad man said as he watched his crew stow their new passenger. He looked and sounded harried, distracted. "People calling in all over the station. Some with ugly spots, some at death's door like this lad. We're already approaching emergency capacity limits." His com chirped and he set a hand to his ear. "Anders. Yes. Well, call up second shift and put third on standby, dammit! Look, just do it! Fuck the union, they can file a complaint!" He rushed off to the cart, hopping aboard even as it raced off, lights flashing and siren wailing.

"It's not Founders'," a woman standing nearby said, and it was not actually a question. "This isn't Founders'."

"No," John replied. "This is something else altogether." Seeing that Wirolen had released her hold on the frightened girl, John took Wirolen by the arm and led her away. Around them, the crowd on the concourse grew larger, and voices from it rose quickly in shrill panic. "Whatever is happening, it's developing quickly. Suspicions be damned, we have to get out of here. *Now!*"

"Did we leave anything in the room that we would miss?" she asked.

"Nothing of mine," he replied.

"Good." Wirolen pulled a round, palm-sized tablet from her jacket pocket and touched it. "The ship is making final preps. Let's go!"

"Station master's office will... "

"They will know nothing until we announce departure," she assured him. "The onboard system is now providing false data to cover what we are doing."

John flashed her a smile and said, "I should've known."

"We have an external dock, so there will be nothing they can do to prevent us from leaving, short of barring access."

"And that might be a problem," he admitted. "If the station master suspects a contagion, he is obliged to lock things down, to prevent spread of the agent to other locations."

"If we can get aboard," she replied, "I can get us out. We should hurry!"

Which they did, taking tubes and, for John's part at least, praying the station's authorities would not immediately implement quarantine procedures. They saw station security at tube transfers, and everywhere frightened people heading for homes or medical facilities. It was far from being a riot, but it was not exactly quiet and orderly. They were in the core and headed to the docks when an announcement blasted from every public address speaker, including the one in their capsule.

"All station residents are to return to their homes immediately. Do not go to a medical facility, as these are currently at capacity. Contact emergency services if you are experiencing any of the following symptoms... " A list was read that matched what John and Wirolen had seen. *"Assistance will come to you as soon as possible. Please remain as calm as you can under the circumstances. Further announcements will be made as soon as information is available."* The message restarted, beginning what John was sure would prove to be an endless series of repetitions.

"Have you noticed that only Humans have this disease?" Wirolen asked.

"Hadn't thought about it, but yes, you're right. Only Humans."

The sensation of weight ebbed as they neared the core. The tube capsule inverted and headed toward the docks, and in moments they floated free of the floor, gripping take-holds and aiming their feet at the panel that now glowed near them. There they would touch off when the tube slowed to a stop, landing on their feet, so to speak. And in a matter of moments they felt a drift toward the panel as the tube capsule decelerated. When the all-clear chimed, they left the capsule and entered the cold, bright docking facility, quickly retracing their route back to the hatch opening to their ship. There were only a few dock workers scattered about, with a somewhat larger than normal contingent of station security on hand. No one stood between them and their hatch, which by some miracle showed green status lights. They made a straight-line jump, and reached it before anyone hailed them, then ignored the shouted command to halt and ducked through the hatch. A short haul down the tube, and they were in their ship.

"Get us out of here!" John said as he fastened the safety harness to his seat.

"The lockdown order just came through," Wirolen said. "They've cut off access to the clamps."

"Not good."

"Hold tight!" And she flashed him a feral, toothy grin. There was a loud, sharp bang, as if something had struck the hull, followed by the vertiginous sensation of a ship drifting quickly to one side. "We are leaving!"

"What just happened?" John demanded.

"I blew up the connection," she said, with the same frightful smile. "They locked the clamps, and I used explosive bolts to jettison our docking probe." She glanced at the golden yellow trouble light flashing rapidly on the boards before her. "Station has registered a protest."

"The node, best possible speed."

"We are already on our way, *sip'ya'a*," she replied. "Please leave the flying to me."

"Yes, ma'am... "

"I have a vector for our point of origin set and... " Alarms shrilled, cutting her off. "Incoming traffic through the node!"

Before John could react, the proximity alert lost its mind. He stared in shock at the readouts as data streamed in from the fleet of ships that suddenly surrounded the node in a standard envelopment pattern as they emerged. The display sprang to life and he could see them. Warships, all of them — there were seven — cruisers of the design used by the RDF. There were no beacons, no ID signals at all, but having served aboard several examples of the most commonly built warship in the RDF fleet, John knew them on sight. Com lit up, on the general channel, and John felt his blood run cold when he heard an all-too-familiar voice.

"This is Admiral Andrew Kester, commander of the Liberated Autonomous Zone fleet. We are aware of your situation and are prepared to render assistance. You are victims of a biological agent created by allied forces from the Confederation and the Commonwealth. When we have secured the station, medical teams will board with an antidote. Station authorities are ordered to a state of martial law. I urge station residents to remain calm. Ships currently docked are to remain docked. All system traffic is to cease until martial law is lifted. Ships moving in violation of this order will be fired upon."

"God save us," John whispered. "And isn't that convenient, that he shows up just now? And where the *hell* did he get those ships? They look like new construction!"

"We are being contacted," Wirolen said. "We are being told to turn about and return to the station." As she spoke John felt the hard shove of sudden acceleration. "I have decided not to comply!"

"How fast can we be moving and still intersect the node with an active field?"

"Very fast, *sip'ya'a. Very* fast." She turned and flashed that feral smile at him again. "Glad now you brought me?"

John grinned back at her, then glanced at the board before them. "How long to the node?"

"We are almost there, now. We are most fortunate that we left when we did. The fleet emerged just as we came in range of the node. We are within their perimeter."

"They can still get a shot at us from the far side of the node," John said.

"Yes, they can. If they do so, we will race missiles. Either way, we will soon be gone." That feral snarl of a smile twisted her face again, then her attention became riveted on the instruments. "*Ha!* Missiles incoming!"

John stared at the boards and berated himself for not getting around to at least rudimentary flight training on Leyra'an systems. He turned his eyes to the schematic display of their surroundings. Their ship raced for the circle of the node, surrounded by seven red marks representing Kester's fleet. The two ships beyond the node had indeed opened fire, and a flock of silver dots closed rapidly on their position, even as the sign of their ship closed in on the node and their matrix field opened up around them. He held his breath and prayed. It *looked* like they would reach the node before being blown up, but it would be a damned close thing.

In an eye blink they were at the node, and Wirolen let out a shout. The schematic now showed a different scene, with just one ship — their own. How she had pulled such a trick John could not guess, not being a pilot. The best pilot he had known up to that point was Robert MacGregor, but now he wondered if Wirolen might not be better. "That was incredible!" he said quietly. "How often have you made that kind of maneuver?"

Wirolen turned toward him, obviously pleased with herself. "For all things there are first times," she replied, and then laughed outright at the look on his face. Almost immediately, she sobered and asked, "What now? Do we go back to base and report?"

It seemed the logical next step, but... "When I lost track of *Vengeance*, Kester had just that one ship under his command. Now he has seven, and announces himself as something *other* than RDF."

"And arrives just as people are growing ill from whatever those people who pretended to be from the Commonwealth gave them," Wirolen said.

John shook his head and said firmly, "No coincidence, not a chance of that."

"I agree," she said.

He thought a moment, then asked, "Where are we?"

"A dark mass system one node transit from base. It is a large mass, an easy target for what I needed to do."

"Vectors out?" he asked.

"Many. This is a commonly used transfer point, by both sides," Wirolen said. And then added, "We dare not linger."

"Show me a list of routes into the Republic from here," he said.

"The *Republic?*"

"Trust me."

Her forehead wrinkled in that way of a puzzled Leyra'an, but she did as he requested. The data shimmered into the air between them, a short list of system names in Leyra'an. As John struggled to stretch his limited ability to read her language, the text shivered and was replaced by words he knew. He nodded thanks as he scanned down the list, then suddenly jabbed a finger at a line. "Perfect! Take us there."

Wirolen ran her finger through the line of text and it blinked. Lights rippled across the board as she said, "*Into* the Republic? What madness is this, John?"

"No, my love, not madness at all." He was suddenly and absolutely sure of his course, just as he had been the day he decided to travel with her into the Confederation. "It's called taking a leap of faith."

Wirolen looked unconvinced, and hesitated. Then she reached out to press her palm against the side of his face. "I will follow you," she said quietly. "That will be *my* leap!" And in another moment they were headed back toward the node at a somewhat saner speed.

CHAPTER TWENTY-EIGHT

Pr'pri System
Bartram Habitat

Alicia and Robert took Drake directly to the same facility that had treated Emerson, where he was examined and determined to be capable of accepting the variant of the Cure created for their friend. This was no real surprise, and the risk of incompatibility was exceedingly low, but not knowing this going into it, Drake was clearly alarmed by the prospect that it might all be for nothing. In less than an hour, however, it was done. The young man walked back with them through the quiet night of the habitat. The Bartram's avian life forms were silent, and the nocturnal crawlers and climbers had begun a soft chorus of chirps and trills. Robert and Drake walked along with Alicia between them, and Drake provided distracted responses to her attempts to engage him in conversation. He gave her very little to work with. It did not seem he was being rude, or evasive, to Robert, who saw the man instead as anxious and ill-at-ease. After a particularly long pause, Robert heard Alicia ask, "Drake, are you feeling all right?"

"Yes, ma'am," he replied quietly. "Well, as far as physical things go. I can't tell anything has happened to me yet, but that doctor said as much."

"Then what troubles you?" she asked.

Drake shrugged and said, "My conscience. I've been very harsh in the past, supporting the hard line. I *believe* in what I'm doing, too, so strongly that I managed to get Emerson recalled when he wouldn't toe the party line." He gave them a sideways glance, gauging their reaction, but Alicia gave nothing away and Robert just kept walking. "Then they tell me I've developed Founders', a form that kills quickly. And where are all my convictions then? Where's the *courage* of my convictions? You read about that sort of thing. About men and women who are willing to die for what they believe in. Me? God forgive me, all I could think was that I *didn't* want to die. I was just ... well... " and he trailed off, shaking his head.

"You chose to live," Alicia said simply. "That's hardly an act of cowardice."

"No? Afraid that's pretty much how it feels, now that all is said and done." Drake shook his head again and looked glum. "And *after* so many things were said, I find myself running to *you*, begging for help. And you say yes, as if I've never done you any harm!"

"You haven't, as a matter of fact," Robert replied. "You represent the views and decisions of your superiors, and apparently agree with them very strongly. Those decisions are slowing down the development of normal relations between our peoples, but," and it was his turn to shrug, "there's still time to work these things out."

"*Some* of us have time," Alicia said quietly. "Drake, how prevalent is Founders' disease these days?"

There was another long pause, then Drake said, "Officially, seven percent of our population suffers from it. But that depends on how you decide to define the problem. Seven percent of us end up like I did. Or almost did. But Founders' isn't just one thing, it's a suite of genetic instabilities. There are other forms, more slow to develop, usually over a lifetime, but ultimately lethal. Something like that was what happened to Emerson. He was sick for years! And then there are lesser abnormalities that don't kill outright, just disable people. Add it all up and you probably have a quarter of the people in the Republic suffering something related to Founders'."

"A quarter... " Robert started to say. And then words failed him.

"And that still doesn't include the number of stillborn children, and kids that are just, well, wrong at birth," Drake added quietly. "Ultimately, the same problem."

"That's the tragedy of how things have unfolded so far," Alicia told him. "We can stop that. We can *eliminate* that, and not just with the repair mechanisms built into the Cure. Over time, we can alter the collective genome of the Republic in a way to re-introduce the diversity you lost, so long ago. It's that loss that's caused this problem. Founders' would be eliminated completely. Forever! We can do all that, and we really want to help, just as we helped you tonight."

"Do you think for a moment I don't understand that? Especially now!" Drake sounded both angry and confused. "There's so much at stake. We're not just doing this to be asses about it. Anything we accept, no matter how helpful, changes us. Changes our way of life. We've worked so hard to become what we are. What the Founders dreamed we would be. The changes you offer, well, it would be too much all at once!"

"But Drake," Alicia said gently, "we have urged only *one* change upon the Republic. And yes, it's an enormous change, one that will take many years of adaptation. But you will, *all of you,* have those years in which to work out how to manage that change, and all the others that might eventually grow out of the Republic knowing the Commonwealth. Some of you act as if we're trying to take over the Republic and run it, change it to suit how we live. But that isn't true at all! There *is* no 'all at once', no sweep of changes being pushed on you by the Commonwealth!"

"Think of how you felt," Robert said. "Think of what you felt when you learned you had Founders'. You've been relieved of that terror. Don't you want everyone else to live free of that fear?"

Drake sighed in exasperation and said, "Of course I do! But I want to see the Republic continue to grow and realize its full potential, as well. Simply accepting your 'Cure' without some sort of preparation would take us a big step toward what your civilization has become, and that is a way of life exactly the opposite of the way we live. I'm not comfortable with that. Many people are uncomfortable with that idea."

"So uncomfortable they would rather watch their own children die?" Alicia asked quietly. And Robert saw her start to raise her right hand to where Paul's sling would have been. Her eyes were round and dark in the lamplight, and not quite looking at Drake.

Drake's response was slow in coming. "No. Obviously."

"You don't think having extra time to live would help the Republic become all it could be?" Robert asked. "I'm serious. It's not a rhetorical question. The Republic isn't as expansive as the Commonwealth, but it still covers a huge sector of the Void, with a large population that isn't going to be in any hurry to give up what they've built for themselves. Think of what you might do, with the system you have now and the burden of Founders' removed? What might you accomplish, within your existing society, if people had all the time they needed to realize their goals?"

Drake made no response, at first. They walked along in silence for a time, in the pale, soft glow of evenly spaced lamps. Their route would take them, eventually, to the Willow Lake Inn. Finally, Drake said, "In a way, this is much worse than what happened when the Leyra'an came along. There were so many possibilities. And look what happened! The reason the Disputed Zone exists at all, and the reason we have so much trouble with bribery and corruption next door to it, is that citizens of the Republic compared our way with that of the Leyra'an and immediately found ours undesirable. If we accept the gifts of the Commonwealth, we won't realize the potential of our way of life. We will abandon it!"

It was the same conclusion that Emerson had shared with them, Robert realized, but where Emerson had sounded a bit wistful and resigned, Drake was angry and bitter. It was obvious to Robert then that their debate was irresolvable.

Alicia apparently saw this as well. "Drake, do you believe our people are behind the incursions?" she asked into the awkward silence that followed.

"No, ma'am," he replied. "It's a gut feeling sort of thing, and nothing rational, but no, somehow I don't think that's who is behind it. But the intel is clear. These *are* Humans traveling through the DZ."

"Well," said Robert, "*my* gut says it's not the Confederation. At least not directly. The Human version of the Cure is available to the disaffected Human population living in the Confederation, so it *seems* plausible these Humans may be the source. What stops me from pointing the finger, though, is the question of how they come to have Commonwealth-type transports. The Humans living in the Confederation wouldn't have been able to build those ships without the Leyra'an knowing of it."

"The answer to that, of course, is that the Leyra'an might very well know about it," Drake said. "They could even have provided the specs that would lead to engine technology of the Republic being used." Drake frowned and added, "We *don't* know. We don't have the proverbial clue. And truth be told, my accusatory approach was meant to provoke the sort of defensiveness that might indicate something hidden. *Provide us with a clue.* But careful analysis of the voices recorded during the meeting turned up nothing. Damned hard to dodge that sort of analysis, if you have even a moderately guilty conscience."

"Whoever it is," Alicia said, "The Republic, Confederation, and Commonwealth need to work together to thwart them. That's *my* gut feeling."

"Yes, ma'am," Drake said. "In that, at least, we do agree." The lights and music of the inn came into view and earshot respectively as they rounded a small woodlot of Leyra'an verdigris trees, gray shapes in the low light, marked by sprays of white, dangling blossoms that just touched the air with a sweet fragrance something like lilacs. Robert and Alicia turned that way, but Drake held up. "Forgive me," he said. "I'm already going to have trouble accounting for my time away, even with Rost'aht Holm covering for me. If I go there with you, attractive as the notion is at the moment, someone is likely to file a report of the sort I did that resulted in Emerson being recalled." He sighed and shook his head. "God pity a prideful fool, but that was a mistake! I should not have called his integrity into question. He's definitely a better man for this job than I am!"

"I don't agree," Alicia said. "I think in the long run you'll do just fine."

"Thanks," he said, looking at her for a long moment. "'In the long run.' Well, now that I have a chance at a *long run*, maybe... Um, look, I really don't know how to thank you. Either of you," Drake added, looking quickly at Robert. "And not just for the Cure, but for showing tolerance to one who did not."

"We're all going to be changed by this," Robert said as he reached out to clasp Drake's offered hand. "And somehow we'll get through it together."

"Have a pleasant night," Alicia said, and kissed Drake on the cheek. "Be welcome in our home."

"God keep you both," he replied, and Robert got the feeling Drake was blushing furiously as he turned and walked away from them without a backward glance.

"I don't envy those people the changes they will endure," Alicia said. "Come on, let's find Holm and Melep. Paul should be getting hungry by now."

Robert took her hand in his, and they followed the stone-paved path toward the light and music of the Willow Lake, where the rest of their family had agreed to wait for them. Familiar faces greeted them from all sides; hands were waved, mugs and glasses raised in salute. They waved back, called out answers to questions, and made their way to the table nearest the lake where they most often gathered. No one requested the pipes. It was well known by all, by then, that when Robert could do so without pain, he would play for them. Melep and Holm, with the infants, were at the table waiting. Little Paul was waiting none too patiently.

"It is about time, he says," as Melep handed him over to Alicia. For all their uncanny biological similarities, neither mother could safely nurse the infant of the other. Alicia took her son and silenced his complaints.

"How was Mr. Bristol?" Holm asked quietly.

"There were no *physical* complications," Robert said. "The med techs say his Founders' will soon be a thing of the past."

"Good!" Holm replied. "He can be a foolishly obtuse man, but *no one* deserves to die in such a way!"

"I believe he understands that, now," Alicia said.

"What he'll do with that understanding remains to be seen," Robert said. "He's nothing like Emerson at all, but that may be his youth and lack of experience getting in the way. He remains reluctant and resistant, but his doubts are beginning to grow. Someday, perhaps, he will realize we're not the monsters he was told to expect."

"He knows that now," Alicia said. "It's what to do with that knowledge, within the bounds of his mission, that troubles him. That, and the self-doubts that plague him."

"Self-doubts?" Holm asked.

"When he knew his days were numbered," she said, "he could not accept it, as his beliefs dictate. He chose life, instead. Now he feels he is a lesser man."

"My feeling is Drake is a stronger man than he realizes," Melep said. "His brush with mortality has opened his eyes a little. Now he just needs to find the strength to accept what he has seen."

"A lot of people in the Republic will die for no reason, if we only convert them one diplomat at a time," Alicia said, slowly shaking her head.

"You know," said Robert, "things he said tonight, added with what we learned from Emerson, really make it clear that nanomed, by itself, isn't the problem. It's the overall life way of the Commonwealth, and the Confederation of Clans before that. If they adopt our production capabilities, our most basic technologies, this system of acquisition they practice would be shattered.

After generations of measuring themselves by that standard, and with hundreds of billions of citizens doing so, are they really being so unreasonable to fear the consequences?"

No one answered at first, and Robert more than half expected the first response to come from either Melep or Alicia. Both had become quite vocal, and adamant, with regard to saving the folk of the Republic from themselves. But it was Holm who spoke first.

"No," he said. "It is not unreasonable. It is regrettable that they resist the Cure, as if it were linked immediately and inextricably to all the rest. But, no, it is not unreasonable for them to resist changes that might bring an end to a life way that has endured for more than two hundred years."

"To say nothing of the millennia before their Founders fled the home system," Robert added with a nod. He leaned back in his chair to let half-formed ideas from earlier in the evening sort themselves out. He accepted a mug of brown ale from Melep with a quiet word of thanks, and reached down to let Gava'mi nuzzle his hand.

"You have something on your mind," Alicia said.

"I've been following the conferences all along, and from that and the reports they've published, I think I may have the beginnings of an idea." He pulled a small projector out of his shirt pocket and set it in the center of the table. It unfolded and activated itself and a holographic image sprang to life in the air less than a third of a meter over the table. It started as a schematic of the galaxy, but swiftly zoomed in on a tiny speck of color until that speck inflated into a lumpy, multi-colored balloon. The lumps touched, off center, and the area of contact, though small, was an easily seen electric blue.

"Our standard map," Holm said. "Red for the Confederation, yellow for the Commonwealth, and green for the Republic. Blue at the interface."

Robert nodded and pushed his finger into the display, waggling it a little. The perspective changed again, with the point of view zooming in. Soon the contact zones between Republic and Commonwealth, and Republic and Confederation dominated the display. Each area was thickly strewn with tiny silver icons and excruciatingly small and sharply resolved identification tags. All three touched in a relatively small volume of space, the systems involved being Eriola for the Commonwealth, Pr'pri for the Confederation, and one named Webster just barely in the Republic. Away from Webster things were messy, and no simple boundary could be drawn. There were two Leyra'an systems and one of the Republic that overlapped Eriola, and this state of affairs was repeated all the way along the interface between the Republic and Confederation, the notorious Disputed Zone.

"To preserve their life way," Robert said, "they need to keep influences from both of our civilizations at bay, or at least under control. Open access to the Leyra'an was, ultimately, the source of their troubles. Simply opening the Republic to the Commonwealth would be a much larger shock to their already fragile economic contrivance."

"Just what Emerson said, is it not?" said Melep. "Only by great effort have they maintained even a little control over the effect of contact with our people."

"The border is not sealed, and because of this, the deezees know about the Cure," said Holm. "Hence the increased instability there, of late."

Robert nodded, not looking away from the bulbous 3-D map hanging in the air over the table. "*They* can't control the DZ entirely, because of the self-imposed limits of their system. But *we* can. The Commonwealth can move resources, ships, stations, whatever is needed, into the DZ in sufficient numbers to monitor everything traveling in and out of the zone. We could turn it into a sort of filter, a buffer zone, that controls how much contact, and of what sort, passes between the three regions. Humans of both realms and the Leyra'an would continue to interact and learn about each other there, but without the leakage of contraband that is making such a mess of things right now. Something like an expanded version of the Trilateral Commission would be needed to manage things, I think. If we were allowed to do such a thing, we might be able to slow the changes the Republic must endure. Maybe that would give the Republic time to adjust and adapt."

"Huh." Holm peered into the display, then at Robert. "Bits and pieces of what you just outlined have been proposed before, but nothing this integrated."

"I've been keeping those bits and pieces in mind all along," Roberts said. "And I doubt I'm the only resident of Bartram doing so. Something about my recent conversation with Drake brought it all together for me."

"It can't possibly be so simple," Alicia said.

"No," Robert agreed. "It can't. And it *won't* be. It will be a work of many years. This is just an outline of the idea, but better to amend a plan as we go than to continue wrangling over one until it's too late."

"My brother," said Holm, with a lopsided and tooth-concealing grin, "you sound more like a Leyra'an all the time!" Then he laughed and said, "Download all of that, and I will propose this at tomorrow's session. They will not, of course, agree to it exactly, but this just might start the conversation that generates that plan of which you speak."

"We need to work it over first," Robert said, holding up a hand. "Let's see how many holes in it *we* can find and plug before you make it known."

"Not just us," Alicia said. "All of us," and she waved a hand around toward the noisy crowd that shared the night with them. "You're almost certainly right that you aren't the only one playing with the bits and pieces. Put it on the station net, and see what becomes of it."

"The other Commissioners will see what is going on," Robert pointed out.

"That does not feel like a bad idea," Holm replied.

And so it was done.

CHAPTER TWENTY-NINE

Grumium System
RDF Fleet Staging Area

Wirolen took them through the node, brows beetled and teeth showing in a grimace that gave her an altogether grim appearance. That she was afraid, John did not doubt, and that she trusted him so much set him to praying fervently that his idea would work. They appeared in Grumium with the RDF ship-in-distress code broadcasting at full power, and luck was with them; no outbound ships were near them with active matix fields. John immediately scanned the schematic of the region around the node and its rather large alpha station, assessing the amount and types of traffic. Even though he expected to find much of the fleet there, he whistled softly to himself when he saw how much *more* of the fleet had now gathered. For all practical purposes, this *was* the RDF fleet as it currently existed, this side of the Rift, all but a handful of frigates and destroyers from the quick count he made. The ships were arrayed in a way that suggested action was imminent, and the node was well guarded.

Wirolen just stared at the display with a lost look. The node itself was fully invested in a standard RDF security pattern made up of a dozen frigates and seven cruisers parked as close to the nodal zone as could be, and still allow safe passage of traffic. Looking at this, Wirolen said, "We will not leave here unless they let us go." The fear in her voice was obvious.

"I know what I'm doing," John assured her. And then prayed again that he was right.

"Ship in distress," said a man's voice over the com. "Remain inertial, or you will be fired upon. State your identification."

"Major John Knowles, RDF, service number 989K632AGY." One of the frigates fired thrusters and moved to cut off their flight path toward the nodal station.

There was a pause, as the com officer had someone run the ID. Then the blunt voice came back with, "That ID is listed as missing in action and presumed dead."

"The listing is incorrect, if understandable," Knowles said. "You should be picking up my PDT by now for verification."

"Affirmative. PDT accessed and verified. State the nature of your emergency and explain your presence on an enemy spacecraft."

"That information is classified. Alpha three seven nine theta one. Refer to highest ranking officer available."

"Hold," said the voice of the com officer.

"John," Wirolen said quietly. "How much of all that is the truth?"

"Some of it." When she made it clear she was in no mood for even gallows humor, John said, "I'll explain it all when we get out of this. We need a data packet with the scans of Kester's ships and his message to Webster system."

"*If* we get out of this," Wirolen muttered as she turned her attention to the task. "There, done. Give the word and I will send it."

"Major Knowles, this is Fleet Admiral Grayson. Mind telling me what the devil is going on? Where have you been?" The stern voice was familiar to John. He'd met Admiral Grayson, knew he did not suffer fools, but that he was a man who would listen, if given a reason.

"Admiral Grayson." It was not a question, it was an expression of surprise that he had been passed all the way up so quickly. He managed to keep his intense relief out of his voice. Apparently his full assignment rating was still in place, despite his MIA status. "Is this channel secure, sir?"

"Yes. Secure and locked."

"Thank you, sir. I'll assume you've done a quick scan of my file and understand why I was assigned to the *Vengeance?*"

"I understand your assignment, Knowles. I supported the investigation."

"Admiral, I've been in the Leyra'an Confederation and in the DZ, using a connection I've made since leaving *Vengeance* to gather intel on reports of Secessionist activities in the DZ, activities that have proven relevant to my assignment." When Wirolen stared at him, John shook his head and held a finger to his lips.

"How exactly is Kester involved in this?"

"I don't have the full answer to that yet, sir, but I have a transmission ready that will tell you what I know. Are you prepared to receive it, sir?"

"Send it."

Wirolen touched a spot on her controls, then nodded. "Stand by, Knowles."

There was a long pause, during which Wirolen asked, "John, were you sent to spy on *us?*" Her eyes were wide with alarm and anticipation. What had been said to that point clearly rattled her.

"No, *sip'ya.* I was assigned to *Vengeance* to spy on *Kester.* My encounter with *Han'anga* and its crew sent me off on a mission of greater purpose, one beyond anything assigned by the RDF, and brought me to you. Never doubt what I've said to you, about how I feel." He nodded toward the board, where the com light blinked pale blue as it waited for the channel to reopen. "They don't know what happened to me, and couldn't know, because Kester went renegade and didn't report on what happened at Attus. I have no doubt they know I left with *Han'anga*, but I'm betting that the stories told by the men who returned to the Republic are confusing enough that no one is entirely sure exactly what my role was. I've just given the Admiral a hint of why I might have left with your crew. Let's hope he believes I took an opportunity to get behind the lines, so to speak, and leaves it at that." He reached over and took her hand firmly, and to his relief felt her immediately hold tight. "*Nas'nala, sip'ya,*" he said. Which was, *Do not doubt me, my love.*

"There are no doubts," she said. "But I *will* have many questions."

"Knowles?"

"Yes, sir?"

"Your report is supported by others from the DZ. Thanks for bringing this to us. Well done."

"Begging the Admiral's pardon, but it's not done, not yet. Even if you go after Kester and bag him — *where did he get those ships?*" John did not feign concern. That a flotilla of brand new warships should suddenly turn up was unprecedented.

"Bigger question than you might realize," Grayson replied. "That's where your report is mostly strongly supported. Kester isn't the only one. We have reports that more than one set of warships has now appeared in the DZ, claiming to respond to the same situation addressed by Kester. And our most recent reports are that these systems claim to have withdrawn from the Republic to form this 'Liberated Autonomous Zone'."

"Admiral, is there any indication at all that the Commonwealth is actually involved with this?"

"Word is they are denying involvement. There's no solid proof one way or the other. They say no, and to be honest, the timely arrival of these new ships with *Kester* of all people in command certainly supports that. The Fleet is being prepared to intervene in the systems that have been invaded. We've decided this poses a clear threat to the Republic."

John considered the Fleet strength he saw before them in the display and nodded to himself. The Fleet could not pacify the entire DZ, but key systems could be controlled well enough to balk an invasion. "One other concern, sir. I believe Pr'pri system and the Trilateral Commission negotiators may be in danger."

"How so?" Grayson demanded.

"Kester holds grudges, holds them tight. He has been vexed time and again by Kr'nai Ersha of the Leyra'an. That individual is reported to be involved with the Commission, and present in Pr'pri. Kester and his ships now have a direct route to Pr'pri. I'm seriously concerned that he won't be able to resist."

There was a long pause, then the Admiral said, "Concern noted and taken into consideration, Major."

"Yes, sir." John paused a moment, then said, "Admiral, I can't stay much longer. I've already violated mission protocol bringing this in."

"Understood, Major. You were never here."

The com light went dark. John shook his head and said quietly, "I can't believe I got away with that!"

"You have not. At least not yet." Wirolen's slim hands did a quick dance across the boards. "It is time for us to go, if they will let us!"

"They will," he said, sure that he was correct. John felt the weight of acceleration as Wirolen turned their ship toward the node and brought the main engines to life. "Take us to the dark node, for the moment, and get us back out of sight."

"And what then?" she asked.

John thought about it for a moment, then asked, "What are the chances of finding a route to Pr'pri system that does not involve a system transit?" It was one of the great ironies of space travel that they could hop from star to star in a heartbeat, but travel within a system could take days or weeks, sometimes months.

"Let me see." Data sprang into the air, and lines of angular Leyra'an characters rippled with swiftly alternating colors of orange and blue as she ran a search. "We will need to return to Tak'ak Na station — we can do that directly from the dark mass — then make it to Pr'pri in three nodal transitions from there."

John frowned a moment as he worked the math in his head to convert Leyra'an units of time shown in the display to those he understood. "Two days. If that's the best we can do, nothing for it! Hope that doesn't turn out to be *too* long! Okay, then, that's our next move."

"Why are we going to Pr'pri?"

"I was serious when I told Grayson that Pr'pri will be Kester's next destination," John replied. "We're going to warn them of the danger a system away, in Webster."

"Do you really believe he will go after Kr'nai Ersha?" Wirolen asked, glancing up from the controls in puzzlement.

"It's partly the logistics of the situation that has me worried," John replied. "From what the Admiral said, what we saw in Webster is not isolated. There's something going on in the other Human-controlled systems of the DZ. Someone is clearly trying to establish control of the region, and Pr'pri marks the portion of the DZ that connects all three realms. It's too important to leave out of the equation. And, of course, he'll go there for revenge as well."

"*Yia*," she said. "Their conflict is a legend in the Confederation."

"It's not exactly unknown in the Republic, either. Kester was, until he killed that Commonwealth ship, our big war hero. People named their children after him." John shook his head again. "From what I learned serving under the bastard, we can't safely assume he'll stop at Webster and leave Pr'pri in peace."

Wirolen did something to the controls and then said, "We are on our way." A few moments later they were in the dark mass system, and Wirolen sent a message buoy through the node. This journey they would behave as calm and civilized travelers, not fugitives barely escaping death. They would wait a while before making the next transit, and make sure the passage was safe. John took a deep breath and tried to will himself to relax.

"So, tell me, *sip'ya'a*, of your life as a spy," Wirolen said.

"First things first, I meant it when I said I was *not* sent out to spy on the Leyra'an," he said.

"I believe you," Wirolen replied.

"It's long been suspected that Kester maintains a connection to a friend who happens to be a criminal, James Calavone. This would be the namesake of the Calavone who tried to take over the Republic, about the time we met your people. It was an ugly thing, I'm told. There are plenty of folk still around old enough to remember it. That Admiral, back there, is one of them. The Calavones set up a conspiracy that spread out through much of the Republic, and when they made their move a lot of innocent people died. The military structure we have now was established to take back systems Calavone controlled. It took several years to restore order. Anyway, many of Calavone's people escaped, some into the general population of frontier systems. The RDF was never able to shut down the entire network, and for years it seemed clear the younger Calavone was pulling its strings.

"And then there was no sign of him, or his network of informers. It just dried up and went away. Andrew Kester was one of the few caught. He was arrested and reformed, being very young and apparently little more than an errand boy. He eventually restored himself to the good graces, if not the complete trust, of the authorities. When the war heated up he seemed to prove himself a staunch patriot, and his past was largely forgiven. But just in case the connection to Calavone's son still somehow existed, RDF intelligence always kept an agent on his ship. I was the last one, before he went rogue. I carried out the normal duties of an officer aboard his ship and kept my eyes open, but sent no reports. What the RDF calls a mole, but don't ask me to explain the term, since I don't know exactly where it comes from, myself."

"So you were there, just in case he made contact with this criminal?"

John nodded. "Eventually I'd have been rotated out, and another agent would have been planted in my place. The incident with the probeship and the events that followed changed all of that. I took a chance that my assignment code would buy me the time I needed to establish credibility, and put the RDF in motion against Kester."

"John, this Calavone person, could he be behind what is going on out here?" she asked.

"I very much doubt that," he replied, shaking his head. "The ships Calavone the elder had were destroyed in a last stand that bought his son and some of their followers time to escape. They had no real base of operations and wherever they went, they certainly haven't had time to build a shipyard!"

"Someone did," she pointed out.

"True," and John frowned. "I can't even guess at what Kester has gotten himself into, out here. The existence of those ships is baffling."

The buoy popped back with the come-ahead message at that moment. Wirolen turned back to her controls and moved them into the node.

CHAPTER THIRTY

Pr'pri System
Bartram Habitat

Robert's augmented outline went into the habitat net with a suitable explanation, and immediately took on a life of its own. Alicia had been quite right; he was far from the only citizen to be considering the matter, just one of the few with direct access to a Commission member. Input was generous and varied. Duplicate ideas cancelled out, contradictory ideas engendered debate, but in a remarkably short time it melded together into a detailed plan that seemed suitable for presentation to the Commission. A vote was taken and the majority agreed it was as good as they could make it. What the Commissioners or their respective staffs might have thought, and they were certainly aware of what was going on, was impossible to say. Even Holm held himself back, fearing a perceived conflict of interest. The synthesis was a lengthy document, so another day was spent extracting a synopsis for review purposes.

It came down to the question of who would present it to the Commission. If Holm or Kr'nai Ersha offered it up, Robert was quite sure the Republic would veto it out of hand. If the Commonwealth Commissioners proposed the buffer zone plan, it would be sent into the Republic for further study, where the idea would simply be shelved, perhaps indefinitely.

"It is simple," said Melep with blunt sarcasm. "We need to get the Republic to suggest it."

Robert turned to stare at her. She sat beside him at the Willow Lake table. "Well, of *course* we do!"

"Drake," Alicia said. "That's the answer."

"Yes, we need to contact Drake," said Holm thoughtfully, brow furrowed as he considered contingencies. "There will be a special session tomorrow, to consider information from the Confederation on the current crisis. See if you can catch him afterwards and suggest a meeting at the Willow Lake."

Melep blinked at them in surprise. "I spoke in jest!"

"Well, here's the funny part," Alicia said. "It's a damned good idea!"

"Yes," Robert said. He leaned over agan and kissed Melep's cheek.

"I wish you would not do that," she muttered, raising her hand to her cheek and frowning. The Leyra'an did not kiss, and found the behavior very strange when Humans did so. "It feels — peculiar."

But Robert only laughed, and tickled little Vurn, who was nestled in her lap. Vurn giggled delightedly and reached for Robert, who obliged by standing and lifting him up into the air to be whirled around once before returning him to Melep.

"So, first we have to convince Drake that this is a good idea, and then convince him to take the responsibility?" Alicia asked. "He *will* balk. Of course he will."

"Perhaps," Holm said. "But this plan provides compromises I believe he will find comfortable, considering his recent experiences. And we have nothing to lose by trying!"

"Do you really believe it will seem more acceptable if it appears to be their idea?" asked Melep.

"Who knows?" Robert replied. Playing fair, he now had Paul high over his head, grinning as his son giggled and screamed. "But it comes from the Bartram habitat, from the very people who made the TC possible in the first place. They've responded well to the opportunity to embrace the survivors of the *William Bartram* before. We're going to play that card one more time."

"Begs the question of how his superiors will react," said Alicia.

"According to Emerson, all but the most hard-core elements of the Republic are heartily sick of the current situation, so Drake is not alone in a tight corner," Holm replied. "The last offensive, which led to the Kester incident, cost the current government much of its credibility. That's apparently why they originally put someone more moderate in charge of their delegation to the Commission."

"Before we parted company," said Robert, "John Knowles told me the Republic was coming apart even without the added stress of the Commonwealth." He set Paul back into Alicia's hands, sat, and poured himself a beer. "Recent debacles can't have stablized things."

"The Republic may already have fractured, in a sense," Holm said. "There is a broad zone of expansion, on the far side of the Republic from the DZ. It is beyond a relatively starless region they call the Rift. Most of those who settle there are people who truly believe the Leyra'an exist for the sole purpose of destroying the Republic's way of life." His forehead dimpled again in a Leyra'an frown as he spoke. "They are trying to build a purer form of the Founders' ideal society. In time, Emerson fears the Republic could become two different entities, likely in conflict with each other."

"What a mess," Alicia said, shaking her head.

"But one that contact with the Commonwealth may ultimately resolve," Holm replied. "The Cure will be difficult to resist, even by the die-hards."

Robert nodded and said, "When the Cure reaches that far and the decades unfold for them, their perspective will gradually change, as they all live long enough to see their worst fears unrealized."

Alicia sighed loudly and muttered, "Gaia, I sure hope you've got that right!"

And so the next day Robert, Alicia, and Melep were waiting outside the chambers to waylay one Drake Bristol. "Hello, Drake!" Alicia said, it having been decided she should lead off. It was obvious to all of them that Drake was attracted to her, in spite of himself. "That was actually a productive meeting."

"It was, and that takes getting used to," he replied with a wry smile. "At least we can rule out the Commonwealth's involvement in the attempt to destabilize the DZ. That analysis of engine design and output by Ho's people will be hard to argue with."

"That's certainly a relief," Alicia said.

"Never thought I'd see us all in agreement on this, when the news broke," Drake said. He looked from one to the other. "Ah, that's not why you're here, is it?"

"No, we're on our way to dinner, and saw you in the corridor," Alicia said. "We wanted to ask you to join us."

"That would not be a good idea," Drake replied. "After Emerson's recall, we're watched more closely than ever. My own fault, of course. My little excursion the other night did not go entirely unnoticed. There were pointed questions."

"I assume you had the right answers?" Melep asked.

"Thanks to Rost'aht Holm." He laughed and said, "It's a shame, really. That Willow Lake Inn has the best beer I've ever tasted, and I could go for a beer right now."

"We'll have to find another way to accommodate you," Robert said. It was obvious their plan was not going to develop as they hoped.

"How are you, otherwise?" Alicia asked.

"I'm fine," he replied with a smile. "I'm just fine, now. Thanks."

Into the awkward pause that followed, Robert stepped forward, and took a chance. "Speaking of beer, when you dropped by the other night you asked about what I did as vineyard manager." He saw Drake's face go blank of expression, as the man tried not to react to the obvious falsehood. Robert pulled the data transfer tab from his pocket and held it out. "I pulled together some information on what we do. Covers *boshna'ti*, grapes, *and* hops," he added as if making an expected point.

"The format will transfer directly to your systems. Maybe people in the Republic can use it to make better beer, who knows? Anyway, you might find it satisfies your curiosity on the matter."

"Why, uh, thanks. This is unexpected," Drake said as he took the tab. "It's also much appreciated. I'll review it, first chance I get."

"Don't read it at bedtime," Alicia said with a wink. "Unless you need help falling asleep."

"I'll keep that in mind," he replied, flicking a glance at Robert and smiling. "Is she always like that?"

"Oh, you have *no* idea," Robert said.

Holm, when he met them at their usual table outside the Willow Lake, listened to their tale with a frown, until Robert described handing over the data transfer device. Then he looked up with a smile that somehow made him look smug. "My brother is one who thinks fast on his feet!"

"He surely knows something is going on," Robert said with a nod. "After all, we never once discussed the cultivation of hops. And the net has been buzzing with the Bartram Protocol for days. But he does love his beer, and it suddenly seemed a completely logical cover."

Holm drained a mug of beer and said, "Well, let us hope he has a chance to review it before his minders do that for him." Another pitcher of beer was brought to the table. Holm refilled their mugs, then raised his own. But where Robert expected the evening toast to their small family, instead Holm said, "To hope."

"To hope," Alicia said softly in reply, and had that dark, faraway look again for a moment as they all drank.

From there they went on to lighter matters, and the evening meal. The Willow Lake became steadily busier as the habitat light levels faded to the usual long twilight, and the lamps on their slim poles around the pub and the lake cast a soft silvery glow on those gathered. The great central lamp overhead sparkled like a cloud of stars. Musicians gathered on the stage, a band that mixed Leyra'an and Human dance tunes, and soon music filled the air and dancers moved all around them. From time to time members of Rost'aht were drawn into the noisy, whirling crowd. Friends came and left, and at times friends were left holding the infants. For the babies, and Vurn and Paul were not the only ones present, such loud and joyful energy was as natural as mother's milk. At one point Robert and Alicia returned to the table to find the proprietor of the Willow Lake with one child on each knee, bouncing each in turn and laughing, as little Paul and Vurn let out ear-piercing shrieks of delight.

"We're not quite finished!" Ira said when Alicia offered to relieve him of his giggling burden. So she and Robert clasped hands and rejoined the circle of dancers. And as he danced, Robert looked into the glittering green eyes of his wife, watching her bright red hair fly around her face, and wondered if her nightmares had truly ended. There hadn't been a bad night since shortly after he took up his pipes again. People danced around him, friends shouted his name, and the woman of his dreams was smiling at him as he whirled her around. The recent past was a dark place in her spirit, and even that evening he had seen a brief sign that the darkness still remained. But the present was a bright and lively thing. Robert embraced it, and her, with a will, always seeking to draw her further from the blackness of the lost *William Bartram*.

His personal com trilled in his ear, signaling a recorded message in the system, addressed to him. He called for immediate, private playback, and heard whispering through the bones of his ear the voice of Drake Bristol. "Robert, thanks ever so much for the information. I stopped at a public terminal on my way back to my office and gave it a quick view. I'll see to it personally that it reaches people who can use it. It should improve access to better beer all around. Wish I could have joined you tonight. Drake Bristol, end message."

"Just heard from Drake," Alicia said with a grin, revealing that she had been included in the message. "Looks like the beer of the Republic might be upgraded soon."

The dance brought her closer, encircled by his arms just long enough for him to say, "That boy has a crush on you."

"Of course he does!" And she whirled away with a laugh and a grin.

CHAPTER THIRTY-ONE

Endmost Station
Disputed Zone

Calavone paced the length of the operations center of Endmost station, contemplating the early reports of success, and eager for more news. The center was no longer the quiet place he had come to know. Every station was occupied and busy, com chatter was constant, and people entered and left the center briskly as they saw to various errands. The big tactical display depicted the constant traffic in and out of the system, and images of ships being prepared for departure floated in the air over many of the work stations.

A new report was announced, and Calavone returned to the station master's chair to scan it. What he saw made him smile. Yet another task force was reporting success, arriving as they did in the proverbial nick of time to rescue citizens of the DZ from panic-stricken chaos. He could picture it in his mind, the heroic teams of medics rushing from ships to stations and habitats, treating the sick and terrified inhabitants, and passing along the tale of a horrible conspiracy unmasked. Of course, those treated would immediately respond; the antidote to their manufactured virus saw to that. Few questions were asked of their saviors, who they were and where they were from. Such questions would come in time, Calavone knew, but he was confident that his carefully prepared answers would get the job done.

Within a few days all the targeted systems would be under his control, which for all practical purposes gave him control of the DZ. Changes long sought but never fully realized would be made by his forces. Many would question the methods, but the results would speak for themselves, and with careful manipulation of the media by his network, he would soon have the distance he needed between what *he* had done, and the excesses of his father.

I am not my father's son in all ways, he would tell the Republic. *I'm not here to control, only to protect. I believe in the Republic, I believe in what the Founders wanted us to do.* Some would accept these words, others would take a great deal of convincing, while a few would surely stand in his way until removed.

The RDF force assigned to the DZ had bottled itself up in a single system. The reason for this strange maneuver remained a mystery. The RDF would need access to Webster system if they were to respond quickly to recent developments. When Kester had control of Webster, the RDF would need more than a month to redeploy effectively. By then, Calavone would be in control of the area.

"Inbound traffic marker," the officer of the watch announced. "Signal ID belongs to the *Vengeance* task force."

"Ah! Last, but not least," Calavone said. "Tell them to come ahead."

The message was beamed to the buoy, which promptly wrapped itself in a matrix field and disappeared. A few minutes passed, and finally a frigate appeared just as Calavone expected. The image of the frigate's captain, a young, dark-haired recruit drawn from a core system by Calavone's network, appeared in the projection area in yet another moment. He did not look happy.

"Report, Captain," Calavone said. "Is Webster system secure?"

"Yessir, we have that one buttoned up. Med teams are in action, but... " he paused, visibly at a loss for words.

"Out with it, Captain. Is there a problem?" Calavone demanded.

"Sir, we passed through two occupied systems getting here. There's trouble in both."

"Trouble?"

"The antidote to the Commonwealth plague isn't working. Not permanently. People are getting sick again." His voice and expression betrayed his anxiety at being the bearer of such news.

"That's impossible!" Calavone snapped.

"Those are the reports, sir. Sorry, sir, but it gets worse. We have some of our own people out here who have contracted it. Whatever the Commonwealth started out spreading around has changed from the intel you received. It's become contagious."

"Hold!" Calavone said abruptly, and closed the voice circuit, though the nervous young captain remained visible before him. "Artie, what the *hell* is he talking about?"

"I am not sure," the quiet voice of Artie said in reply. "However, there *was* a risk of our bioweapon mutating over time, as I explained in the beginning."

"You said the odds against such a thing were huge!"

"That is true," Artie replied. "But the odds were not zero."

Oh, good God! Calavone drew a deep breath to calm himself, fighting the feel of ice in his blood. "What do we do? How do we stop this?"

"I will need samples," Artie replied.

Calavone nodded and reopened the channel to the frigate. "Captain, are members of your crew infected?"

"I'm afraid so, sir. Not many, but the disease has appeared in crew who went stationside. We can't dock with Endmost."

"Understood," Calavone said, trying to project concern. "Believe it or not, Captain, that's to our advantage. We need samples from your crew in order to determine how to respond to this turn of events. A med crew will be on its way."

"Thank you, sir," the young man replied, looking as relieved as he sounded.

"Whatever you and your crew need, we'll get it to you," Calavone said. No deception in this case; Calavone did feel loyalty to those who followed him, and the people of Endmost had always looked after their own. "Any word from Admiral Kester?"

"Uh, yes, sir. There's a recording. He made it before we left, of course. To the best of my knowledge he is not yet aware of the situation. The new bug wasn't loose back at Webster." He looked very nervous again. "It's about, uh, something else entirely, I believe."

"That's fine, Captain. Go ahead and transmit now."

The young captain looked away from the forward pickup and nodded to someone out of sight. "You should have it now."

"Run it," Calavone said to the watch crew around him.

Kester's image appeared before him, standing with hands clasped behind his back and not quite meeting Calavone's gaze — an artifact of how the three-dimensional image happened to be oriented. Kester sounded perfectly at ease. "Since you're receiving the same reports I am, you know that your plan is working pretty much as you expected. I'm convinced that, by the time the RDF is able to organize a response, we *will* have complete control of the DZ, making it very expensive and risky to dislodge us. Whether or not they'll try *anyway* remains to be seen. The propaganda gang is working on the populace, and reports that, in Webster at least, they're having no difficulty convincing residents that the Republic has let them down, and left them vulnerable to a sneak attack. The general understanding here is that our ships were RDF, but that we've mutinied and are no longer under the control of the central government. We even have Secessionists coming out of the ductwork and allying themselves to us. We'll have established the first phase of that semi-autonomous zone of yours in short order."

Calavone was nodding as his friend spoke, glad that the main event was mostly done, recent complications notwithstanding. Then he froze in place, a chill rippling up his spine, as Kester went on.

"I will leave two cruisers and the support ships of my task force here at Webster, and move on to Pr'pri. I fully realize that you do not agree with the necessity of such a move, but upon considerable reflection I've decided to trust my military knowledge and experience in this matter. From a purely military point of view, we need to control Pr'pri system too, if we want this to work out. This presents a risk, of course. I'm convinced leaving the Commonwealth in complete control of the current contact point is the greater hazard. I'll send word when we have Pr'pri under our protection. Kester, end recording."

"Military point of view *my ass!*" Calavone's voice rose in pitch with each word. "Captain!"

"Sir." The young man's image replaced the frozen view of Kester.

"To the best of your knowledge, has Admiral Kester departed Webster System?"

"He was preparing to invade Pr'pri system as we headed out. We needed to make four nodal shifts and one short system transit to get here. We, uh, left Webster more than two days ago. If the Admiral followed through on his decision, he's done it by now." His eyes shifted about nervously and he added, "For what it's worth, sir, and for the record, senior staff objected."

"Noted." Calavone took a breath and calmed himself. "There's a shuttle on its way to you now, son. Tell your crew to stay calm. We'll fix this!"

"Understood, sir. And thank you." The frigate captain vanished from sight.

Attack a neutral system, one under the ward of the most powerful force in known space, a strategic *necessity?* The bio-agent was a knife that had turned in his hand, and Kester was off on a damned fool's errand. He could already see his plan coming apart. He could *feel* the inevitability of it. Calavone felt his jaw muscles begin to cramp and tried to unclench his teeth. He had trusted Kester, wanted his experience in the system most likely to see action when the Republic tried to keep open what was currently their only route to the Commonwealth. It was that *corridor* he needed to control, not Pr'pri system itself! *Sure, let's poke the sleeping giant with a steel rod, Andrew. And to hell with the military standpoint. You want revenge. You want Kr'nai Ersha! You're going to throw it all away for the sake of vengeance!*

"Kester," Calavone muttered. The crew in station ops bent over key pads and displays, doing their level best to be invisible. "You stupid, obsessive, *son of a bitch!*"

His shout of outrage carried no further than the limits of the room. Kester would never know, and the crew on hand carefully pretended not to hear.

CHAPTER THIRTY-TWO

Somewhere in Confederation Space

John and Wirolen broadcast news of the threat growing in the DZ to each Confederation system they used on their way to Pr'pri. Each message included an appeal to send aid to the defense of Serch'nach station and the habitats around it. In no system did they linger for long, intent on reaching Pr'pri as quickly as possible. There was no way of knowing how soon Kester would make what John assumed to be the obvious next move. Knowing Kester, John was quite sure the man would not wait one hour longer than necessary.

A probe was sent at last to Pr'pri, and a come-ahead returned to them swiftly enough that John took it as a sign that Kester had not yet invaded. "Let's go!" he said to Wirolen, and with a softly uttered *"Yia,"* she flew into the node, centered them as she flew, and set the vector. And they were, at last, in Pr'pri. Peaceful, neutral Pr'pri system, and no sign of Kester's task force. Just the ships allowed by the truce: a probeship for the Commonwealth, and a cruiser each for the Republic and the Confederation.

"All quiet," Wirolen said softly. Her head dropped forward a moment in relief.

"Yes," John replied. "Just the peaceful scene we hoped to see. Unfortunately, we need to change that." With the touch of a key he opened their com system and began his transmission, prepared in advance. Anyone who was receiving in any way at all would pick up the distress signal and warning they sent. The station proper would also receive the same data already provided to Admiral Grayson. A response was not long in coming.

"*Eli'ahtna*, stand by for the station master."

"Will they believe us?" Wirolen asked suddenly.

"If they don't believe the data that went out with the message, they won't need to wait long for additional proof. Count on that!"

Wirolen muttered a Leyra'an profanity under her breath. "We want to be further from the node, as soon as possible."

"*Yia!*"

"*Eli'ahtna*, this is station master Rir'lek Olersa," a female Leyra'an voice said, speaking Leyra'an. An image of her popped into view between Wirolen and John, a mature Leyra'an with the usual bright amber eyes, nearly black hair tied back severely as was the habit of station workers, and brown scales that shaded to the color of coffee around her eyes. "Can you provide an ETA for Kester's fleet?"

"No. He had only just arrived in Webster system as we prepared to leave. That was more than two days ago. I can only guess how long it would take for him to secure that system before coming here."

Olersa's eyes narrowed. "Do you know for certain he *will* come here?"

"No," John admitted. "But I know Kester quite well, and know all about the matter that stands between him and Kr'nai Ersha."

"Station master," Wirolen said with a respectful nod toward the image. "May I suggest that you seek out Kr'nai Ersha and gain his insight? I see from the presence of *Han'anga* that he is here."

"He is, indeed," Olersa replied. "He has been informed of the danger, and even now reviews the data you brought. In the meantime, *Han'anga, Perseverance,* and *Newcomb* have assumed alert status."

John scanned the system readout, and was relieved to see that the *Han'anga* and the RDF *Perseverance* were in good positions to defend the station. Not far from Serch'nach loomed the incredible bulk of a Commonwealth probeship, tagged as *Newcomb* by the onboard computer. Even knowing that these ships were an order of magnitude larger than any ships ever built by the Republic, John found himself gaping in astonishment at the huge vessel. It was not a warship, but it was present, and John could only hope it was capable of making its presence felt. By some miracle the gigantic ship was parked directly between Serch'nach station and the node. Near the docking pole of the station was parked an RDF frigate tagged *Cygnet.* It took a moment, but John remembered that frigates were being used to keep open the line of communication between the Republic and Pr'pri. A bit of luck; the *Cygnet* was a small ship, but a warship all the same.

The station master signed off and traffic control came back on, directing them to an open docking port at Serch'nach. "Respectfully decline," Wirolen replied. "For the duration of the situation, we prefer to remain free and clear to navigate. Please assign a position."

John nodded approval and said, "We're well stocked and almost fully fueled."

"Enough to easily take us trans-system to the other prime node," Wirolen said. "We can escape to the Commonwealth if we must, and summon assistance."

"Let's hope it doesn't come to that," John said. "It's almost a complete system transit to reach Eriola from here."

Com came back on. "*Eli'ahtna,* Kr'nai Ersha desires contact."

"We are honored," John replied, speaking Leyra'an.

"John Knowles?" Kr'nai Ersha's image appeared, a dark-scaled face familiar from the time John spent aboard *Han'anga.* "I am very pleased to see you are alive and well, though I could think of better circumstances in which to meet again!"

"No argument, sir," John replied. Ersha had addressed him using the Human language, and so John switched languages yet again.

"I have done a quick review of your data, not enough for a complete understanding, of course, but I must agree with your assessment. *Han'anga* stands ready. I have been told that the *Perseverance* has been officially ordered by the Republic's representative to stand in defense of Serch'nach."

"Even with yonder probeship," said Wirolen, "that is a very slim line!"

"Greetings, Eb'shra Wirolen," and he bowed slightly. "I am pleased to see you and John traveling together, though the *Han'anga* misses you at the helm! What is the status of your ship?"

"Fuel at ninety seven, full stock of consumables," she replied.

"Then I have a request," Ersha said. "Emble'rast system is within range of your drive field generator. We have military assets there that could be here in a matter of hours. Are you up to the trip?"

She glanced at John, who nodded firmly. "We are on our way," she replied.

"I have encoded a message ordering those ships here," Ersha said. "You have it now."

"Sir," John said quickly, before the other stepped away from the pickup. "Does Robert MacGregor remain a resident of Serch'nach?"

"He and his family reside within a habitat not far from here," Ersha replied.

"Give him, I mean them, my regards, if you would?"

Ersha bowed before the pickup and said, "I will do so."

They were left to themselves, and John could feel a gentle sideways pressure as Wirolen turned their ship end over end, then a solid shove back into his seat cushion as the main engines fired. It took time to kill their momentum and build up speed for the return to the node. John took the opportunity to relax a bit, even dozing off briefly. Wirolen announced the launch of their navigation buoy; he looked up in time to see it dart away and vanish though the node. A few minutes later Emble'rast sent it back with the word to come ahead.

"Our vector is set," Wirolen announced. "Field closure in... Ah, *no!*"

As her cry of denial burst forth, John felt a thing then that should never be felt in a ship so small, that vertiginous turning and twisting sensation of nodal distortion that grew ever more prevalent as a ship's mass increased. Their small ship was somehow interacting with the node as if they were a much, much *larger* mass, and that could mean only one thing.

"Abort!" he shouted. All of this in an eye blink.

"Too late!" Wirolen replied, her hands dancing over the boards as she fought to pull them free of a dangerous situation.

The twisted feeling swiftly grew into outright pain that ran down his spine from the base of his skull, rippling like cramps out into his limbs. John grunted and clamped his teeth on a wordless cry of agony. Wirolen was panting and whimpering pitifully, but still fighting to work her controls. And then the collision alert went off. There was an instant's glimpse of the display showing the appearance of ships, big ships, all around them, exiting the focus of the node even as they entered, a thing that could never be done without terrible risk. And now, all unwitting, they had crossed their matrix field with the vastly more powerful — and combined — fields of Kester's fleet.

Their field collapsed and sent them elsewhere.

In the instant of transition John heard Wirolen scream, a sound higher in pitch than any Human voice could reach, almost birdlike in its shrillness. His own pain was bad enough that he would have answered her cry, but he couldn't breathe. A moment later, the point was moot.

CHAPTER THIRTY-THREE

Pr'pri System
Bartram Habitat

The hour-long shuttle flight to Serch'nach from Bartram had just ended and Robert was in the queue for the lift tubes leading into the station, when the general alert sounded. Robert stopped where he was, frozen like everyone else by the sound of the alarm, and listened for instructions. The people around him all had puzzled or worried looks on their faces.

The explanation, when it came, was overridden by the voice of Kr'nai Ersha over his personal com. "Robert, the monitor system shows you aboard Serch'nach."

"Yes, *par'aman*," he replied quietly. "I just got off the shuttle. What's going on? What's wrong?"

"Andrew Kester is on his way to Pr'pri with a small fleet of warships!"

"*Warships?* I don't understand. We're being attacked by the Republic?"

"No," Ersha said flatly. "Not the Republic. The information we have makes that very clear."

"Then who... ?"

"We do not know," Ersha said. "Perhaps the same people responsible for those impersonating the Commonwealth's medical teams."

"Gaia," Robert said. The chill of the dock seemed to seep into his blood. "We're not well prepared to defend ourselves, are we?"

"No, we are not. That is why I have called. We need any combat-ready personnel we have available, and that will pull in people who would otherwise be managing rescue and recovery missions. You are rated on Leyra'an flight systems, and could fill one of those vacancies. I truly hate to ask, but... "

His immediate impulse was to refuse. Stark visions of war flashed through his mind, smoke and explosions, the searing flash of lasers, screams and the smell of blood and charred flesh, all of it vivid in his natural memory for a heartbeat. Robert shuddered and clutched the come-along pole, trying to catch his breath as the brief flashback sent his heart racing. Chance and coincidence once put Robert in a place he would rather not be. Was history about to repeat itself? He fought to calm his breathing and racing pulse. His palms were wet and he felt the flow of station air chilling sweat on his brow. Unbidden came words learned during his Gaian schooling.

Courage comes when you feel the fear, but do the thing anyway.

The *boshna'ti* vine cuttings he'd come for would have to wait.

"I'm in," he said. "Where do I report?"

Ersha gave him directions; Robert could see the facility in question from where he was, clinging to a come-along pole. "Thank you, my friend," Ersha said as Robert cast off to cross the brightly lit space. "By the way, John Knowles and Eb'shra Wirolen send their regards."

"Knowles?"

"Yes. They brought the warning, and are even now on their way out to summon help."

"If you can, let them know I'm aware, and wish them well."

"I will send it," Ersha replied. "Be safe, Robert."

Safe? War had caught up with him again. Where was safety?

He wanted absolutely no part of this, but how could he sit back and remain idle while men and women risked their lives on his behalf? On behalf of those he loved? As a pilot for a rescue crew he could at least do something, and while it might not be *safe*, he'd be saving lives, not taking them. He flew in a straight line to his destination, but his hands were so wet with perspiration he slipped off the next pole. The crowd gathered there saw him coming and scale-backed hands grasped at his arms as he started to tumble, catching and steadying him. Voices shouted orders, and crews assembled outside access tubes. Most were dressed in green uniform coveralls, but others in civilian garb were mixed in, volunteers like Robert, though he was the only Human among them. Robert pulled himself into the thick of things and spotted the person who seemed to be in charge, a Leyra'an woman also clad in the green coveralls of emergency services. "I am Robert MacGregor," he said in Leyra'an when his arrival caused her to look up. He raised his voice to be heard over the crowd noise. "Kr'nai Ersha said you need another pilot."

She quickly scanned the small tablet tethered to her hand. "Ah, yes, there is a notation. It just came through. You are expected. How are you with *Par'apa* systems and protocols?"

"Class one rating," he replied.

"Ah! That is good news!" she said, and pointing to a tube with a brace of Leyra'an around it, gave him the access number. "Tell them you are first pilot."

Robert blinked at her for a moment, surprised by the assigned position on the flight crew, then nodded and pushed away to join the crew assembling where she pointed. They looked in his direction just as he moved, six green-clad Leyra'an men with a variety of scale colors. Somehow the supervisor had alerted them, for they seemed anything but surprised by his arrival. Hands reached out to catch him as he arrived, hardly necessary this time, but a welcome courtesy all the same.

"You are MacGregor?" one man asked in Leyra'an. "Good! Are you comfortable as first pilot?"

"For my part, yes. Who have I displaced?"

"Me!" The man smiled as much as a Leyra'an could without teeth appearing. "But your reputation is well known, Robert MacGregor. I willingly stand aside to be your second pilot." He somehow managed a formal bow in zero-gee, without tumbling. "It is an honor to fly with you."

Robert returned the bow as best he could, clasped forearms with him, and then there were quick introductions all around. His second pilot was Eb'shra Pori. The other names went into his memory hoard, tagged to images; he would know them when they were needed. Robert and Pori passed through the tube into the boat first, and as he sailed through it, Robert glanced around at the medical gear and life support pods that lined the main compartment walls. The five non-flight rescue crew immediately donned EVA suits, helmets and all, ready to work outside the boat at a moment's notice. Robert and Pori pulled themselves into the control cabin.

They strapped themselves in and ran a quick check of instrumentation and systems, a task that took only a few minutes in the well-maintained craft. It was a lightweight spacecraft with very powerful engines and thrusters, clearly designed for quick, precise maneuvers. The flight system status display included an image of the boat, a boxy, angular craft with heavy duty clamps and extendable hatches on each of the four sides. It was not a pretty thing, but the design perfectly matched its purpose. The crew reported all secure, and in moments the boat, named *Ara'mu*, was undocked and clear to navigate. Robert flew them to their assigned standby position manually, to gain a feel for the controls and the responses of the *Ara'mu*. He found the *Ara'mu* to be both powerful and nimble. Under other circumstances the strange-looking little spacecraft would have been a joy to fly.

Pori brought up the main display to supplement the schematic of the region around the station, revealing a flurry of activity around them as traffic was cleared from around the node. If a group of large ships were to come through of a sudden — and Ersha seemed to think invasion was imminent — the presence of other ships near or, worse, in the node could be disastrous.

One modest vessel continued to approach the node at a significant speed. The onboard computer labeled it as a Leyra'an ship, the *Eli'ahtna*, presumably the ship containing his friends. They were not far from the node, and would soon be safely away. Between the station and the node the probeship *Newcomb* was parked; above the docking pole of Serch'nach was the frigate *Cygnet,* still in the system on courier duty. Farther off, toward the node, the *Han'anga* had taken a position that blocked the direct path to the station. Not far from the Leyra'an ship was another of noticeably different design, but equal size. The cruiser from the Republic, the RDF *Perseverence*, stood on guard with the *Han'anga*.

In a moment it registered, what he was seeing. The Republic and the Confederation, preparing to fight shoulder to shoulder, facing a common foe.

"Did you ever think you would live to see this?" he muttered, pointing to the warships.

"No," was Pori's simply reply.

"We have reached our assigned position," Robert said. "Signal that we stand ready."

"Done," Pori said.

"And now we wait... " Robert started to say.

He saw the ships appear even as Pori gave a wordless cry of alarm. There were five of them, all warships, each comparable in mass to the *Perseverance*. The warships dispersed into a wider formation as they approached, which they did at a reckless pace.

"Gaia!" Robert said.

A moment later, a high-power signal from the invading fleet's flagship overrode the com chatter.

"This is Admiral Andrew Kester, commander of the Liberated Autonomous Zone Fleet, aboard the flagship *Vengeance*. This system is within LAZ space and is now under our protection. Cooperate, and no one will be harmed. All members of the Leyra'an species are ordered to leave by the quickest means possible. Commonwealth citizens are free to go or stay as they wish. Resistance will not be tolerated. Immediate compliance with all LAZ instructions is mandatory. The warships in our path are to stand down at once. RDF *Perseverance,* we have no quarrel with you. You may pass and return to the Republic. Warship *Han'anga,* surrender and prepare to be boarded, or you will be… "

At that moment both the *Han'anga* and the *Perseverance* opened fire on the lead ship. The defensive fields of the *Newcomb* were already active, for all practical purposes screening Serch'nach station from weapons fire. The lead ship of the small fleet returned fire as the other cruisers changed formation to envelop the defenders. Missiles leaped out, intensely bright sparks of light that swiftly crossed the distance between the ships. Gunners wielding laser batteries snuffed the missiles, but could not shoot though the defense fields the way missiles did.

It was a horrible game of chance. However effective the computer-aided covering fire, a missile was bound to get through somewhere, and in moments, the LAZ flagship was hit. A brilliant flare of blue-white light erupted from the hull of the *Vengeance.* A moment later a flare appeared amidships on the Leyra'an vessel, as a second attacker surged forward and fired repeated salvoes.

The *Perseverance* made a sudden lateral maneuver, the flare from thrusters visible all over the ship, placing itself between the beleaguered *Han'anga* and the second LAZ ship, blocking its attack on *Han'anga.* Sparks swarmed from *Perseverance* and overwhelmed the defenses of the enemy cruiser. Flares of blue fire bloomed in several places, then the cruiser seemed to swell up and fill with light; it exploded, and where a moment before had been a warship they now saw only a swiftly expanding field of incandescent debris. The *Perseverance* disappeared briefly into that horrible nebula.

"All those people!" Pori whispered in horror. "All those people!"

As this happened, *Han'anga* and *Vengeance* continued to exchange fire at a ferocious rate, as if desperately determined to settle their long conflict once and for all. The remaining ships fired their thrusters and maneuvered past the fight, advancing directly on Serch'nach station. It was a fair distance to the station, but only the probeship stood between them and Serch'nach. For the moment it was enough. An order was broadcast by the attackers, demanding that the *Newcomb* surrender. There was no reply, and the enemy cruisers opened fire. The defensive systems of the probeship, wielded by the hyper-fast reflexes of the shipmind, proved an utterly impenetrable defense, while its shields prevented stray shots from harming the defenseless station.

Perseverance reappeared, having done an end-over-end maneuver and fired its immense main engines, moving up quickly and attacking the three station-bound LAZ ships from behind. One sustained damage that shut down its engines before its crew recognized the danger, then all three diverted their fire power aft, and the RDF cruiser was suddenly in grave danger. Fire erupted from near its engine pack, then the stern of the ship broke apart into a cloud of glittering debris. A distress beacon went active, but even so, *Perseverance* kept firing, and taking fire from ships now thoroughly balked by the defenses of the probeship. The fire from the *Perseverance* faltered, and in another moment the invaders left it for dead, focusing their attack on the *Newcomb*.

Robert glanced at his copilot, who simply said, "*Yia!*" He engaged the engines and *Ara'mu* came to life, flying to the aid of the stricken warship. Several other rescue ships followed suit, all of them broadcasting non-combatant intent to rescue.

"Civilian craft!" a voice shouted over the com. "Hold positions or you will be fired upon!"

Pori stared at Robert in shock and alarm.

Outrage shook him, and Robert shouted back over the com, "These are unarmed medical vessels. Go on and shoot, you fecken coward! Show everyone what you're made of!" He was on the open channel; everyone within range heard him.

Pori bared his teeth, snarled, and said something profane in Leyra'an.

They flew on, intent on their errand of mercy, waiting for the flash and the flame that would mean the end. But before the enemy could make good on its threat, the *Cygnet* suddenly appeared from behind the bulk of the *Newcomb,* flying fast and launching everything she had at the enemy cruiser sending the signal. The frigate took the enemy completely by surprise and the lead ship took several hits before being able to respond. By then, the frigate had taken a position between the rescue boats and the attacking ships. Robert's heart sank as he saw fire from the enemy lash out at the smaller warship, which would not long survive the assault.

"Ships!" Pori shouted. "More ships!"

Warships appeared in the node, three at a time in rapid succession, until a dozen of them were in the system, moving as fast as such could go and still survive nodal passage. A message rang out over the com system on all channels.

"Cease fire! Cease fire! This is the RDF. Ships under the command of Kester are ordered to cease fire and stand down *immediately*, or you will be destroyed. This is your only warning. *Stand down or die!*"

More ships appeared, all of them tagged as RDF. Ten more. In a moment the only ships still exchanging fire were *Han'anga* and *Vengeance.* The rest of Kester's ships suddenly went inertial, their only hope of survival in the face of overwhelming odds.

Han'anga was clearly in trouble, no longer launching missiles and barely mounting enough of a defense against those from the *Vengeance,* which ignored the RDF order and kept up its attack. Two RDF ships, equal to Kester's flagship, altered course and fell upon *Vengeance.* True to the given word, they opened fire on the rogue warship, a withering and merciless assault that almost immediately overwhelmed the defenders. Suddenly light erupted in multiple locations, and the matrix drive module floated away. *Vengeance* was dead in space. *Han'anga* limped away from the combat zone on thrusters and issued a distress signal, drawing a swarm of rescuers into its vicinity.

Escape pods flew from Kester's warship in all directions, all broadcasting distress calls of their own. Like the other ship in Kester's fleet, the warship seemed to swell and glow with a strange blue-white inner light, before flashing into another hellish nebula of war. Robert stared in shock. The rogue warship of Andrew Kester was no more.

It seemed so sudden, the end of the battle. The RDF ships moved in, some of them maneuvering to surround what was left of Kester's fleet, the others launching a flotilla of small craft to assist in the recovery of the life pods that now swarmed through the space near the station. Boats were launched from the probe ship as well. Perhaps most incredible of all was the signal, on open com, from the lead vessel of the RDF fleet. "*Hamilton to Han'anga. Hold position. We will assist.*"

Robert held his original course and brought them to the *Perseverance*. "RDF *Perseverance*," he said. "Can you extend your emergency docking probes?"

"Affirmative," said a harried, clearly frightened voice over a none-too-clear channel. A familiar voice.

"Drake!"

"Who... ?"

"Robert MacGregor. Our ETA is less than a minute."

"Robert? *God be praised!* Yes, we can extend the emergency docking probes. Doing that now." There was a pause. "We're in bad shape, here. Life support and containment are failing. We can't find the breach to lock it down!"

"Your engines were shot off!" Robert replied. "You can't seal that breach. Abandon ship!"

"Understood. Sending wounded out in pods. Releasing those now. Most of us can't get to pods, though. We'll be at the emergency bays. Docking port beacons are active."

"Coming in now," Robert said. The ship turned suddenly, creating a disturbing sensation in the pit of his stomach. There was a loud bang and everything shook.

"Hard dock. Pressure is good." In the display he saw a swarm of Leyra'an boats like the *Ara'mu* fastening themselves to what was left of the warship. "More help is on the way. Hold on!"

"Good!" Drake said, sounding relieved. "I'll take you up on that beer, when this is over." The transmission ended.

Robert idled the *Ara'mu* and monitored conditions. With a nod he sent Pori back to assist the crew; it needed only one of them to keep the *Ara'mu* stable. When alone, he studied the visual pickup and the schematic display. He felt numb, and there was a sour adrenaline aftertaste in his mouth, as he looked out at the wreckage and glowing gases that marked where ships had died. How many people were aboard? How many crew had perished in sudden moments of fire and fear and then the merciless cold of the Void? *Han'anga* had a crew of more than two hundred men and women; surely comparable numbers crewed the ships under Kester's command? Some had escaped the destruction of *Vengeance*, but that first ship had died too suddenly, and no pods had launched. It made him sick to his stomach to realize he had just seen so many lives snuffed out in an instant.

Com was buzzing as the rescuers coordinated efforts and chased after the flocks of escape pods slowly drifting away from the scene of the brief battle. One message suddenly stood out.

"Eta-nine-one *Cygnet*. Kester is alive and in our custody."

The *Cygnet* had him. Kester had somehow survived and been captured by the brave crew of the frigate. It seemed appropriate.

CHAPTER THIRTY-FOUR

Pr'pri System
Serch'nach Station

The hours that followed ran together in his memory, never completely clear, and yet somehow inescapable. His crew gathered survivors from the *Perseverance* and shuttled them to the station, then Robert flew back to the wounded warship for another set. Most were injured, some grievously, and far too many died along the way for all the care they were given. Over the com he heard a terribly litany of injuries sustained. Bruises and sprains and broken bones, fractured skulls, severed limbs, massive burns and radiation poisoning, and of course all the damages a Human body could sustain from decompression. He saw none of it as he flew, but he heard. That was bad enough.

More than one man, carried from the warship, or hauled in from the Void aboard a pod, panicked when he saw that he was in the hands of the enemy. Robert heard this tale told over the com dozens of times, even though the Admiral of the RDF fleet issued a general order to remain calm and to cooperate with the Leyra'an. But for many the belief that the Leyra'an were implacable foes ran too deep, and there were a few who chose death over what they saw as surrender.

Among the crew rescued by Robert's team from the *Perseverance* was Drake Bristol. Drake was one of the last men to leave. After receiving treatment for his own injuries, Drake suited up and joined Robert's Leyra'an crew in searching the doomed warship, seeking men trapped in life pockets and sealed cabins. When they had exhausted the possibilities, he remained aboard the *Ama'ru* as Robert joined the search for escape pods, offering reassurance to frightened Humans when they hauled the pods in, convincing them that they were truly safe.

Those rescued, most of them hurt in some way, were taken to the station for treatment, but the station medical personnel were soon overwhelmed. Robert heard the station master request medical teams from the RDF, and to Robert's surprise the fleet Admiral immediately responded by sending medical crews and the necessary supplies.

When the last pod signal was accounted for, and a sweep was made of the area for survivors in EVA suits, Robert and his exhausted crew re-docked with the station. Pori was in the copilot's seat, nearly asleep where he sat. The bump of the shuttle docking roused him, and he grinned toothily at Robert, saying, "We did well!"

"We did, indeed, my friend!" And they had. So many lives lost, but so many saved in part by their efforts. Robert felt a deep sadness, even knowing lives had been spared by his actions. Most of all, he was just plain tired, worn out by the need to endure, and the knowledge that war had once more intruded upon his life.

The docks were bright and noisy, with here and there a med crew still shuttling a wounded man into the lift tubes for transport into the station. Most of those present, however, were members of the rescue force, worn out and moving slowly without words, wanting only food and rest. Drake floated near the hatch, looking as rumpled and weary as his RDF uniform coveralls. When Robert appeared, Drake caught him by the shoulder and said, "Thanks." No more than that. Robert merely nodded in response. They then joined the migration into more comfortable regions of the station. There was little conversation along the way; for Robert at least there seemed too much to say. Drake went off to see to the men with whom he had served.

Robert made his way to the transport schedule display in the lounge, where he logged on to a flight tentatively scheduled to leave for Bartram in a couple of hours. He wanted nothing more than to go home, but the delay was inevitable, all things considered. He found a comfortable chair and curled into it with a sigh, too tired to be hungry. Too tired to care. People passed to and fro, and he paid them no mind until Drake appeared to awaken him from his drowsiness with a plate piled with seasoned meat rolls and two large mugs of *mi'pat*.

"Saw that you were waiting for the same shuttle as me. Thought you might be hungry," Drake said as he shared the food and handed Robert a mug

Robert murmured thanks and as the bittersweet aroma of *mi'pat* mingled with the savory smell of the food he realized he was *not* too tired to eat. The rolls were soon gone and they were left sipping the *mi'pat* in companionable silence.

"Wouldn't have figured you for a fan of Leyra'an cuisine," Robert said at last.

"Whatever else can be said about them, they know how to cook." Drake took a sip, then added, "As for *mi'pat*, this stuff caught on before the war, so I've been drinking it all my life. We don't call it by its Leyra'an name these days, of course. Real coffee is a rare commodity. The synthetic version, well, you really don't need to know about that stuff!"

"I'll take your word for it."

Relaxing as they drank, Robert let the sounds from the torus concourse below wash over him as so much white noise. He knew this sound as the steady gathering of Leyra'an for a huge celebration, a response to being rescued from grave danger. The lounge was set in the rim balcony above it all, and from where he sat he could just see the tops of trees set against the afternoon glow of the station's central lamps. "It's going to be a noisy place tonight," Robert observed.

"I wish them the joy of it," Drake said. He leaned his head back, eyes closed, exhaustion adding years to the appearance of his face. "Don't know about you, but I'm going back to Bartram and sleeping for a couple of days."

"That sounds good." Robert paused, hesitated, then asked, "Why were you aboard the *Perseverance*?"

"I'm a Reservist. When there's a long enough break between sessions, I shuttle over and log a few shifts to maintain my rating." He sipped from his mug and frowned. "And I had a long enough break. How did *you* get mixed up in this?"

"I was here to pick up new vines. Could have had them shipped, I suppose, but I wanted to pick from the best of the best. Just arrived as the call for pilots came."

Drake laughed, but not for long, and then said, "Damn the luck!"

Robert could not find it in himself to laugh, but the irony did produce a rueful smile. "Willingly," he replied. And in response to the gesture Drake made then, he touched his mug to that of the other man.

Four people wandered into the lounge and over to the rail of the balcony, looking out over and into the main torus of Serch'nach. Two were Leyra'an, and one of these was none other than Kr'nai Ersha; after a moment Robert recognized the woman with him as the station master of Serch'nach. The other two were Human, men in the dark blue, gold-trimmed uniforms of the Republic Defense Force. As they looked out at the station, the sounds from below grew suddenly louder. Robert got up and wandered over, mug in hand, to see what was going on; Drake was only a step behind him. The quartet at the rail did not immediately notice their presence.

"Good God," said the older of the RDF duo. "Are they so upset by the sight of us?"

"They are not upset or unhappy, Admiral Grayson," Ersha replied. "The noise you hear is a greeting. And gratitude."

"Unbelievable!" the Admiral said, raising his voice over the growing noise.

"Not really," Robert said. They all turned their heads to look at Robert and Drake as they came forward to stand at the rail beside the station master. "After all, you and your ships came to their rescue." He met the Admiral's eyes and added, "These people were never *really* your enemies." The words came out harder, harsher, than he intended. Robert struggled to suppress the surge of sudden and not quite rational anger that rose within him. He clenched his jaw to keep back even angrier words. *All those people dead,* he wanted to demand. *Why?* He wanted to scream the question out loud. Kester would have been the one from whom to demand an accounting, but he wasn't here, and they were all part of it, had played their roles in the long years of war that led to the disaster he had just witnessed. Robert was too tired and too horrified to be reasonable, but had enough presence of mind left to clench his jaw against the words he wanted to shout, knowing no good could possibly come of it.

Ersha stepped in to make quick introductions and first Grayson and then the younger officer offered Robert a hand to shake. Grayson was a tall, slim man with dark eyes and brown hair going gray. Robert stopped just short of using the forearm grasp of the Leyra'an instead of the old-fashioned Human handshake. Drake saluted them, looking acutely self-conscious in his worse-for-the-wear uniform.

"Gregory Milhouse," the other RDF officer said when Ersha hesitated over his name. "Captain of the RDF frigate *Cygnet*."

"*Cygnet!*" Robert grasped the man's hand tightly and held it for a long moment. "You and yours went into harm's way for my sake," he said gravely. "That was bravely done!"

Milhouse had a sheepish grin on his face. He released Robert's hand and just said, "It had to be done."

"It *was* well done," Grayson said to the younger officer. Then he looked at Robert with one eyebrow raised and said, "Your name seems familiar to me for some reason."

"One of the rescue pilots," Ersha offered.

"Saving citizens of the Republic," Grayson said. Then, more quietly, "And not for the first time, either."

"No," Robert replied carefully, still rattled by his near loss of composure. Grayson surely made reference to the Attus station incident. "Not the first time."

"I have men under my command who are alive, thanks to you," Grayson said. "The Republic is doubly in your debt." He reached out to shake Robert's hand again. "An honor to meet you, sir."

"Both times I was glad to help," Robert said as he released the Admiral's hand. "And both times... I wish it hadn't been necessary at all."

Grayson merely nodded in agreement, then turned to Drake. "You've been put up for a commendation, along with Captain Milhouse and his crew."

"Thank you, sir," Drake replied. Milhouse echoed the sentiment.

Grayson looked out over the noisy crowd again and, seemingly on impulse, gave them a wave. The shouting that erupted was almost deafening. "My God! How does one respond to such a thing?"

"Put your left hand over your heart, Admiral," Ersha replied. "Then bow to them. They will be acknowledged, and you will be free to make a graceful departure, without seeming rude."

The Admiral did as suggested and the response was a long, loud, howling cheer. They moved back out of sight and the noise gradually subsided to the level of a Leyra'an crowd in full party mode. Grayson had a rueful half-smile on his face, while his escort laughed outright. The Admiral looked at the man and asked, "Who would have thought it?"

"Perhaps a sign of things to come," said the station master.

"Perhaps," the Admiral replied gravely.

"We cannot thank you enough for your help, Robert," Ersha said with a bow. He used the Human language, as had the station master, likely as a courtesy to the RDF officers. "Many were saved because we had one more pilot."

Robert bowed to them in silence, rather than repeat words already spoken. "Yours was a most timely arrival," Robert said, instead.

"We were warned by an RDF operative that an attack was imminent," the Admiral said. "Seems someone, and we still don't know how this came to be, built a fleet out there and tried to take over the DZ. The informant seemed to think they were the same ones responsible for a fraud involving med crews claiming to be from the Commonwealth. Whatever they dispensed, it wasn't medicine. There's some sort of plague on the loose out there! Well, we made our best speed to get here. Would have been better if we'd gotten here first."

"You were here when you could be," said Ersha. "It made a difference. For that, we are grateful."

A wry smile touched the Admiral's face. "Just when I thought life couldn't surprise me anymore. No one could *ever* have convinced me that I would lead a combat rescue mission to save a Leyra'an space station!"

"Tell me about it!" Drake said. "I mean, um, sir!"

A smile for a brief moment brightened Grayson's face. "Hardly need to, do I, son?" The Admiral sobered. "We're on our way over to the *Newcomb*. To make a formal appeal to the Commonwealth for help in the DZ. It's an ugly situation there. That plague is everywhere the fake Commonwealth teams visited, and we're afraid it will spread into the Republic proper."

"We'll help," Robert said. "I have no doubt of that." He hesitated, then went on to ask, "Admiral, what's to become of Kester?"

"We have him in custody," Grayson replied. "We'll take him back to the Republic. Beyond that, well, his fate is not mine to decide."

"As long as he isn't able to do more harm," Robert said.

"Reasonably sure he's done with such things," Grayson said. "Beyond saying that, I'm afraid you'll just have to trust us to deal with him effectively."

"We will not keep you longer," Ersha said into the awkward pause that followed. "Go home, my friend. Be with your family. Drake, rest well."

"Be well, uncle," Robert said in Leyra'an, and returned the bow. Drake stood there, as if not sure what to do, then saluted the Admiral, who smiled at him and returned the salute. The party walked away, and Robert saw that it was time to catch their flight home to Bartram.

It was a quiet flight, as most traffic was flowing *toward* Serch'nach. The handful of passengers sharing the flight were all Leyra'an, residents of Bartram who recognized him and quickly realized who Drake must be. They greeted both with enthusiasm, then recognized their weariness and left them to sleep the hour it took to make the passage. Robert knew the trip ended when a young Leyra'an woman gently roused him from his nap. Muzzy from exhaustion, that single mug of *mi'pat* having worn off, he allowed his fellow passengers to steer him through the Bartram docking facilities and into the lifts. Drake seemed more up to handling the trip into the habitat, but did not shake off the kindly nudges and grasping of arms as they made their way to the lifts. When they came to the stop for his residence, Drake shook Robert's hand firmly and, bowing to the Leyra'an, went on his way.

When Robert left the lift capsule at last, he found what looked to be the entire habitat population crowding the terminal, a throng that spilled out from the paved deck outside the lift station and spread into the park beyond farther than he could see. The murmur of noise that greeted him at first became a great shout that trailed off into a chorus of voices calling his Human and Leyra'an names. His family was there, front and center, and they practically leaped upon him. All of them wept, and Holm somehow managed to get his arms around Robert, Melep, and Alicia at the same time. The babies, frightened and confused, began to wail; Gava'mi stood stoically by his pack members, looking around sternly, a han'anga on guard. They stood a little apart from the cheering crowd, laughing and crying, and set to work reassuring their children.

Robert had very little awareness of making his way to their home. There was a celebration going on all around them, of course. The Leyra'an were what they were, and the Human population had never shown any reluctance to follow suit. Robert begged off, wanting only to go home, clean up, and sleep. Then at last they *were* home, and Holm said to Alicia, "Put him to bed before he falls down."

Somehow Robert managed to stumble on his own into the bedroom. Alicia laid Paul in his crib and came to the bed, where Robert found himself seated, and helped him undress. She steered him into the shower, where after a long while with hot water pouring over him, he remember that one applied soap under such circumstances. Then he was sitting on the bed again, without remembering how he got there.

"Are you feeling all right?" Alicia asked softly.

"Just tired," he said. He fell back onto the bed and felt Alicia lifting the covers over them both. He drew her close beside him and held on tight. "No, I'm not all right. Gaia!" He paused and caught his breath. "I ran into Ersha on the way home. He praised me for helping save so many lives, and it was all I could do not to scream at him, and at the RDF people with him. Alicia, I watched two ships die! Two ships full of Humans, 'Licia! *Two!* They were there on the screen, and then they weren't. Just big clouds of glowing plasma. All those people incinerated in an instant, or thrown out into the Void. *Dead*, either way! People who might have lived a thousand years! Why? They've been at this for five decades, and still they go on killing each other! I wish someone could explain why they... " He hauled himself up short, aware that he was babbling. "I just don't understand!"

Alicia pulled his head to her breast and he felt her hand gently brush away the tears that finally came. "Maybe there's no understanding it," she said. The catch in her voice, the words barely a whisper, made him look up. Alicia had that lost in the dark look to her eyes, and finally Robert really understood it. "No understanding. Not for you, not for me. Our lives before Contact gave us nothing to prepare us for this. Or what happened to the

William Bartram." Alicia closed her eyes tight and shivered.

"It's got to end," Robert whispered. A strange numbness took him, his feelings suddenly muted, and a great drowsiness like a soft, heavy weight settled over him.

"Sleep, my love," Alicia whispered in his ear as he felt himself fade from the world. "Just sleep. And do not dream."

CHAPTER THIRTY-FIVE

Pr'pri System
Bartram Habitat

The depression that settled over him the next day evaporated when Robert learned that John Knowles and Eb'shra Wirolen never appeared at their intended destination. With a sharp pang of anxiety he remembered how close they must have been to the node when Kester's fleet arrived. With the help of the shipmind of the *Newcomb*, he examined the sensor data gathered just before the battle, and what he learned only deepened his fears, even as it suggested a course of action. He contacted Kr'nai Ersha immediately to enlist his aid.

"They had an active field when Kester came through with all those ships, and the fields intersected after they set their vector," he explained.

"Cross amplification," Ersha said, with a grimace that revealed his pointed teeth.

"Exactly. Their vector was probably set properly but the node reacted to their field as if it were roughly a thousand times stronger. They were kicked out along that vector, but with an uncontrolled surge of field strength. I doubt the mass of their target system could have pulled them in."

"They overshot."

"Essentially, yes," Robert replied.

"How far might they have gone?" Ersha asked.

And it was Robert's turn to shrug, which he did Leyra'an style, without thinking. "Not even the shipmind can give a precise answer at this point. The distortions produced by Kester's ships make it impossible to get a completely clear reading on the *Eli'ahtna's* field strength at that moment. What I *can* tell you is that they would have remained on that vector until the field power dissipated enough for *something* to pull them back into real space. And that vector crosses much of the Confederation."

"Ah, I see! I shall put out the word, and have all the systems along that vector contacted. We will find them, my friend."

"Those who search should be warned that the ship might be damaged. John and Wirolen were likely injured."

"They will be warned," Ersha said gravely. "And the word will spread with the greatest possible speed."

Which was as much as could be done. All Robert could do at that point was wait and hope, though he was not allowed to be idle as he did so.

A month after the failed invasion, it was decided to publicly honor the heroism of the Serch'nach station emergency crews, an idea put forward first by the Republic, but adopted readily by the other governments. Robert really wanted no part of it, and was far from the only one, but the Confederation, Commonwealth, and Republic all seemed for once to be in complete agreement. The emergency service crews who had saved the lives of so many were to be publicly honored for their courage. To Robert's chagrin, even Holm thought it was important.

"It has been more than fifty Human years since cooperation to such a degree took place between the Confederation and the Republic," Holm told him. "We must do everything we can to encourage this. The moderates in the Republic have placed a high value on what took place here. If we can do anything to support the point they are trying to make to the people of the Republic, then we must do so."

And so Robert, with a host of others, found himself standing before a large audience seated in a many-tiered auditorium in the main torus of Serch'nach. He stood on the raised platform stage with fellow pilots and med techs, dressed like them in simple, pale green coveralls, his being borrowed for the occasion. He was the only Human, but like the Leyra'an, he wore a twisted braid of colored cloth, the *es'ava* bearing the colors of his family. In the front row were three others with the same *es'ava*, and seeing them seated there, eyes shining with pride and love, he felt his reluctance to receive such attention fall away. Looking at his children, and thinking of their futures, he realized Holm was right.

The speeches were predictable, though no less sincere for all of that. The Leyra'an who rushed to the aid of the RDF *Perseverance* received special praise, even from fellow emergency crews, for they had gone into the line of fire to save the men in the battered warship. Nor was the crew of the *Cygnet* forgotten; most were in the audience, but Captain Milhouse and his officers stood with Robert and the others.

"They responded to the desperate need of fellow space-farers," Ersha said when it was his time to speak. "They did so for the same reason we went to the aid of those who came here meaning to do us harm, for against this thing the Gaians of the Commonwealth call the Great Void we must all stand together, if *any* are to survive."

The officials from the Commonwealth and the Republic expressed similar sentiments, with the latter also expressing gratitude to the Commonwealth for the outpouring of medical aid from the probeship, including the use of a variant of nanomed to save victims of radiation exposure. The Leyra'an were thanked, simply and plainly and sincerely, for saving Human lives.

They *thanked* the Leyra'an. The significance of it was clearly not lost on the audience.

Something had changed. Something about these new representatives from the Republic was different, their attitudes less stiff and guarded. It was all the more surprising that some of them were career military officers, for whom 'career' meant fighting the long war with the Leyra'an. Robert compared these men with the first RDF officers and political leaders of the Republic to visit Pr'pri, before the loss of the *William Bartram*. Those representatives were of Drake Bristol's kind, or at least the kind of man he had *been*. Admiral Grayson and his associates reminded Robert more of Emerson.

Afterwards there was a great deal of milling about, meeting and greeting. Robert introduced Eb'shra Pori and the rest of the crew of the *Ama'ru* to his family. As was traditional for the Leyra'an, the children were passed around for proper admiration, and the expressions of the Leyra'an who had never seen, much less held, a Human toddler, were a delight to behold. Strange as the experience clearly was, they lavished no less praise over Paul than Vurn, before the child was handed back to Holm, who cradled the Human child in the crook of one strong arm.

They were joined then by Ersha and Admiral Grayson, who was accompanied by Drake and Captain Milhouse. The RDF officers in their dark uniforms stood out in stark contrast to the colorfully dressed people — Human and Leyra'an — gathered around them. And yet there was something splendid about their appearance and bearing that allowed them to fit in all the same. Pori bowed to the Admiral, and Grayson proved himself a quick study in Leyra'an courtesies by bowing in return, without hesitation. In a heartbeat, Milhouse did the same. Pori clapped Robert on the shoulder and wished him well, then with his crew drifted off to the grand celebration just beginning to develop in the low hills sculpted into the floor of the torus around them. Robert turned and introduced his family to Admiral Grayson and the man gave a respectful bow as he said, "Ladies, sir, a pleasure to meet you." He nodded toward the departing crew and said, "For not the first time recently, I have seen something amazing, a thing I would not have imagined. Leyra'an fussing over a Human child!" Holm, still holding Paul, who looked around bright-eyed and waved his hands about, inclined his head in a half-bow. Melep, standing beside him with Vurn, did the same. Grayson smiled — carefully — and added, "You have a beautiful family, Mr. MacGregor. You must feel yourself blessed."

"I do, sir," Robert replied.

"As do we all," Holm said. "Very much so."

"Mr. Bristol made a recording of the encounter, just now," the Admiral said. "I took a chance that it would not seem too intrusive. Would anyone mind terribly if it were made public? It is quite acceptable to say no, of course. The record would be erased at once."

"Why do you want to publish it?" Alicia asked, though she sounded more curious than taken aback.

"It would be good for people to see a different side of the Leyra'an, especially in the core systems," Drake explained. "There are years of unfortunate perceptions to overcome, if there is to be peace."

"That would be a significant departure from previous policies," said Holm.

"There are changes unfolding in the Republic," said the Admiral. "News of Commonwealth med tech is out. With Commonwealth crews spreading through the DZ to help clean up that plague, it's no longer possible to conceal the truth."

"I'm surprised they trusted any of us, after the ruse used to trick them in the first place," Alicia said.

"Well, we had to trick them again. At least, to get things started. We put your crews in RDF uniforms." Grayson gave them a rueful smile. "It's going to take months, but matters in the DZ are coming back under control. Some of the task forces under Kester's command surrendered as soon as RDF ships appeared. The plague took the fight out of them. A few others declared for seccession, so we have some pockets of potential armed resistance." The smile faded. "We still don't know where they got the ships in the first place. Our economic system hasn't produced that many cruisers at one time since before the war began."

"There are no records in the navigation logs?" Robert asked.

"Not of ship origins, no. The recorders were set to start recording data only *after* a ship reached its primary target. Everything before then was wiped as soon as the ship entered that system." Grayson glanced down, shaking his head a bit, a look of grave concern on his face. "And without that information, there's no way short of keeping a massive fleet presence in the DZ to prevent another incursion. We simply don't know what these people have for a resource base."

"What of their crews?" Alicia asked.

"So far, none of them have told us anything useful in that regard," Grayson replied. "The majority of them were recruited in the Republic and taken elsewhere, but that location was not disclosed to them. If any of the prisoners taken were actually from this mystery star system, we haven't found them out. Yet."

"Whatever the source of the threat, it clearly did not originate within the DZ," Ersha said.

"We're quite sure of that," Grayson said with a nod. "And that's worrisome, since it implies a rogue settlement, or a set of them, out somewhere beyond our charts. Whoever these people are, they came in and tried to *use* the DZ, but they were not *from* the DZ."

"So yet again the region of contact draws trouble," said Holm.

"In more ways than one," Drake said. "It was a recent decision by the Executive Council, directing the RDF to take extreme measures in the DZ, that tipped the balance of power in the Republic."

Grayson slowly shook his head and sighed. "We were instructed to put in harm's way the citizens of the Republic that, by oath, we are bound to protect. So we chose to protect them. The bulk of the fleet is drawn aside and idle. Technically, we're in a state of mutiny against the elected government of the Republic."

"In support of your people,"Alicia said.

"Yes, ma'am. We will stand ready to defend the Republic from any further external threats, but we *will not* intervene in civilian politics."

"There may be a way to stabilize the situation in the DZ," Drake said to the Admiral. "A great deal of thought has gone into it," and his eyes shifted for a second to the members of Rost'aht, "and I believe it, or some variation, will render the DZ incapable of destabilizing the Republic in the future. I intend to introduce it tomorrow, in outline form."

"Sounds like I should attend," said Grayson.

"I would urge you to do so," said Holm.

"The rest of you, too," Drake said. "That way we can all go off for that beer I've been offered."

Grayson laughed and grinned, heedless of Human teeth showing. "You know, I just might go along for that, too!"

"You would be most welcome, of course," said Melep. "And you as well," she added to Milhouse, who stood a little outside the conversation, as if unsure of his place.

"Why, thank you!" Milhouse replied.

"I can't help wondering why the rulers of the Republic decided on such a rash act, with regards to the DZ, I mean," Robert said. "Has word of our nanomed technology spread so far, so quickly into the Republic from the border?"

"Well, it's spreading quickly," Grayson replied. "And you're close to the mark about it being the trigger. I believe you know Emerson Worth?"

"Very well," said Melep. "And we miss him greatly!"

"He speaks well of you and yours, as a matter of fact. Mr. Worth came home cured of Founders' disease, one of the slow and difficult-to-treat manifestations. Full remission, a thing that has never happened before. And contrary to the instructions he received, he's made it known how that cure was achieved."

"Did he, now?" Alicia said. There was a wide smile on her face, and her green eyes were shining. "Did he, indeed? I'm surprised he was allowed to get away with that!"

"Oh, the current government tried to shut him down, with threats of arrest and a rather clever disinformation campaign. But people desperately *want* to believe that the Commonwealth can end this scourge. Fortunately, what they all want to believe happens to be true! And then there are the rumors spreading from the DZ that the Commonwealth has brought an end to old age for the Leyra'an, using that same medical technology." To Robert's eye the man suddenly looked rather sad. "That's hard to believe, even after hearing both Emerson and Ersha verify it."

"It's true, Admiral," Alicia replied. "The people of the Commonwealth do not age, are rarely ill, and recover quickly from all but the most devastating injuries. You saw this, in the wounded men brought here. We used a form of our nanomed tech that does not persist, to heal their injuries." Then she laughed and said, "We call that one the Worth Variant."

"In that case," Grayson said, "the current government won't last much longer, now that the news is out. There's a vote of no confidence being held even as we speak. The results from the first systems to check in are not in the current regime's favor."

"You do not fear the repercussions of such a thing?" Melep asked. "It will, after all, bring great changes."

"I have no doubt it will," Grayson admitted. "But then, so does death. Commonwealth medicine is a change we can, well, learn to live with." He hesitated, and then Robert saw sadness in the man's face, beyond any doubt. "I lost my wife to Founders', six years ago," he added quietly. Grayson then gave them a little bow, and before anyone could think of a thing to say, departed. Drake hesitated a moment, then when Robert nodded, he and Milhouse went off after their commanding officer, the two new Commissioners trailing along behind.

"Friend Drake need not feel ashamed that the fear of mortality overcame him," said Holm. "He now has that in common with all his folk."

"Emerson was right all along," Alicia said.

"And so, my friends," said Ersha, "it may yet be that the Commonwealth brings an end to the war, as I have long hoped and believed, though not by any means I might have guessed!"

"Let us join this celebration," Holm suggested. The

noise of it was becoming ever harder to speak over. "Tomorrow we will meet at Commission headquarters, and hear what friend Drake has in mind for our scheme."

CHAPTER THIRTY-SIX

Pr'pri System
Bartram Habitat

From the look of the crowd already on hand when they arrived, the chance of getting any seat at all seemed slim, let alone one near the front. Rumor had it that the Bartram Protocol was to be discussed, so the crowd, while inconvenient, was anything but a surprise.

"Maybe we should find a remote site, or just go home and watch," Robert suggested.

"Wait, *par'aman* is waving to us," said Melep. She waved back, and so did little Vurn from his perch behind her head, adding an ear-piercing shriek as he did so. Not to be outdone, Paul answered in kind. And indeed, Kr'nai Ersha was waving, urging them toward the front. As they worked their collective way forward, the sergeant at arms for the session, a tall, young Human male in the dark dress uniform of the RDF, appeared out of the crowd and escorted them to a trio of seats in the front row. He reached down and removed the bright sapphire blue ribbon draped across the seats, then helped Melep set the carrier containing Vurn on the floor. Robert did the same for Alicia and little Paul. He saw his Leyra'an name in the angular script of written Leyra'an on the middle of the ribbon.

"Being married to a hero has its advantages," Alicia said as they settled in.

"Yes, it does," Melep said, and nudged Robert playfully with her elbow.

"Once in a while," Robert admitted as he sat, unable to resist a grin. Paul was suddenly fixed on his father and began to fuss a bit, so Alicia handed him over. Having what he wanted, for whatever reason, the little one settled down and drifted into a nap.

The members of the Commission walked into the room and stood for a moment behind their seats at the curved table. Rost'aht Holm and Kr'nai Ersha represented the Leyra'an, Yu Sei Ho and Sarah Badesha the Commonwealth, and Drake Bristol with Admiral Franklin Grayson for the Republic occupied the bend of the table. The Leyra'an bowed politely, a gesture the Commonwealth Commissioners duplicated, and for a wonder — this time — the representatives of the Republic did the same. For some reason that, more than anything else seen and heard in the days before, gave Robert a sense of certainty that something had changed.

"Today I am scheduled to hold the chair," Drake began. "But due to the nature of what I need to bring to your attention, protocol requires me to yield the chair to another. It should go to Kr'nai Ersha, according to the normal sequence. Is this acceptable?"

"The Commonwealth has no objection," said Sarah.

"I will chair this session," Ersha agreed with another bow. "I ask the members to please be seated. Drake Bristol of the Republic will address us."

"Thank you, sir," Drake said with a nod of his head toward Ersha. In a moment, he alone remained standing. "The first thing I must say is that we've secured the Disputed Zone systems with vectors leading to Pr'pri system. This was accomplished more quickly than might have been expected due to the impact of the plague on the crews of Kester's ships. If there are renegades unaccounted for, they will not be able to come here without running a most formidable gauntlet. The recent confrontation will not be repeated."

"I believe I speak for us all in expressing our deep gratitude," said Ersha.

"You do indeed," said Ho. "And if I may, and Mr. Bristol will pardon these interruptions, let the record also show that the residents of this system recognize the courage and sacrifice of the crews of the RDF *Perseverance* and Confederation warship *Han'anga*. May those who were lost *always* be remembered."

A murmur of ascent rose from those crowded into the hall, Human and Leyra'an voices mingled. Drake stood quietly for a moment as it subsided, clearly working to maintain his composure as memory intruded. He had seen men die that day, some of them close friends, an experience he'd admitted to Robert was new for him, and one he found hard to bear. "Thank you," he said at last, addressing all those gathered. "Much of what I say here, this session, is aimed at an attempt to make such sacrifices unnecessary in the future. But first, some details on what happened in the Republic's part of the DZ need to be heard."

"Please proceed," said Ersha.

"The attempt to take over the DZ and turn it into a separate state by those led by Andrew Kester has failed. The artificial plague turned loose in several systems has been contained, and with the help of the Commonwealth, the contagion will soon be eradicated. There were, I am sorry to report, a significant number of deaths as a result of this artificial viral agent. The ships sent by Kester into the DZ are under control of the RDF, with the exception of half a dozen that went over to the DZ Secessionist cause. These have agreed to a truce, and are for now of no concern. Of great concern, of course, is how all of this came to be. Interrogation of the crews of captured ships reveals a vast and intricate recruitment network throughout the Republic. We have only just begun to investigate the matter. A renegade organization following an extremist agenda has apparently existed, and in fact has been growing quietly in the Republic, for some time. How it was funded or managed, we don't yet know. How they were able to build a small fleet of warships is a *complete* mystery."

"How could such a thing be done without *anyone* in the Republic being aware?" Sarah asked.

"Clearly there is some source of funding to at least cover their activities," Drake replied. "It may extend up into the central government. At this time we simply don't know, and if the vote of no confidence goes forward, removing those responsible from power, we may *never* know. At this point we are only sure of two things," and he flicked a glance to where the Admiral sat. Grayson nodded slightly. "First, the ships were all of designs used by the Republic, down to the last wire and bolt. *But they were not built in the Republic.* They came from somewhere else, a system outside the Republic, from a facility for which we have no record. Second, Kester was not the leader of these renegades. They follow a man named James Calavone, who happens to be the son of the man who caused the Republic's civil war more than fifty years ago."

The other Commissioners looked at each other and the sound of whispered conversations rose from the gallery. Ersha silenced them with a raised hand.

"If this James Calavone remains in control of a shipyard, a threat still exists," said Holm.

"We need to assume such is the case," said Drake. "We will continue to work toward uncovering this clandestine facility, but for the time being the threat exists. However, the search is not so broad as it might seem at first. That they first tried to take over the DZ suggests they came from a region with systems or mass points that provide several direct vectors to systems in the DZ. Given enough time, we will determine the possible vectors used for entry into each system attacked, and backtrack."

"With your permission, I will contact the probeship *Newcomb*," said Ho. "The shipmind would surely be willing to assist in making those calculations."

Drake hesitated, then glanced down at the Admiral, who gave him the tiniest of nods. "I will see that you receive the necessary data. And thank you. The sooner we find these people, the sooner we'll all be safe." He reach down to tap a key on the desk and a star map appeared in the U-shaped space of the table. "And now, to the main reason I requested this session. What you see is the region of space centered here, at Pr'pri system." A bright blue spark appeared and gleamed steadily in the heart of the three-dimensional chart. "And these are the regions claimed by the Republic, the Confederation of Clans, and the Commonwealth." Areas in the map assumed color as he named the three realms, pale blue, rust, and green, respectively. "As you can see, the border is anything but smooth. The Commonwealth system named Eriola is within the Confederation, and Pr'pri is linked by nodes to a region of space settled by the Republic." The projection zoomed in to focus on the convolutions of the DZ. "It only grows worse when you examine the complete interface between the Confederation and the Republic. The war has essentially been an effort to regularize the shape of this region and make it easier to manage." He looked gravely out at the gallery. "The resulting stalemate has come at great cost to both sides."

Alicia leaned over and whispered into Robert's ear. "He sounds like Emerson!" Robert just nodded.

"When I came here to assist in the negotiations," Drake said, "our task was essentially to insure that nothing of substance came of them until the Republic could deal with the Disputed Zone. Somehow, we were to do so without making adversaries of the Commonwealth. By dealing with, I mean the use of military power to solidify control of systems settled by the Republic in which a secessionist movement had taken root. Such an action would have been legally and morally questionable, and for that reason alone the Fleet wisely refused to comply. News that the government of the Republic meant to use force on our own people, combined with weak support for continued hostilities against the Leyra'an, and word that the government has blocked availability of a cure for Founders' disease, all have worked to discredit the leaders for whom I worked. In fact, as we speak, a poll is underway in the Republic, and the overwhelming result so far is a vote of no confidence. Should the trend hold, the government that has led the Republic since the start of the war with the Leyra'an will fall. It will take years for all of that to unfold, and for a new governing council to be formed. In the meantime, for the sake of the peace and security of us all, the Disputed Zone must be pacified.

"The plan I have to suggest for doing this is not entirely my own. Friends I've made, from both the Commonwealth and the Confederation, have opened my eyes to some possibilities. Based on their suggestions, vetted it seems by nearly the entire population of this habitat, I propose that the region known as the DZ be made, in fact, a semi-autonomous zone. I'm not unaware of the irony in this suggestion, of course. We need to use the DZ as a sort of buffer zone, a region of controlled contact where my people can study the impact of new ideas and technologies from our neighbors by seeing their affects in a limited area." Drake paused to allow the quiet muttering of the gallery to run its course.

Holm held out his hand for permission to interrupt, and Drake nodded to him. "How would this buffer be managed? Or should I say, by whom?"

"When this proposal is brought to the Republic, I intend to suggest that the Trilateral Commission be charged with that task. It will be managed by us all, by all three nations." He waited a moment for another murmur of reaction to subside. "I'm presenting the plan here, first, to give the Trilateral Commission a chance to examine it for flaws before it is forwarded to our respective governments. Since it will likely be resisted by certain interests within the Republic, it must be as airtight as possible. This plan will end the flow of Leyra'an items into the Republic, and that will make some people *very* unhappy."

"Such control, by itself, will be quite a challenge," said Ersha.

"Indeed it will," said the Admiral, speaking for the first time. "And it will require the assistance of the Leyra'an to control availability of such things to begin with."

"A good point," Ersha replied, calmly accepting the implied criticism. "I will urge my government to enforce strict controls over such matters in our DZ systems."

"Sir, I believe we need to go a step further than that." Drake made a gesture, and all the overlapping systems of the DZ took on a wash of gold, Republic and Confederation alike. So did Pr'pri and Eriola. "All of these systems must be in the autonomous zone, completely neutral, and under the jurisdiction of the Commission. We cannot afford to have any of them answer to one government or another."

Ersha and Holm simply sat and stared at Drake. The Commonwealth Commissioners looked at each other and exchanged small nods of agreement of some sort. A louder noise arose from the gallery, one that included expressions of disagreement. Ersha raised a hand and the crowd subsided. "That presents a difficulty," said Ersha mildly.

"No doubt," Drake replied. "The very same difficulty I will face when I propose this to my government. I cannot ask them to give up territory unilaterally. If all sides cannot agree that this is a worthy sacrifice, I fear we will be right back where we started, and no good can come of that."

After a long moment, Ersha looked from Drake to Holm, who whispered something to him. "Indeed?" Ersha said in response, though no one else heard the comment. "We are in full agreement, then. I will advise my government accordingly. I can, however, make no promises."

"Well, neither can I, of course," Drake said. "This plan... Well, what I've presented here is no more than a broad brush view of what will be a far more complicated agreement, and process, once all is said and done. We could go on, but it might be best for all involved to study the detailed proposal before we go any further."

"Yes," said Ho. "Let's agree to give it three days' review, then meet here again to begin in earnest."

"If there are no other questions," said Ersha. No one spoke. "Then this session is adjourned. We will reassemble three days hence, at the usual starting time."

CHAPTER THIRTY-SEVEN

Endmost System
Disputed Zone

"I am sorry, Jim, but the latest tests failed to produce useful results."

"That's *not* acceptable, Artie," Calavone said.

"I am sorry," Artie said again. The bland voice coming over the com showed no trace of regret, defensiveness, or impatience. "The information brought to me is simply insufficient. There are too many variables that cannot be estimated. I suspect some of my data may not even be relevant to the question. Inferences drawn from other aspects of Commonwealth technology are inadequate. The mere existence of stealth tech is not of itself a clue to how it is done. We will not be able to conceal any of the facilities of Endmost, should the RDF find a way to trace Andrew Kester and the fleet back here."

Calavone clamped his jaw against anything stronger than what he'd already said. Artie did not respond to emotional outbursts very well, since he did not really understand emotions. The machine mind was many orders of magnitude beyond any computer system Calavone had ever encountered, but still lacked the ability to decipher the meaning of a tone of voice. Venting on the machine was pointless. "Tell me what you think of the chances that the RDF can find their way here?"

"If they persist in calculating vectors long enough, it is inevitable," Artie replied. "However, it will take a very long time, on the order of years. Each calculation will lead them to a mass point, from which a great many new vectors must be calculated. They will need to spend a significant amount of time exploring vectors that lead to habitable systems, and more time examining carefully systems in which an operation such as ours would be viable. Even with the use of automated probes sent out in large numbers, I would estimate a search period of five to seven years."

Calavone nodded thoughtfully, then came up with a disturbing thought. His face reflected in the polished desk surface frowned back at him. "How would it change your estimate if the Commonwealth's computer technology is added in?"

"I could not make an accurate estimate with that parameter," Artie replied. "Data on artificial intelligence, along with stealth and weapons technology, was automatically erased when calamity befell the *William Bartram*. I can only state with certainty that, based on the technology I have studied from the Commonwealth, the necessary calculations could be done in a fraction of the time. However, I do not believe it is possible for calculations of any power to reduce the options far enough to significantly shorten the necessary physical searches."

"How firm is that conclusion?"

"I have significant confidence in it," Artie replied. "However, I am in fact rendering the equivalent of an educated guess. There is insufficient information available for anything more."

Calavone grunted and settled back into his chair. "Educated guesses are not to be trusted, Artie. It would be a good habit to learn not to rely on such."

"Yes, Jim."

He sat with his eyes closed for a very long time, running recent events over in his mind, and inwardly cursing Kester. The man's lust for revenge had utterly ruined the plan and, through the capture of so many of their recruits, seriously compromised the network within the Republic that Calavone had built over the years with such care. Now, according to Artie, there was a good chance that Kester's failed attempt to annex Pr'pri would lead to the discovery of Endmost, and the end of everything the Calavone family had built out in the deep dark. The advantage Commonwealth technology gave them would be for nothing, if the RDF found them now. Endmost, even with its currently augmented defenses, would be no match for the full strength of the RDF Fleet, and even if they had years in which to prepare, with only a single star system for support, it would become a siege that he could not hope to outlast. For all that Artie was sure of his conclusions, that it would take years to ferret out Endmost even with the help of the Commonwealth, Calavone's instincts were prickling in his brain with a sense of great danger.

They could not wait.

Calavone rubbed his chin. "Okay, effective immediately, we're shutting down the net. No further information in or out. Complete blackout." Cutting the net meant abandoning good people, but they had known of the possibility when they volunteered, and with the network compromised, he could not take the chance of trying to extract them. "Sort through the records we've created of unsettled systems along vectors out from Endmost, and away from the three civilizations. End points as far from here as we have options. We need a fallback position that will give us time to regroup. Chart courses that use multiple dark masses and nodal transfer points, if they can be found. We'll send out probes to scout those systems and make sure that our first stop isn't already on somebody's charts."

"I am running the sort and search now. If we are to depart, should I shut down manufacturing operations?"

"Hmm, no. Don't start anything new, but follow through on the ships currently under construction.

Especially the transports. We'll need them. I want to haul away as much as I can, then destroy what I can't. We'll leave the RDF a hell of a puzzle when they do finally get here. Better than that, I'd like them to find an empty system."

"That might be a bit unrealistic, Jim," the computer pointed out.

"I suppose you're right," Calavone replied. "Still, that's the standard to shoot for."

"Of course," Artie agreed.

Calavone began the monstrous administrative task of abandoning a place so many had come to call home. The news would not be well received, and from some quarters, he knew he would have a fight on his hands. Calavone knew how to handle internal dissent, however; it was why he encouraged the growth of families among those who had fallen back to Endmost with him. Fear for the safety of loved ones was a powerful lever, when held in capable hands.

With that, a thought occurred. A temptation, in fact, and one in which he decided to indulge. "Artie, before you institute the blackout, send into the net that Andrew Kester is to be killed."

"Yes, Jim."

CHAPTER THIRTY-EIGHT

Pr'pri System
Bartram Habitat

The day before the Bartram Proposal was to be sent out to the three nations, Drake Bristol joined family Rost'aht for an evening at the Willow Lake for what proved to be the last time. He'd become a regular following the Second Battle of Pr'pri, a big fan of Ira Ashe's beer and sausages. He'd also taught Gava'mi a game called "fetch." This night he revealed to them his decision to return to the Republic.

"It won't be a quick trip to the regional capital this time," he explained as they settled around the Rost'aht table that night, between the dance floor and the smooth, dark lake. A mixed band of Leyra'an and Human musicians were tuning up and preparing to play; it was a night scheduled for music from the long lost Scottish Highlands. It promised to be a noisy start for the evening, with no small amount of dancing. "Simply briefing the governor so his aides can prepare yet another report won't do. He is firmly attached to the current ruling party, and I can't trust him to convey the message accurately, or at all."

"Where will you go, then?"Alicia asked.

"I'll be going straight to join Emerson in his home system, where he leads the opposition party. I believe he'll find the Bartram Proposal a very useful tool in his campaign to unseat the current government. It provides a nice alternative to using military force against fellow citizens." He paused and a half-smile quirked his lips. "I'm also sending my resignation to the powers that be, of course. I can't do this job and help Emerson in his run for the council chair of the Republic."

"I hope it all works out smoothly, for you," Robert said.

"Oh, it won't," Drake replied with a sudden grin. Then he seemed to remember Leyra'an customs and hid the smile behind his mug of beer. "The hardliners will find something to use to counter the work we've done here. They have everything to lose, and I don't doubt for a moment there will be some ugly politics in the Republic soon. Ugly and dirty. Worse than usual, I mean. And all of that means a delay in bringing new Commissioners here from the Republic. We need to decide who gets to pick them, first!" He drank and lowered the mug, looking pleased. "Of course, we could just brew up a huge batch of this stuff and distribute it. Ought to be at least as influential as the Cure!" When they laughed at that and drank a toast to good beer, he looked at Robert and said, "In all seriousness, sending the horticultural packages in ahead of time will have enormous influence, especially with the messages preceding it with pictures of roses and such. And sending it as a gift to multiple systems, was an excellent idea!"

"We had it all ready to go before Emerson was recalled," Robert said. "Admiral Grayson had the idea of sending it to more than one location."

"He had that one dead right," Drake said. "They won't be able to intercept all of them, and it'll only take one or two, combined with word of the Cure, to make even more people wonder what the government ministers could possibly be thinking." He drank again and smiled, Leyra'an style. "I could wish we'd allowed this earlier."

"We were caught up in matters to do with war and social upheaval," said Holm. He sat with his son in the crook of one thick arm, poking Vurn in the belly to the obvious delight of the child. "Matters of life and death. Why would anyone think of roses and grape vines?"

"That we did not," said Alicia, "says something rather unflattering about us, when you think about it."

"Not of you, ma'am. Or any of you." Drake looked a bit troubled, but did not go on from there to lay the blame where they all knew it belonged.

Alicia gave an exasperated sigh, glared at Drake and raised an admonitory finger toward him. "Drake, if you call me 'ma'am' *one more time...!*"

"Sorry, Alicia!" Drake replied with an embarrassed grin.

"To lessons learned," Robert said with a smile. He raised his mug and the rest followed suit, until all met with multiple sharp, glassy clunks over the heart of the table.

"We have no roses in the Republic," Drake said. "Just pictures. The Founders brought some out with them, but during the settlement of the central system they were lost." He looked thoughtful, then said, "You know, I think I'll suggest that Emerson adopt the rose as the emblem of his movement."

"Make it a rose bud," Melep suggested.

"Perfect," Alicia said, beaming at her sister-wife. "A hopeful symbol of something beautiful about to unfold."

Drake nodded, then said, "I like that." And he laughed. "Sounds like something Emerson would say, in fact, so I'm willing to bet he takes to the idea. I'm coming to understand his fondness for the four of you." Little Paul squealed shrilly. "So sorry, I meant to say six. Er, ah, seven." Gava'mi was giving him a peculiar look.

Robert looked on and wondered at the change in the man. He had been such a staunch defender of the status quo at the beginning, and when given charge of the Republic's diplomatic mission had turned into a veritable titanium bulkhead to ideas aimed at open relations with the Commonwealth. Never mind his apparent attitude toward the Leyra'an! And now he sat with them just as Emerson had done, a friend of the family, a man clearly and deeply changed by his experiences. Robert thought back on the process he had seen unfold when John Knowles was forced to confront the lie he had been living. In that case a Leyra'an man had risked and then lost his life coming to John's aid. For Drake it was the sudden and dreadful knowledge that his own life was coming to a horrible end. In each case mortal peril, a brush with death, opened the eyes of a man from the Republic.

Just as fear and death had upended the quiet world in which he and Alicia had for so long lived.

Robert turned his attention to the band on the stage, and for not the first time noted that they lacked a piper. He wondered if he would ever find the strength to play in public again. And suddenly knew very clearly that he would.

The conversation moved on without him as Robert contemplated such things, and when he turned his attention back to those around the table, he realized they were indulging in speculation on what sorts of changes roses, grapes, and coffee trees might spark. Listening to them he saw just how right Emerson was likely to be, just because of all the things in the horticultural gift that the Republic lacked, or had lost. The ways of the Republic would soon be changed by the mere existence of the Commonwealth. Roses would bloom for citizens of the Republic for the first time in almost two centuries. Old age and illness would be banished. All of this without solid leadership to guide the process. It could well be something like striking a spark in an oxygen-charged environment. He could not help wondering if this would be an entirely good thing.

"You know," he said, "I was bothered at first by the travel restrictions you imposed in and out of the autonomous zone. But the more I think of it, the less troubled I am by the idea."

Drake nodded and said, "For the foreseeable future, it needs to be a buffer zone for real. The government was not entirely wrong to fear the influence of the Commonwealth. The turmoil that an open outflow of ideas and technology would create could have terrible consequences. Our society disrupts itself all too easily as it is — we really don't need any help! We need to be able to control the changes that are to come to the Republic, if we can't resist them outright. And we can't resist them, of course. So we'll start with medicine, and roses."

And they drank a toast to that sentiment as well.

The volume of the music rose and the number of dancers grew, until people were whirling past their table, laughing and shouting as they rushed by. For a while conversation became difficult, so they all sat back to watch the enthusiastic folk spinning past their table. Their evening meal was brought, standard pub fare from a bygone time in Earth's history, and the consumption of food reduced the conversation to lighter matters, a strong Leyra'an tradition.

"It is a sad thing that you must leave us," Melep said when they were through. "You will be missed." Her sentiment was immediately echoed by the others. "But the path you intend to follow seems to me a wise one."

"It is regrettable that we will not finish the work here together," said Holm. "But I believe Melep is quite right. We will suspend the Trilateral Commission until things are as resolved as can be in the Republic."

"That's probably for the best. It may take some time for my replacements to arrive," Drake said. "I have no idea who they'll be, of course, but I doubt they'll be selected by the current government. Its days are numbered."

"Is it possible elements of the military will interfere with this transition?" Holm asked.

"Only if the councillors and their chairman attempt to block the vote, or the elections likely to come after, at which point the RDF would step in and enforce free elections. Admiral Grayson was very clear on that. The fleet, at least, will not take sides, just see to it the letter of the law is met."

"What of RDF resources elsewhere in the Republic?" Robert asked.

"Few in number, and thinly spread," Drake replied. "If they cast their lot with the current government and not the bulk of the Fleet, that could be a problem. We can only pray that they will respect the legality of what is unfolding."

Someone approached the table, and Robert looked over in time to see Kr'nai Ersha take a seat beside Melep. They greeted each other quietly, uncle and niece, then Ersha looked gravely at Robert. "We have received word from half the systems along their recorded vector," he said. There was no need to explain what he meant. "So far there is no sign of them."

"How long to the far edge of the Confederation?" Robert asked.

"A bit more than a month," Ersha said. "So we should not give up hope just yet."

Robert sighed and shook his head. "The further the cross-amplification kicked them, the harder it would have been to endure. Their ship was almost certainly damaged." Alicia put her hand on his arm and squeezed it gently.

"Word is traveling outward," Ersha said. "If they survived, they will be found. We will not end the search until they are recovered, one way or the other. More than this, we cannot do. We can only accept that they are missing, and endure with the patience that acceptance provides."

"May God grant them his divine protection," Drake said softly.

EPILOGUE

Unknown...

John Knowles was awake and aware, in darkness and silence so profound it provoked only terror. No sight, no sound, no touch — just awareness and fear. The Great Void was in his soul. John was naked in the dark. He tried to call out Wirolen's name, but had no voice, and the empty darkness and the silence and fear went on forever...

Interested in knowing, ahead of time, when my next book will be available? I could beg an email address from you and add you to yet another email marketing list. But these days, who needs more unnecessary stuff in the inbox? Or another concern regarding email security and privacy?

A simple way to keep up with me is to follow me on Facebook, Instagram, or through my weblog. New releases will always be announced in these venues well in advance, along with special promotions, access to signed copies, and the rare public appearance. The necessary links:

Facebook Page
https://www.facebook.com/desertstarspublishing

Weblog
https://underdesertstars.com/

Instagram
https://www.instagram.com/underdesertstars/